"It's a poltergeist."

A sudden burst of noise stopped them outside the music room. Side by side, they carefully peered through the glass at a choir practice.

"It's in there." Brianna muttered as one of the altos reached out to turn a page. Her music stand fell, and the whole row went crashing down.

"I think you're right."

The choir mistress' baton snapped.

Brianna snorted. "I know I'm right."

"Come on, I've seen enough. It's a poltergeist," Tony told her as they headed back to Ashley. "They like to hang around the uh . . . emotional turmoil of young girls."

"So it's not here because of me?"

"It might have come to this school instead of another school because of you. Your power might have attracted it."

"Like you attracted that girl who tried to kill you by sucking your . . ."

"We aren't going to talk about that," Tony interrupted, ears burning. "We, you and me, we aren't *ever* going to talk about that."

"Not even when I grow up?"

"Not even."

—From "After School Specials"
by Tanya Huff

CHILDREN
of MAGIC

EDITED BY
Martin H. Greenberg
and Kerrie Hughes

DAW BOOKS, INC.
DONALD A. WOLLHEIM, FOUNDER
375 Hudson Street, New York, NY 10014
ELIZABETH R. WOLLHEIM
SHEILA E. GILBERT
PUBLISHERS
http://www.dawbooks.com

First Printing, June 2006
1 2 3 4 5 6 7 8 9

DAW TRADEMARK REGISTERED
U.S. PAT. OFF. AND FOREIGN COUNTRIES
—MARCA REGISTRADA
HECHO EN U.S.A.

PRINTED IN THE U.S.A.

ACKNOWLEDGMENTS

Introduction © 2006 by Kerrie Hughes
Mr. Death Goes to Washington © 2006 by Thranx, Inc.
Nethan's Magic © 2006 by Jody Lynn Nye
Touching Faith © 2006 by Alexander B. Potter
The Horses of the High Hills © 2006 by Brenda Cooper
An End to All Things © 2006 by Karina Sumner-Smith
After School Specials © 2006 by Tanya Huff
Titan © 2006 by Sarah A. Hoyt
Shades of Truth © 2006 by Jana Paniccia
The Winter of Our Discontent © 2006 by Nancy Holder
The Rustle of Wings © 2006 by Ruth Stuart
Basic Magic © 2006 by Jean Rabe
Fever Waking © 2006 by Jane Lindskold
Starchild Wondersmith © 2006 by Louise Marley
Far From the Tree © 2006 by Melissa Lee Shaw
The Weight of Wishes © 2006 by Nina Kiriki Hoffman
The Trade © 2006 by Fiona Patton
Shahira © 2006 by Michelle West

CONTENTS

INTRODUCTION

Kerrie Hughes

WHEN I WAS A CHILD I thought I was magick. I tried to move objects with my mind, change the color of crayons and transform my cat into a cougar. As an adult I still believe in magick and when I saw the first Harry Potter film I was enraptured. Surely this is the way life was meant to be for me! Learning the mysteries of sorcery in a castle, away from parents and reality. Better yet, I could be a professor who taught the little prodigies how to use their talents! My son was with me at the movie and patted my hand in sympathy; he knew I longed to be a wizard. He also knows he is the best magick I have ever made and does his best to entertain me.

But what if children really were magickal in our normal world? What could they do and how would they learn to use their powers? With this anthology I asked my writer/magicians to create a story about a child with magick. In this world or one of their own making I wanted to know, how does the gifted child develop their skills? Perhaps the craft is forbidden or secret? What if the child has no teacher or one with malice in their heart? Intriguing.

They have, in my opinion, risen to the challenge and I would like to thank them all for their enchanting stories. Alakazam!

1

MR. DEATH GOES TO WASHINGTON

Alan Dean Foster

Alan Dean Foster's writing career began when August Derleth bought a long Lovecraftian letter of Foster's in 1968 and much to his surprise, published it as a short story in Derleth's bi-annual magazine *The Arkham Collector*. His first attempt at a novel, *The Tar-Aiym Krang*, was bought by Betty Ballantine and published by Ballantine Books in 1972. It incorporates a number of suggestions from famed SF editor John W. Campbell. Since then, Foster's sometimes humorous, occasionally poignant, but always entertaining short fiction has appeared in all the major SF magazines as well as in original anthologies and several "Best of the Year" compendiums. Six collections of his short form work have also been published. His work to date includes excursions into hard science fiction, fantasy, horror, detective, western, historical, and contemporary fiction. In addition to publication in English, his work has appeared and won awards throughout the world. His novel *Cyber Way* won the Southwest Book Award for Fiction in 1990, the first work of science fiction ever to do so.

PERHAPS UNSURPRISINGLY, Melody encountered Mr. Death at the memorial to the veterans of the Vietnam War. He was standing there staring at the smooth, polished black wall, studying the inscribed names as if a relative of his own had been memorialized therein. In a sense, they were all his relatives. He had not killed any of them; no, not a one. But he had taken them all; lo, every one.

She recognized him immediately, of course. Death is a hard entity to miss, even on a late winter's day in the nation's capital. There were plenty of ordinary folk about who trailed behind them the aspect or aroma of death. They entered or emerged from buildings that were heavily if cunningly guarded, and to which a teen-age visitor and would-be political intern like Melody Johannsen from Minnesota was denied access. Being sensitive, and unusually schooled, she was able to recognize many of these people. Not only because they could not shake from their spirits the unpleasant odor of death and dying, but because they usually had the fashion sense of a parade of slugs.

Death himself, now—that was another matter of matter indeed.

Her widowed mother had always taught her to be straightforward and curious. "Doing nothing is safe, but that's not how you learn about the world." Melody was not afraid of Death. He looked like a lonely old man, albeit one badly in need of a good home cooked Midwestern meal. He was tall and slender, with a mournful expression, but far from intimidating in appearance. He wore, as one would have thought, a black suit, though from the cut of it she could not tell if it was a casual outfit meant for daily wear or a uniform. None of the other people who were wandering slowly back and forth in front of the memorial, many of them sobbing quietly, noticed him. Perhaps, in a place of death, Death himself is harder for most people to distinguish.

More likely, identification came easily because Melody was a sorceress.

Well, to be entirely truthful, an apprentice sorceress. They were scarce in Minnesota, though shamans were plentiful. Being of Swedish descent, her source for serious sorceressness was Norse, arising from the myth and

mystery of ancient Scandinavian legend, of tales of great
gods and goddesses. Melody was blond and very pretty,
but no goddess. Not even the boys on the football team
who kept trying to date her thought that, though some
of their false compliments approached it in presumption.

Thanks to her mother's patient instruction, Melody
had gumption, if not presumption. So after watching the
lanky figure inspect the sweeping black stone litany of
loss for several minutes, she took a slightly deeper breath
than usual, walked up to him, and as soon as she had
attracted his attention, inquired straightforwardly but
not innocently, "What are you doing here?"

Death looked down at her and smiled. It was not an
attractive smile, but it was tolerable. Although it might
well have sent a non-sorceress (all right, just an apprentice) to screaming.

"I beg your pardon?"

Taking the notion that Death might beg anyone's pardon as encouragement, she pressed on. "You're Death,
and I'm interested to know what you're up to here in
the capital on this very fine day in March."

The smile widened slightly, but became no more pleasant. She took no umbrage. It wasn't his fault, she knew.
We are who (and what) we are. "You are a very percep-
tive young woman. I am Martin Mulvaney, of 435 East
Delaware Way, in Chevy Chase. Apartment 8B."

"You may very well live at 435 East Delaware in
Chevy Chase. No one knows where Death abides. At
least, not on a daily basis. Besides, I'm from out of town
and I don't know the local neighborhoods. But I am sure
that you are not Martin Mulvaney, or any of the Mulvaney clan. You are Death."

The angular shape looked around, craning to see if
anyone was watching them. No one was. Everyone else's
attention was on loved ones, be they living or locked in
marble. He turned back to the girl confronting him, and
this time there was a depth and a darkness to his eyes
into which a careless soul could plunge and drown.

"If I am Death, then shouldn't you be a little afraid
of me?"

"Why should I be afraid of you? You're a component

of everyday life, as natural and as a part of it as the air and the water. I wasn't raised to be afraid of Death, though I really never thought I'd get to meet him. At least, not until time."

The polite smile turned to a disapproving frown. "I am no entertainment celebrity, to be gawked at and casually mocked."

"Am I being flippant?" she inquired.

He pursued his lips, which when he did so turned very, very white. "No, you are not being flippant. I perceive, somewhat to my astonishment, that you are being quite serious, as well as friendly and respectful. Respectful is advisable." The voice dropped to a dangerous rumble that hinted of dimensions unknown. "Friendly is dangerous."

"I'm not afraid of you," she repeated unflinchingly. Cocking her head slightly to one side, she eyed him intently. "You don't look like what I'd imagined."

"A lot of people say that. Just before the end." That grim smile again. "The face of death is not blank. My job isn't to scare people. Quite the contrary. I dislike a fuss. My work is taxing enough as it is." He leaned toward her then, and Melody found she could smell him. Like his appearance, it wasn't especially foul. Not when it was this fresh, anyway. She had an aunt in St. Paul whose attic smelled much the same.

"You're charming and pretty," Death told her. "Would you be interested in coming to work for me? Good help is always hard to find."

"No thanks," she replied. "I already have enough homework. I want to come to work here and represent my state. I want to be a senator and help people."

"Oh dear," he hissed softly. "We'll be seeing a lot of each other, then." As if that concluded the conversation, he turned away from her.

Absently, she noted that he cast no reflection in the wall of polished black marble. That was to be expected from a specter. "Why are you here?" she asked quickly, repeating her initial question before he could fade to a shade.

He paused and turned back to her, his expression a knowing scowl. "You really are a bold little girl."

"I'm not a little girl," she snapped. "I'm fifteen."

A different sort of smirk this time: still ominous, but also slightly wistful. "I am somewhat older. Listen to me, um, young lady: you'd best mind your own business. Even though it's not your prescribed time, I am allowed a certain leeway in these things." He inhaled audibly, but not of air. "Since you seem determined to discover that which you would be better off not knowing, I am here to pick up a number of people." Turning, he raised an arm and pointed. "In a short while there's going to be quite a dramatic crash just over that way involving a pair of tour buses going too fast in opposite directions. By coincidence, I believe that several elderly couples from your state are on board one of the vehicles. For a moment or two thereafter I expect to be quite busy."

Death's remorseless description of what was poised to ensue did not upset her. It was his indifference that got her small-town dander up.

"No," she said.

It's not easy to surprise Death, but she succeeded. Heavy eyebrows rising, he eyed her evenly. "*No?*"

"No." She made sure her purse was securely slung over her shoulder, the better to keep her hands free. "I have nothing against death in the course of things, but I'm dead-set against these kinds of unnatural tragedies. Especially when one of my possible future constituents may be involved."

"Dear me," Death murmured sardonically. "Should I be afraid? What are you going to do if I proceed? Kill me?" Death might not be proud, but he was affluent with irony.

"Stop you," she replied calmly. "If I'm going to be a worthy senator, I have to be able to stop bad things from happening."

The pale death's-head nodded slowly. "A sensible observation. In that case, I suggest you prepare to begin with protecting yourself. As I am not constituted to brook any interference in my work, I expect I'd better start this afternoon's work with you." He glanced briefly southward again. "I have a little time yet." And with that, he extended a long, skinny arm in her direction, the fingers of the hand opening toward her like the white grapples of a cargo crane. One touch of those cold, cold digits, and she would pass immediately and irrevocably from the realm of the living.

No one seemed to be looking in their direction. It was as if the two contending figures had suddenly entered into an isolated pocket of reality where only they existed: Melody Johannsen, of Remsburg, Minnesota (pop. 2,342, and static), and Death, of the Hereafter (pop. unknown, and ever-growing). Remembering everything she had studied over the past several years in the course of her desire to become a senator as well as maintain her family tradition, she raised both arms high, inclined her fingers forward, and proceeded to intone with solemn force.

"An objection may be made to the consideration of any original main motion, and to no others, provided it is made before there is any debate or before any subsidiary motion is stated. Thus, it may be applied to petitions and to communications that are not from a superior body, as well as to resolutions. It cannot be applied to incidental main motions, such as amendments to by-laws, or to reports of committees on subjects referred to them."

The reaching claw of a hand halted, the grasping fingers stopping more than a foot from the front of her neatly starched blouse. Death blinked. A bemused expression came over his face. It took a few seconds and a violent shake of his head to clear the cobwebby enchantment from his mind. Any suggestion of a smile had vanished from his face, that now assumed a thoroughly grave and grim expression. It was the look of imminent demise, of incipient destruction, that would brook no turning. Once more, he reached for her.

Holding her ground, Melody modulated her tone so that it became as monotonous, as boring, as entirely enervating a dreary drone as could be produced by the otherwise captivating human voice. One could properly and accurately call it deadly dull.

"Incidental motions are such as arise out of another question which is pending, and therefore take precedence of and must be decided before the question out of which they rise; or, they are incidental to a question that has just been pending and should be decided before any other business is taken up. They yield to privileged motions, and generally to the motion to lay on the table. They are undebatable, except an appeal under certain circumstances as shown in section 21. They cannot be amended except where they relate to the division of a question, or to the method of considering a question, or to methods of voting, or to the time when nominations or the polls shall be closed. No subsidiary motion, except to amend, can be applied to any of them except a debatable appeal. Whenever it is stated that all incidental motions take precedence of a certain motion, the incidental motions referred to are only those that are legitimately incidental at the time they are made. Thus, incidental motions take precedence of subsidiary motions, but the incidental motion to object to the consideration of a question cannot be made while a subsidiary motion is pending, as the objection is only legitimate against an original main motion just after it is stated, before it has been debated or there has been any subsidiary motion stated."

Letting out a cry of pain, Death staggered backward. For a third time he raised his hands—only now they were employed not in trying to reach her, but to cover his ears. If it had not been Death uttering it, the cry of pain expressed by the tall figure would have been truly pitiable. Following up her advantage, Melody advanced relentlessly, lowering her arms and shaking one finger portentously at the gaunt figure that was trying to stumble away from her.

"Furthermore," she continued while channeling the implacable insensitivity of only the most accomplished parliamentarians, "the motion to suspend the rules may be made at any time when no question is pending; or while a question is pending, provided it is for a purpose connected with that question. It yields to all the privileged motions (except a call for the orders of the day), to the motion to lay on the table, and to incidental motions arising out of itself. It is undebatable and cannot be amended or have any other subsidiary motion applied to it, nor can a vote on it be reconsidered, nor can a motion to suspend the rules for the same purpose be renewed at the same meeting except by unanimous consent, though it may be renewed after an adjournment, even if the next meeting is held the same day."

"Stop, stop!" Unable to take any more, Death threw the back of one forearm across his eyes and turned away. There was a blast of noisome air, like the collapsing of a balloon, and then he was gone.

Aware that at least one passing couple was now staring in her direction, Melody lowered her arms to her sides, adopted a look of small-town innocence, and headed for the memorial's east exit. No one paid any attention to her as she departed. She had arranged to meet her mother back at the hotel in time for lunch. The recent confrontation would provide food for thought, and she was sure her mother would have both reprimands and suggestions to make. From somewhere not far south of the memorial, there was a screeching of brakes as one fully-loaded tour bus swerved violently to just miss another entering the intersection from the opposite direction. The occupants of both vehicles continued on their way, blissfully unaware of how close many of them had just come to having their visit to the nation's capital shockingly and lethally terminated.

North of them and closer to the Capitol building, one of the state of Minnesota's future senators, and most accomplished sorceresses, made sure to look both ways before crossing the street on the way back to her hotel. True to her word, she had done her homework well. While proud of that, she was not one to rest on her laurels, however accomplished. Prevailing over Death had been easy enough.

Getting something that would actually help people through Congress was going to require a great deal more knowledge, both legislative and sorceral, than she had managed to master to date.

NETHAN'S MAGIC

Jody Lynn Nye

Jody Lynn Nye lists her main career activity as "spoiling cats." She lives northwest of Chicago with two of the above and her husband, author and packager Bill Fawcett. She has published thirty books, including six contemporary fantasies, four SF novels, four novels in collaboration with Anne McCaffrey, including *The Ship Who Won*; edited a humorous anthology about mothers, *Don't Forget Your Spacesuit, Dear!*; and published over seventy short stories. Her latest books are *The Lady and The Tiger*, third in her Taylor's Ark series, *Strong Arm Tactics* (Meisha Merlin Publishing) and *Class Dis-Mythed*, co-written with Robert Asprin.

THE LAUGHING, curly-haired tot wasn't looking where he was going when he cannoned into Morrah's leg. He looked up the long body clad in embroidered, red silk robes, took in the narrow face framed by wings of dark hair going silver at the temples and the deepset, black eyes, and the expression of glee he had shared with his small friends died away to a stare of fear tinged with respect.

"My apologies, Honorable," he stammered. Morrah inclined her head slightly, and the little boy shot away, his small feet chattering on the cobblestones. Morrah watched him go, bemused and a trifle envious. He knew where he was going off to. For the first time in her life, she did not.

Peace bloomed throughout Ternagorina. It wasn't an accident; Morrah, King's Wizardess, overseeing hundreds of ministers, soldiers, spies, negotiators and lesser wizards, had been working toward peace for decades. The labor of her lifetime, helping to halt the everpresent wars between this land and the great nations around it, had come to fruition. She had shown her king through crystal mirror and candle flame the movements of his rivals' troops, and the thoughts of the lords who commanded them. She had advised him not to destroy the opposition, but to make allies out of them. He had taken her advice. The surrounding nations had at last been pushed, persuaded or beaten into agreement, and trade was now more important than conquest. Tribute was being paid into the treasury, and permanent guests of the castle, too comfortable and spoiled to be called hostages, ensured that no further attacks would be endured without repercussions. Her job was over.

The king had gratefully bestowed upon her and the generals and elders statesmen many honors and handsome gifts of land and valuables, then dismissed them from his service. The king, as did all men of power, took the victory to himself, dismissing the notion that anyone else might have been too instrumental in helping him to gain it. He was likely to call upon none of them again unless the unlikely event of war broke out again. Morrah was content. She had enough money to live well for the rest of her very long life.

And to do what with it? She wasn't old for her kind, only 105 years of age. But what hadn't she done? She had ridden dragons, split mountains, walked through flame and flood more or less unscathed. She had learned the language of the animals and the songs of stars. She'd befriended trolls and tritons, and even defeated her greatest rival, the wizard who served Ternagorina's greatest enemy.

"Good day, Honorable," a woman greeted her, waking her up from her reverie. She nodded deeply to the wizardess. The babe in her arms, perhaps six months of age, stared at her in awe, a wet finger in its mouth. Another child clinging to the woman's skirts offered a shy smile. Morrah smiled back, and the little one disappeared behind the fold of cloth.

Ah, children.

"Children just happen," an unfortunate maidservant had once said to her. The girl's noble lover had dismissed her upon learning of her condition, and she was running to throw herself in the river when Morrah had intercepted her. At a quiet word from wizardess to the king, the brute of a knight was sent out to the arctic wastes to command the front lines, and the maidservant was put to work in the palace nursery tending the royal heir.

Well, children *didn't* just happen, Morrah knew. They never had to her. Oh, she was aware of all the bodily reasons why she had never been visited with offspring; she wasn't a fool or an innocent. Yet how the women whom she had attended in childbed had suffered during the birthing, she was sure there must be a better way to have one.

Perhaps . . . perhaps the time had come for her to have a child of her own. She liked children, no doubt about that, and they liked her, once they came to know that her formidable face concealed a tender heart, loving and patient with the innocent. The more she thought about the idea, the more she wondered why it had not occurred to her before.

She had always been too busy to think about the needs of her body. When she was young, the hours of studying had grown into years, and potential mates had gone from rivals to colleagues, usually removed by many leagues, if not countries. And when she had come to this city to be its wizardess, she was too busy to consider taking the time away from her duties to bear children. All around her she saw women with two, four, six, eight children tottering along behind, with one at the breast. These women had no time to contemplate the movements of the stars, nor of kings.

Well, time she had in plenty, now. Stirred by the thought

of a new challenge, Morrah turned her feet back toward her grand new home at the north edge of the city. It would be a fine place to raise a child. She must begin making preparations.

"The trouble with babies," she explained to Oakleaf and Tansy, the tree elves who had served her for the last thirty-five years, "is that they are so needy. They drool, soil and wet, and they are hungry at such strange times. This one won't have any of those needs. And they are so easily injured. That is why I shall make my child out of wood. It is a substance that resists injury."

"Another willow shaving, mistress?" piped Oakleaf.

"No," Morrah said, standing back in her spacious tower workroom. She surveyed the small form lying on the work table. "I think it's finished now."

The pale slips of wood well approximated the delicate skin of a baby. Swan's down made fine, fluffy hair, and under the rounded eyelids were a pair of precious round sapphires given to her as earrings. They made beautiful, clear blue eyes. Morrah put her hands palm down over the simulacrum, and drew energy from the earth and sky. The skin warmed and joined together in one seamless piece.

The eyes opened. Morrah admired their glitter and took the child in her arms. It lay looking up at her. She smiled down at it. Such a beautiful thing. She rocked it from side to side. It felt like a real human child. She admired the tiny fingers and toes, and stroked the delicate little face. The small mouth, made of pink rosebuds, moved.

"I love you, Mother," it said.

Morrah embraced the child. It was perfect. And all without her having to grunt or cry or sweat for a single moment!

"Here is where you will sleep, little one," she said. She brought the wooden infant nearer the fire, to a cradle that Oakleaf had carved by hand from a single piece of cherry wood.

The sapphire eyes surveyed the little bed. "It is beautiful, Mother."

She pulled the knitted silk coverlet up to the child's chin. "Sleep now."

"As you wish, Mother."

The infant closed its eyes. Morrah sat in her reading chair beside the fire, constantly looking over to admire the little creature. How beautiful it was! She looked forward to caring for it. It would grow a tiny bit each day. It would learn to play among the clouds, and make friends with the spirits of stones. When it was old enough, she would teach it magic. What a beautiful future lay ahead of them.

She fell asleep in the great chair, her head pillowed on her hand. She stirred about daybreak as the elves were making tea. Morrah rolled her neck to get the cricks out of it. She glanced over at the cradle. The child had not awoken at the noise.

Tansy whisked over to her with a steaming, fragrant cup. Morrah sipped the tea gratefully.

"You should warm some milk for the child. Did it demand food in the night?"

"No, Honorable," Tansy said. "It didn't make a fuss at all."

Perhaps it had died. With breath indrawn, Morrah leaned over the cradle.

The child's eyes flew open, surprising Morrah with their brightness. "Good morning, Mother," the wooden infant said.

"Good morning, child," Morrah replied. "Are you hungry?"

"No, Mother. Do you want me to be?"

"Not if . . . it is not your nature," Morrah said, taken aback.

"No, Mother," the baby said placidly.

Morrah drew it from the cradle and held it close to her. It was of a comfortable weight, just a trifle lighter than her cat, Whisper, and of a satisfying firmness. The scent was not like that of a human baby's. Instead, it had the sweet, tangy smell of new-cut wood and milkweed. She breathed in the essence and hugged the baby tightly.

It didn't move. That was odd. Babies normally nestled closer to her for reassurance or affection. This child did neither. But it wasn't a normal baby, she reminded herself. She'd made it out of bits of wood and plant. Her spell, powerful as it was, couldn't change wood's fundamental nature. Hastily, she put it down. It smiled at her out of those unearthly eyes. Morrah turned away.

She tried many times over the next few days to warm to her creation. She felt ashamed that she felt nothing for it. There was no bond between them. It did not need her. It was content to lie in the cradle, or sit on her knee, or be placed anywhere she liked for as long as she liked. It could converse with her, but it knew nothing interesting, and received all information from her with "that is very interesting, Mother," but no reply evincing curiosity. Morrah found herself avoiding it.

She should have felt pride in her creation, but there was nothing. Where was the surge of maternal warmth she experienced when she watched the children of the court? Where was the protectiveness she felt toward the babies she helped to be born? Why did the baby she had created with her own hands not plead for her attention? The cat clamored more to spend time in her lap than the doll did.

There, she had told herself the truth at last: it was a doll, not a baby. She didn't even care enough about it to give it a name.

With the greatest reluctance, she removed the enchantment that animated it. She left it wrapped in a blanket next to the cat's basket. Whisper used it as a headrest, and occasionally rabbit-kicked it.

Morrah investigated other materials for creating her child. She hesitated to use hide or leather lest the soul of the animal from which it came remained behind, but that left plenty of other possibilities at hand. When market day dawned, she browsed the aisles of tents, tables and huts thoroughly, frowning at each display in search of inspiration. As she looked over this bolt of cloth or that block of wax she ran her palm over them, feeling for a spark of sympathetic magic. At the far end of the market, in the shadow of the castle itself, she found a golden-skinned peddler who had shining silks for sale. One pale-blue bolt set up a tingle in her palm.

"This will be perfect for my child," Morrah told the peddler.

"Ah, yes, it will look very fine wearing this cloth," he replied.

She looked at him coldly. "It is not for the child to wear. It is for *making* the child."

"Ah," the man said, nervously.

"I must cut it," she insisted. "I would not want it hurt."

The peddler might be a foreigner, but he clearly knew who she was. His deep brown eyes wide with awe, he handed over his shears and pocketed the gold coin she gave him.

But the blue silken doll she made from the cloth was no more satisfactory than the wooden doll. Pretty as it was, Morrah didn't love it or care about it. Whisper batted the light form all around the floor while Morrah contemplated the fire sadly, wondering if she would never have a child to cherish.

The stone effigy that followed the cloth doll moved and talked, but it had no more personality than the material of which it was made. She sent it as a present to the Duke of Dwarrowhelm. The wax baby she made laughed shrilly at everything. Morrah's patience lasted less than an hour before she removed the animation spell from the wax and threw the wax into the basket of candle stubs. None of these creations made an emotional connection with Morrah. Once the joy of making was over, she lost all interest in them.

Morrah began to despair. She hated to fail at any task. This one seemed so straightforward at the beginning. Nations had moved at her word. Why, with all the techniques and power at her hand, was it difficult to order the making of one single, perfect child?

Shunning the cheerful bustle of the town, she walked instead along the dirt roads that led into the gorse-studded hills to the north, to be alone with her thoughts.

Cool air and stark sunlight revived her and brought

out her honest streak. The decision to have a child had been an impulse. Never before had she considered whether or not she had to have progeny, someone to take after her, to inherit her power or her wealth. She had always been content before in her isolation. Interruptions made her impatient. She barely tolerated the elves who were her servants and messengers, let alone the pixies who invaded once in a while to spread their mischief.

It had been a whim, she realized, as she sank exhausted beneath the boughs of a gnarled old tree. She didn't really need to be a mother. The clear truth made her sad, but she would rather have known it than continue to pursue a task needlessly. It had seemed like the only thing she had not done in her long life, and she had pursued it as an intellectual exercise, not an emotional one. Therefore it was wise to stop. Loneliness was not enough of a reason. She would have had to put the interests of a child ahead of her own, and none of her creations had been worthy of subsuming herself. If she was missing something in her life, then she would go on missing it. Discontent but relieved, she walked home in the gathering twilight. On the morrow she would seek more worthy pursuits for her retirement.

"Honorable, come quickly!" Tansy piped, waking Morrah from her sleep.

Morrah was glad to leave behind the dream in which she had been reliving that last desperate, bloody rout of the Ngan pirates. The house elf seemed agitated.

"What is wrong?"

"Nothing! A good thing!"

The little female jumped down from the bed and glided out of the room toward the stairs. Morrah, shaking her head, slipped on her heavy robe over her night dress, and followed.

At the bottom of the steps the tower door was open. In the morning's cool light Oakleaf and Tansy stood over a basket.

"See, Honorable! A proper baby comes to you! It is beautiful!"

Eagerly Morrah bent over the basket and pulled the light blanket away. Blessed chance might have brought her what her own work had failed to do.

Beautiful? No, that was a sad joke. If she hadn't known better she would say this was a changeling, a troll's child put in place of a human baby. It was as ugly as a toad. The muddy-colored eyes bulged halfway out of the round, parchment-skinned face, and the mouth was a wide slit. The rest of the child was wrapped in some rough, dark-colored rags. Some poor girl unable to care for it had left it here in hopes of finding it a better life.

Morrah opened her mouth to say, "Get rid of it," when the child lifted its bulging eyes to hers. It smiled, the wide, toothless mouth crinkling up at the corners. The smile was truly beautiful. Morrah's heart twisted inside her. She stood up. "We must find who this child belongs to. Take it upstairs."

She turned away, the moment she did, the child burst out crying.

She turned back. The child quieted and looked hopefully at her through tear-wet lashes. It cooed. Tenderly, Morrah reached down and gathered up the pathetic bundle. It nestled close to her with a contented noise. Morrah cuddled it against her, discovering the sensation of warmth and protectiveness that she had craved and failed to find with any of the babies she had created. Here was the child she had been seeking.

In that moment, in that single sublime moment, she discovered how very wet this child was. She held out one hand, dripping with urine.

"Ugh!" Morrah exclaimed. She breathed a short incantation, and her hand was clean and dry once again.

The child gurgled and beamed at her.

"Well," she said, her gaze caught by the adoration in the baby's eyes. "Children do get messy. We must clean you, too, little one."

The house elves had shot upstairs ahead of her, and were waiting to show them off when she reached her bed chamber.

"We have many cloths that can be used for swaddling," Oakleaf said, holding up his finds.

"Not that," Morrah said, discarding one piece after another. "Nor that. The cloth of gold will scratch its skin. Oh, Oakleaf, not my court dress!"

"It is soft," the elf said apologetically. "And absorbent."

"Use this, Honorable," Tansy suggested. She held up the remnants of the blue silk.

Morrah hesitated.

"What better use?" the little female asked. "The doll-baby does not need it. My children would have liked the softness on the bottom."

"You are right, Tansy," Morrah said. "I hadn't planned on diapers. I hadn't planned on any of this."

The child was a boy, she discovered when she unwrapped him. She gave him a bath in her scrying basin, as no other appropriate sized vessel was available. So many things she lacked, since she hadn't been planning to raise a human child. She was now, of course, she thought in satisfaction, knotting a ribbon from one of her many orders around the makeshift diaper.

"I should seek out his real mother," Morrah said, picking up the baby. Once again, the little one nestled into the crook of her arm as if that was his proper place. "Oakleaf, prepare for the ritual of seeking."

The two wood elves hesitated.

"Well, what are you waiting for? A girl has lost her baby. What if she wants it back? What if she doesn't mean me to have him?"

"If she wanted to be found," Tansy said reasonably, "she would have waited on our step and said 'please take him.' But she didn't. She doesn't want him, and doesn't wish to say so out loud. But you do."

"Ah," Morrah said. "You are right. I do. Well, then, he needs many things. We must go and get them. For Nethan."

"Is that his name?" Tansy asked.

"Yes. He must not go unnamed. He is not a doll or an effigy, but a real child." Morrah smiled down at him. "You are Nethan."

The child kicked and waved his fists amiably.

"Will you leave him with us while you visit the market?"

That seemed like sense. Morrah began to hand him over to the two little people, but was reluctant to let him go.

"I'll take him with me," she said.

Shopping for a child was an unprecedented experience. Townsfolk who had treated her with respect and awe before changed to indulgent and friendly at the sight of a child in her arm. They seemed astonished to see her do something so ordinary. For once, Morrah reveled in the ordinary.

Morrah suddenly found herself the focus of a torrent of advice, good and otherwise. She listened to everything, even absurdities, with the reserved smile she had always kept for ministers out to further their own particular interests. Like the courtiers' needs, she planned to balance the townspeople's advice as it pertained to Nethan's well-being.

As for the child, no one could look at him, asleep and wrapped warmly in blue silk cloth, and do anything but gulp deeply and lie.

"A beautiful child, Honorable," they all said.

Morrah didn't care. She loved Nethan deeply, whatever he looked like. He loved her back with all the devotion she had ever wished for. She hated to be parted from him at any time. He hardly touched the ground during his first six months of life. When she permitted him to crawl it was upon a priceless silken carpet she had received from a weaver whose life she had saved.

She made inquiries widely, offering a reward for anyone who knew of a mother missing her newborn. No true replies. A few treasure-seekers tried for the reward, of course, but a mere glance in the truth mirror told her they were lying. She sent them all away with a tongue of flame speeding them hence. In truth, she was glad. She loved Nethan with all her heart. Here was the little life she would shape. One day he, too, would be a great wizard, beloved and respected by every nation.

Nethan slept most of the time, waking to cry in a thin

voice like that of her cat's. Morrah watched him sleep, needing little herself. She wondered at the soft, warm breaths that stirred the soft lips. At first she was appalled by the constant wetting and soiling, leaving the elves to clean it up, but then she started to envy them the look of relief and gratitude the clean baby gave them. Those happy coos ought to be for her alone! She took back the task. She had had worse jobs in her life. The elves tittered at her behind her back. She didn't care.

One night in Nethan's ninth month, Morrah became aware of little lights dancing past her eyes as she sat at her table eating supper. She squinted, concentrating on using her second sight, and the lights coalesced into human forms no larger than her hand. Pixies! At last they had managed to work a hole through the magical shield she had placed around her tower. She could figure out where the weak place was later on. In the meanwhile, she had to get them out as soon as possible before they caused too much mischief. She rose, seeking about her for her staff.

"Oakleaf! Tansy!"

"We see them," the house elves chorused. A crash echoed from her work room. The pixies had already upset something. A loud "Rraow!" told her that they were also tormenting Whisper. Morrah whipped up the household guardians. The ancient spirits, embodied as blue-white mists, seeped out of the very stone of the building.

"Kill them swiftly," Morrah ordered. She swept upstairs to Nethan's nursery.

The baby lay in his crib, crying. The pixies pinched his plump flesh, leaving red marks. He looked about him in confusion. Morrah became aware that he wasn't looking at the tiny lights that dipped and swooped over him. Every assault was a surprise. He couldn't see them! She grabbed him up.

"You're safe, little one."

"Mama!" he wailed.

The stream of pixies increased. They had hated her ever since she was part of a triumvirate of wizards who drove them out of the forest of Calum, the country to the northeast. Whether she could force them back through the mystic door to the land between times in which they had been imprisoned alone bothered her less than the realization that Nethan did not have the fairy sight. It was almost the least of the senses possessed by natural magicians. If he couldn't see those beyond normal sight, then he probably couldn't understand animal speech, nor feel magical energies . . .

"Oh, no you don't!" she said, reaching out to snap a large blue pixie in two. It had tried to land right on Nethan's head. Being broken in half destroyed the pixie's presence in this world. It dissolved in a blaze of diamond-bright light. Nethan didn't flinch or blink. He couldn't see them.

It took all night and half the next day to stem the flood of angry invaders. When it was over, Morrah placed Nethan back in his cradle. He had been bewildered by his mother's waving and shouting. He showed no sensitivity to the power flying about him. That would explain why he had never shown any awareness that there was anything different about her and the elves from the people they met in the market.

She scryed in the enameled basin for his true soul. His did not contain the marks even of an apprentice.

"What is that?" asked one of her colleagues who visited one day. Hervin appeared before her in his astral form, a translucent image bounded by a circle chalked on the floor. He pointed to Nethan, who sat on the floor building a tower from Morrah's alchemical equipment.

"That is my son," Morrah said proudly.

"Ugly little ferret." Hervin frowned. "He's spirit-blind. Did you know?"

"I did," Morrah replied. "He was a foundling."

"Well, what good is he if he lacks power?"

"What good is he?" Morrah asked indignantly. "What good is any child?"

"No, dear, what good is he to *you?*"

"I love him, Hervin."

The elder wizard looked amused. "That's a tiny word to saddle yourself with sixty years of caring for a magic-less tot with the face of a toad, dear. But, please yourself.''

Once he had departed, Morrah did sit down to think about his words. Nethan's lack of power did not matter to her, and would never matter, however long he lived. The love of that little child was a spell that gave her the youth she had never had.

Morrah had been old before her time. Blessed with the power when she was very small, she found herself a pawn of fate. To keep her power under control she had had to grow up and forsake all young-woman things. Here was something she could not and never would be able to control completely. How Nethan grew, what he showed interest in, what he liked to eat, what made him laugh, were all out of her realm of influence. He turned over her pots, pulled the cat's tail, tasted a variety of herbs, some quite dangerous, all with the same cheerful optimism that nothing bad could happen to him. That randomness was a joy that had been missing from the constructed children, and from Morrah's life in general. For a woman and wizard who had always planned events to the last detail his childish abandon was frightening, but intriguing. She felt that living backwards, from wisdom to impulse, made her a stronger mage.

Nethan, for his part, explored his world with an ever-growing curiosity. By the time he was a year old and taking his first steps, Morrah dared not leave him unsupervised lest he cause some fresh disaster.

"Mistress, this message comes for you!" Tansy chirped, dropping a scroll in her lap.

She had no sooner unfurled it when she heard a crash and a yowl that sent her running into her work room. She found Nethan sitting staring at a heap of glass shards she recognized as an alembic that had been made especially for her from the rose-quartz sand of the far desert. Morrah's hands shook with rage. How dare he destroy something so precious and rare that she had crossed a world to bring home?

"Mama?" Nethan said, offering her a hopeful smile. He pointed. "Pretty!"

Morrah pulled herself together. He couldn't know and did not understand the power inherent in the object he had just casually destroyed. She had to forgive him as she had never forgiven herself for mistakes. Reasoning with him at this age was pointless. She had never *not* known how dangerous or important something was, and envied this child its innocence. He only understood his own point of view. It was her own fault. She had to learn not to put temptation in its way.

"Yes, Nethan," she sighed as she caused a small whirl-wind to pick up all the pieces and deposit them far away from the tower. "It was pretty."

Morrah learned that no matter how many toys she provided for him, *her* things always seemed more inter-esting. She learned to form a magical tether preventing each from being removed from its place except by her. Her heart was torn two ways when he sat and cried with frustration at not being able to dislodge precious crystal phials containing water from the seven great dark wells. Her friends at the market were sympathetic but amused.

"Of course you must get all of your good things up out of his way," the weaver's wife said, with a laugh. "Wait until he starts climbing!"

Trouble as Nethan was, Morrah reveled in the joy he took. When a lightning storm lit up the sky over the town he clapped his hands and shouted "More! More, Mama!"

Dutifully, she caused the clouds to crash together over and over again, as he laughed gleefully at his own pri-vate light show. He had no idea as to what the use of power cost her, but she never grudged it. To Morrah there was no cost that shouldn't be paid for Nethan's joy. Her responsibility to him was to provide the best life possible, and with her resources, that was a fine life, indeed. If she went to bed exhausted and couldn't so much as scry the weather for the next week, what of it? It made Nethan happy.

She took to her old studies with new eyes. Her life's work had always been to serve others. She now made her focus to ensure that Nethan would be able to do whatever he wanted. She would find a way to make it happen. It caused her to view the ancient texts in new ways. Morrah sought to expand her own horizons simply by trying whatever came into her mind, instead of sticking by the old caveats and prohibitions. It took time to shed the ways of a lifetime, but she felt the years fall away from her. In her early life all things need to have had a purpose. How liberating it was to try things just for fun.

Following Nethan's example, she learned to enjoy events as they happened, just to watch them unfold. His experimentation with words as he learned to speak led her to play with the ancient spells, toying with the rhymes and bringing them up to date. Wait until she read the revisions to Hervin! They were half as long as the traditional chants, and twice as effective. What good was this spell-less toad-child? Why, he was revolutionizing magic, and all without casting a single spell!

"And so, my lord begs your help, Honorable," the page stammered. "He fears that his daughter is in the hands of the Troksir."

Morrah pursed her lips. With a quick swipe of magic she pulled Nethan away from the bookshelf and the *Tome of Animals* he was yanking therefrom. "I am familiar with the Troksir," she said. "If Princess Imrie is their prisoner, I will find her."

"Thank you, Honorable," the page said. He retreated from her study as quickly as he could, away from the ugly baby, the two hovering elves, and the formidable woman in red silks.

Morrah put her chin in her palm. It would be easy to spy upon the Troksir. Those troll-kin were surprisingly beautiful to behold but greedy and evil by nature. The spell to see into their realm was straightforward, made more so by her recent tinkering. Entrusting Nethan to the care of the house elves, she began her preparations.

The circle on the floor must be a particular shade of deep blue chalk. If properly drawn, no demon had ever been able to break free of that ring in all the history of magic. She lit candles of yellow for clear-sight, red for love, and gold for strength, and added a brimstone-heavy incense to her thurifer. These would lend her extra power if she had trouble maintaining the vision, which was really an insubstantial door into the Troksir's realm. Morrah sat down at arm's length from the edge of the circle, and drew power from deep within herself to open that door.

If Imrie had been taken, she would be in the hands of the Margrave, the Troksir's violent master. Morrah steered her vision in the direction of the greatest concentration of evil power, the black, fork-topped mountain. Beneath it was the Margrave's fastness.

Through soil, stone and wood her vision moved. She passed unseen among guards in helmets bearing spears. Troksir needed no armor with that thick hide of theirs, gold bright and studded with colored spots so like jewels that it had led many unwary treasure hunters to their doom. Morrah searched the entire fortress from attic to dungeons, yet saw no sign of the princess. Only one place remained: the audience chamber. With a flicker of thought she saw it. The Margrave sat on his throne made of his enemies' bones, hand propped on fist as if he was a human being, listening to several bright-skinned henchmen speaking. Was that a girl at his feet? She leaned close to look.

"Pretty!" Nethan crowed. He lurched forward into the room, making for the glittering figure of the Margrave.

Where were the house elves? "Not now, child! No!"

Morrah sprang up to catch him, but her old bones were too slow. He dashed over the chalk line, breaking the spell.

Suddenly, wizard and child burst into the Troksir's midst. The Margrave sprang up from his throne.

"Kill them!" he shouted.

Morrah threw up a shield spell. The first three Troksir that ran into it burst apart like rotten fruit. Nethan sat stunned at her feet. Morrah gathered him close to her, keeping him from straying beyond the sheltering enchantment. Now, where had she seen that girl? There, at the foot of the throne. Was that Imrie? It was! The young woman's face was dirty and bruised, and her lovely violet dress had been torn and soiled, but she had the wide green eyes and decided nose that had been in the royal family for generations. She reached out a beseeching hand to Morrah.

More Troksir threw themselves upon Morrah's defenses. The bodies momentarily blocked her vision. She pushed forward, and found herself treading upon gobbets of flesh and pools of ochre-colored blood.

"Ich!" Nethan wailed. "Messy!"

"Kill them!" the Margrave bellowed again. Behind her the doors of the audience chamber were flung open. No time to waste. Morrah pressed ahead. The Margrave sidestepped and seized a sword from one of his soldiers. He brought it crashing down on the top of the shield bubble. It bounded away, but not without doing damage to the spell. Morrah felt the energy weaken. Her attention was drawn two ways, managing the enchantments and keeping Nethan near her. He trembled in her arm.

Closer . . . closer . . . there! Morrah let the spell drop for a moment as she stretched out her staff. The girl, her wits still about her, grasped hold of it and was pulled hastily in. Morrah had to let go of Nethan to recast the protection. Just in time, the glowing globe reasserted itself in her mind's eye. Jagged-bladed weapons clattered inches from her face, and fell to the ground. Now, they must escape!

She sought about her for the broken line that represented what was left of her circle. It could not be too far away. If she could just reach it, she could redraw it.

Nethan clung to her leg, crying, as a hot red light enveloped them. The Margrave's wizard was at last responding to the threat. The fire spell drove Morrah to her knees, but she could not let Nethan or the princess be harmed. The new incantation for protection sprang to her lips. She recited it before the second spell could broil them. Cool air, like a shower of snow, fell around them. The Troksir wizard looked furious. Morrah wasted no time. She swept her son up in one arm and ran to the broken blue line on the floor. The girl stumbled behind. The Troksir wizard sent a golden arc of power after them, but Morrah swiftly redrew the line with her staff. The spell shattered in a shower of flame that stopped inches from their faces.

"Mama!" Nethan wept. Morrah dropped her staff and wiped his tears with her sleeve.

"There, now, dearest one," she said. "We are safe again, do you see? Lift your eyes."

The angry Troksir sought about them for the vanished intruders. The Margrave was berating his wizard for letting them go.

"All safe?" Nethan asked, his lip trembling.

"All safe." She helped the trembling girl to her own deeply cushioned armchair and settled her in with a warm shawl tucked around her shoulders. "You are safe, too, my dear."

"Thank you, Honorable," the girl said, quietly. She was pale under the grime and bruises, but she had regained her dignity now that they were out of danger.

Morrah turned to Oakleaf and Tansy, who stood at the circle's edge, their hands clasped tightly and their heads lowered in shame. "All is well. I am not angry. Tansy, take care of her highness. Oakleaf, take a message to the king. His daughter has been rescued. We await an escort to convey her safely home."

"We obey, Honorable!" Oakleaf exclaimed, much relieved. The elves sprang to fulfill their duties. Oakleaf disappeared out the window, and Tansy flitted over to pour a glass of wine for their guest. Morrah turned to Nethan, who sat on the floor, his lower lip trembling.

"Now, I've told you and told you to stay away when I am performing the great works," Morrah said, sitting down and gathering him onto her knee. "Why did you run into the circle? It was dangerous."

Nethan pointed to the glittering faces of the Margrave and his court. "They pretty," he said. "Fun watching."

Morrah raised an eyebrow. Their brief appearance in the court had caused chaos to descend. The Troksir were rushing around, pushing one another and turning over furniture, looking for the escaped hostage. The Margrave shouted and jumped up and down, his golden face gleaming with fury. More guards rushed into the room, responding to their lord's commands. They slipped on the bodies of their fallen comrades, landing with a loud crash on the floor. The wizard threw red balls of flame into corners, hoping to surprise invisible enemies. All he succeeded in doing was setting fire to the mismatched arrases that hung on the walls. More guards ran in with buckets of water, trying to extinguish the blaze, only to douse one another and the hapless wizard. The confusion caused the Margrave to become ever angrier. Morrah laughed, her face suddenly young. It was as good as a comedy play! It even elicited a low chuckle from the princess huddled in the armchair. Morrah embraced Nethan, enchanted once again by his own brand of magic.

"You know, my son," she said, plumping him on her knee, "it *is* fun. Let us watch together."

TOUCHING FAITH

Alexander B. Potter

Alexander B. Potter resides in the wilds of Vermont, editing anthologies and writing both fiction and nonfiction. His short stories have appeared in a wide variety of anthologies including the award-winning *Bending the Landscape: Horror* volume. He edited *Assassin Fantastic* and the award-winning *Sirius: The Dog Star* for DAW Books. A third anthology, *Women of War*, co-edited with Tanya Huff, was published by DAW in 2005.

SOMETHING TELLS ME to look up even before the *whump* of impact. Looking right at it, I still feel more than see the dark fluffy shape hit the kitchen window with a sound like it should break the glass. The tiny bird drops like a stone.

I jump up, heading for the front door at a run, but Mama calls me back from her place at the sink, washing dishes. "Don't touch it, punkin'. Call the cats in if you want, but don't touch it. It's probably just stunned and you know the mother might reject it if you handle it."

She's right, I do know that. Nine years of *Wild Kingdom* and *Animal Planet* obsession hasn't gone to waste on me. I also know she's a lot more concerned about whatever bugs might be on a bird than if the baby might be rejected. She doesn't even like me picking up old feathers off the ground. I have some hid under my bed anyway, but I never tell anyone because of the time Cat brought home a shoe box with salamanders in it and hid it under her bed and they got out and disappeared. Mama was convinced the things would get into the walls and grow bigger.

I actually sort of like the idea of giant salamanders living in our walls. I sometimes put my ear up to the wood paneling to listen for them, but I never hear anything. I think probably they hide from me. They know when I'm listening, and get all still and quiet.

The salamanders drop from my mind as I run down the front steps, hollering back "I'll be careful." I think I spend most of my life saying "I'll be careful." Well, that and "Yes, I washed my hands." Bouncing off the steps, I round the corner of our trailer at a run, skidding to a stop and searching the side yard. No cats in sight, to my relief. But the bird? The little fluff ball almost disappears in the grass, and I kneel carefully beside it.

The lawn is cool under my knees. The sun doesn't hit this side of the house, the western side, because of the tree line. I sit within touching distance, but just breathe. It's so small. Definitely just a baby. The tiny eye I can see glitters at me, open. It's aware, but the head is cocked off at a funny angle. I don't think it's just stunned.

I lean down, closer and closer, until the pointy green blades tickle my chin. The feathers on the puffy breast barely lift. My left fingers enter my field of vision and for a minute I almost think they're someone else's. I don't remember giving them permission to move. But that hangnail on the thumb is definitely mine and then the feel of the downy feathers registers on my fingertips, in my brain.

A pulse of heat flares down my arm, the blood pounding in every one of my fingers. The two fingers resting against the bird almost sizzle, as if I'm touching coals like the one Jennifer picked up by accident when she was a baby, because it was so pretty and orange. Her first finger is still slightly bent with the scar tissue. Never did straighten out fully, after that. Red hot coals burn in my mind as I jerk back from the bird, surprised.

But not half so surprised as when those little wings

suddenly twitch and spread, the tiny head realigning. The baby draws in on itself, then flutters into a takeoff, rising and falling down the lawn until it finally gets enough lift to stay in the air.

I push myself back to my feet, staring after it. *It must have been just stunned after all*, my brain says, like a good little soldier. It tries, my brain does. Doesn't do much good though, because I always know when the brain is just lying to make everybody feel better.

That bird wasn't stunned.

More to the point, I knew I could help before I ever touched it. I don't know why I knew, I just did. Whatever it was drew me up and out of the house, got me onto the grass beside it in the first place, knew. And I believed it before I'd even thought about it. The same belief got my hand out and moving before my brain could tell me it wouldn't do any good.

The same way I believe it now. I know what just happened. I know I healed a baby bird with my hand. No one *else* would believe me and everyone would say the little bird was just stunned and . . . well, that's fine, really. Doesn't much matter, the way I see it.

I stare down at my perfectly ordinary looking hand. Yep, it's a hand. My hand. With red paint from the picture I'd been working on, the one with the wheelbarrow that was sort of ending up in the sky, for some reason. I flex my fingers. Nothing happens. No heat, no sizzle, no nothing.

And I just know. It's right there. Inside. Waiting. It'll be back. Because I believe in it.

Very, very cool.

I turn to go back into the house. Gherkin now sits a few feet away, staring up at me with accusing yellow eyes. Blames me for letting lunch get away, I suppose. On my way past I scoop him up and bury my face in his sun-warm grey fur. He purrs. Forgiven, I think.

I go back inside and seeing me with the cat, Mama asks me if the bird is still out there. "No," I say, shaking my head. "It's fine. It flew away."

I don't say anything else to her. I don't say anything to anyone. Not even Cat. Not any of my sisters, or my dad. I know it was . . . special. Somehow, I know it means *I'm* special.

People have called me special all my life.

I just don't think this is what they meant.

At school "special" has a meaning all its own, and it's not a good one. Nobody wants to be in the special group, or go to special classes, or special sessions with the reading tutor lady or the speech therapist or the school counselor.

I get to go to all of them, except for speech therapy. I talk okay, just a little slow.

After my latest discovery with the bird, school seems even less important. Just another month or so before summer vacation anyway. But since I'm here, I figure I might as well put the place to use. I need more information and that's supposed to be what school is about. So I try to find out more from the library, about healing with your hands. About faith healers.

This is Vermont. There isn't much. Yankee practicality gets in the way of this sort of thing. 'Round these parts, seeing is believing. The only thing we take on faith is weather, and we don't trust that.

Of course, I am looking in a grade school library at a little country school. The pickings are slim by definition. *Highlights* and *Ranger Rick* and junior *Time* just aren't going to cut it.

I need more and I use the quiet of the library to try to puzzle out how to get it. The television has been a mixed bag. Nothing on my favorites . . . *Discovery* doesn't do much with faith healing, not even on *Unexplained Mysteries*. *Animal Planet* has weird stories every once in a while about animals who sense something wrong with their humans, like dogs who smell tumors or whatever, but I knew that wasn't what I was after. Flipping through channels I ran across some guy laying on hands. He'd call up sick people out of all the rows and rows of watchers, and put his hands on them and heal them. It didn't look exactly like what had happened to me, but it was the closest I've seen yet.

I made note of the channel number, and checked the

other religious stations too. My sisters thought it was downright weird when they'd catch me watching TV preachers, but Mama told them to leave me alone. She didn't think much of TV preachers and didn't mind saying so, but all she said was "watch out who you let tell you what the Bible says." I nodded and told her I wasn't exactly watching for religious or Biblical reasons.

She paused, looked at me in that way she does when my two and two just doesn't add up to four, and then nodded and handed me a piece of rolled up pie dough with cinnamon and sugar baked into it. And told my sisters to let me watch what I wanted, and that they could take over the programming at 8 o'clock.

My sisters made too much of a thing about it, anyway. Not like I'm always watching the religious channels. After all, they don't always play the healing shows. Sometimes it's a nun with an eye patch.

The few healing shows I did see had a weird similarity I was starting to clue in to. They were all grown *men*, in suits. They either did the "laying on of hands," as they called it, and shouted out or prayed, asking for the person to be healed, or they put their hands on the person's head and . . . well, pretty much it looked like the preacher man would smack the sick person on the forehead. They always seemed to fall over. The sick person, that is. The preacher man generally stayed on his feet.

I didn't see how that could be good for a sick person, but I was willing to assume they knew something I didn't. For the time being, anyway. I wondered if that's what my life was going to be. Doesn't inspire much in the way of job prospects, but I guess that's what people do, what people are, who do what I do.

Oddest of all, though, they all talked southern. Heavy accents, one and all. I've been practicing and I think I've got that down. I watch the *Golden Girls* in reruns with Mama and Daddy, and Blanche is perfect. If I keep her in my head and think "how would Blanche say it?" then I can hold onto the accent no problem. It's starting to be second nature.

But because all the preacher men doing television healing were so much the same, I knew I needed more information before I went out and got a suit and a . . . congregation, I guess. I'd been raised to not trust the television, in general, and I didn't trust the religious shows, in specific. They just didn't ring any of my bells, and felt a little sketchy besides.

Seems like the healers out there now all think it's the Lord working through them. Not exactly what it feels like to me. I know about the Lord, but I'm not completely sold. We don't go to church but Mama reads the Bible and, well, Daddy owns one. He gave it to me last year. Didn't look like it had ever been opened and Mama joked about that.

I've read parts of it, when I can make the words hold still. There are even a couple healing people in there. Overall it doesn't feel much like me, and I'm not so sure about this Lord. Mama doesn't push it even though she quotes it. She pretty much goes her own way on the whole religion thing. Which is maybe why these big churches and preacher men don't make much sense to me.

But I tend to think it's just because the whole religion thing doesn't make much sense to me. The fact that healing is so connected to religion for all these other people is starting to worry me, actually. If you have to be religious to do this . . . I don't know.

So I'm standing in my tiny Guilford School Library realizing that none of the magazine subscriptions here are going to help me. Forget the books. The *Hardy Boys* I don't need. A book on Bigfoot is fascinating and a little scary, but not exactly helpful. My eyes wander over to the row of computers lined against the right side of the room. But we can only touch those when we're assigned to, and I'm not. And when I am assigned to, there will be someone looking over my shoulder.

A sigh rises and falls in my chest. Not for the first time I wish we had one of the magic machines in our house. But Mama and Daddy and computers don't mix. We couldn't afford one even if they would get one.

"Come on, Evan. You don't want to spend another entire recess inside. You've been here three days this week already and your class has library tomorrow." Ms.

Marks, the librarian, pops up on my left. "It's beautiful out."

I jerk my eyes away from the computers and look up at her. She has really black hair, but what always make me stare are her nails. She's got nails like no other teacher here. Every single one is perfect, and long, and bright red. She even handles books funny because of it.

"Evan? Don't you want to go outside?"

I blink and force my attention away from her nails to her face. "No," I answer truthfully, before I remember I'm not supposed to say things like that. Normal kids like recess best. Normal kids always want to go outside. I hate recess. It's one of the worst parts of school.

Teachers are always going on about how we need exercise, and should go out and get fresh air. I don't mind the fresh air so much, but I don't need exercise when all it involves is me making sure I stay far enough away from some of the more . . . aggressive kids.

Besides, the teachers just want us to go outside so they can get a break from us. It occurs to me that probably Ms. Marks wants to eat lunch. She's looking at me with that puzzled look adults get around me. "But, yeah. I'll go outside now," I mumble, and skitter out from under her gaze.

Out on the playground I look around carefully, analyzing the various clusters of kids for levels of safety. That one is a definite no—the group playing basketball. The ones around the swings are reasonably safe to at least walk near, and the girls on the jungle gym won't bother me. Won't talk to me, probably, but won't bother me. My course plotted out, I start off the long way around for the jungle gym.

"Hey retard . . ."

The voice comes from the direction of the basketball hoop. Just great. I keep walking, ignoring it, but within seconds I can sense them closing in from the right. Dylan steps directly in front of me.

I don't bother to try to get by him. My eyes flick left and right. The recess monitor isn't within sight. She must be up the other end of the field. The kids on the swings are carefully ignoring us. Big surprise. I sigh and stare at Dylan silently. I just need to wait until the monitor gets back down here.

"Where you been, sped? Tying your shoelaces? Or practicing the alphabet . . ."

His friends laugh. I just stand there. Considering some of the grades I've seen on his social studies tests, you wouldn't think Dylan would be in the business of calling other people stupid. Doesn't take much to ignore him though, since I know I'm not. Stupid, I mean. The doctors that the school wanted Mama to take me to all said so. They couldn't quite figure out what was wrong with me, but they all said I was perfectly intelligent, given enough time to work things out. They think I might have some "learning disabilities" but they don't know exactly what.

"Playing dolls with the kindergartners?" chimes in Julie from beside Dylan. "That's about your speed."

I shift my eyes to her and continue the blank stare. I've had adults tell me to stop looking at them like that. I don't know what it is exactly, but something about my stare makes some people a little jumpy. I figure I can use all the jumpy I can get at the moment. Inside I sort of wish I *had* dropped by the kindergarten room to play dolls. Sounds kind of fun.

A shadow falls across us and I immediately think with relief that the monitor finally noticed something. But when I look up, it's not the monitor. It's Cat, and Jennifer is standing behind her, arms crossed. The wash of happy feeling starts at my toes and floods up through me at the glares on my sisters' faces and the way Dylan and Julie and their friends back up. I see other heads turning to watch us from the swings, and the jungle gym. When seventh and eighth graders show up down here on our playground, the third and fourth graders notice.

"Everything all right, Evan?" Cat asks, tossing her hair behind her shoulder and leveling a stare at Dylan that would ice over the cafeteria's vegetable beef soup.

Jennifer takes a step toward the other kids. "Back off, you little maggots," she snaps. "Catch you bothering our brother again and get ready to eat your damned basketball."

Two of the kids turn and walk off, fast. Besides being two of the prettiest girls in the junior high classes, Jen scares people and Cat intimidates the hell out of everyone. I beam at them both and step closer. Jen feints at the remaining kids, and they all turn and run off. I look up at my sisters. "How'd ya'll know?"

Cat leans down, hands braced on her knees. "You glow, Ev." She flicks her eyes up to my blonde hair and grins. "When it's sunny out, you're hard to miss. We saw you come out and we saw the basketball game slow down and break up."

"We keep an eye on you," Jennifer adds, still glaring at the knot of kids who are back to dribbling and shooting the basketball and casting worried looks over at her. "Besides, we were watching for you because you haven't been out at recess for a couple days."

"I've been in the library." I walk between them as we head across the playground. I know they need to get back to the upper field or they'll get in trouble. "Sort of research. But I need the computer."

"Yeah? We're doing Reading Buddies with you guys this afternoon. How about if I tell your buddy to take you to the library and you guys can get on the computer? That's allowed. I did it with my third grader a couple weeks ago. You can read articles."

"Really?" I bounce in place. "That would be awesome! Will you ask her?"

"Sure. You've got Terry, don't you?" She turns as Jennifer tugs her arm and nods toward the junior high teacher crossing the upper field. "Whoops, see you later, munchkin. We've got to get back up top."

We're almost at the jungle gym. I nod, happy with the new plan. "Thanks," I call after them as they walk away up the hill. They both wave and Jennifer calls back, "and stop *talking* like that."

I just smile, and walk to the bars. I climb up about halfway, then settle in, draping my arms over the crosspiece at chest level. From above, a girl from my class peers down at me. Rachel. She treats me okay when no one else is around to hear her be nice to me. I smile at her.

She looks at me, then at my sisters walking away, then back at me. "Your sisters are wicked pretty," she finally says.

I nod. "I know."

My Reading Buddy, Terry, is awful nice. I wish I could spend all my time with my sisters' classes. Their friends are even nicer to me than they are. I remember when I was little, a couple years ago, I used to think that I'd get to be in classes with their classmates when I got to the grade they were in. Then it finally occurred to me that everyone keeps moving up the grades, not just me. So I would always be with this group of kids I'm with now.

What a depressing thought.

But Cat talked to Terry and she takes me to the library and gets us onto the computer. I'm so excited it didn't even occur to me that Terry would be watching what I looked up. The thought finally hits me as I call up the browser. I pause. This is going to be interesting.

"So what do you want to look up?" Terry asks.

I try to think fast. Speed isn't my strong suit and I don't lie well at all. All I can think of is my sisters calling me weird for watching the TV preachers. "How about . . . something strange and kind of, you know, out there," I offer tentatively.

Terry grins. "Cool! Like UFOs? Or Bigfoot?"

Huh . . . Bigfoot twice in one day. I wonder what that might mean. Before I can get sidetracked, I force myself back on task. I get distracted way too easy. It's one of the reasons I don't pay attention so well in class. And it sounds like my ploy is working, so I need to focus. "Yeah, like that. Like . . . people who heal with their bare hands."

"Oh, I've heard about that," Terry points to the screen. "Put in 'faith healers'. Or maybe 'healing hands'."

I'm already typing. The hits are immediate and plentiful. Terry helps me pick out which ones to click. The words start jumping around right off, so Terry also helps me read, which is another big plus to this whole Reading Buddy thing. I really owe Cat big time for thinking of this. With Terry reading and helping me decipher what all the website articles say, this is going a lot faster than if I did it alone. As a rule, letters and numbers just won't stay still for me. When I first tried to explain that to the teachers, they thought I was dyslexic.

I'm not. They just move. If I concentrate real hard, and go very slowly, I can get them to settle down, but sometimes they don't settle down in the right order.

At least half of the hits are all trying to sell something. Either a healing hands massager, or a book, or natural medicines, or an appointment with someone who has golden hands and charges $90 to put them next to people. I wonder if his hands are really gold, and if he paints them. Terry and I both start giggling when we get to the part where the website says that one of the side effects is women experience firmer, more erect boobs after sessions with this guy. They even use those words . . . boobs.

I really don't think I want to spend my life giving women firmer boobs.

We agree that we should have expected the sales pitches, the internet being what it is.

With Terry's help, I get past the advertisements to the articles. The browser doesn't distinguish between the pro and con articles, and it looks like there is no middle ground with faith healing. This makes me wonder. None? How can that be? The articles are very clear though. They are split right down the center, with a little more than half of them going off about how all faith healers are charlatans (my new word for the day . . . Terry and I both had to look it up) and con-people and even dangerous because they keep sick folks from getting real help. The authors are frank in their disgust, and the stories range from silly to scary. Doctors and stage magicians wrote them, and people who research fakes.

The positive articles are almost all personal testimonials, talking about "true stories." Where the doctors and research people tried to document things all scientific-like, and did definitely find some frauds, the pro side of the arguments are mostly people talking about what they've seen or felt, and making a strong connection between the power of the healer and the healer's faith.

There are women in both sets of articles. That's the first big difference I notice, even with the horror stories crowding my brain. Not just men in suits. That's a relief. I don't know why, but that part was really worrying me. Religion is still all over the place, though. I'm not sure how to take that. Some of it is very "New Age," according to Terry, but it's all still connected with a "Higher Power" moving through the healer and touching the sick.

I'm not sure it felt like some force moving *through* me. It felt more like something already inside me, coiled up and ready to stretch out and get bigger at any moment.

On the whole, the internet gets me a lot more information, but doesn't leave me any more convinced I want to jump on board with these people who call themselves faith healers. The people who are against it make rational arguments and the people who are for it sound all kooky. Terry and I both get a little depressed with it all and we switch over to stories about Bigfoot.

For the rest of the afternoon, the thought hangs in the back of my head that maybe I imagined the whole thing. Maybe I'm a fake just like the internet said about everyone else. They made really good cases and some of the researchers went in with open minds and tried hard to find someone doing real healing. They just ended up disappointed and watching "healers" pretend to pull bits of cow and pig intestines from sick people's guts.

I feel a little sick to my stomach. By the time I head for home I'm downright miserable.

The following week I've got another check up appointment with the doctors the school told Mama about. Last time they put me in a big machine that made a lot of noise and they let me listen to music on headphones. They said they were scanning my brain, which I thought was so cool. I had to stay very, very still. They were surprised at how good I was at being still, and I think they thought I was going to be really scared. I just thought it was kind of neat.

We drive over to Keene to see them. Now that they've ruled out me being dyslexic, they are still trying to figure out what I am.

Me too.

The teachers and doctors don't understand because I can talk fine—just a little slow—and I guess sometimes I say things that make them think I'm really smart but that doesn't make any sense with the rest of me. Or at least the rest of me as they experience me. People see me staring out the window or trying to work out a math problem and they hear me talking slow and they just jump to conclusions.

As we're driving through town we pass the little restaurant on Canal Street and there is a big easel sign out front that says STOP STUFFED CABBAGE AND CHICKEN FINGERS. I giggle. Stopping stuffed cabbage sounds like a fine idea, but I don't have any thing against chicken fingers. I know what they meant—they wanted people to stop and eat—but they didn't put in any punctuation so it looks like a protest sign. I laugh all the way to Keene about the idea of people marching against stuffed cabbage. I feel bad for the chicken fingers though, caught up in all the vegetable anger.

Thinking about food puts me in mind of how Mama always buys me jelly donuts after going to the dentist. Or a cookie as big as my hand, from the bakery downtown. But this isn't the dentist, so I don't know.

We get to the medical center in Keene, go in, and find the elevator. Mama doesn't really like elevators, but the directions to the doctor's office told us to use it, and we don't know how to find the office using the stairs. It's like a little maze over here. Well, a big maze. This is one of those really expensive places, you can tell by the smell. And the carpet. Mama and Daddy were really worried about that until the school people said they could help us because the state would pay for the tests they wanted me to have.

We get on the elevator with two little old ladies and a guy in pink pajamas wearing a big name tag that means he works here. His name is David. I can't make his last name stay still long enough to read it. I also can't help but stare. He has dark hair and really blue eyes behind glasses with black frames.

Instead of telling me to stop looking at him, he smiles at me. He looks nice. "Hi there," he says.

"Hello." I drop my voice to a whisper. "Why are you wearing pajamas at work?"

He coughs and grins. "They do look like pajamas, don't they? They're called scrubs. Lots of people who work in hospitals wear them."

"Ah." I nod my head and he smiles again. Mama's hand closes on my upper arm and she gives me a stern look. Mama always tells me not to talk to just any person I see but sometimes I can't help it. I've tried to explain to her that it's okay, that I know who to talk to and who not. Everybody has dots around them. Some people have bright shiny yellow dots and they shine like little individual suns. Other people—the people I don't tend to talk to—have little swirly dots around them that look like itty-bitty violet purple tornados. Some people are sort of a mix.

Even the kids at school have dots. Usually kids are mostly bright and shiny but some of them have dark spots, too—like Dylan. It's a little unusual to see somebody my age looking that dark that early, but I've seen it more than once. Sometimes I think I've almost got it figured out why some kids are so much darker than others. But then it slips away.

One thing I have definitely figured out is that other people don't see the dots. So I stopped talking about it a *long* time ago.

Either way, the guy in the pink pajamas is all shiny. I'd like to keep talking to him, but he gets off on another floor.

We get to the doctor's offices and as usual they have me sit in a little room with books and toys while the doctor talks to my mom in his office. The door is open and I can hear them but I always pretend I'm not listening. Today is interesting. My brain is normal.

For some reason that strikes me as really funny.

"I'm sorry I don't have anything more conclusive, Mrs. Trevalyen. The good news is the scans look great. Developmentally his brain is fine. From our previous tests, he's obviously intelligent. We're thinking perhaps his thought processes just work in a slightly different way than we're used to . . . and that he needs a little more time than most kids. He can obviously reason and come to conclusions. His conclusions are just . . . very different."

My mother snorts. "That's all well and good, Doctor, but the school isn't so convinced of his obvious intelligence. They still want me to take him out and enroll him in a special school."

Ah, a special school. For special kids. Like me. I smile down at my book about bees and giant jam sandwiches. It's really old, but I like it, and I dig it out of the basket every time I come here.

"Well, I understand the school's concerns, given he isn't truly operating on his grade level despite his innate intelligence. He doesn't seem to come at learning in a direct, logical progression. In some ways normal development *is* definitely off. The bottom line is there doesn't appear to be an organic brain issue at work, though, which is good news. I still believe we're looking at a form of learning disability, that just isn't easily quantifiable."

Quan-ti-viable. I need to remember that one. Another one to look up. I'll get Cat to help me, and I'll clomp-beast her leg if she doesn't.

"There's so much about the brain we still don't understand, Mrs. Trevalyen."

"And there's so much about my son *no one* seems to understand. He's still saying completely nonsensical things. We're in the grocery store and the woman—who is a perfect stranger, mind you—this woman next to me is saying something about the green beans to me and Evan looks up at her and says 'Don't worry. He still loves you. He's just really angry right now. Give him a little time.' I thought the woman was going to burst out crying. And now? He's started speaking in a southern accent. He says it's going to be expected of him."

I can't hear the doctor say anything. His silence actually sounds pretty funny to me.

"We are Vermonters, Doctor. We do not speak in Southern accents."

There is another long pause and I can almost see the doctor's face as he struggles to find something to say. Finally he says, "I'd like to arrange for further testing."

I sigh.

Now Mama is the one who is silent. Finally I hear her voice. "I don't think testing is what my son needs."

"But an extended study . . . your son is obviously different, and we may yet be able to determine what's going on. There are more extensive imaging tools." There is another, shorter, awkward pause, then the doctor clears his throat. "In the meantime . . . have you considered therapy?"

"My son does NOT need therapy." My mother's voice is ice, and I can hear exactly where Cat gets that tone.

I can also almost hear the silent "we are Vermonters, Doctor, we do NOT need therapy." I think the doctor can too, from the way he hurries on.

"I understand your hesitation, but I have some excellent referral sources, and I think-"

"I think we're done, Doctor. Thank you for all your . . . help." I hear the chair scrape as Mama stands up, then her heels are clicking across the floor and she's back in the room with me. "Ready to go, Evan?" She holds her hand out to me.

"But Mrs. Trevalyen—"

Mama walks out, my hand held tightly in hers. I glance back at the doctor, standing there with a distressed face, watching me walk away. Even though I don't want any more tests and I want to jump up and down that Mama said no, I still feel bad. His dots are yellow, they're just really faded, so they're almost beige. I smile at him, and wave. The corners of his mouth lift, and he waves back.

As we walk back to the elevator I look up at Mama. She's got her worried face on. Mama worries too much. I tug on her hand. "Can I have a jelly donut?" I ask hopefully.

She looks down at me, and smiles. "Sure. Let's go to

the cafeteria." We know where that is too, because when I had to come over for tests they didn't let me eat before. So they gave me a free breakfast after. We ride the elevator down, walk around two corners, and find a table. "Sit and wait here. I'll go get the donuts," Mama instructs.

I nod and sit. The cafeteria is busy. At the table next to ours an old man with hearing aids just like Daddy's sits with an old woman in a bathrobe, with a cane leaned up against her chair. He's got a worried face just like Mama's. He holds the woman's hand and I can see from here that she has his gripped so tight her knuckles are white.

Pain. Pain is everywhere in her face, and her dots are practically wincing with every breath she takes.

Something warm uncoils in my chest. Reaches through my arms, spreading like the heat of the wood stove in the middle of our Vermont winters. And I need to go to her.

When the man leans over and says something to her, she nods, and he rises with both her cup and his own, and heads for the table of juices and coffee and tea. I'm standing beside her without any memory of moving.

She smiles at me, a pained stretch of her lips that tries hard to climb to her eyes. "Well, hello there."

"Hello." I smile back at her and my hand is settling on her arm, gently. I feel the heat stretch and grow, arching like Gherkin after he's just taken a nap in a sunbeam. I can almost picture the heat inside me stretching out paws and kneading like Gherkin does. The sizzle is in my hand and bursting from every finger and finding her bones and going straight to her hip. I can feel it, I can feel the burst of fire when it settles in her hip and explodes, healing the bone that has collapsed from something called avascular necrosis and I don't know what that means and I don't know how I know the words at all but it's just there and all that really matters is the reformed bone and the look of surprise and relief flooding her face.

"What—" she breathes, and then a voice beside us speaks.

"Well, well, who is this?" The old man is back, setting down two cups of tea and smiling at me.

"Hello. I'm Evan." I beam at him and then look back at his wife, still staring at me, now with tears in her eyes. "And I'm not a fake," I add happily, patting her arm. "Feel better, now," I whisper and start to turn back to my table. Her hands stop me, as she pulls me back around and closer, pressing a kiss to the top of my head.

"I don't know what . . . how . . ."

I shake my head. Don't try to figure it out, lady. Nobody else can, either. "Just feel better," I repeat. I let her hug me one last time and walk back to my table. Mama isn't back yet. The cafeteria is really crowded. Behind me I can hear her telling her husband that she can't feel any pain, that she feels like she can walk without the cane. I climb back into my chair and wait for my donut.

Almost immediately, I feel a prickly sensation on the back of my neck, and I look in the other direction. The man in the pink pajamas is standing a few feet away, with a puzzled look on his face. Something about the way he stands there makes me think he's been watching me with the old woman.

I can't help smiling at him. His dots bounce like the little happy faces from the Wal-Mart commercials. He smiles back, and I remember my word of the day from a few days ago—bemused. I giggle. He walks past my table and sits down with the old couple.

Mama comes across the cafeteria with a little bag of donuts. I jump up and grab her hand and we head back out to the dreaded elevator. I actually like riding the elevator but I feel bad because she hates it so much.

I start humming as we ride back up to the main floor to leave. I decide not to go with the suit or the congregation at all. I think maybe a pair of pink pajamas might be in my future.

But I'm going to keep the Southern accent.

THE HORSES OF THE HIGH HILLS

Brenda Cooper

Brenda Cooper has published fiction and poetry in *Analog, Oceans of the Mind, Strange Horizons,* and *The Salal Review,* and been included in the anthologies *Sun In Glory* and *Maiden, Matron, Crone.* Brenda's collaborative fiction with Larry Niven has appeared in *Analog* and *Asimov's.* She and Larry have a new novel, *Building Harlequin's Moon.* Brenda lives in Bellevue, Washington, with her partner Toni, Toni's daughter Katie, a border collie, two gerbils, and a hamster. By day, she works as the City of Kirkland's CIO, applying her interests in science, technology, and the future to day-to-day computer operations and strategic planning. She writes for *Futurist.com* and can sometimes be found speaking about the future, and suggesting that science fiction books make great reading. The rest of the time, she's writing, reading, exercising, or exploring life with her family.

MORNING SUN PAINTED the wood chips on the path under Carly's slender feet red and orange and soft yellow. Soon, the Sawdust Festival would open and the nearly-empty byways would fill with tourists come to mingle with the Laguna Beach artists, listen to the buskers, and eat hot dogs and popcorn and chips. For now, it was just the artists, sipping strong coffee and hoping for a good Saturday crowd. Maybe Carly's mom, Suzanne, would sell enough pottery today to bring another load from the garage studio they rented up-canyon. If Carly brought her coffee, maybe she could jump-start a good mood; make the day one of those rare ones when her mom stayed with her.

Marla, the women's shelter lady who served coffee in the morning, sat behind a big yellow picnic table with stick-figure families hand-painted on its top in bright colors. A blue and white family planning banner fluttered above her head and two coffee pots stood on a cart off to the side. She smiled softly at Carly. "Good morning, little one. Come for your mom's coffee?"

"Yes, please." Carly eyed the bench beside the tall blond woman.

"Sit."

Carly sat. Marla reached in her purse for a brush and started in on Carly's wild hair. "When I was eleven," she said, "my mother made me cut my hair off because I never brushed it."

Like her mom would bother. Carly smiled, grateful for the way Marla held her hair so pulling out the tangles didn't hurt. Much. She sat, silent, while Marla combed through her red-blond hair until it lay shining along her arms, falling nearly to her elbows.

"You know, you can come by the shelter any time."

Going would be defeat, would be like she couldn't handle her mom, and she could. Besides, her mom needed Carly to keep her from screwing up too bad. "No thanks. Mom needs me, and we take care of ourselves."

Marla smiled softly. "Sometimes, caretakers need to be taken care of—just so they can go on helping. You, or your mom, are welcome any time."

It wasn't the first time Carly had heard Marla's offer, and it wouldn't be the last. But she and her mom didn't need help. Not from outside.

Marla put the brush away, then poured a cup of coffee. "Here, take this to your mom." Her gray-blue eyes gathered the clouds of worry that she wore so often. "And take care of yourself today, okay?"

Carly curled her fingers around the warm cardboard cup and looked down at the ground. "I'll be okay." She turned, not wanting to see Marla's face, knowing the exact sad smile Marla would be wearing, the one she used for all the women and girls she worried for.

Back at the pottery booth, Carly's mom, Suzanne, reached for the coffee, her face crumpled up with her usual morning headache. Her hands shook. "Thank you, honey," she said, actually smiling. "Go on now."

"Don't you want me to help you this morning?" Carly asked.

Guilt flashed briefly in Suzanne's eyes, then she brushed her short red-brown hair back and looked right through Carly, the guilt gone to cunning. "When I was a kid, I would never have wanted to hang around with my mom. You go on, play." She fished into her pocket and handed Carly a dollar. "Go on—you can come back after it gets busy."

Carly balled the bill in her fist and walked away. If she wasn't in trouble for not being around, then she was in trouble for being around. Just past the first curve she ducked below John Kiley's silver booth, careful not to rattle the glass cases, and peeked back at her mom through the wooden slats. Sure enough, Suzanne poured whisky from the dark-glass bottle she kept in the bottom of her cash drawer into her coffee. Suzanne glanced in Carly's direction, but looked up instead of down. Later in the day, she wouldn't even bother to hide the bottle, but she always tried in the morning.

Some mornings like this, Carly sat by Marla and helped hand out coffee and brochures about AIDS and birth control and family violence, but she'd told Marla she'd be okay.

Well, fine. There was still one place she could go. Carly stepped aside to avoid Jack the caretaker as he passed by, mumbling about fixing the back wall. He called hello at her. She nodded and raised a hand, hiding her face and the tears hovering at the edge of her eyes.

She liked Jack all right, but she didn't want to explain her mood.

She leaned on the rail at the highest public place in the festival—a wide bridge with tables for gathering and a good view. From up here, she could see most of the festival: three acres of unique hand-crafted booths lining winding pathways, and all of it enclosed in a wooden wall, except the back, where a natural scrabble and stone cliff made most of the back wall without any help. The food booths were to her right the right, the stage below her. As festival-goers starting filling the paths, she faded back toward the waterfall behind her, feeling the tug of the water as if it called to her unshed tears. She turned, closed her eyes, and stepped through, water falling on her face, her back, heavy and sweet and bracing. Hands in front of her, Carly felt the soft give of the stone wall as it enveloped her, the thickness of the shimmering black and gray fog of the stone, and emerged on the far side. Stars shone above her.

She'd found the water-door during the first week of the festival, and she ended up back here almost every day, though she usually went later since the time was oddly skewed on this side of the doorway—almost two hours behind.

Carly let out a long breath, and wrapped her arms around herself, blinking at the early-morning dark. She shivered, wet from the waterfall. The pre-dawn stillness of the High Hills felt good. A soft wind blew through the trees below her, and three coyotes called the end of night from up-canyon. She started carefully down the path to Gisele's studio.

The stars began to fade and the black humps of hills to resolve into details like low trees and boulders and ravines in the rising light. The High Hills looked like Laguna Canyon might have before the town came. Carly squinted down to the sea, watching it turn from gray to blue as the sun rose behind her. Beyond the river, a little town nestled in oak trees and big boulders, but Carly had never been that far. What if she got lost, and couldn't find her way back to her mom?

She crossed the river at the stone ford and turned back toward a small wooden workroom perched on the river bank under a stand of oak. She glanced back at the cliff that held this side of the doorway between her world and the High Hills, reassuring herself, even though it was always there.

Carly pushed the door open and let the morning light into the dark room. An old woman sat bent over her desk, shaping a tiny wooden bird with a small file held perfectly between bent and twisted fingers. Carly sighed, slightly cheered to be here, but as confused as always— as if crossing through the water-door bent the world sideways; it was hard to make sense of the High Hills. Gisele looked up, her wrinkled eyes narrowing. "Well, there you are."

"Good morning, Gisele."

Gisele's voice was matter-of-fact, cool, as she said, "Can you stay long enough to finish the horse?"

"I bet I can be gone half the day," Carly muttered. Not that Gisele cared about her other life. Why should she? Carly looked over at Gisele, noting how deep the darkness under her eyes was this morning. Gisele had her own problems, she'd lost her son and granddaughter to Carly's world five years ago and not seen them since, and her husband had died this past winter. She should feel sorry for Gisele, but she was pretty sure this was a made-up world anyway. It had to be, right? But even if the High Hills was really just her imagination, she didn't have to act as crazy and rude as the drink made her mom. She could be nice. "Did you sleep well last night?"

Gisele held the little bird up to the light with her right hand, stroking its wooden head with her right finger. "From midnight till a few hours ago. Go on with you, girl, get started."

Gisele must have a tender heart for all that she never really gave Carly a break. No one without a good heart could possibly make some magical little animals. Carly sighed and went to her little workbench, picking up the fist-sized wooden horse that lay half-painted in front of her. She turned it over and over in her hands, searching for its soul. She'd given it a dark coat, and painted a star on its forehead and two white socks, one on each front foot. She forgot Gisele's sternness as her hands roamed the perfect musculature, the tiny hooves, the long tail that curled gracefully down to the horse's hocks. Gisele had given the horse its perfect shape, and taught Carly to hear its dreams and paint it awake. That used to be Gisele's husband's job, and Carly was new at it, and slow. A whole box of carved wooden animals sat waiting for Carly's paintbrush. She'd never finish them all this summer, not with the festival closing in two weeks, closing off her access to the water-door. Gisele had warned her that the waterfall-door stopped working when the festival closed, and didn't start again until it had been open a few days.

Carly mixed a dark sienna, streaking it with off-white, and swabbed her brush softly through it. Always good to do the hooves early. As she dabbed the paint on, it smoothed itself, filling in cracks, as if it knew exactly where to go.

She finished the white tail and started on the mane. The wood felt bristly under her hands, beginning to soften until Carly stroked it, getting white on her fingers, murmuring, "Be still, little one, let me paint your spirit, your strength, your speed."

As she reached for the dark eye-black Gisele came and stood behind her, one gnarled hand on Carly's shoulder. "Speak it softly with that one," Gisele whispered.

"Come alive, little one, come and dance." She dabbed one eye with paint and turned the horse over. "Come now," she whispered, brushing the other eye on, and the horse raised its head in her hand and looked at her calmly. Carly flattened her palm for the little horse to stand up on. It struggled up, its back hooves digging in near her wrist, its front feet settling in just where her middle and index fingers joined her palm. It tossed its head and flicked its tail, and she reached down and stroked it. It shuddered. She crooned, and it finally calmed, whickering softly and nosing her finger.

"Nice job," Gisele said.

Carly kissed the little horse back to sleep and set it

carefully in the box Gisele had made for it. "I wish I could take it with me."

"It might sleep forever in that world," Gisele said, her voice rough.

Carly swallowed her longing. The horse could be such a friend! "I know." And suddenly the tears she'd hidden from Jack and drowned in the waterfall and blinked away in the cold on this side of the rock poured out of her, falling on the sleeping little horse, on Carly's hands, on Gisele's hands. Gisele turned Carly's head up and looked deep into Carly's eyes. Gisele's eyes were such a soft blue they were almost white. As if the years had thinned them. Carly shuddered a little. Why did she come here anyway? Surely the High Hills were a dream. Gisele was the only person she'd seen here, but there had to be more, people to bring the wood and make the tea and buy the little animals Gisele made. People that lived in the little town in the distance. "Can't I stay here? I like being magic."

Gisele brushed at Carly's hair, a gesture like Marla's, but with no worry for Carly in her eyes. Just sadness, and magic, and age. "Take the horse with you. Just bring it back." She gestured to the box by Carly's arm. "I made it a family, and families should stay together."

So that was Gisele's answer about staying. "Why doesn't the magic go with me?"

The edges of Gisele's mouth turned into a thoughtful frown. "Doesn't it?" she asked.

"How would I know?" Carly glanced at the box, furrowing her brow. "Can I take a waiting one, too? Paint it over there?"

Gisele took her hand from Carly's shoulder and turned away. "Be careful with them. Go on now, go home."

Carly sighed. Gisele's sadness reminded her of her mom, except Gisele just kept going, making magic instead of pots. She didn't try to distract herself, and her only addiction was her craft.

Carly patted the sleeping little horse, watching it breathe softly. She closed the lid over it. Then she picked out a small mare from the box. She found a box for it, too, and put one horse in each pocket, then walked back to the ford, across the meadow, and up to the doorway. From this side, she had to close her eyes and trust, and her hands always went first, feeling for water, needing the wet on her fingertips before she could make her body walk through the stone.

It was past lunch at the festival and the summer sun beat down on the pond below the waterfall. She had to step around two little boys splashing each other and laughing while their mom took pictures. The woman looked at her and smiled patiently, waiting for Carly to step out of the space between the camera and the boys. Somehow no one ever asked her how she appeared from inside the waterfall, even though the stone wall shone wet and solid behind it. It must be part of the magic.

Carly walked back down the path until she could see her mom talking earnestly with an old woman about a vase. Satisfied that her mom was okay, she clambered up behind Paula's leather booth to a rock ledge and wriggled until she could get the two horses out of her damp pockets. The first box she opened held the unpainted mare, looking as warm and alive as wood-tools could make it, like it looked in the High Hills. Waiting. She opened the other box, and the black horse lay with its legs tucked into the same position as she'd seen it last. It didn't breathe, but its mane lay tangled and the paint that filled in its eyes was too perfect to have been done by a clumsy brush: the whites showed, thin as a hair, and the center of each eye glowed just slightly darker than the outside. The little horse felt caught—not dead, not alive. Perhaps its spirit had gone back to the same place the other carved animals waited before Carly painted them. She closed each box, confused that they were still there, pleased that life still whispered through the black horse's stillness. Only then did she realize she truly hadn't expected the boxes to pass through the waterfall. The meant the High Hills were real, right? She wasn't making it up, and suddenly she knew she had known that, but she couldn't really believe it, and now she had to. It made her tremble and want to sing, both at the same time, and she just sat there and held the boxes in her hands, not opening them again, but

holding them and looking from one to the other. It took
almost a half-hour before she was ready to tuck the
boxes back into her pockets.

All afternoon she kept them in her pockets while she
fetched lunch for her mom and helped wrap up two sets
of candlesticks, a vase, and a salt and pepper set her
mother had fashioned into a cat and a mouse, each so
fat it would take two hands to use them. She tried to
ignore the horses as hard as she tried to ignore the coming night.

Dark came anyway.

As day faded, the festival crowd shifted. Families and
busloads of gray-haired grandparents with canes and
canvas shopping bags gave way to young women with
bare bellies and young men with pierced eyebrows
prowling for the women or for other men, to a mix of
locals and tougher, edgier tourists come to feed on the
festival's drug trade and guzzle beer from Coke cans.

Carly eyed the change with distaste while her mom
began to fidget and started excusing herself for long
bathroom breaks. What would tonight's excuse be?

Suzanne's eyes were already too-shiny when she
looked away and said, "My friend Janice is sick and
I need to bring her dinner. Can you watch the booth
until closing?"

Carly's hands moved easily through the routine of
turning on the lights she and her mom had strung around
the top of the booth to add to the path lighting and
draw customers' eyes. "Can someone else do it?" Sometimes it worked to ask.

"I . . . I want to see if she's okay." Suzanne reached
for her purse.

Carly stopped and held Suzanne's eyes with her own.
"Can you come back soon? As soon as she eats? I . . .
I think it might be busy. It's Saturday night."

A flash of conflict and guilt clouded Suzanne's eyes,
then she looked away. "It's not very crowded yet. I don't
think it will get worse, and it should be quiet." She
licked her lips. "Marla said she'd watch out for you. It's
important to take care of my friends."

Carly swallowed. "Best not leave your friend waiting."

After Suzanne had walked away, Carly whispered under her breath, "It's important to take care of your daughter." She blinked, trying to keep the edges of the jars and pots and vases clear in her vision, balling her fists. There was nothing to hit, nothing to do but be ready to smile for the customers, and no way to go to the High Hills and get away, not when she had to try and sell enough pottery to help pay for their winter.

She thrust her hands in her pockets and pulled out the little black horse. It wasn't real. It couldn't be real. She squeezed it tight, so the little wooden hooves and pointed ears dug furrows in her palm. She heard a muffled crack, and opened her palm to find the tail broken off, with nothing more than a stub left. Her chest hurt, like when Suzanne hit her on a late, bad, night. She sank down onto the booth's sawdust floor and just stared at her open hand, at the little black horse and the broken tail.

A woman picked up a tall blue-glazed candlestick, but when she looked at Carly she set it back down and left. She must look a sight, sitting on the bare sawdust, almost crying. Familiar footsteps came up behind her.

"Are you okay?" Marla's voice sounded worried, but there was a tinge of wonder in it.

Carly looked up to the tall woman bending down near her. "Yes." She closed her fist, loosely this time, and started to struggle up. The little bit of tail slipped through her fingers and lay still and accusing in the bright sawdust.

Marla reached down and picked it up, holding it reverently. "I thought," she whispered, "I thought maybe you were the girl Gisele told me about."

Carly glanced up, surprised. "You know Gisele?"

Marla smiled, her expression wistful. "I still go a few times a year. I went more when I was a girl." She held her hand out, palm open, and Carly released the horse's hard little broken body into Marla's open hand.

"I'm sorry," Carly said. "I didn't mean it. I didn't mean to break it."

"I know." Marla wore the worried look again, her brow furrowed, her eyes a little clouded. She held Carly's eyes with hers. "Can you stay here? I need to go get Jack."

Jack? Carly didn't want to ask. "Like I have someplace to go? Sure, I'll stay here." She held the box out for the horse. "But, please, I need to keep the horse with me."

"Jack is from the High Hills. Didn't you guess?" Marla set the horse and tail down carefully in the box, and walked quickly away. Carly watched her slender back until a young woman asked about an incense burner, stealing Carly's attention.

Three sales later, the booth emptied again. Carly busied herself rearranging cups and bowls on shelves, unable to stand or sit still, trying to see every direction at once, looking for Jack or Marla or her mom. Even so, Jack and Marla managed to sneak up on her while she was wrapping up a set of wine goblets for a young couple in matching designer jeans and denim shirts with matching black glasses. Just as Carly wished the pair a good night, Jack cleared his throat from right behind her. She jumped and turned. "H . . . hello."

Jack stood and looked at her for a bit, his deep blue eyes dancing with questions. "I hear you broke something important." He grinned. "If you'll let Marla watch the booth, I can help. If you want." He was short and wide, just a bit taller than Carly, and all muscle. Curly dark blond hair contrasted with dark-brown skin.

He looked so—so helpful—that Carly just nodded and pulled the box out of her pocket and held it out to him.

Jack shook his head. "You keep it. I'm going to help you fix it, not fix it for you."

Carly looked over at Marla. Marla had watched the booth three days ago when Suzanne had been too sick to drag herself in and wanted Carly home. So maybe it would be okay. "You don't mind?"

Marla shook her head. "I'd like to help."

Carly swallowed, torn between obeying her mom and fixing the little horse. "Tell mom I'll be back as soon as I can." She turned and started toward the waterfall.

Just four steps in, Jack said, "Where are you going?"

"To the High Hills."

"No need. Follow me." Jack started toward his little workroom at the back of the festival. Puzzled, Carly followed, fingering the box, dodging small knots of people. She nearly bumped into him as he picked through his keys to unlock the heavy door. The room had three wood walls and one stone wall, a part of the cliff that rose up above the festival. Was the cliff a doorway to the High Hills, too?

But Jack led her to a bench that lined one wall, and pulled a little wooden table up close to the bench. "Now, take it out and let me see what you've done."

She set the box on the table and opened the lid, grateful to see the horse hadn't moved or changed position. She'd hurt it! "But . . . but how can I make it whole again?"

He reached into a steel toolbox and brought out a shred of sandpaper and a tube of liquid glue, setting them on the table. "How did it get made in the first place?" Jack asked mildly, sitting down beside her on the bench and staring at the broken tail.

"Gisele made it. Do you know her?"

He smiled. "I came from there. Sometimes I still winter in the High Hills."

"But you're not her lost son?"

Jack shook his head. "No. That's a sorry tale, best left. Some people come here and lose their magic, and they can't find their way back. Some are like me, and can move back and forth pretty easy. And some are like you and find a doorway and cross when they need to. Maybe you can keep that ability, maybe not." She shrugged, looking directly at Carly. "That'll be up to you." He stood up and retrieved a sign for the bathroom that someone had written graffiti on and another piece of sandpaper. He started smoothing the edges. "Gisele carved it, but how did it come alive? I can see it woke ·up, even though, thankfully, it's not got a spark o' life right now. Did you breathe it alive?"

Carly frowned. "I just . . . I think about the animal I'm painting, and I can feel what colors go where. And at the end, when the last bit goes on, the animal wakes up."

"Start out erasing the rough edges—see here, where

it splintered a little when it broke? He'll have a little smaller tail when you're done, but it'll grow."

"But the glue—it won't hurt?"

"Have you ever broken an arm or anything? Know how it takes some time to heal? Well, this is like that. If you're good at fixing what you broke, and you mean it to get well, really mean it, well then you can fix it right up."

Carly picked up the sandpaper and the tail, and held them up to the light, looking carefully at the rough broken edge. Then she picked up the horse, and looked at where the tail had broken, and frowned. Jack was quiet as she looked a second time, and he stayed quiet as she sanded carefully. After the first few tentative swipes, it started to feel like when the paint went on, like the paper knew what little bits to sand off and what to leave untouched. She held the two pieces together; they fit exactly right. He handed her the glue, and she dabbed it on as if it were paint. She made a vise with her hands, holding the long part of the tail tightly onto the broken stub, looking over at Jack. "How many people know about the High Hills?"

He laughed. "Just a few. Every year some young people find the door and get through it, and some years older folk, but not usually."

"So how come I found it?"

Jack pursed his lips and brushed the fresh wood dust from the sign, holding it up and turning it over. "Everyone over there has magic. I figure everyone here does too, but this version of the world teaches it out of them. I notice it's mostly kids that find the door and get through, and mostly kids who are hurt, at that."

Carly frowned. He meant hurt like her. Tears stung the edges of her eyes but she swallowed hard and didn't let them fall. "I didn't think it was a real place."

Jack laughed and stood up to get a paint can and brush. "It's as real as you believe it is." They were both silent for a few long minutes while Jack applied a coat of paint to the front of the sign and set it down on two rocks to dry. "Why don't you look at your little horse?"

Carly carefully lifted the black horse and squinted at

the tail. The line of glue was completely invisible. "Will it wake up?"

Jack smiled. "Over there it will. But the tail might hurt a bit—you'll have to tell Gisele you broke it."

Carly held the horse loosely in her right hand, not wanting to let go. "Why can I fix a little magic horse and not my life?"

Jack grunted. "Who says you can't? The thing is, you can only fix what you break. I can fix stuff other people break—" Jack waved a hand around the workroom, "—but I can't fix people. They can only fix themselves. And the same goes for you. You've got to fix things in yourself that need help." He paused. "Though sometimes the first step to helping yourself is asking for help. Maybe you were doing that when you found the gate."

Carly sat the horse down and pulled the other box out of her pocket, making sure the little raw wooden mare looked all right. "Jack? I asked Gisele if I could paint this horse over here, and she said yes, but that I might not like what I found. Do you know what she meant?"

"Why don't you try it?" He fetched her a brush and a paint palette. "Here—I use these for fine work. You might try them. I'm going to make a quick round of the festival. Paint your horse while I'm gone. I'll stop and check on Marla."

Carly nodded and held the little mare to her chest while Jack walked out the door. Maybe some of the magic from the High Hills lived here, in Jack's place. It smelled like Gisele's hut: wood and paint, with soft hints of oils and grease. She looked at the little jars of color, but none of them called to her. But sometimes she didn't know with her mind, even when she sat in Gisele's workshop. Black? It was family to the other horse. Her hand reached past the black all by itself and settled on a light tan. She began to paint.

The colors went on like they did before, filling in, looking brighter on the horse than on her brush, drying quickly. She painted a soft yellow mane, almost white, and a strip of the same color down the mare's nose. Carly dabbed the nostrils and inner ears with light pink and mixed the eye-black with a prayer for life and energy like Gisele had taught her, applied it carefully to the tiny round eyes.

Nothing happened.

The horse looked as alive as its partner, and stayed as still and dead. She blew into its face gently, hoping to send it life, like she had to sometimes with the slow animals, like the turtles.

Nothing.

The door opened and Jack came in. "Everything's all right. Your mom's not back yet, though." He stepped nearer and looked at the little tan horse. "That looks good."

Carly sighed. "It's not alive."

Jack squinted at it. "But it looks good enough to come alive. That's the best you can do over here. You'll have to take it back to Gisele's to see if it wakes up."

"What good is that? In a few weeks, I won't even be able to go to the High Hills. I can't get to the door once the festival closes."

He nodded as if agreeing. "But you can make something magical now. Your mom, she does the same. She makes some of the best pottery in this show. And that little horse, it looks more alive than anything they sell around here."

Carly frowned. There were two booths that sold toys, and Jack was right, none of them looked nearly this good.

"If you remember your magic, you can get back there next year." He smiled. "And you still have two weeks."

She looked at the little horses again, already feeling the empty winter looming behind the summer sun. "Maybe. I'd like to go there between festivals. We live close by."

"Well, that's a tough one. Part of what opens the gate is all the creative people here at Festival. But you'll have your memories, and your imagination, and there's magic there." He squatted down and looked into Carly's eyes. "Magic to help you get through the tough times."

Carly looked away from him. "I'd like to have magic to help my mom. This doesn't do any good at all, not really." She made a silent apology to the horses.

"Well, maybe your work on them will help you understand your mom better. And you're old enough to help her with her work." He stood up. "Come on, we should get you back. You've only got an hour left until closing."

Carly followed him out, clutching both horses to her. Maybe if her mom didn't come back by closing, she would go to the shelter with Marla. Maybe it was time to start taking care of herself. Letting someone else help her didn't mean she couldn't still help her mom. Somehow she thought Gisele would agree, and the idea made her smile. Maybe Gisele would let her keep a family of horses all winter, just so she'd remember the magic.

AN END TO ALL THINGS

Karina Sumner-Smith

Karina Sumner-Smith is a twenty-something re-
cluse, short fiction author and novelist-in-the-
making. A graduate of Clarion 2001, Karina has
had her work appear in the anthology *Summoned to Destiny* and magazines including
Strange Horizons and *Lady Churchill's Rosebud
Wristlet*. Though constantly in a state of flux,
her day job(s) usually involve research, educa-
tional technology, blogging evangelism and a
fair sprinkling of administrative busywork. She
currently lives in Toronto.

SITTING IN THE RAISED concrete alcove of what
had once been a doorway, her feet pulled beneath
her to keep them from the wet, Xhea watched a middle-
aged man awkwardly pretend to fumble with the catch
of a newspaper vending machine. Magic sparkled above
him in a shape like an upturned tulip, deflecting the
heavy rain and letting it pour to the ground around him,
tracing a circle in the puddles at his feet. He was, of
course, watching her.

It was not his attention that had caught her notice,
nor the way he was slowly but surely making his way
down the street towards her, but rather the ghost of a
teenaged girl tethered to him with a line of energy more
felt than seen. She could not be much older than Xhea

herself—fourteen, she supposed, perhaps fifteen—and she floated an arm's span above the man at the end of her tether like a girl-shaped helium balloon.

As Xhea waited, she tied a coin to the end of a thin braid of her hair with a bit of discarded ribbon. The coin was an old and dirtied thing, found in the concrete labyrinth of tunnels beneath the City. Once it would have bought her bread, cigarettes, a warm place to sleep. Now it was nothing but a bit of shiny metal, a decoration that watched with the pressed eyes of a dead Queen, no magic in its essence other than a sense of the past that hung about it like the faint scent of something sweet.

What was it, Xhea wondered, that made the ghost-afflicted wait until the darkest, rainiest days to seek her out? She snorted softly, a sound without care or pity. They didn't want to be seen with her, that was the truth of it, as if her very presence could leave a shadow that wouldn't burn away. In a city built upon the bright, sparkling magic of life, who would admit to needing the help of the thin and sickly talents of a girl who could see ghosts?

Xhea had started braiding another section of her dark hair before the man at last made up his mind to approach. He shuffled forward. He glanced about. He walked right past as if intending to keep going, then stopped and turned. Xhea watched as he came to stand before her and her narrow shelter, the heavy rain falling between them like a beaded curtain.

Xhea held his eyes as she slowly pulled a cigarette from one of her oversized jacket's many pockets and placed it against her lips. He blinked. From another pocket she drew forth a single match, thankfully dry, which she struck with a practiced flick of a chip-painted nail. Cigarette lit, she leaned back against the concrete alcove and exhaled.

"Well?" he said impatiently. He stood looking down at her, back straight as if to get every last intimidating inch out of his average-sized frame. She knew his kind.

"Well what?"

"Aren't you going to help me?" he said. "I have a ghost."

"I can see that," Xhea replied, returning the cigarette to her lips.

"I was told," the man said slowly, as if she were younger than her fourteen years and dreadfully slow, "that you can help people with ghosts."

Xhea raised an eyebrow and watched him until he began to squirm, hearing his words and finding them foolish.

"Forget this!" he muttered and turned angrily away. Xhea let him leave without watching him go. He remained blithely unaware that his ghost had remained right where she was, floating before Xhea's shelter with her tether stretching like a long elastic band, a clear indication that the man would return.

Xhea smoked slowly, watching the ghost. She floated serenely, eyes closed and her legs folded beneath her like a dreaming Buddha. The ghost's hair was pale—blonde, Xhea supposed—her skin even paler, each appearing in Xhea's black-and-white vision as a faintly luminescent gray. The ghost girl's dress was more vivid, hanging in loose folds that appeared almost to shimmer as they moved in an unfelt breeze, the fabric untouched by rain.

Red, Xhea guessed, from the energy it exuded. She rather appreciated the contrast.

What was their story, she wondered. Too young to be his wife, unless his tastes ran to the illegal; too calm and familiar to be the victim of a hit and run or the unlucky bystander in a spell gone awry. His daughter, maybe. How touching.

Was it disease that had taken her? Suicide? Perhaps her father had killed her.

Xhea exhaled a long breath of smoke as the man again approached. Come to my temple, she thought to him mockingly. Four walls of concrete and one of rain; a cloud of tobacco for incense. Come pray for your ghost.

He stood for a long moment, staring at her. "You're too young to be smoking," he said at last.

"And she's too young to be dead," Xhea replied, nodding towards the ghost that once again hovered above his head. The coins in her hair clinked together at the movement.

She had to give him this: he started, but nothing more. Most of those who came to her searched wildly about themselves when she revealed the location of their hauntings, though they had told her that the ghosts were there themselves.

"So tell me," Xhea said, "this help you've come to me for—do you want her gone, your pale ghost? Or is it something you need to say to her? Maybe something you think she has to say to you?"

The man watched her in an angry, uncomfortable silence.

"Ah." Xhea sighed. "You don't know. Just came to see what the freak girl could offer."

It was only then that Xhea realized how thin his umbrella of magic had become, and how dark the circles beneath his eyes looked. She squelched what little sympathy she felt. Even if he had lost everything, if everyone he loved had died, he still had a bright magical signature, a gift of nature and blood. Doors opened to his touch; vendors could sell him food; the City acknowledged he existed. He was, in a word, normal.

Unlike herself. There was no brightness in her, only a dark stillness that she could only think of as absence.

"I'll tell you what," she said at last. "I'll take your ghost for a day, maybe two, give you a little break. If that turns out okay, we can discuss something . . . more permanent."

"How much?" he said brusquely.

"A week's worth of food chits," she said, "and five hundred unshaped *renai*."

"Five hundred!"

"You'd use less to get a taxi across the City."

"But unshaped?" he asked, confused that she didn't want the *renai*, the magical equivalent of the old-world currency, to be spelled to her own unique signature, but raw. "Gods—*why*?"

"I didn't ask you how you got a ghost," she said. "Don't ask what I'll do with the payment."

His protective umbrella flickered and failed, and the rain poured down on his unprotected head. Xhea watched as, to her eyes, his hair and clothing changed from mottled grays to tones of charcoal and black, the fabric slicking itself to his middle-aged body. Water dribbled in his eyes and trickled from his nose.

"You *are* a freak," he said at last in a voice she would have called dangerous had not the frustration in the words revealed his helplessness. "A monstrosity. Your mother should have drowned you at birth."

Xhea ground her cigarette against the wet concrete, watching the bright ember at the end sizzle and dull to black. A line of smoke rose upwards, vanishing.

"You're the one standing in the rain," she said.

Fourteen years old and Xhea knew how to fight with a knife, how to scream like someone dying, how to steal food from children and business people distracted on long-distance calls—and yes, how to get the best of a sad and sorry man in mourning.

A deal was struck. The rest was only negotiation.

Changing the anchor of a ghost's tether was not an easy thing, but it was something that Xhea knew how to do and do well: a bit of magic that she could perform without failure and one that had given her a reputation in the lower levels of the City. Throughout known history, ghosts were said to remain in the living world because of unfinished business—something they couldn't leave behind. What few knew was that ghosts were literally bound to that unfinished business.

Unless, of course, one had a really sharp knife.

Xhea's knife was a small silver blade that folded into a handle inlaid with mother of pearl. The man, soaked to the bone, stood rigidly as Xhea climbed onto an overturned fruit crate, knife extended, and began to examine the tether above his head.

"Don't cut me," he said.

"Don't complain," she replied.

The pockets of her jacket were full with food chits, little plastic tabs imprinted with just enough *renai* to buy her a single serving at a time. They were designed for children too young to be trusted to share their own magical energy safely or wisely, more likely to buy heaps of candy or be drained by a predator than to purchase a balanced meal. Though she looked younger than her age, even with her eyes darkened with black eyeliner and nails painted some shade of dark, Xhea knew she looked far too old to be using chits. She couldn't bring herself to care.

It was that, steal, or starve.

The other half of the man's payment he had spelled to be transferred to her upon completion of their bargain. The little light of the uncompleted transfer hovered about Xhea's face like her own shining ghost, awaiting its time to leap into her body.

When Xhea took hold of the tether, the ghost of the girl jerked. Xhea watched her carefully as she adjusted her hand, trying to get a better grip on a section of energized air that felt as if it had been oiled.

"Hurry," the man said. "Please, just . . . hurry."

Xhea's knife flashed down. The ghost's eyes flew open and she recoiled, springing back to the end of the tether that Xhea refused to release. The ghost opened her mouth as if to scream, her once-perfect calm gone, but she only watched in silence as Xhea took the sliced end of the tether and pressed it to her own chest. It sank in like the rain into a storm sewer, vanishing completely.

"That's it?"

"You want to pay more?"

"I—"

"Then that's it."

The rain had slowed to a drizzle; he stepped back, away from her concrete shelter and into the center of the street. He stood for a moment, watching her with a confused and unnerved look on his face, then turned and walked away without another word.

Xhea's payment—a mere five hundred *renai* of pure magic—brightened for a moment, then sped forward and slammed into the exact center of her forehead. Xhea stumbled back, falling from the crate to her knees, a sound like the ocean roaring in her ears. In the back of her throat she tasted bile as her stomach attempted to return what little food she'd eaten that day. Head in her hands, she focused on not throwing up.

"Breathe," she whispered. Her head spun. She reached out to grab at the concrete wall as a sudden rush of vertigo seemed to flip the world on its side and tilt it back again. Xhea gagged and clutched at her stomach. "Breathe . . . breathe . . ."

It was in these moments, with the raw magic coursing through her body, that she always swore she would never ask for *renai* in payment ever again. For someone with so little talent, such a strange magic as she had, it was a waste, a rush of energy without use or end. She would stick to food chits and pity.

Then the vertigo began to subside, her dizziness to fade, the terrible churning in her stomach settling like the wind after a storm. She could hear the rain again, pattering down on the wet concrete, and the wind as it sighed through the City's towering corridors of mirror and steel. She felt . . . she almost had to struggle for the word . . . alive. For as long as the bright magic coursed within her, the dark stillness that always seemed to fill her body was absent. Like sun burning away heavy fog, the magic banished the darkness: she was light, empty, on fire.

She ignored the thought that murmured in the back of her mind, as it always did, that this was strange, foreign, *wrong*; this, she replied, is what normal people must feel every day.

Slowly, Xhea opened her eyes. Instead of black and white, a world of unending grays, she saw color. No matter how many times she did this, the sudden brilliance of the world around her made her want to gasp, unsure if she should stare or cover her eyes.

The ghost hovered above her, legs again curled in a meditative pose, though it was Xhea's sprawled body that now held her attention rather than the flowing dreams of her death. She was blonde, Xhea noted, and her eyes were a pale electric blue, but her dress wasn't red but a deep plum. It reminded Xhea of new spring blossoms—something she so rarely saw, trapped as she was at the concrete base of the City.

"That looked like it hurt," the ghost said, her voice tentative.

"A good observation."

Xhea felt that she had but to lift her arms to float up beside the ghost-girl, untethered by weight or the world. Reality had other ideas. Xhea struggled to her feet, holding the wall of her little alcove until she was certain that her unsteady legs could hold her.

Breathe, she reminded herself, and after a moment the rush of dizziness and nausea again subsided. Xhea stepped down onto the long-deserted roadway, tilting her head upwards to feel the rain wash down her face. There was a sensation of tugging against her ribcage as the ghost's tether tightened and stretched, then the ghost was dragged inevitably after her.

"Why . . ." the ghost started, "why . . . why am I here?"

"That was the bargain," Xhea replied, glancing over her shoulder. The world spun about her as she turned. "Nothing personal, I assure you."

Everything was so bright—the ghost-girl's dress, the mirrored surfaces of the City buildings, the magical glow of aircars shimmering across the sky high above her. Color stabbed at her eyes, strange and vivid, and somewhere in the back of her head Xhea felt the faint beginnings of pain. There was too much, too bright, but she wanted it all.

"Bargain? I was just sleeping. And now . . ." The ghost looked down, apparently only just realizing that she inhabited a space without gravity, hovering about five feet from the ground and skimming forward without walking.

"Oh," said Xhea. "That. You're dead."

"I can't be," the ghost whispered, peering over her crossed legs and watching the pavement speed by. "No. I was just asleep."

Great, Xhea thought. A talker. She had seemed so quiet at first, so serene; Xhea had thought that she might dream away her death until the City crumbled to dust and the sun burned away the sky. It would have made things so much easier. Perhaps this was why the man had wanted to get rid of her—a sense that an unseen speaker was doing her best to talk his ear off.

Well, she had only committed to a day, perhaps two, and then she could let the tether go. The girl would catapult back to her original anchor and would be out of Xhea's hair unless the man wanted to pay her significantly more.

"I was asleep," the ghost insisted, "only asleep."

"Then this must be a very bad dream."

On any day the ground level of the City was sparsely populated, the magic-weak bottom dwellers hidden away in their homes, but with the rain coming down the streets were all but deserted. Buildings' doorways and elevators, usually oblivious to her presence, flickered now as she went past, registering the *renai* burning in her body. For these brief moments, she had but to touch the keypad to have doors open for her. As always, she was tempted to get inside an elevator and ride it to the top, never mind how she would get down again with the bright magic gone from her system. Whatever magic gave her the ability to see and speak to ghosts, the magic that tainted her vision and seemed to pool inside her like a black and silent lake, was not enough for the City's systems. She could only wonder what the world would look like from so high.

The ground level was a terrible place, rough and edged or falling apart entirely, old foundations crumbling away and the bases of magically-reinforced buildings standing in their stead. But even the ground level was too much for Xhea, filled with magic and its relentless brightness. Still dragging the ghost behind her, she came at last to the entrance to her home: a heavy metal grate pushed aside to reveal a dark hole and the rusted rungs of a ladder leading down.

Squinting already with a magic-induced headache, Xhea lowered herself into the darkness.

Once, Xhea knew, the City had been different, delving downwards instead of relentlessly up, up, up. But with magic came a craving for all things growing, for light and life and open air, and much of the old infrastructure was discarded. All that was left now of the old City were

tunnels, some filled with broken roadways or rusting
train tracks, others flooded or boarded up or too dangerous to explore. Xhea knew them all.

Her normal sight needed little light; shades of gray
were easier to tell apart than the startling array of colors
that magical sight brought—and, worse, the unnerving
absence that accompanied darkness. She kept a flashlight
in a jacket pocket for just such an occasion.

She shone the beam down the tunnel and began to
pick her way forward, stepping over rusted nails and
dried refuse with confidence borne of long practice. The
ghost made a low noise, almost a whimper; Xhea glanced
back to see the ghost-girl grimace, her eyes closed, one
hand over her mouth in disgust. Even dead, few City-
dwellers had the nerve to travel the roads and passage-
ways in which she lived.

Xhea's home was a small room, once maintenance
space, up a small set of stairs that led off a train tunnel.
The door creaked open at her touch and she shone the
flashlight around the room, checking that everything was
safe before entering.

There was something comforting about concrete, Xhea
thought. Even with her sight burning with magic, it was
still gray. In one corner were the bits and pieces of the
past that she'd found in one tunnel or another, shoes and
coins and books, dirty and mildewed but still intriguing.
Against the far wall she had created a bed from a pile
of blankets.

It was on this pile that she dropped without even
thinking of first changing her wet clothes. She closed her
eyes, opened them, and let the magic take her over. The
pain at the back of her head was still there, as was that
lingering sense of wrongness, but Xhea couldn't bring
herself to care. With this magic inside her she could leap,
spin, dance, fly.

"I don't think . . ." the ghost began quietly.

"Not now," Xhea said.

"It's just that . . . well, I—"

"Not. Now."

Later she would have time to talk to the ghost, discover what held her to this life and see what she could

do about it—if the right payment was offered. But the days were long and the magic stayed with her for such a short time. She just wanted to lay still and feel the possibilities before it all burned away.

Xhea woke, drained of bright magic, to discover that the ghost was gone. She opened her eyes, touching her chest; the tether was still there, slippery and elusive beneath her fingers, but within an arm's length it vanished. As if she had cut her lead and fled, the ghost was nowhere to be seen.

But it was not this that had woken her.

Where the magic had shone inside her there now lay blackness, as if that dark pool of calm that she always felt lay hidden in the depths of her self had risen to fill her entirely. It was the opposite of everything she had felt with the *renai* of payment burning through her system: a magic slow and dark. Xhea suddenly felt cold.

As she watched, the darkness began to overflow. Like a fog, soft as breath, it poured from her body, falling not down but gently up, through the concrete ceiling and beyond. She could feel it even as it left her sight: an extension of herself questing outwards.

It was the ghost, Xhea thought desperately. What had she done?

Before the ghost had come to her, she'd always been able to keep the darkness in check, burn it away with snatches of bright magic or hold it down by sheer force of will. But now it coiled out from the depths of Xhea's self, a seeping magic that followed the broken line of the tether. Try as she did, this time Xhea couldn't hold it back; it was drawn to the ghost.

What was her name? Xhea was sure that in the past hours, as the bright magic and its colors slipped from her body and vision, the ghost had tried to introduce herself.

"Shai?" Xhea called, and the name felt right in her mouth. Her voice echoed around the bare walls. "Shai?"

Later, Xhea was never sure if it was the darkness, the tether or the sound of her name that called her back, but Shai returned to the room with an audible *crack*, then hung in the air by the door at the end of her tether.

Her shoulders were hunched, her arms pulled in tight to her chest, her blonde hair—gray now to Xhea's vision—all but covering her face. There was a noise, too, like the distant sound of leaves pushed across pavement: she was whispering.

Xhea climbed on top of a salvaged chair, balancing carefully as she raised herself up on tiptoe, head tilted as she strained to hear the ghost's quiet litany.

"*It doesn't end,*" Shai said, eyes closed, lips barely moving. The words seemed to slip from her mouth like a soft exhalation. "*It doesn't end, it doesn't end, it doesn't end.*"

As Xhea watched, the ghost of the girl slowly began to straighten, uncurling from her hunched position, her head rising like a flower seeking the sun. Though she couldn't harm her, Xhea took a step back to avoid Shai's leg as it swung forward and folded beneath her, the smooth length of skin vanishing beneath the folds of her dress. The whispering ceased and Shai became as Xhea had first seen her: calm and serene, a picture of ghostly stillness.

"Shai?" Xhea said again, and the ghost opened her eyes.

"I'm only dreaming," she said. She sounded heartbroken, too sad to cry.

Xhea opened her mouth to reply, easy denials coming to her lips—and stopped. For there was something different about Shai, something that set her apart from every ghost Xhea had yet known. Only in black and white could she see it, made plain by the shifting grays of her vision and the intensity of the attention that she had not paid to the ghost-girl before: at her core, deep within herself, Shai sparkled with bright magic.

But ghosts were dead and Xhea knew that the dead had no magic.

She could only stare. How was it that she, living and breathing, could not hold magical brightness within herself, while the ghost of dead Shai still shone with it?

The bright magic that was the City's foundation was the very essence of life, an embodiment of light and growth. Looking upwards at its towering buildings, the

City had always glowed in Xhea's sight, a white beacon even in the darkest nights. But what she felt rising from the depths of her self—the shadow she'd always sensed inside—was just the opposite: a force of stillness and dark, a slow movement that spoke of endings and of death.

Xhea looked around herself, at the concrete walls of her home deep beneath the ground, at the past braided into her hair, at the ghost that hovered in the air before her.

Yes, she thought, the word like a cold breath of fear. Yes.

And still the dark magic flowed from her, pulling towards Shai and the imbalance of a dead girl full of life. The fog seeped towards the ghost that hung before her— but then continued upwards, outwards, in the direction that the broken tether had led.

One slow step at a time, Xhea walked towards the door, following it, trusting her instinct to lead her. But as the tether binding her to the ghost tightened, she stopped. Slowly, she turned back. The ghost looked down at her, that heartbroken look still in her eyes.

"You'll have to help me," Xhea said at last, her voice trembling as she spoke. "I've never been to the top of the City before."

She swallowed and extended her hand. It was a long moment before Shai understood her meaning and still longer before she moved. Like a falling petal, her dress fanning out around her, Shai sank until they stood eye-to-eye, then slowly, deliberately, placed her palm against Xhea's own. Xhea curled her fingers around Shai's hand and felt a glow of warmth, like a memory of living skin.

Hand in hand, the girls rose towards the City.

It was late, the afternoon all but dying, before they at last came to the right building. The air was cool, damp with the earlier rain that still lingered in puddles. Xhea stared at the elevator touchpad. The only times City workings had ever responded to her touch was right after she'd been paid, *renai* strong in her system. She'd thought her dark magical signature too weak for the City; now she wondered if was not strength, but the type of her magic that had confused the sensors.

Still hand-in-hand with Shai, Xhea pressed the touch-pad and held her breath. The sensor blinked once, twice, detecting the warmth of her skin and the magic sparkling through Shai's ghostly flesh.

The elevator doors slid open.

Xhea stepped inside, heart hammering, and Shai followed before the doors shut behind her. Shai indicated the floor button with a single finger that trembled as she pointed, and together they pressed it. Xhea watched the numbers move, floor by floor, to keep from panicking; she had never been in an elevator before.

When at last the doors opened Xhea stepped back, unprepared for the inside of a City building. Light, more than could possibly come through the building's windows, streamed into the hall from every direction. She squinted at its intensity. The walls were a riot of foliage that seemed to come up through the floor and rise through the ceiling, and the carpet beneath her feet felt like moss.

Shai moved towards a door at the end of the hall so quickly that Xhea felt a firm tug on her end of the tether. She didn't protest, but followed; instinct, embodied in seeping fog, led her in the same direction.

Xhea's knock was answered by the man from that afternoon. He had changed from his wet clothes, but if anything he looked more haggard than before. He recoiled at the sight of her, and Xhea used his distraction to duck under his arm and into the room.

"You can't come in here!" he protested.

"I already did."

To Shai she said, "Is this the place?" But with a cry the ghost curled in upon herself again, doubling over in midair before vanishing. Xhea swore.

She had no choice. Closing her eyes, she released the last of her hold on the rising tide within herself, and let the darkness seep out around her. Like a magnet, one direction pulled. She followed, hurrying down a hall.

Soon, there was no doubting her destination: the light of magic shone blindingly bright around the edge of one door and the small sign tacked to its surface read *Shai*.

Xhea pushed the door inwards.

There, in the center of a bed, lay a body. Xhea stepped slowly into the room until she stood at the bedside and looked down at the girl who lay so still. She knew that face, that hair, those eyes, though never had she seen Shai's ghost look so ill. Her pale hair was plastered to her head, heavy with sweat, and the hands that lay against the blankets seemed but wasted bones. Beneath her closed lids, Shai's eyes roamed, caught in dreams and visions of ghostly walking.

To Xhea's sight, Shai burned far too brightly. White-hot, as if at any moment her skin could ignite.

Life raged through Shai's body, building upon itself, multiplying: life without end. It was magic, yes, but without control. In its wake it left only brightness and disease: cancer.

Looking down at the girl's wasted flesh, Xhea could see spells whose glimmers she'd seen mirrored in the ghost. There were so many of them: one to stem the growth of the tumor on her liver, another to slow the tumors in her lungs, still another attacking the growths that spread through her bones. There were more spells, spells upon spells, staunching bleeding and energizing her faltering heart, repairing the damage that medicine and magic had left in their wake.

And all of the spells leaked magic, more magic, bright magic that because of its very nature said to her body and tumors alike: live, grow.

From the doorway behind her, a voice spoke. "I cannot save her," Shai's father said, and at last Xhea understood his failing power, the heavy weariness that marked his face. "I didn't know what else to do."

If he had been able to sense Shai's ghost around him, Xhea thought, he must have known it was too late; but how could he simply let go?

Perhaps he had gone to her for a simple reprieve from his dying daughter's ghost; perhaps he had thought that setting the ghost free would let her body finally die. Or perhaps he had sought Xhea not knowing what it was he wanted, what she could possibly do to help, only desperate to try something, anything while he still could.

"I know," she told him, not daring to look back. "This is why you came to me."

With her right hand, Xhea brushed back the hair from Shai's forehead, the skin beneath her fingertips fevered and flushed. Her left she placed on the center of Shai's chest in the exact point where the ghost's tether had been attached. Beneath her palm, Xhea could feel Shai's heartbeat, quick and erratic like the fluttering of a small bird's wings.

"Shai," Xhea said gently, softly, calling to the girl as she had the ghost. "Shai."

Shai opened her eyes. They were glazed with fever, unfocused, black pupils dilated wide within the pale rings of her irises. Looking down, Xhea knew it wasn't her own sight that made Shai's blue eyes look so empty or so gray.

"Shai, listen to me," Xhea said, still stroking her hair, speaking slowly to the dying girl and the bright ghost that she knew lay trapped somewhere inside. "Shai, it's okay. You're only dreaming. Relax," she said. "Breathe. It'll all be okay soon."

To Shai, to Shai's father, to herself, she whispered, "There must be an end to all things."

Slowly, Xhea leaned down and brushed her lips against Shai's fevered forehead. The coins braided into her hair chimed, their small, high notes ringing like prayer. Her hands steady, Xhea let her magic flow and watched as the dark fog sank into Shai's broken body like rain vanishing into soil. One by one, the spells began to flicker, their harsh brightness fading beneath a tide of shadow. One by one they uncoiled, lines of magic releasing their hold on Shai's dying flesh, the power unraveling and spinning into nothingness.

When she was finished, Shai's body lay still. The room was silent, the air as peaceful as the depths of a deep lake and as quiet. To Xhea's sight Shai was no longer the harsh white of burning magic, nor the black of emptiness, but gray. Merely gray.

"Balance," Xhea whispered, and with that word she understood her magic and her role in the world. She could have no part of the life of the City or its bright magic; she was its opposite, its balance, its end.

Behind her, Shai's father crumpled, sliding down the wall to the floor with his face lost in his hands. As she left, Xhea touched him once, stroking back the hair from his forehead as she had his daughter's, as if by touch alone she could convey all the things that had risen within her, thoughts and feelings for which she knew no words. He did not move or acknowledge her presence, but sat still and unmoving until she had left his side.

As she walked away, Xhea heard the quiet sound of his weeping.

Outside, the sun was setting. Xhea stood atop the building feeling as if she stood atop the City itself, watching the sun set in brilliant tones of ash and rainwater. It was the first sunset she'd ever seen, and she did not need color to know it was beautiful. Around her, in the towers and homes of the City, she could see the glow of life, the minutiae of lives being lived: all nature of magic, bright in her eyes.

"Balance," she said as the day faded to night.

In the darkness above the City, stars began to come out.

AFTER SCHOOL SPECIALS

Tanya Huff

Her most recent novels are *Smoke and Shadows, Smoke and Mirrors,* and *Smoke and Ashes,* which were spun off from her Henry Fitzroy vampire series and feature Henry and his young friend, the streetwise Tony. "After School Special" is set in this world.

"ASHLEY, your freak sister is doing it again."

The drawl was unmistakable; Sandra Ohi, Ashley's only serious competition. Having come back from South Carolina for second term after having actually worked on a movie with her mother, a movie where she had lines and got to cry on camera, a movie shown in class during Black History month, Ashley would have ruled the eighth grade girls at The Nellie Parks Academy except for one thing.

Arranging her face in the expression her mother usually saved for her father—somewhere between "Oh, it's you" and "Drop dead"—Ashley turned to face Sandra and the trio of girls currently in her inner circle. "Why so interested in a grade five, Sandra? Oh that's right," she continued too sweetly, "you were told to stop hanging around with the grade threes."

As Ashley's posse snickered, Sandra tossed a perfect fall of blue-black hair back over her shoulder. "As much as I would have preferred to avoid her, the little weirdo is standing in the middle of the atrium talking to the *ceiling*. She's *impossible* to avoid. *Everyone* has noticed her. I'm glad you don't mind that's she's so *noticeable*."

"Well, you'd know about having a sister who's noticeable, wouldn't you?"

"What do you mean by *that*?"

"Last I heard the whole entire senior year of Mackenzie College had *noticed* your sister."

Sandra's eyes narrowed and the nostrils of her extremely expensive made-in-America nose flared. "Your father's show is stupid."

Her father had taught her to never bother arguing an unarguable position. "Yeah, well, that doesn't change the fact that your sister is a slut."

Apparently Sandra's father had taught her the same thing. "At least my sister is a slut in a different school!"

Embarrassing family members might be the norm but they could be denied as long as they weren't sharing the same cafeterias and hallways and extracurricular activity rooms. Unfortunately, until she graduated and moved on to high school at the end of the year, Ashley was stuck with Brianna intruding on her space.

Well aware that she'd scored the final point, Sandra sneered and swept past, trailed by her three acolytes— also sneering.

Ashley took a deep breath, and then another because after a certain age screaming wasn't cool. "I'll be in the atrium," she snarled and stalked off.

Her girls were smart. They didn't follow.

"Ow! You're hurting me, you big cow!"

Ashley tightened her grip on Brianna's arm and dragged her out the front door of the school. "Stop being such a baby."

"I'm telling!"

An extra yank kept the little dweeb off balance and unable to kick. "I'm telling first because you promised to stop the freak show at school!"

"I wasn't doing nothing."

"You were staring at the ceiling," Ashley snapped,

pulling her sister close and spitting the words right into her face. "And you were talking to yourself."

"I was talking to my *familiar*."

"It's not a familiar; it's a bug in a box!"

"Well it's smarter than you!" Brianna rubbed her arm and scowled up at the older girl. "And better looking too!"

"There's the car." Pushing the brat in front of their father's Lexus would have consequences. They'd so almost be worth it. "Come on!"

"I don't have to do what you say."

"I'll *drag* you."

Brianna glanced down at the pavement and then up at the car, clearly considering it but when Ashley started forward, she hurried to keep up. Once strapped into the back seat she pulled a small gold jewelry box out of the breast pocket of her uniform jacket, opened it a crack and peered inside. Opened it a little wider. "Oh great. My familiar is dead."

Ashley rolled her eyes. "It's a bug!"

"Probably died from having to be in the same car as you." She dumped the dead cricket out on her palm and poked it once or twice. "Hey." Two hard kicks to the back of the driver's seat. "Hey, Theodore, unlock the window. I gotta open it."

"Your father says no. Not after what happened the last time."

"I didn't actually go anywhere!"

"Still no."

"Suit yourself." She flicked the dead cricket at the back of the driver's head. It bounced off his hair and against all odds dropped into the space between collar and skin.

Rubber shrieked against asphalt as he braked.

"Next time let her open the window, dumb ass," Ashley sighed.

"CB Productions, may I help you?" Phone tucked under her chin, Amy continued to sort and staple the next day's sides. "No, the box company is long gone.

You've reached CB Productions; home of *Darkest Night,* the highest rated vampire detective show in syndication. What? Well, we've never heard of you either. Ah, the glamour of show business," she muttered as she hung up, slammed in another staple, and added one more set to the finished pile. "There are days . . ." Sort. Staple. Stack. ". . . when I think I should have stuck with NASCAR." Sort. Staple. "Crap!" More and more, this was one of those days. She hurriedly put the stapler away as the boss' daughters came through the front door.

They were better than they used to be. Although it was a DEFCON 4 as opposed to a DEFCON 5 kind of better.

"You're wearing too much black stuff on your eyes," Ashley sneered. "Are you trying to look like a raccoon?"

"Why, yes I am." Amy smiled broadly, insincerely, and threateningly. "Thank you for noticing. Your father is waiting for you on the soundstage and . . ."

"Is Mason there?" Ashley interrupted, having taken a careful step back from the desk.

"He is." And star of the show or not, Mason could be sacrificed for the greater good.

"Then I'm going in to see *him.*"

"Happy days. And Tony is in your father's office waiting for you," she told Brianna as Ashley rolled up her uniform skirt another inch and left for the sound stage.

"She thinks Mason likes her but Mason thinks she's a creepy little girl," Brianna snorted.

"Mason's not usually such a good judge of character."

"My familiar died."

"Again? Girl, you're hard on crickets."

"I need something sturdier."

"Why do you need a familiar at all?"

Brianna stared at her for a long moment, brows draw in to a deep vee over her nose. "Because," she said at last.

Amy nodded, a little unnerved by how well she was getting along with CB's younger daughter. "Not a good reason but it'll do."

* * *

"Come on, Brianna, concentrate. You have to learn to focus before you can learn to do anything else."

"Why?"

"Because it's the first lesson."

"You never started at the first lesson."

"I'm not eight."

"Nine!"

"Whatever. The point is . . ." Tony cut off his "I'm a grown-up and you're a little girl" speech as Brianna's eyes narrowed. That was never a good sign. "Look, it's important that you learn this right because someday I may need you to fix something I've screwed up."

"That's what's in if for you. What's in it for me?"

"I won't turn you into a smoking pile of ash and tell your father you did it to yourself by accident."

"Oh. Okay then." She sighed and slumped further down in the chair, kicking one foot against the desk. "My familiar died."

"The bumble bee?"

"That was two familiars ago!"

"Sorry. The uh . . ."

"The cricket!"

"Right." He sent a silent prayer to whatever gods might be listening—and at this point he was pretty damned sure that there were gods listening—that CB keep refusing to get her a cat. "Bri, maybe you're not meant to have a familiar."

"Yes I am. It makes me feel . . ." She closed her lips tightly around what she felt.

Tony didn't need her to tell him that it made her feel less alone. Because after all, he was the grown-up and she was the little girl. "Come on, Bri, focus your power in one spot." He sketched a sparkling blue circle in the air. "You can do this."

"I want a wand."

"You don't need a wand."

"I *want* a wand."

"Use your finger." He sighed. "Use a different finger."

* * *

CB had his daughters one weekend a month and three days a week after school. He gave them free run of his studio, had his people supervise their homework—and in Brianna's case the word homework had taken on a whole new meaning—and at some point in there, he saw that they were fed. Sometimes, when Ashley refused to be parted from Mason Reed, they ate from the catering truck. Sometimes, when volume won out over his patience and they swore an oath to never tell their mother, they ate fast food with one of the writers. Sometimes, they went to nice restaurants so he could show his beautiful daughters off to the world.

Over the years he'd learned that enough money excused anything up to and including biting the waiter.

"Tony won't teach me to blow things up," Brianna complained, pushing the last of her smoked salmon and spinach fettuccini around the bowl. "He won't teach me to do anything good."

"Tony's just doing what Daddy tells him," Ashley sniped.

CB winced as his youngest narrowed her eyes. His eldest was obviously still annoyed at having to leave Mason. "I'm sure Mr. Foster will teach you to blow things up when he thinks you're ready."

"I'm ready now!"

"Oh yeah, like you're so ready to be trusted, Cheese. You can't even keep a cricket alive!"

Cooper colored sparks danced on the end of Brianna's fork. "You've got one of Mason's socks in your back pack!"

"Girls, indoor voi . . ."

"Liar!"

"Am not! You're pathetic, Ashes!"

"Girls, don't raise . . ."

"You don't even know what pathetic means, you freak!"

Crushing the linen napkin in her fist, Brianna leaned forward, her eyes barely slitted open. "Mason thinks you're creepy!"

"Daddy!"

"Twenty dollars each to keep your voices down."

Ashley sniffed and Brianna looked mutinous but they held out their hands. As CB passed out the money, he could feel the restaurant staff breath a sigh of relief. Fortunately, they were too early for the crowds and the only other diners had been seated as far away as possible. Over the years, he'd also learned that it was best to show his beautiful daughters off to a little bit of the world at a time.

Ashley sniffed again and stuffed the bill in her pocket. "I'm going to the ladies room."

CB moved to block her way. "What do you do if someone approaches you?"

She rolled her eyes. "Scream blue murder and if it's a guy kick him in the nuts so hard his eyeballs bleed."

"Good girl."

"I'd blow him up if Tony'd teach me," Brianna muttered, as her sister crossed the restaurant, pinging the empty water glasses with a fork as she passed.

"He'll teach you someday."

"Promise."

"Yes." He beckoned the waiter over with the check. Lingering was seldom a good idea.

"My cricket died."

"So my driver informed me."

"It made me very sad."

He pulled out his pen to sign the bill. He usually took the girls somewhere he could run a tab in case of unexpected expenses.

"Very, very sad. Very very very sad."

A tear trembled on her lower lashes and he shuddered. "What will it take for you to feel better?"

Her gaze flickered around the table. "Your pen."

"My pen?" He stared down at it. He'd had it specially carved from Brazilian rose wood, had it made to fit his hand. Most pens were far too small for him to use comfortably. The gold inlay was eighteen carat.

A second tear trembled and her lower lip went out.

Tony Foster couldn't teach her anything more dangerous than that.

He handed her the pen and said, without much hope: "Don't tell your sister."

Teresa Neill hadn't wanted to be a teacher but she hadn't wanted to starve either and teaching paid the bills. She tried not to resent the time it took from her real work, from the great literature she could create if only the world supported talent as it should. She was less successful at not resenting the oh so privileged girls she taught who would always have enough money to follow their muse should any of the spoiled brats ever find a muse willing to allow their . . .

The chalk snapped under her fingers and before she could stop herself she'd drawn a jagged white line across the board.

When she reached for the brush, it fell from the shelf.

When she stepped back to retrieve it, she nearly tripped over her desk chair.

When she threw out a hand to save herself, she knocked a stack of books off the edge of her desk.

When she turned to face her fifth grade math class, all but one of the girls was laughing. Brianna Bane was chewing on the end of an oversized pen and staring at the floor. No, not staring, watching something run along the base of the far wall.

Oh bloody wonderful, she thought as she picked up a fresh piece of chalk and returned to the problem on the board. *The last thing this dump needs is mice.*

"Ashley, your freak sister is at it again only *this* time she's talking to the floor outside the science lab."

"I didn't think you knew where the science lab was."

Sandra's lip curled at that lame evidence that she'd thrown Ashley off her game. "It's right next to your *freak* sister."

The science lab was on the second floor at the front of the building. Brianna was on her knees in the hall outside the classroom door, ear to the floor. Ashley grabbed her arm, yanked her to her feet, and pushed her up against the wall before anyone else saw them. "Now, what are you doing?"

"I can hear something," Brianna told her sulkily after a short, unsuccessful fight for freedom.

"You can what?"

"Hear something in the floor." She looked down at the scuffed tile. "It's a lot easier to hear from up here than downstairs."

"Yesterday, you were listening to something in the ceiling?" When Brianna nodded Ashley gave her a short, sharp, shake. "You said you were talking to your cricket!"

"I was! But I was *listening* to the ceiling!"

"Is it something . . . you know, weird?"

"You mean is it something freaky like me?"

"Yes." A short shake for emphasis. "That's exactly what I mean."

"I think so."

There was, unfortunately, no way she could lift both feet off the floor at the same time. "Is it something bad?"

Brianna shrugged. "I dunno."

"That's it." Still holding her sister, Ashley headed for the stairs. "We're calling daddy."

"What can daddy do?"

"Send Tony."

"Calling the men in the white coats to come and take away your freak sister?" Sandra called across the lawn.

"Calling the newspaper to report a sasquatch roaming around," Ashley yelled back as she pocketed her phone and dragged Brianna over by the sidewalk. "Okay. We wait right here for him."

Brianna's lower lip went out and for a moment, Ashley was afraid there'd be trouble. "She wouldn't call me freak if she knew I was a wizard."

Okay. Different trouble. "Yeah, she would and you know it." Ashley had a hundred cutting replies ready for *"Your sister thinks she's a wizard!"* So far, she hadn't had to use them. "You can't tell people!"

"I know that, stupid-head!" One loafer kick a muddy swath through the new spring growth. "It doesn't matter, they wouldn't believe me. I'm *nine*! Besides, there's no point in telling people you're a wizard until you can *be* a wizard."

"Frustrating?"

Brianna's sigh sounded a lot older than nine. "You have no idea."

After a moment, Ashley moved closer and bumped the younger girl with her hip. "I'm sorry I called you a freak last night."

"Okay."

"And you're sorry you said that Mason thinks I'm creepy."

"Sure."

From behind the hedge came Sandra's distinctive laugh. Ashley's lip curled. "The moment you can blow things up . . ."

Brianna nodded. "She's top of the list."

In the final approach to The Nellie Parks Academy, Tony closed out his uplink and began to power down. It was always best to approach CB's daughters with both hands free.

"They're out there waitin' for you, dude."

He leaned around Theo, CB's driver, and sighed. "Yeah. I see them."

"Man, you must've acquired some powerful bad karma in your last life to get stuck babysitting those two in this one."

"I hear you." He snapped the laptop closed and zipped the case shut. "But I'm not the one locked in a car with them."

"Yeah." Theo snorted. "I hear that. I figure I was like a slave trader or something last life and that's why little black girls are making this life a living hell."

"But only three days a week."

"So maybe I wasn't one of them really bad slave traders, you know. Hey!" he called as Tony opened the door. "I can't park here so you call me when you need me to come back."

"And you'll be . . . ?"

"Off looking for better karma, dude."

"Good luck with that." Tony slammed the door, slung the computer case off his shoulder, and turned as the car drove away.

"Oh, that's lovely," Ashley sneered.

He looked down at his classic and paint-stained *The Apprentice* sweatshirt.

"Thanks for dressing up," she continued, through an impressively curled lip. "I thought gay guys were supposed to have taste.

"I thought little girls were supposed to be made of sugar and spice." He smiled down at her. "Seems like we were both wrong." And switching a slightly more sincere smile to her sister. "What's up, Bri?"

"Didn't Daddy tell you? She's hearing things in the floor!"

"Is your name Brianna too? That must be really awkward, both of you having the same name."

"Bite me!"

"If only it wouldn't get me fired. Bri?"

Arms folded over her uniform jacket, she rolled her eyes. "I can hear something in the floor."

"What?"

"Muttering and moving and the muttering moves."

CB had been quite clear that he was to deal with whatever it was Brianna had heard. "Well, let's go have a listen shall we?"

"If you don't quit patronizing me, you're gonna be second on the list!"

Tony didn't need to ask what list. Besides, he was impressed by a nine year old using *patronizing* correctly in a sentence. He couldn't have done it when he was nine. "Sorry. Ashley's call upset your dad and you know how he likes to share the joy."

"He yelled."

"He did."

The three of them shared a moment then Brianna sighed. "It's not a big deal or anything. Ashley got all stupid."

"Oh 'cause hearing things in the floor is normal," her sister muttered as they went inside the building.

The school smelled better than Tony remembered schools smelling.

"I sort of know it's there all day," Brianna explained on the way up the stairs. "But I can't really hear it until most everyone leaves."

"Does it sound angry?" he asked.

"More cranky."

"Do things ever happen while you can hear it? Like, if you hear it in a room, do things happen in that room?"

"Things that aren't supposed to happen? Like chalks breaking and books falling and that kind of stuff?"

"Yeah. That kind of stuff."

"You know, if a teacher sees you, they're not going to like it that you're here," Ashley pointed out as they reached the second floor.

"I'll tell them I'm Brianna's tutor." Which was even the truth. When Brianna went to turn right, Tony reached out and turned her in the opposite direction. "No, it's gone this way now."

"You can hear it." She made it more an accusation than a question.

"No. But unless there's a lot going on behind the walls, there's something this way. Come on. Ashley?"

Hands shoved into her jacket pockets, the older girl shook her head. "You guys go wandering. Do that weird stuff you do. I'll wait here."

"You're sure?"

Her lip curled. "I don't do weird."

They walked slowly through the halls, Tony following the feeling that a bit of the world was cock-eyed, and Brianna sticking close by his side. After a while he noticed that their steps were synchronized so perfectly he could only hear one set of foot steps. "Are you lost?"

"No." He matched Brianna's near whisper. "Reach out. Can you feel it?"

"Reach where? And what am I s'posed to feel?"

"It's hard to describe."

"Totally *not* helpful!"

"Sorry." Trouble was, most of his analogies weren't particularly age appropriate. "Okay, concentrate, and focus. You're groping the world. It's an orange and you're feeling for a seed."

"I'm groping the *whole* world?"

"Not the whole world, just this part of the world."

She frowned, stumbled, and would have fallen had he

not grabbed for her. When she looked up at him, she was smiling. "I can feel a seed!"

"Because you focused and you concentrated." A little reinforcement couldn't hurt although it didn't look like she believed him.

The frown returned. "It's really close. What is it?"

Good question. "It might be a Brownie."

"Students aren't allowed to be Brownies. The principal is *always* on a diet."

"What does that . . ."

"The cookies." Brianna interrupted impatiently. "If you have Brownies you have cookies."

It took Tony a minute to work that out. By the time he realized they were talking about two different things, it was past time to mention it.

A sudden burst of noise stopped them outside the music room. Side by side, they carefully peered through the glass at a choir practice.

"It's in there." Brianna muttered as one of the altos reached out to turn a page. Her music stand fell, and the whole row went crashing down.

"I think you're right."

The choir mistress' baton snapped.

Brianna snorted. "I know I'm right."

"Come on, I've seen enough. It's a poltergeist," Tony told her as they headed back to Ashley. "They like to hang around the uh . . . emotional turmoil of young girls."

"So it's not here because of me?"

"It might have come to this school instead of another school because of you. Your power might have attracted it."

"Like you attracted that girl who tried to kill you by sucking your . . ."

"We aren't going to talk about that," Tony interrupted, ears burning. "We, you and me, we aren't *ever* going to talk about that."

"Not even when I grow up?"

"Not even."

They walked in silence for a moment or two then Brianna asked, "Are they dangerous?"

Tony hoped she was asking about poltergeists because, right now, that was all he was willing to discuss with the boss' youngest daughter. "They can be. But mostly they're just trouble makers, not too bright but not actually malicious. Do you know what malicious means?" He took her snort as a yes. "They're hard to get rid of so we'll just let this one be, okay. You keep listening and the moment it sounds actually angry, you call me and we'll deal with it."

"You'll teach me how?"

"Sure." The heat of her regard warmed the side of his face.

"You don't even know how!"

"Not right now, no. But I'll work it out by the time we need to know it." He heaved the computer case back up onto his shoulder. "We're wizards. It's what we do."

In a just world, Ashley thought the next afternoon when once again, Brianna was late meeting her at the curb, *I'd be the wizard and then I could stuff her into a jar and keep her in my pocket.*

"Lose your freak?" Sandra sniffed as she sashayed past, hem of her kilt flipping rhythmically, her posse giggling reinforcement behind her.

Ashley ignored the lot of them as she went back up the stairs and into the school. No Brianna in the atrium. No Brianna in the hall outside the science room. Where the hell was she?

Brianna sat on an overturned bucket in the custodian's closet by the library.

She heard things in the floor and Ashley called daddy. Daddy yelled at Tony. Tony found out about poltergeists on his computer in the car on the way to the school because if he knew what it was she'd heard he wouldn't have brought the computer with him.

She had a computer. And Ashley'd got rid of the Net Nanny about twenty minutes after their mom's last boyfriend had put it in. They'd found out all sorts of good stuff about mom's last boyfriend.

Last night, she'd found out all sorts of good stuff

about poltergeists. Even though it took her a bunch of tries to spell it right.

The seed was moving around in the orange but she couldn't get it to come close. Tony said it was attracted to her power. But it wasn't. She frowned and kicked at the side of the metal bucket. Wizards worked things out. Tony said it was what they did.

There were still some other girls in the school being all emotionally turmoiled so maybe she needed more power to make it leave them.

Tony said she needed to learn to focus.

Fine.

And to concentrate.

Whatever.

Tony just pointed and drew blue lines in the air.

She wasn't Tony. Maybe he was right and she didn't *need* a wand. Maybe he was a jerk. Reaching into her backpack, she pulled out the pen. It was wood. And smooth. And it smelled a little like her father's cologne.

She pointed the pen at the floor and she concentrated on being focused. She concentrated as hard as she could but nothing happened.

Because it wasn't a *real* wand! The pen bounced off the wall when she threw it and an instant later a bag of rags bounced off the shelf and landed beside it. The muttering in the walls wasn't muttering now. It was laughing. Laughing at her.

Her lip curled. She kicked the rags aside and snatched up the pen.

A copper colored spark gleamed on the pointy end. By the time she'd carefully spelled poltergeist in sparkling cursive script about an inch above the tiles, it wasn't a pen anymore.

She didn't have to wait very long.

The mops fell over first. Brianna covered her head with her arms as they clattered around the tiny room, biting back a shriek as they whacked against her shoulders. The paper towels flew off the shelf and unrolled. She batted them aside. The lids flew off two bottles of floor cleaner and the contents sprayed toward the ceiling. Cleaner couldn't hurt her.

She felt it touch her pattern.

She gripped her wand, ducked a flying bar of soap, and smiled.

"There you are!" Ashley grabbed her sister's arm and dragged her along the hall toward the front doors. "Mom's going to be here in a minute and you know she throws a total fit when we're late." She glanced down at what Brianna had clutched in one hand. "Tell me you weren't hunting for another bug."

"I wasn't."

"Yay. Why do you smell like floor cleaner? Never mind. Don't tell me." She brushed at Brianna's jacket as they walked. "You've got bits of paper towel all over you."

Narrow shoulders rose and fall. "Some got shredded."

"Were you fighting?" Ashley asked as they emerged out onto the broad stone steps. She stopped on the path and pulled Brianna around to face her. "You'd better tell me."

"Sort of."

"Did you win?"

"Totally."

"Good. You know what Daddy always says . . ."

". . . no point in fighting if you don't win." Brianna grinned up at her.

"I see you found your freak," Sandra called from the lawn. "Maybe you should put a leash on it."

"All right. That's it." Ashley began unbuttoning her jacket. "This school isn't big enough for all three of us. I'm going to rip her hair out and stuff it in her bra with all those socks!"

Brianna's hand on her arm stopped her. "It's okay. Let it go."

Ashley looked from the hand to her little sister. "She keeps calling you . . ."

"I know. But mom's here." As the car pulled up, Brianna pocketed the little gold jewelry box, the new copper clasp gleaming for an instant in the late afternoon sun. "We'll deal with Sandra tomorrow."

TITAN

Sarah A. Hoyt

Sarah A. Hoyt has sold over three dozen stories
to places that include *Asimov's*, *Amazing* and
Analog. Her Shakespearean fantasy trilogy was
published by Berkley Ace. She has a time-travel/
adventure novel (a collaboration with Eric Flint)
forthcoming from Baen books, and a Three Mus-
keteers mystery trilogy forthcoming from Berkley Prime Crime.

"LEONARDO, we will be burned," I said. "If anyone
finds out, the church's tribunal will have us
burned."

He looked back at me and didn't say anything, but
his lip curled up in a sneer that looked like the expression his grandfather, Ser Antonio, made when someone
made a mistake in household accounts.

At ten, Leonardo was a handsome boy—I knew this
for a fact because Ser Antonio would put his age-gnarled
hand on Leonardo's head and say, "Such a handsome
boy. Such a pity."

I didn't understand the pity part but I understood
handsome. He was larger than most of us, the children
of Vinci, at his age, and he had gold-red hair, like newly
polished copper, in a frill of curls around his head and
bright green eyes, like spring leaves. Those eyes glinted
now by the light of the oil lamp I carried. It was covered

almost all the way in a metal shade, to avoid showing the path of our walk through the fields. But I'd left the bottom just a little open so we could see the stones on the way and not fall on our faces.

"Fool," Leonardo hissed at me, between clenched teeth. "Cover that lantern."

"But it is dark," I said

"It is darker where we're going," Leonardo said, his small voice acquiring a tone of great weight and thought.

"Leonardo," I said, my voice trembling just a little at the thought of what we meant to do. "You know the priest says the old gods are truly demons and that—"

Leonardo shook his head, impatient. "He would say that, would he not? Come on, Antonio. Tonight we do magic."

I trembled from head to foot, but I followed. I always followed Leonardo. It wasn't just that he was the grandson of the weathy Ser Antonio or the son of Ser Piero—a notary with a big business in Pisa—while I was just the son of a local farmer with mud between his toes. No, it was much more than that. Leonardo had life in him, a vitality, a hunger, a need I couldn't either understand or resist. I followed him, where he went. I did what he told me. His need was stronger than any of my smaller wants or thoughts. He needed to be noticed. He needed to be someone important.

I had realized why he had this need just a few months before. I was the same age as Leonardo and his playmate since we were both about five, when my father, hired to help with the harvest at the great house of Vinci, had taken me along. I'd never given Leonardo's birth or his position much thought.

I'd known that Leonardo's family was wealthier than mine, because his grandfather's kitchen had piped in water and he had servants and fields that other people tended. But I hadn't thought much about it, or about their allowing their grandson to play with me, till my parents talked about it.

It was at the dinner table, as we sipped soup from our coarse clay bowls, and ate bread mother had bought from the baker in Vinci. I'd come in disheveled and sweaty from running in the fields with Leonardo. Leonard was ever like that, active, restless, climbing walls and running through the fields, exploring caves, riding horses—his grandfather's and anyone else's he could get on.

My father had grunted—not exactly reproaching me—as I pulled a wooden stool to the table, and sat down.

My mother, setting the steaming bowl of soup in front of me, gave my father a sharp glance. "It's Ser Piero's boy," she said. "He's wild and Antonio will follow him."

Father grunted again. He ate a spoon full of soup, then tore at the bread with his broad, calloused hands. "I suppose," he said at last. "He'll be going to live with his father in Pisa soon? And be apprenticed into his father's trade?"

Mother clicked her tongue on the roof of her mouth, as if Father spoke great foolishness. She shook her head slightly and threw me a sharp glance.

"What?" Father said. He sounded somewhat annoyed.

Mother sighed. It was clear to me she didn't wish to talk about it and hoped he would understand her expression. But Father was never good at subtle signals. Instead, he got annoyed when she spoke in a way that he didn't fully understand. "What, woman? What's this foolishness? Mean you to say the boy won't be apprenticed to his father's trade?"

Mother sighed again. "He is not . . ." she said. "The son of his wife." And then, as Father looked at her, she added, "The notaries will never accept him, his not being . . ." she threw me a glance. "Legitimate."

Father looked as struck as I felt. Clearly the idea that Leonardo's birth might have something to do with his future had never occurred to him. "What will they do with the boy, then?" he asked.

"None of the better guilds will take him," my mother said. "He will have to learn some lower trade."

"What?" Father asked. "Work the land? A boy raised as the son of his grandfather's house as he has been?"

"A pity," mother said. "And a great shame. He's been taught to want more than he can have."

And that was when I understood what drove Leonardo—why he talked of commanding armies, or of conquering cities, of creating great buildings, of changing the world and everything around him. So that his being born outside marriage wouldn't matter and he could have the great destiny he'd been taught to expect.

In our explorations of the region, some time back, we'd found a cave where the gods lived.

Listen, I know what the priests say, and what has been written by great learned men: that the ancient gods never existed, that they were people's ways of explaining the wind and the sun and those other things for which they lacked a cause. I knew that back then, too. Like any other good Catholic boy I'd been taught there was only one God and he ruled all and the others were demons and monsters, ready to deceive and take one's soul.

But Caterina, Leonardo's mother, had a reputation in the villages around for being able to see the future. She had a bag of bones that she'd inherited from her mother, and which she could cast this way and that and tell you what lay in store for you in days not yet dawned.

Everyone knew it, in all the area. Probably even the priest knew it. But by tacit consent no one spoke of it. The girls would go to Caterina, now and then, when they were crossed in love. And sometimes wives went when they suspected their husbands played them false. Or old people would go to find out to which of their sons they should leave their fields and house. No one talked about it, but everyone knew there were supernatural powers beyond those of which the priest spoke in Mass.

Besides no boy, growing up in Tuscany, could doubt the existence of gods. Amid the steep hills, the precipitous crags, the low fields planted with sweet-fruited vines, who could doubt that some elemental power had thrown the rocks this way and that, and that some creature or other gave soul and heart to the twisted oak trees that projected the only shadow onto the soft, warm earth of the summer fields?

Leonardo and I walked along the beaten path around

one of those fields—his grandfather's—in the dark of a fall night, headed back to the cave we'd found.

"Do you really think there are gods in there, Leonardo?" I asked, half knowing what his answer would be, but needing his rebuke and certainty nonetheless.

He'd forced me to cover the lantern completely, and above the sky was dark, with only the merest pinpoints of stars showing, too distant and dim to give any light. Underfoot, my bare soles felt the pebbles and rocks smoothed by thousands of feet over the generations. A breeze blowing from the south brought with it the tang of ripening wine. To the North, the ground fell away precipitously in crags and chasms, from the terraced field to the depths of a ravine, from which it climbed again, to someone else's terraced field.

"Of course they were gods," Leonardo said. "What else would they be?"

I could hear the sneer in his voice and, indeed, how could I think those figures, carved and drawn in the rock were anything else? There were powerful men painted on the dark granite of Tuscany, their faces suddenly emerging from the living rock as if they slumbered beneath it and could push forward, at any moment, like a man tossing off his covers and wakening.

We'd found them one drowsy summer afternoon, when Leonardo had fallen through an opening to the cave below. I'd thought him lost, or hurt, but he'd emerged laughing and called me below, to see his discovery. We'd walked down long corridors seemingly carved by a giant's hand into the rock. Down and down and down.

"As if we're going to the womb of the Earth," Leonardo muttered, at a point, down the corridor.

I'd followed in hushed silence, till we emerged into a vast cavern, echoing, with a domed ceiling like I imagined a Cathedral would look—having only heard one discussed and never having seen a larger church than Vinci's tiny chapel. And like a Cathedral, it was peopled by statues and paintings, but such paintings had never been seen in the Christian churches.

A single ray of light coming in through a narrow shaft in the ceiling lit the interior and revealed . . . art.

At first I got an impression of men, muscular men—mostly naked or near naked, painted in poses of movement. They were so realistic looking that I jumped back, shocked. Before I realized that they were not alive, and were not in fact human—not as such—but creatures that resembled humans as a rock or a tree grown in the right shape might resemble a human. Humans with the vitality and the feel of immutable earth. And the scene painted on the wall was a dance.

Leonardo walked around the wall, fascinated, his fingers touching the paint which looked as fresh as if it had just been painted. "The gods, Antonio. It is the gods. They lived here." He turned to me. "La Caterina said the ancient gods were worshiped in a cave, by initiates who found their way in and passed tests. And those who got to the cave could get anything they wanted. Anything, Antonio."

His eyes glimmered with that nameless need of his, that need for more than his life could give him.

He walked around the cave, looking, besieging. His mouth formed words I could not decipher from their movement. His fingers traced the figures. He seemed to be begging, asking for something.

When nothing happened, he looked back at me. He looked like a blind man trying to discern someone's face.

At the time I didn't know what to tell him. But I knew he'd asked for something. And that it had not come true.

Our entire friendship, I'd been the follower and he the leader, but now he looked exactly like a small child who asks his mother for a treat and is refused.

I said the first thing I could think of. "You probably have to do something," I said. "Some sort of ritual. To . . . Wake them up?"

Like that Leonardo's eyes lit up. He punched his open palm with the closed fist of his other hand. "That's it," he said. "We'll need to wake the gods. They've been sleeping too long."

Two weeks after we'd found the cave, we had managed to slip away from Vinci and walk through the fields to see Leonardo's mother in Campo Zeppi.

Leonardo never called Caterina mother. He called her la Caterina. When he was just a year old, she'd given him to his grandparents to raise. Then she'd got married and had a brood of brats.

When we got to her home—a small farmhouse amid verdant fields—she was sitting in the yard, in the sun, mending clothes while her three younger children, a toddling boy and two crawling girls, played around her.

She looked up as we approached and smiled at us. She looked much like Leonardo—same high cheekbones, same straight nose, same leaf-green eyes and brassy red hair. But in Caterina the endless energy and ambition of her son became a placid certainty and self-contentment.

She smiled and returned to her sewing without a word. Leonardo moved to sit at her feet. The toddlers neared to play around him, never quite touching him, but staying close by. They were never fully at home near Leonardo, and yet he fascinated them.

Caterina sewed with uneven, broad stitches and Leonardo sat at her feet. I sat in a low wall nearby that protected a flowerbed filled with late blooming roses.

One of the spiny branches worried at my back and I wondered how long it would take Caterina and Leonardo to talk. But their protocols moved in their own way, and in their own way were as prickly as the rites of any court.

After a long while, without seeming to take any more notice of us, Caterina reached over and lay her broad hand on Leonardo's head.

He looked towards her and smiled. "Caterina, the gods," he said at last. "The old gods you talked to me about . . . How were they worshiped? If they were asleep . . . how would you wake them?"

Caterina didn't seem to hear. She removed her hand from his hair, and returned to her sewing. At length, she spoke, her voice slow and filled with the lilting accent my own mother's voice had. "Well," she said. "They've been sleeping a long time." She sewed some more. "There are dates when it's easier to wake them, but midsummer's night is past. So you'd have to go in late fall, when the time turns around to winter. The last day of October. You should go late at night, in reverence, expecting to be challenged, expecting to hear from them. You should fast beforehand."

She went on, her voice even, as she gave him the instructions for waking the old ones.

It seemed to me as though it were all a lot of nonsense, and my mind fell into a drowsy half-dreaming. There was a twist to Caterina's mouth, just at the corner, a placid smile that made me suspect that she was playing one of her practical jokes.

And I hoped I was wrong. Because I did not want to see the lost and confused look in Leonardo's face ever again.

And thus we were on our way, through the darkened fields to the cave, once again.

As we neared the way got rougher. We left the fields behind altogether and went across an area of low scrub. Nimble-footed shepherds herded goats in this place, the goats climbing and jumping across the uneven ground. Past that, we started getting into deeper and deeper forest, the trees growing increasingly thicker all around.

Pasture I'd crossed unthinking hundreds of times in the day, forests where I played, now seemed a land of danger and fear.

A wolf howled in the distance, and I thought I heard a growl nearby. Was it a bear?

"You can uncover the lantern now, Antonio," Leonardo said. "We're far enough no one from my grandfather's house will see us."

Grateful, I pulled the tin cover up to allow the light to shine fully on the path underfoot. But the light only seemed to make the shadows more threatening and the trees leaning towards us looked like the outstretched arms of some monster come to collect us.

Was this a test? Were the trees the guardians that Leonardo's mother had talked of, who protected the approach to the sacred cave? "Are you quite sure you can find the cave again? In the dark?"

He looked over his shoulder and nodded once, and in that nod I knew he'd been to the cave often since our first visit together, worrying at the ancient portraits like a dog at a bone.

All too soon we got to the cave. Just at the entrance, it seemed to me something uncoiled and snarled. I did not know what it was, or even if there was anything. Leonardo whispered a word I did not understand, and the moonlight shone on an empty patch of ground and the cleft in the rock that led to the cave beyond.

We walked into the cleft and, in the dark, it seemed to me that shadows flitted and that dark beings or ghosts or animals ran just outside our field of vision. Rats, I thought to myself. It would be rats. But the thought was hardly reassuring. After all, one or two people could easily be eaten by a tribe of rats.

"It's all right, Antonio," Leonardo said, evenly. "It's all right. We are protected. Caterina told me what to say."

She had? I didn't remember. Somewhere, amid the buzz of Caterina's words, I'd lost track of what she'd told him.

But I stepped close to Leonardo's heels, and I told myself I was imagining the movement, the scurrying. That it meant nothing. That I was a fool. My own heartbeat was so loud that it sounded like a drum in my ears.

We stepped into the cave and I stopped, drawing breath sharply. The cave was lit with a big bonfire. A fire, burning brightly. Someone had to have made the fire. How?

"What—" I said.

"I came earlier today," Leonardo said. He whispered, as if we were at church. "I came at sunset and laid it all in readiness. It only needs a little stoking." As he spoke, quietly, he added wood to the fire. The wood was laid by, in a neat pile, and my mind spun around this thought because I could neither imagine Leonardo cutting the wood nor making the fire. Leonardo, in the normal way of his life, avoided such tasks as much as he possibly could.

Then Leonardo pulled from his lamb's skin vest a packet of herbs, which he filtered between his fingers onto the fire. He murmured words, under his breath.

I didn't understand the words and started to open my mouth to ask him about it, but he only shook his head, wordlessly telling me to be quiet.

So I remained quiet and watched Leonardo throw herbs on the fire and mutter words in an increasing tone of exasperation.

The smoke from the burnt herbs writhed around me like incense at church, but much stronger.

I knew it. Caterina had made a joke. She'd lied to him and now . . .

I realized I was sitting cross-legged on the rough ground of the cave, and there was music. I did not remember sitting and where did the music come from? Who was making it?

Startled, I started to rise. And then I realized that the figures in the wall were dancing—moving round and round with vigorous movements, stomping their feet into the ground with such vigor the entire cave trembled.

I rose, confused, trembling. Was I dreaming? Leonardo stood, without moving, smiling a little with a curious but serene expression much like his mother's.

"Leonardo," I said, and grabbed for his sleeve. I wanted to tell him we must be out of here, we must run, we must—But this was what he wanted, wasn't it? Didn't he want to to wake the gods?

I hadn't wanted to see him disappointed. I'd never thought . . .

"What do you wish, pilgrims?" The voice that wasn't a voice was all around us, demanding, absolute.

And in that voice, my own wishes rose up. I wanted to be like Leonardo. I wanted a life just like he had—to belong to a powerful family with a big house, and be wealthy enough to have piped water in the kitchen. Even if I were nothing but an illegitimate member. I wanted . . . to be better than I was.

I heard my own voice say all this, fumblingly, but the god was waiting, was waiting—waiting, I realized for Leonardo. It sensed Leonardo's greater hunger, his greater need, and it would hear from him.

"I want to be so important that everyone in the world knows me," Leonardo said. "I want to be remembered long after I'm dead."

The naked feet of the dancing creatures on the walls made a final stomp, and there was a sound like laughter. Not mocking laughter, but bitter laughter.

And out of the middle of the creatures, one walked, who stood head and shoulders above the rest. He had flying white hair and beard, but his side was gashed open, bleeding. He pressed a hand to it, seemingly without any pain, and smiled at us, a smile full of curiosity and of a hunger at least as strong as Leonardo's.

"Long ago," he said, and spoke in a voice that seemed wholly human and echoed with the sing-song tone of the peasants of the region. "Long ago we could have granted you all that and more, little one. But we are old ones. Old. We were old when Rome was new. When their Jove shackled us. We are the gods who danced at the dawn of humanity." He pointed with his free hand at the fire. "I gave humans fire and farming and letters. And for it I must be devoured endlessly by Jove's eagle. My name is Prometheus and all those others—" he pointed to the wall, and to the other creatures now frozen in the act of dancing. "Those others, my brothers, my cousins, my uncles, all of them lie in their own prisons, unable to die, but unable to live. We have just life enough to present ourselves to you. But we are shadows . . . shadows and nothing more."

He looked at me, and for a moment I read such nobility and humanity in his gaze, that I felt sorry for him.

And then he spoke. "And I cannot do what you wish . . . unless . . . you would allow us to merge with you?"

"Merge?" I asked, trembling.

This earned me a quick smile. "Yes," he said. He picked a sharp sliver of stone to the ground and handed it to me. "If you prick your finger and let the blood drop into this fire, we'll be able to come to you, to use your body to make you what you want to be. To make your wish come true."

My mother had told me, long ago, that everything had a price. And so I asked, "What will it cost me?"

The noble features turned towards me and the mouth opened fully in a smile that revealed sharp, needle-like teeth. "To be devoured," he said.

I let the sliver of stone drop. I heard it fall to the ground of the cave as if very far away. And I was already running, running, past the scurrying shadows and the darkness, past the narrow corridor to the outside, past the forest and the pasture and the vineyard, till I was snug and still in my pallet in my father's house, crossing myself and muttering pater nosters to sleep, seeking to interpose the new God before the old.

Before going to sleep, I realized, I knew, that Leonardo had taken the bait and cut his finger. And I wondered what it would mean.

What it meant was that I lost my friend. Oh, nothing was changed, not really, not outwardly.

The scab in Leonardo's finger healed. And instead of spending his days running wild in the fields, he started to draw. He would take pieces of his grandfather's papers, the scrap left over from household accounts, and, with deft strokes draw a face, to the life. Or a horse so real it might have been running through the pasture outside. Or strange devices, machines that, he said, would one day fly through the skies.

I wondered if that was the gift the gods gave him and sometimes I felt sorry that I had not pricked my finger, but not sorry enough to return to the cave. Still, when Leonardo was taken to Florence, to become an apprentice painter, and when his painting and the costumes he designed for the elegant set in town became all the talk in tiny Vinci, I wondered why if I had missed my one chance of getting my wish. And what it meant being devoured. Leonardo seemed whole to me.

But life went on, in the way life does, and I acquired fields and married a woman who brought me a little in her stocking foot, with which I bought yet more fields.

I had three sons, all strong men who married and gave me grandsons.

Two years ago my eldest grandson took me to Florence with him. Leonardo was there. He had been away a long while, but came back to finish a fresco under contract.

My grandson left me at the door to Leonardo's workshop, while he went to talk to some notaries about the purchase of a vineyard.

I went in, hesitant, tapping my cane on the floor, more for reassurance than out of real need. My legs were yet steady enough.

The workshop was a busy place, full of apprentices of all ages, sketching and talking and calling to each other and making bawdy jokes. I asked the nearest one, an impish young man of maybe twenty where Leonardo was.

He pointed me towards a wall where a man knelt, painting the hem of a cloak in small feathery strokes. Under his hand, the hem had the look of real silk, flowing in an unfelt wind.

"Leonardo," I said.

He turned to look at me, and a look of recognition sparked in his eyes. "Antonio," he said, softly. "I remember . . . long ago. You ran."

I swallowed. I could not speak. Because the face looking at mine—flying hair and white beard—looked like a face in a cave, long ago. Not Leonardo's.

When we got back to Vinci, I made my grandsons take me back to the cave, and I walked the great length of its corridors, tapping my cane as I went along.

We took lanterns. I was not about to light the old fire once again.

The figures were still there, one and the other arms linked, eternally frozen in their primeval dance.

But the figure with the flying white hair wasn't there. Prometheus was gone. He had become Leonardo and was making Leonardo's name immortal.

I walked back out and ordered my grandsons to seal the cave shut with the biggest boulders they could find.

To this day, it remains sealed.

SHADES OF TRUTH

Jana Paniccia

Jana Paniccia was born in Windsor, Ontario, but grew up in the country—just outside the town of Essex. After extended stops in Ottawa, Vancouver, Australia, and Japan, Jana moved to Toronto, where she now works at an advisory services firm. Jana's work can also be found in the anthologies *Women of War* and *Summoned to Destiny*. She is also co-editing the upcoming DAW anthology *Under Cover of Darkness* with Julie E. Czerneda.

*I*GNORE THE COLORS.
   Standing on the banks of the Melrada River, his back to the ancient oaks whose wood was essential to the livelihood of Arboran's secluded mountain community, Jaryn Dalsayan tried to remember his sister's words of caution even as he tensed under the onslaught of new perceptions.

Once clear water now glowed a luminescent aquamarine, deepening in richness as it swirled downstream. Silver-grey sparkles pierced its flow, singing with the lives of young salmon and trout. Trees whose branches' shadowy pall had once brought shivers of unexpected nervousness running through him picked up an emerald lustre none could consider frightening. And the sky . . . the sky danced with streaks of gilded gold whose brilliance melted all thought and offered a promise of change.

Without thought for consequences, Jaryn reached out with both hands seeking to grasp the radiance giving the entire world a new face. His arms and legs tingled as arrows of rainbow light pierced his skin. With each new touch came emotional knowledge—awareness. Maple trees on the eastern bank wallowed in the warm spring air, their branches growing outward as water trickled in through their roots. A sparrow twittered in one of the trees, calling out to another farther down the river. He *knew* the joy in the bird's song, and echoed with its faint sense of longing. Sunbeams shimmered along the tanned skin revealed by his short-sleeved tunic, working to relax taut muscles and draw him into a new alignment.

For long moments, he revelled in the vision granted by the connection—vibrated with its crystal note of *life*.

Ignore the colors.

Shuddering, he clenched his eyes shut and dropped to his knees in the damp grass, trying to push out the knowledge of worms slinking their way beneath the soil. Tightening his hands into fists, he refused to accept the new awareness.

None of this is real!

There was no joyful bird. No questing worms. No energy coursing through his spine, seeking to change his being.

There was only himself and the Trial of the Lowest God.

Closed eyelids did nothing to dispel the attraction impinging on his every conscious thought. Struggling to deny the sense of power taking root in his soul, Jaryn cursed the Lowest God.

Please—let Alya be right. Let me reject this. Give your temptation to someone else!

At fourteen years and a season, Jaryn had believed the Lowest God had passed him by . . . ignored him to offer temptation to his more mischievous year-mates. He would not have been surprised. Most of the people in the settlement took his maturity for granted and had begun treating him as an adult. Already he was allowed to tend to the nets at the edge of the river a candle's mark east of the town's gates. Collecting fish was a chore; it added benefit to the provisions of the town. It was a man's job, and one he took pride in.

He had been certain the Lowest God would chose not to lure him, that he would slip into adulthood without experiencing the moment of temptation his elder sister had described—the temptation that had killed several in the town including her closest year-mate. He had believed this without thought, forgetting the truth that without exception every child of Arboran would at the turning to adulthood face the Trial of the Lowest God: the moment where he had to reject the powers of the Lowest God and accept instead the struggles and challenges of life without gifted, tainted aid. Or at least he had forgotten the Trial until the events of that morning had proved his assumption disastrously wrong.

Alya had noticed the signs even before he had. Waking before the sunrise, Jaryn had eaten the cold breakfast of cheese and crusty bread his mother had left out, then stood to make his way down to the shed to pick up the fish netting his father had mended the night before. As he was moving his dishes to the sink, his sister's gasp from the stair had forced him still. It was she who had pointed to his face and called him *demon*. As she stood by, he had torn off his woolen cloak, certain of her mistake, only to be confronted by the sight of golden lines twisting an otherworldly glow through his skin. Lines spreading downward from his shoulders toward his wrists.

Please, Highest Lord—turn the Lowest God's eyes away from me!

Silence met his stark plea. Neither the Highest Lord nor the Lowest God appeared to take back the temptation arousing in his very blood. A temptation that could cost him his soul as the town elders had warned.

"The power the demons in Lianshiavel call the Sanri, comes from the Lowest God. As you become a man, his minions will offer you power and bid you accept his evil into your heart. Yes, this power would give you immense abilities but to use it would cast you into the Lowest

*God's hells. All in Arboran understand this; it is why
we live apart. Living among the damned would taint us
beyond reckoning."*

Kneeling on the grass, cornered by the intensity of the
sensations ringing through him—merging with him,
Jaryn wondered how he could deny such power. Trying
to bar the new impressions, he focused on details: the
dampness seeping through the knees of his pants, the
impressions his nails were leaving in his palms, the swish-
ing sound of his sister pacing along the ridge overlooking
the river, surely wondering at their next move.

His sister, who had hurried him out of town even
though they both had been taught that once lines of
the Lowest God's power had reshaped a person's body
nothing could be done. Killing then became a mercy.
Better death than the betrayal of all the values they were
taught to hold dear.

"Help!" he cried, forcing the words out loud to draw
her attention.

From within, a murmuring came: a voice struggling to
speak through the rush of an azure waterfall. A mantle
of comfort brushed over his senses, muting them into a
deep calm. Relishing in the gifted quiet, he turned his
focus inward to search for the giver, for a line of sapphire light he knew was not *his*.

*::Lord of the Sanri, brother. What's happened to you?
I can sense your pain from Lianshiavel. Hold on. I'm
coming.::* It was a man's voice, deep and filled with
shock. His words echoed through Jaryn's mind, sound-
less yet filled with concern.

Before he could respond to the strange words, a hand
came down on his shoulder breaking the connection.
Anxiety washed over him, tinged with an increasing fear.

"Brother, are you all right?" A halo of palest green
wrapped his sister, brushing ghostly edges against his
skin. With shuttered eyes, Jaryn shouldn't have been
able to see at all, but he could see her. He reeled as
his senses merged with hers, giving him a taste of her
growing apprehension.

*Please, not like Felora. Please don't take him . . . let
him fight it!* Her thoughts—not his own.

Shivering, he managed to straighten, using the knowledge of her to ground his awareness in the present and not in the singing offering he had no choice but to ignore. Opening his eyes, he met her concern while trying to disregard the glowing outline of her presence. "Lowest God's Trial. I never expected it to be this hard . . ."

"Oh!" Alya turned to take in their surroundings, her anxiety no less apparent with her back to him. Her movement drew his attention to a log held captive in the depths of the river's center. Golden tufts of sea grass had taken root in its rotting husk and waved precariously in the light wind. Dark shadows crept through the rotting wood, clashing with the sense of living he received from its passenger.

"It might be hard," she continued, unaware he could sense her every emotion. "But you have to fight him. You can't give in. You have to live." Alya reached out to him, her fingers shaking, tears painting her cheeks with liquid silver light. "Prove the elders wrong. Prove Felora wrong . . . You can still reject him. You *can*."

Tensing, Jaryn took her offered hand and stood, leaning against her smaller frame when his own threatened to give. As they touched, her clear thoughts shouted through her fingertips. *Maybe I was wrong. Maybe a quick death would be better. Highest Lord, what can I do?* He braced himself against her growing panic, shutting his eyes tightly and trusting her to take the lead.

Alya led him north of the town, along the ridge overlooking the Melrada, using a high trail they often travelled to gather herbs and berries. If anyone had noted their departure, there was not yet sign of pursuit. Once their parents noticed them missing, all in the community would be out to search; and when and if they found him . . . he could not think of that. He knew his death might be preordained but he had no desire to face it. Not before he had a chance to fight off the Lowest God. All the adults in the town had done so, surely he could. He *would*.

Stones crunched under Jaryn's feet as he walked, as

did a scattering of hardy wild flowers working up through the rocky path. He winced at the death his steps brought to one of the weeds he had always ignored. Shaking from the strength of its ending, he concentrated on the colors of the forest he sensed even behind closed eyes, sidestepping patches of even the dullest shades of life.

With each step, his consciousness deepened, strengthening into a bone deep awareness of imminent change. He shuddered as bumps arose on his skin, sending a cacophony of sensations running through his back, intense almost to the point of pain. At his side, Alya's thoughts flickered between worry and fear—the intimate knowledge of her only raising his own anxiety.

I have to reject him. I must. I will.

His body undermined his silent vow with each breath of living air. Without allowing defiance, lines of silken power infused his being with colors and emotions, thoughts and impressing need. Closing off thoughts of failure, he kept moving forward hoping outright denial of the Lowest God's power would break his strengthening hold.

They had walked for half a candle's mark when he noticed their steps levelling off, footfalls coming down on bare rock rising from the encrusted ground rather than on loose stones. Trees fell back as they approached the crest of the ridge overlooking the split in the river that separated the town's domain from the marshlands. As they came into the open above the flowing water, a wild blue radiance swamped his blossoming perceptions.

Yelping, Jaryn opened his eyes to find his growing awareness even clearer. A blue shadow hung on the horizon, approaching ahead of a line of crisp white clouds marching through the gold-laced sky. Stepping away from Alya, he marvelled at the brightness surrounding the one approaching, at the well of raw energy raying outward. A translucent line of blue spiralled forward until it brushed through him, bringing an infusion of calm. As the being closed on their position, the connection strengthened. Words trickled through the link, echoing silently through his thoughts.

::You're not yet Sanrian? But I thought you one of our kin—:: It was the same voice Jaryn had heard once before.

"Kin? I don't know you." His words came haltingly through the blanket dulling his regular senses. He blinked as the shape of purest blue grew before his eyes: an outline of a man with the wings of a devil. Jaryn cringed backward as the glowing presence lit upon the ridge, terror fighting for precedence with the gentle calm the man exuded. He denied the encroaching emotion with all the will of Arboran. This was the one who brought change. This was the Lowest God's messenger.

"Demon," he shouted. As the word left his lips, his sister jumped forward, coming between him and the devil without any thought for her personal safety.

"Get away from him. You can't have him," she said, voice filled with tension. *Highest God, please—save us.* Her thoughts reverberated through his mind, even without touch, carried on the strength of her passion.

Within Jaryn's new vision, the demon's aura dimmed until its true shape came through, leaving only a fine mist of color shadowing its figure. Blinking, he found he could see the demon clearly: a thin, dark skinned man with deep brown eyes, short, trimmed hair and gold-veined wings.

The man stepped back to the edge of the ridge, letting Jaryn see his entire form without Alya's blocking presence. A sleeveless shirt covered his chest, dangling ties that looked to keep material from interfering with his wings. The loose-fitting pants matched the shirt; both were of the same sapphire shade that held Jaryn's senses captive. A shade his sister could not see, innocent as she was from the Lowest God's taint.

"Hasn't your family taught you anything of the Sanri? I felt your change from Lianshiavel. You'll kill yourself if you don't accept it." The man's words held a lilting burr, tinted with confidence. For a moment, Jaryn let himself be lulled by the tone of authority, forgetting everything but the onrush of energy seeping into his body from the thickening lines of light.

"Don't talk to him, brother. Back away—he wants you

to give in. He's meant to tempt you!" Jaryn stumbled as Alya pushed him backward. One look in her eyes was enough to realize her peaking fear. Her face had paled and her thoughts were jagged. "Remember Arboran!" she told him.

Ignore the colors.

Mindful of the first words she had offered upon escaping the town, he regained his balance. Whatever the Lowest God threw at him, he needed to reject it. As he stood on the ridge, power ringing through him with the promise of change and welcome, he understood why the town elders had decided death was a mercy to those touched by the Lowest God.

Accepting this would make me more than I am. More than any of us have a right to be. It would be everything I've been taught to abhor.

"I won't accept your gift. I reject it. I reject you." He stepped forward, motioning his sister aside. She cast him a worried glance, a question in her deep green eyes—which he met with a slight nod. In his vision, the glow of the Lowest God's power continued to shine. Jaryn refused to let it affect him, refused to acknowledge the knowledge it bore of Alya's worry changing to relief. "Go away, and take His offering with you. I am not the Lowest God's," he said to the winged demon.

"Oh, young one." The man reached a hand out in placation. "The Lowest God has nothing to do with this change. What's being done to you is a crime to the Highest Lord. Normal people can reject the Sanri, if they so choose—though most do not. You, however, will be Sanrian. What is your home to not teach you the difference? You have to accept the change."

"You're wrong. It's wrong to give into the temptation to live with power. It's our duty and responsibility to accept life's struggles—that is the way to salvation. Arboran is the one place where people live true to the Highest Lord's wishes." As he spoke, the intensity of sensation growing through Jaryn multiplied, setting his limbs to shaking. Unable to hold himself up, he collapsed to his knees on a bed of moss holding court between two protruding rocks. Goosebumps rose on the backs of his arms as he realised the moss was striving to sooth his anxious nerves. He would have shifted to bare rock, but there was no strength left in his muscles, even as more and more power crested over his head.

"A rejection of the Sanri is a rejection of *life*. Choose to live, child. I'll teach you of the true power of the Sanrian. Our power is a gift; we don't live outside of the Highest Lord's domain. I promise you." The man made to step closer but Alya was there to block him.

"He's already told you—he won't accept it. Leave him alone. Isn't it enough that Felora had to die? Do you have to take my brother's life too?" she demanded. Her brown-black hair waved out behind her, framing her taut face with an aura Jaryn sensed should have been a bold green and not the dulled echo of color it was.

"Felora?" Confusion radiated through the man's presence, tinted with shock.

"Don't tell me you don't know her—your Master stole her life too. Our elders had to give her death because of your so-named gift."

"Another Sanrian?" A whisper this time, accompanied by the sound of the man stepping forward. Closer. Golden-laced wings folded back, their tips just brushing the ground. "How many?"

"More than our town has cared for! Felora. Dionir. Kesalri. More, I'm sure, but I'm not that old. I only know what our father and mother have shared. Except for Felora. I was there for—" Her voice broke as she took a step toward the stranger, one hand raised. "Your powers touched her. The elders said they couldn't stop it—said there was no way but the Aldraswood to keep her from giving in to the Lowest God. They said there was no way."

Jaryn longed to offer comfort, to reach out and give aid. Her grief poured over him, bringing up tears in his eyes. Even the winged man had runnels of wetness down his cheeks.

As he watched, the aura surrounding the man deepened. Tendrils of sapphire reached out, encircling Alya. He shifted his weight, thinking to intervene, but the tendrils only brushed over his sister, faltering as if they could not match her resonance.

He smiled, relief freeing him for a moment from his sister's emotions. "Your power won't touch her. She's already rejected the Lowest God."

"I would have offered comfort," the man said. "But your town has taken even that gift away. Sanrian are *meant* to heal. Yes, you may call the power use of most in Lianshiavel frivolous. The Sanrian are more than that. Only we can give healing to the sick, deepen the connections of others to the natural world, and work the most difficult magics in Lianshiavel. By rejecting the Sanri, this one has lost all access to it. All of it."

"That's only right," his sister broke in. "We are meant to live our lives as we will, not as others would make us." She stepped closer, blocking his view of the stranger: the Sanrian. Her eyes focused on his, impressing him with her confidence. With her courage. "Deny him. Even this demon has said it; by rejecting the power, you won't be able to access it. Do what Felora couldn't—reject the Lowest God."

Jaryn raised his own hands until they covered hers. He noticed the gray shirt she was wearing had gained a tear. It was the small things he needed to focus on. Let the power ebb. Let it flow back into the ocean of the world like the sea after high tide. He could fight it down.

"It won't get easier," the winged man said, this time not letting Alya block his path. The demon didn't hurt her, only pulled Jaryn out of her reach, forcing the lines of blue connecting them to stream wide open. Jaryn lost himself in the flow burning through them both. He *became* the man named Irek Remoan of the Sanrian.

Flying through a crisp spring air, moonlit singing through the skies. Laughter as a child played in the grass who only a candle's mark before had lain unconscious. A yellow flag flapping over a red sandstone city carved out of a mountainside. Winged Sanrian hovering around a central table, arguing on the best way to heal the rift left by a forest fire. A bird's eye view of the Melrada. A child in need, and a desperate desire to reach him.

Shivering, Jaryn fell out of the connection. Light rolled over him and he twisted to get out of the Sanrian's hands. "Stay away from me," he said as he pulled away, taking two steps toward the tree line.

Light dazzled his eyes; the world faded beneath the array of colors and sensations. A living world danced through him, harnessing him with the vibrant song of birds in flight, of the drumming of fish through the water below and the staid ancient view of trees watching the land change beneath their branches. Reds and golds, greens and yellows, bound by lines of gold and sapphire blue. Crystalline, vibrant shades, dizzying beyond anything he had every known. A sweet sensation that offered him a connection, pulling him into an embrace of life and growth, wanting—needing him.

Fumbling over a rock, he fell, mashing an elbow against the hard ground. Pain shattered over his head; not his own. Moss and grass and a beetle crushed beneath one of his boots. Struggling like a fish caught out of water, he reached for air—reached toward the one dull presence in the brilliance of the world. Alya.

She clasped his hand in her own, verbal words unheard but her thoughts begging him to live. *Highest God, none should have to fight this. Why? What good is his death? What need for it? Let him live. Let him live.*

Jaryn shrouded himself in her presence, remembering the times he had hid from her when it had been her duty to watch him. Her life was unattached from the auras of light breaking over him; the colors sliding off her gave him no release. Blinking, he sensed nothing of normal life—nothing of the world he knew. No foothold to deny the Lowest God and to succeed in his trial.

Felora had the right of it. The elders. Death would be a mercy.

A chill swept through him as his eyes darted around the ridge. Light. Essence. Color. A shimmering web of brightness masking all other sight. The well within him brimmed to overflowing as the Lowest God's change hovered beyond his eyes. All he had to do was reach out for it.

No! Rising up on a last wind of physical energy, he

moved forward without thought, only the intense desire to end the trial without giving in. One step. Two. The sky opened up before him where the rocky ledge ended. Standing on the precipice, colors swirling around his form, Jaryn decided.

Lowest God—I reject you.

Alya's fear enveloped him, her thoughts turning against everything their entire town stood for. "Don't die. I don't want you dead. Arboran is about life!"

Thoughts touched his own, carrying with them remorse and desperation. *::Don't give in. A rejection of the Sanri is a rejection of life. Become what you are meant to be. Live. I'll help you.::*

A rejection of the Sanri is a rejection of life. The thought resonated. How could this connection be evil? This golden connection that filled him with the glory of his surroundings from the moss at his feet to the fish in the river. Always the Lowest God was the god of evil— of dissonance—of all things granted out of place.

All in Arboran accepted the struggles and challenges of life without gifted aid. To live in the town was to reject the power, to give up the magic of the world— the Sanri—and live.

But this is no gift; this is who I am. To be without it is to die. And while his foot touched the edge of the ridge, reached out to step into empty air, he did not want to die. He wanted to live. The Highest Lord asked each child to accept the struggles and challenges of life. Of life. Not death. Not of a poison meant to shred a life from the heart of the world.

Life. Life was the challenge. With or without the gifts the Highest Lord offered.

Reject the Lowest God and *accept* who he was meant to be.

Jaryn placed his foot back on the ridge, savouring the sense of stone cradling his choice, giving him balance. Reaching his hands to the warm glow of the sky, he welcomed *life* into his soul.

Color flared up, an intense blue fire. *What have I done?* A single thought before the power of the world remade him in a blaze of acceptance.

* * *

He came awake surrounded by a fuzzy glow of warmth, a gentle glow that dissipated as he looked upon the world with new clarity. And saw nothing but two faces staring down, both worried: his sister's and the demon's. *Irek's.*

Startled, Jaryn scrambled backward.

"Wait!" Alya grasped his arm, stopped him a bare handspan from the edge of the ridge overlooking the Melrada. *Don't kill yourself by accident, you toad,* she vented silently.

"Toad, am I?" He relished her shocked look at his response to her thoughts, then glanced around, realising just how close he had come to giving up his life.

A shudder ran through his body and down his wings: a new sensation that brought laughter to his lips. With a nervousness he couldn't quite grasp, Jaryn looked upon the changes wrought in a moment of desperation. A terrified scream froze in his throat. *Changed!* Wings of muscle and bone sheathed in a thin layer of skin, tinted with gold and copper. He wondered if he could . . .

"Of course you can fly." Irek said quietly, "The wings are the physical manifestation of the Sanri. Our bodies take in too much of the world's life than can be carried in a human form, even the form of a full bodied man. The wings are a symbol of our gift. Our responsibility." He grinned. "But you can still fly."

"Gift? Responsibility?" Jaryn repeated, caught up short by the remembrance of his duty to reject the Lowest God. He had become what all in Arboran had rejected. What he should have rejected. He struggled to stand, looking for a place to go and unable to make a choice. There were no choices left. If he went back to the town, they would kill him. He had become one of their demons.

"No," Alya said, her nervousness plain in her awkward movements as she came to stand before him. As she laid warm fingers on his shoulders and gazed knowingly into his eyes. "No. I saw it. I saw you. You are no demon. You did no wrong—you accepted life."

"Accepted life, but at what cost?" he asked her.

"You? Mother and Father. The town? I can't go back now."

She sighed, radiating a loss akin to if he had died, had plummeted over the ridge or drank the poison Felora had accepted without protest. "I know. I know, younger brother. But the Highest Lord gives us each our challenges. Yours is just a little harder than most." She turned toward the Sanrian—the *other* Sanrian—Irek. "You'll take care of him—he's still a child, even if he doesn't act like it sometimes."

"If he so chooses, we'll be glad to take him in. I would be honoured to teach him." A tendril of blue reached out from the Sanrian, tinged with gentle welcome.

"I have a choice?"

"Always," the man said. "The Sanrian do not all serve Lianshiavel—some have chosen their own service. None will hold you bound."

Jaryn touched the fine skin of one wing, relishing in the excitement it sparked through his mind. Tensing at the power flowing through them, he wondered whether his decision had been the right one. Wordless music resonated through his body as his sight gained a second dimension. Irek of the Sanrian's dark skin glowed with an intense blue, a blue as vibrant as the billowing clothing he wore. Vibrant with *life*.

He relaxed. *Accepted.* Later would be the time for questions. Time for wondering if he was damned in the Highest Lord's eyes. Maybe one day he would accept that it was his destiny to reject the elders' teachings, but not now. Not yet.

He looked over at his sister standing forlorn a few steps away, her eyes turned from them; tears wet her cheeks, sparkling silver in the sun. It was she who would have to explain his absence to their parents—to the town.

Alya had *accepted* him. In a way, she too was now a stranger to Arboran, no longer bound by their beliefs. Her emotions churned with recognition of this discovery, with the wild realization that Felora's death had not been needed. He resonated with her sadness, with her inability to put her jumbled emotions into words. He longed to let her share in his own thoughts, though that road was barred by her own rejection of the Sanri.

He could not imagine a life without her, but he sensed she would not willingly go with him. This was his challenge.

Turning back to the Sanrian, Jaryn said, "Let me come learn about the outside world then—" For a moment, he glanced back toward the trees, toward where he knew Arboran stood, its gates now closed to him. Then he turned and looked outward, up into a sky filled with gold and a land where life would no longer be certain. "Prove to me that I have done the right thing."

THE WINTER OF OUR DISCONTENT

Nancy Holder

Nancy Holder's work has appeared on the *L.A. Times*, Amazon.com, Waldenbooks, LOCUS, and other bestseller lists. A four-time winner of the Bram Stoker Award from the Horror Writers Association, she has also received accolades from the American Library Association, the American Reading Association, the New York Public Library, and *The Romantic Times*. She has sold approximately five-dozen book-length projects, many of them set in the *Buffy the Vampire Slayer*, *Angel*, and *Smallville* universes. *Wicked*, her recent series for Simon and Schuster, was coauthored with her former Maui Writers Retreat student, Debbie Viguie. She has also sold approximately two hundred short stories, essays, and articles, mostly recently to *Hot Blood XI* and *BTVS: Tales of the Slayer 3*.

WE ARE CREATURES OF such darkness, those of my House. I never knew it until today. They are bringing Annelise down to the courtyard, and the sand in the glass is almost gone. It is diamond dust. We are wealthy, still, despite our defeat.

I thought I was resolved, but now that I see her, I have no idea if I can go through with it. My heart wants to rip from my chest. My hands are shaking around the hilt of my sword, and tears spring in my eyes at the sight of her. Of course, no one can tell that I am crying, because of the rain.

Dressed in silvery furs and silks, Annelise descends the last stair, hooded like a falcon in gray leather. The twin plaits of her white hair dangle from beneath the hood. The strands are caught up with gray tassels.

I am fully armored. I am only thirteen, and she is but nine.

No one is prepared for what is to come if she should fail. No one can guess.

I cannot do it.

I will not do it.

There is no way Annelise can know that this is her final test. Nor anyone else, of the hundreds who are waiting inside the castle. Scores are straining to peer out the windows. I see their colorless gowns, their cloaks of ebon and metale. Many wear masks, which are the fashion: swans, nymphs, Gorgons. The rain obscures their view, of course. No hardship for those who watch: we are used to obscure vision, and shadows.

We are unused to treachery.

But my mother says that it's not treachery. She wept as she told me what I must do. She would rather cut out her own heart, she said, weeping. But that is not the choice at hand.

But our kingdom lies in the balance. The world.

No one suspects a thing. It is not unusual that I should stand inside the Circle with my sword unsheathed. Since the death of my father, I am my family's Long Arm of the Law. It is I who protects the Circle when the High Priestess casts the magicks. I have battled crimson demons and chartreuse Golems that tried to stop her. There are scars on my face and shoulders. They are marks of distinction. My mother laments that I was born too late: if I had lived when our Enemy attacked, we would have prevailed.

My mother. She stands beside me, her face unlined, her beauty unparalleled. She comes by it through her magick. She is regal in her black robes and diadem of silver. Her hair is white, like mine. We have been bleached of color, by the rains.

Where there were dozens in our family, there are now only six of us. The other three—my little sisters, of five, four, and three—remain in the Room of Life, completely oblivious to what is happening. Protected from it, one might say.

I, too, am protected. Though it is said that in earlier times, our sacred salt was spilled directly onto the earth, a ring of small boxes containing the salt surrounds me. We learned the hard way that if our High Priestess poured it on the bare mud, the rain would leach both salt and magicks away.

As it has leached everything. Sky, stone, moor, montaña, bog—it is all the same to our sad eyes. Our world is the color of my sword, and has been since our Enemy prevailed in the Last Battle, when my grandmother served as High Priestess.

In the Last Battle, They killed the sun and enshrouded it. Since then, it has never stopped raining. Ever. This has not always been the case, and we have the Room of Life to prove it. That chamber is an exquisite bower, hung with tapestries of roses and violets and sprays of purple irises. The windows are magnificent colored patterns of magenta, cyan, and amaryllis. The hangings shimmer with morado and chartreuse; the thick warm carpets are vibrant tumblings of blanco, cerise, and noire.

The Room of Life is where Annelise has lived since the instant of her birth. It is the only place she has ever been, with the exception of the courtyard. She has never stood at a window and looked out across the gray land, drowning beneath the rain. She has never reveled in the feast hall, which rumbles with thunder and startles with lightning.

She has never seen our catacombs and our crypts. I'm not even certain she understands what death is, despite losing our father three years ago . . . the day after the birth of my youngest sister, Marialuz.

She envies me because I have had the run of the castle. Now that I know what lies upon her shoulders, I no longer envy my sisters for living in the Room of Life. When I was much younger, I used to wish Annelise would die so that I could live there. I didn't realize, of course, that I never could have claimed all that color for my own.

For then the sisters arrived, and I understood that the Room of Life is reserved for the females of my family. My mother spent her girlhood there. She produced a fabulous rosebush when she was six, and then nothing. But she lived there until her marriage. My grandmother was High Priestess then, and she was loath to let her out at all. It was not until the birth of Annelise that she truly forgave my mother for making only the single rosebush . . . or so my mother has told me. I am uncertain if my grandmother ever forgave her.

But the rosebush is a greater achievement than Annelise has yet managed.

And today is her last chance.

Now the drumbeats of my heart sound the alarm. Her four ladies hold poles to which a decorated dragon skin has been stretched above her head, to protect her from the rain. I am likewise protected by skins, as is my lady mother. It is not so much the force as the constancy of the rain that dissolves stone and softens bone. The rivulets of gray long ago melted sight, sound and touch to one silvery sense. I would not have even known that one could touch warmth in a living person, had I not long ago, once touched Annelise. I am not permitted to so much as breathe upon her, my other sisters, or my mother; and as I remember my fingertip upon her baby cheek, I wonder if I am to blame for these past three years of failure. If so, I should fall upon my sword, rather than put her to it.

I am silently crying as Annelise glides toward me, clasping and unclasping her fists. Her sweet little shoes are gray upon the stone floor of the courtyard. The rain falls steadily on her handmaidens. The youngest one is practically dancing with excitement. The tallest— Bellaclarissa—is so nervous I wonder if she suspects what may come. But that is impossible.

The courtyard is the only place they have ever lifted her hood, save for the Room of Life. The only spot in the courtyard she may see is the where her rose grew, for a spell.

And then there is my mother's vibrant crimson rosebush, which still lives.

The rosebush was my mother's greatest achievement, and she managed it when she was six. After a lifetime of studying the Room of Life, while troubadours sang the ballads of the world before the rains, Annelise coaxed forth a red rose when she was four. I shall describe it in the High Language, which we of the Blood whisper in our magicks:

Burgundy, cardinal, carmine, cerise, cherry, chestnut, claret, crimson, flaming, florid, flushed, fuchsia, garnet, magenta, maroon, ruby, sanguine, scarlet, titian, vermilion, wine, rojo, abracadabra, abracadabra.

Her success was hailed as the end of all our sorrows. We held great feasts. My mother couldn't stop laughing; and my father wept with joy.

A second red rose sprouted in the courtyard on her fifth birthday. The parties! The rejoicing!

But those living things are dead now, and she is nine this dawn. And she has made nothing bloom since then.

The birth of flowers presaged the cessation of the rains, or so my mother had told us. She had read the auguries, and so the Goddess had told her. But the rains are still with us, and Annelise's flowers are not. The rosebush still grows, but the rains still come.

I believe my father died because grief cleaved his heart. Not even our blood holds much color. It is tinged with scarlet, but I am told that in the old days, it was as thick and red as the carpets and tapestries in the Room of Life.

My heart is breaking now, the only surviving male heart of our house. I am anticipating her failure. I'm certain that speaks of treason. She is the heiress to the legacy of High Priestess. My mother says her death must come if she no longer believes in magicks. She says that is likely. Because the rains have come down so long, only children cling to legends of sunlight and once-upon-a-time. The Room of Life surrounds the females—the holders of magicks—with visions of what was, and what could be again. Only females, who carry the magick of creation, can bring forth the flowers again.

But the sands rush through the glass, and her death is what *I* bring forth.

I am a warrior; I can make it painless. And I will make it happen so fast that she will never know it happened.

Our dead . . . are their specters as gray as our land? The shrouds we wind them in are colorless. Everything is colorless.

Except the Room of Life, which is the dreaming chamber of our people, and the monsters of our Enemy.

I remember shortly before my father died, he clutched my sleeve and whispered, "Are her eyes blue? Are they blue?"

He was speaking of my baby sister. I told him that I couldn't really tell. I wasn't allowed to touch her.

"I think they might be silver," I told him.

He died hours later. I don't know what he really wanted to know. The eyes of our family are silver. None of us has blue eyes.

Now they are walking Annelise to the little shrine where her two roses grew. The petals have been placed inside statues of the roses, gray monuments to her faded glory.

I think it is a mistake to make her look at the statues. The thought is to remind her that she managed to create color and life before. But I believe that her memory is of her failures, since they are fresher. Or so it seemed last year, when we performed this ritual. Bringing her out on her birthday marks the passage of time, as well. Her hands tremble; it is clear, at least to me, that it makes her anxious.

She is so slight, a reed in the tempest. My mother steps forward, murmuring spells to her; then she lifts up the hood. My heart constricts. She looks so frightened.

My sister blinks rapidly, then her eyes go wide. She stares at my mother, whom she sees everyday, and then her gaze travels to me.

She saw me a moon ago, when I came by the Room

of Life to watch my sisters dance. They wore their gray shifts, with scarves of silk wrapped around their arms. They were beautiful.

I didn't speak to them. But Annelise smiled at me over her shoulder. Then she danced on. I know their reels make magicks.

She smiles now, fleetingly. I try to smile back, and I am grateful for the faceplate that conceals everything but my eyes. In this rain, she cannot know how hard I am weeping.

I cannot do it.

I must do it.

My mother has explained that the magick flows from female to female in our line. It extends from generation to generation, and there is a finite amount of it. When only one daughter is born, she receives all of it, through her mother. When four are born . . .

. . . they share it.

My mother learned that once she is past the age of dreaming, she could no longer grow flowers. No matter the years in trancelike states, staring at the colors in the Room of Life. No matter the pavanes and the spells. Once she can no longer believe, she can no longer bring forth.

The magick is wasted on her.

So, to prevent waste . . .

She is the only sister I truly know. The one I love.

But I understand my mother. I believe her. And I am the Long Arm of the Law. I protect the Circle.

They help her kneel. The dragon skin hangs over her head. I imagine for a moment the arc of my sword as I heft it against the back of her neck. My hands tremble. My heart quakes.

We hold our breaths, she, her maids, my mother, and I. My gaze ticks to the castle windows, filled with steam and shapes.

My sister holds out her hands. She takes a breath.

I will her to prevail.

My mother glances at me, as if reminding me of my duty. How could I forget it?

Words spill from Annelise's lips. I do not know the

language, much less truly hear the separate sounds. It is an alien, magical language. Nothing that has to do with such as I.

And everything to do with me. I am the Prince of this house, the son of this world. The rain falls on me just as it falls on every peasant and priestess.

I think, *Troubadours will sing of this.* I am not naive; I know there will be consequences. My mother has sworn I shall be unharmed, even celebrated. I cannot let that decide me. Unless I am sure of my actions, I cannot . . . act.

Annelise continues to cast her spell, and I wish I could pray to her Goddess, too. But my God lives in my sword, and He is already listening to me. The strength and skill to make a clean cut. That is all I should be asking for.

But in the spaces between my heartbeats—which are narrow, and few—I plead, *Tell me what to do. I beg of you.* Although it is not His province.

The rain spatters the stones at Annelise's feet. The little shrine is dark inside. I do not see the stone flowers. I see the tension in her shoulders as she chants, and nothing happens.

I sob in silence. I grieve. When our father died, I thought I would stop living. I was suddenly, surely aware that I was the only male in a house of magical women, and I thought for a moment that I might die, too.

I have asked myself is that is why I am here, in the rain beside the High Priestess, preparing myself to slay her heiress. Not for the sake of the kingdom, or the world, but to save myself.

It is clear that our High Priestess will sacrifice her children for the greater good.

Annelise falters; perhaps she has forgotten the next word. Perhaps she knows it is futile.

My mother gives me a sharp nod.

I remember the scent of her cheek when I touched it. It was not dull and gray. It smelled of sweetness, and loveliness.

I can feel a fissure in my heart; the blood is pumping out of it into my chest. I will drown in it soon, unless I do what I must.

And so I take a slow, steadying breath, and swallow hard. My world pinpricks to the back of Annelise's neck, and I tighten my grip around the sword hilt.

Adieu, mi hermosa, I whisper to her. *Well met in heaven.*

It happens in a clang of thunder and a flash of lightning.

Annelise leaps to her feet, whirls around, and grabs my sword. I am a warrior; I am the Long Arm of the Law. But she yanks it from me, barely able to lift it—but she does—

—thunder clangs; lightning flashes—

—and she takes a step forward, staggering beneath its weight. Her face is white. Her silver eyes stare at me.

I can take it from her, but I do not.

I do not.

It happens so quickly; everything is happening so quickly; she has the sword and she steps forward and

tip, blade, hilt

She runs my mother through.

The blood is astonishing, though I know what a sword can do. It is a brilliant red. It is *burgundy, cardinal, carmine, cerise, cherry, chestnut, claret, crimson, flaming, florid, flushed, fuchsia, garnet, magenta, maroon, ruby, sanguine, scarlet, titian, vermilion, wine, rojo, abracadabra, abracadabra.*

My mother does not scream. She does not gasp as the blood pumps from her chest onto her gown. She looks neither at Annelise nor at me. As she crumples to the wet stones, Annelise's ladies are screaming and running toward us.

But we are in the Circle and none can enter.

The courtiers are flooding out of the castle. The uproar is deafening. Voices are crying for death, for succor, for—

The sun.

The sun.

I fall to my knees and cover my head from the blinding heat.

The rain stops. Immediately.

It is not raining.

No one speaks. No one moves. Our kingdom holds its breath, gazes in wonder.

I close my eyes, overcome. I sway, and then I retch, hard.

I fall forward.

I swoon.

When I awaken, Annelise lifts me up with a touch of her hand. I stand and sway, and she holds me in place with a pointed finger.

She wears a blue gown and scarlet robes and a crown of gems that sparkle and glitter. Her fingers are covered with rings and her eyes are blue.

Her eyes are blue.

She is not the High Priestess. She is the Goddess.

There is no rain, none. And the earth is *dry* beneath my feet. I cannot fathom it. I would fall, if she did not hold me up. I take no breaths; is my heart beating?

The earth is sand. The wind is howling. All around me . . . it is brown. The gray is gone, but the colors are not here.

"Not yet," she says, as if she can read my mind.

What if they do not come, for her? What will she do? What will she command me to do?

I do not ask about my mother. I have so many questions, but I do have that answer already.

I think to myself, *The sands will not run out for Annelise.*

But what of me? What of me now? The world has changed, staggeringly, and yet I cannot stop thinking about myself.

We are creatures of such darkness, those of my House.

I never knew it until today.

THE RUSTLE OF WINGS

Ruth Stuart

Ruth Stuart is a Canadian fantasy author whose first novel, *Kin to Chaos*, is presently under consideration by a major U.S. publisher. She has been active in the Canadian SF/F community for many years. Her first short fiction sales appeared in 2004 in *Haunted Holidays* (DAW Books) and *Summoned to Destiny* (Fitzhenry & Whiteside). This story, her third sale, is set in the world of her fantasy novels—a fact that thrills her beyond words.

"HE IS NOT MY SON."

"Rayenn, keep your voice down. Do you want them to hear?"

Anden, ear pressed against the wall of the sleeping chamber, heard the voices clearly.

"Little late to think about that," said a voice close to his other ear. "We've heard it before. Right, Anden?"

He waved his younger brother Lienn to silence. They had heard it before but maybe this time their father would explain why.

In his mind, he could see the cottage's main room on the other side of the wall.

His mother Jullie sat in the fireside chair, hands busy mending a rent in Lienn's tunic. His father worked a

135

*whetstone along the blade of a hoe, the rhythmic rasping
a soothing sound.*

"The boy is strange. Even you must see it."

Jullie smiled. "Anden is more mature than most thirteen year olds, I will grant you." She glanced at the pile
of mending beside her chair. "Definitely growing taller
every day. That doesn't make him strange."

"Mature?" Rayenn's voice rose again. "He knows
things he shouldn't. I've never caught him but I swear he
watches from the shadows." The rhythm faltered. "Despite all our efforts, crops fail and the weather turns in
a heartbeat."

She looked up from her work, locking eyes with her
husband. "You think our son—"

Rayenn broke in. "He is not my son." The stone
skipped on a chip, tearing a layer of skin from his
hand. "Gods!"

As Jullie dropped the tunic and reached for his hand,
Rayenn twisted to look toward the sleeping chamber.
"Curse the child."

Anden jerked away from the wall. There had been
anger and fear in Rayenn's eyes. He was certain his father had seen him.

Was it real? How could I have seen them?

"Anden."

Lienn's low call drew him back to the chamber. And
alerted him to the sound of approaching footsteps. He
threw himself face down on the cot twitching the thin
blanket over his legs as the heavy tapestry blocking the
entrance was flung aside. He lay still, fighting to control
his breathing, to slow his racing heart.

A long moment passed before a breeze blew across
his back and two sets of footsteps retreated toward the
main room. He lifted his head long enough to see the
tapestry again hung over the entrance and Lienn was
still on his cot before letting it fall to his pillow.

Did I truly see them? Anden closed his eyes. *Is Father
right? Am I strange? Could I be the cause of our failures?*

As sleep claimed him, one question crowded out all
others. *Am I his son?*

* * *

"Time for a break."

Anden glanced up at the sound of his mother's voice. Jullie stood at the edge of the field, a covered basket hooked on her arm. Over the stunted grain, he could see the jug at her feet. Rayenn, hoe resting on his shoulder, strode toward her. He watched her welcoming smile fade as his father stopped. *Likely telling her not to waste water on us,* he thought.

He bent to loosen the compact soil surrounding the root ball of a prickle weed. Experience had taught him to wait until his father called to him before stopping work. Sweat stung Anden's eyes and he spared a moment to drag his tunic sleeve across his forehead and glance into the cloudless sky. He could wish for shade but the only trees in Trella grew in the Godswood. The village stood between their field and the gods' home in the mortal realm.

As close as I wish to be, he thought as he continued weeding. He had been working in the fields from the time he could walk. Now, nearing his fourteenth birthday, he knew something was wrong. The sun grew hotter and the rains came less. The last few harvests had dwindled, making winter meals lean.

The whole village suffered, not just their family. *How can Father think I would hurt everyone?* Even his talent with plants—*another thing to mark me as different*—had not helped.

"Anden."

Jullie's normally calm voice held an edge. Anden drove his hoe into the weed and began working his way across the rows.

"I forbid it." He heard Rayenn say as he drew close. "We need to save water for the crops."

Anden carefully stepped over the row of small rocks marking the edge of the field and shook his head. "It won't help," he mumbled.

Rayenn spun to face him. "What did you say?"

Silently cursing himself for speaking, Anden looked over his father's shoulder to see his mother. She shook her head in warning, short black braid bouncing on her shoulder.

"Answer me!" Rayenn demanded.

Anden met his angry gaze. One part of his mind noticed their eyes were level and their shoulders nearly as broad. *Father always seemed so large,* he thought. *When did that change?*

A blow to his shoulder rocked him. He took a step back, trying to keep his balance and avoid the plants. His eyes snapped to his father's.

"Do you question my decisions?"

Another push, another step back.

"Rayenn, stop. You aren't thinking." Jullie reached for her husband's arm. He shook her loose and swung for Anden.

Anden raised his arm, catching his father's wrist in his hand. "The small amount of water we drink will not save the crops. We need it as much as the fields," he said quietly. When his father's expression did not change, he added, "I know you have noticed the change in the weather."

Rayenn easily pulled free. "And whose fault is that?"

Jullie's hand fell to Rayenn's forearm, her fingers tightening. "No. I've told you before."

"A mother's blindness," he snapped.

In his confusion, Anden found himself stepping closer to them. Heartbeat quickening, he looked from one to the other. "Mother? Father?"

"You," Rayenn brought up both hands, striking him in the chest. "You are not my son."

Anden staggered back. Jullie's voice rose above the blood pounding in his ears. "Rayenn, don't."

"I have prayed," Rayenn said. "I have made offerings to the gods. Still the rains don't come." He advanced. "You are a cursed bastard, changing the weather and ruining the crops. Nothing but trouble."

Anden prayed his father would stop. A *touch* on his mind accompanied by the caress of fingers along his cheek distracted him. When Rayenn pushed him again, he lost his balance, slamming to the ground hard. Pain flared behind his ear. As his mother's gasp faded into silence, Anden heard the rustle of wings.

*   *   *

Birdsong filled Anden's ears. He lay still, eyes closed, listening for the cry of the morning lark. Once its raucous call came, he would have to leave his cot and prepare for another day of helping his father in the fields.

Help Father in the fields? His eyes flew open as memory filled him. One hand rose to find a tender spot behind his ear. He sat up and swung his feet to the floor. Heart pounding, he glanced around the chamber. "This isn't my room."

"No, child. It isn't," a quavering voice replied.

He had mistaken the darkness beside the window for simple shadow. Jumping to his feet, he faced her, bowing his head. "Healer Brianne."

"Be at ease, Anden. Sit."

He swayed but remained standing. "My mother taught me to respect my elders."

A low chuckle came from the shadow. "Then respect my request before you fall down."

Anden lowered himself to the cot, hands grasping the edge. How had he come to be here? The Healer's cottage lay far from their field, beyond the village wall, on the path leading to the Godswood.

His mind shied away from the thought. Once on a dare, he had approached the line of trees marking the boundary of the gods' home and the source of their power. The darkness within the wood had not been marred by the bright sunlight. Despite assurances the gods and goddesses seldom walked in the mortal realm, he had been certain something watched him, measured his worth. He shivered in remembrance.

"Are you cold?"

He looked into Healer Brianne's wrinkled face. She sat before him now, somehow moving silently across the room while he was lost in memory. His mother's training coming to the fore, he dropped his gaze to his lap and shook his head.

"Anden, look at me."

Her voice was gentle but left no room for argument. He glanced up and found himself caught by the shifting color of her eyes. First brown, then a subtle slide into green. He saw concern, anger and understanding in their depths. Above all, he sensed *someone* studying him. She grasped his chin with surprisingly strong fingers.

"Do not fear."

Another voice echoed the words in his mind. A wave of calm washed over him. His heart raced as he fought whatever—*whoever*—tried to control him. Another wave of calm, stronger this time, settled around him, numbing him. He kept fighting, clawing the webbing away from his thoughts.

Who are you?

A feminine sigh, at once old and young, accompanied by the thought, *Peace, child* filled his mind. Then silence.

Healer Brianne released him, dropping her hands to her lap. "You are strong, but—"

"But what?" Anden leaned closer to her. Her eyes, brown again, filled with sadness. He touched her hand. "Healer?"

"I fear you will need all of that strength and more." She captured his hand between hers, squeezing as he began to shake.

"For what? To face my father?" He was still a half cycle from his fourteenth birthday, the day he would be considered an adult under Trellan law and able to leave home. Still, to be under his father's rule even for so short a time frightened him. The memory of his mother's restraining hand on Rayenn's arm as they had argued filled him with dread. "Has something happened to Mother? Or Lienn?"

"Jullie and your brother are fine," she assured him.

"Did she bring me here?

The healer drew a small stoppered bottle from her pocket and gave it to him. She waited for him to drink it before standing. "You simply appeared at my door. Your mother came earlier to check on you. She said a voice in her mind had told her where to seek you." Retrieving the bottle, she motioned him to lie down. "For now, rest. You will be safe here a little longer."

He hesitated. "Safe?"

She placed a hand on his shoulder and gave a little push. "Rest."

The presence in his mind echoed the healer's order. *How can I rest? What other things must I face?*

Warmth filled him as the healer's medicine spread through his body. This time when the feeling of calm eased through his mind, Anden did not have the strength to fight it.

Anden pulled another weed from between the velen plants, finding calm in the repetitive motion. When he had awoken and quickly bored of bed rest, Healer Brianne had put him to work, saying she trusted him to know which of the greenery should remain. He had been reluctant to ask her again why he would need strength, why the healer's cottage would not be a safe place.

His fingers brushed the leaves of a tiny plant topped with purple blossoms. A sharp odor filled his nostrils, making him sneeze. He drew his hand away.

"Why not that one?"

He jumped and looked up. The healer leaned against the garden gate, studying him. He glanced down at the plant. "I don't know. It doesn't *feel* like a weed." Her smile surprised him. "I'm right, aren't I?"

"It's known as feverbane," she replied. "Few are found outside my Lady's home. They require just the right conditions to thrive."

He nodded. Rayenn had made certain he understood each crop's needs. He had enjoyed those lessons before the weather had changed and his father with it. "Your Lady?" He thought a moment, trying to determine who the healer meant. "Do you speak of the goddess Ayrmid?"

Her smile broadened. "Aye, the goddess of healing. Who else?"

The sound of someone banging on the front door drove his response from his mind.

"Where is he?"

At his father's bellow, Anden jumped to his feet. Healer Brianne opened the gate and held out her hand.

As Rayenn burst around the corner of the cottage, she grasped Anden's arm, pulled him from the garden and shoved him toward the path leading to the Godswood.

"Run, child. I'll delay him as long as I can."

"But Healer."

She gave him another push. "Go!"

In the face of his father's approach and the healer's determination, Anden turned and fled down the path.

He could no longer hear his father's voice and the path behind him remained empty but Anden continued to run. Barely breaking stride at the dark Godswood border, he plunged between the trees, dodging low-hanging branches until he stumbled over an exposed root. He flung his arms around the nearest trunk to break his fall.

Gasping for breath, he closed his eyes. The tree thrummed where his cheek pressed against the rough bark. "Gods," he whispered, "what have I done?"

Nothing, child.

He winced as the words tore through his mind. Gentle fingers brushed the hair away from his face. His eyes flew open.

Before him stood a young woman. A long blonde braid festooned with feathers hung over one shoulder. Pinned to her tunic at the other shoulder was a circle of velen leaves pierced by a tiny dagger. He looked closer. *Not a dagger. A staff.*

She cocked her head to the side, studying him as he did her. Embarrassed, he began to look away until he heard the rustle of wings. Anden met her eyes.

"You were there," he said slowly. "In the field."

She nodded. "You asked the gods for aid."

His arms tightened around the tree and he swallowed hard. "Goddess."

Peace, child.

His knees buckled and his eyes filled with tears. The goddess closed the distance between them and took his arm.

"Ayrmid did not mean to cause you pain, Anden."

Her voice was low and soothing. He blinked and met her grey eyes. "That wasn't you?"

As she shook her head, another voice answered. "Brianne was correct."

Anden's head snapped up. An older woman, russet hair pulled into a loose bun at the base of her neck, stood a body-length away, watching them. She stepped closer and caught his chin in strong fingers, much as Healer Brianne had done. Eyes as green as his own captured him. The intensity of her regard froze his tongue. He felt her presence, the same presence which had tried to control him at the Healer's cottage, in his mind, testing him, probing his thoughts. This time, when he tried to fight her, she easily brushed him aside.

The younger goddess was distant but he could feel her distress. He tried to touch her hand where it still rested on his arm but he could not move.

A heartbeat passed—or an eternity—he could not tell which. When Ayrmid released him, she looked pleased. His arms spasmed and he slid to the ground, slumping against the trunk. From the tree came the same distress he had felt from the younger goddess.

She crouched beside him, peering into his face. Her eyes hardened.

"What have you done? He is only a child!" she snapped.

"Much more than that, Birte."

Anden struggled to raise his head. Birte was glaring at Ayrmid but the older goddess watched him. He blinked, trying and failing to hold her gaze. He heard her sigh.

"Rise, Anden. After you rest, we will talk."

He closed his eyes and took a deep breath. *I'm not certain I can,* he thought.

Fingers brushed his arm. Opening his eyes, he took in Birte's angry and worried look. She held out her hand. He stared at it a moment, then took it. As she helped him to his feet, Anden could not help smiling at her muttered "We will certainly talk."

*   *   *

Anden drew his knees to his chest, allowing the hearth stone beneath his feet to ground him. They had traveled within the spirit realm to reach this dwelling. The trees around them had become orange-red glowing columns within a field of light. Shadows and fog had confused him until he had closed his eyes and allowed Birte to guide him.

He glanced to his right at the room of plants beyond the doorway. Among the pots they passed, he had seen feverbane. *This must be Ayrmid's home*, he realized.

From his vantage point on the edge of the hearth, Anden looked from one silent goddess to the other. Ayrmid sat enthroned on the cottage's only chair. Birte seemed unable to remain still, pacing from the fireplace to the window and back. Each time she turned, her pace quickened. She came to an abrupt stop, her back against the fireplace stone.

In the buzzing suddenly filling his ears, he could almost discern words. Tension, palpable enough to touch, grew, the pressure tightening against his temples. He squeezed shut his eyes.

Stop, he thought. *Please, stop.*

The pressure eased immediately. He opened his eyes to see both women staring at him. Sliding until he felt the fireplace at his back, he sat straight and met Ayrmid's gaze. He swallowed hard, searching for a way to break the silence. From memory came the first words she had said.

"Goddess, what was Healer Brianne correct about?"

Her hands rose to rest on the chair's arms. "Your strength."

"Strength?" He remembered how easily his father had knocked him down. How helpless he had been when the goddess had tested him.

"Not all strength is physical," she said gently. "And I have an advantage here that you do not."

His eyes snapped back to hers. He could not sense her in his mind. "What?" he asked aloud.

Ayrmid leaned closer. "I can hear your thoughts, child. Any of our kind can."

"Our kind?"

Birte crouched beside him, her hand on his arm. He turned to her. Her grey eyes were wide as she looked from Anden to the other goddess.

"In truth?" she asked.

Ayrmid nodded. Anden felt a surge of joy from the younger goddess. Her hand tightened on his arm.

"Goddess?" He did not try to hide his confusion. "What truth? What do you mean 'our kind'?"

Ayrmid stood and moved to the hearth. Gracefully, she sat at its edge. Uncomfortably aware he was caught between the goddesses, Anden wriggled.

"There are a number of truths," she replied. "For you, the most important is that Rayenn is correct."

A shiver ran down his spine. Heart pounding, he whispered, "I am not his son? I am to blame for the crops failing and the weather?"

Birte's hand captured his wrist while Ayrmid's touched his foot. He was nearly overwhelmed by the compassion and denial that swept over and through him. Taking a deep steadying breath, he looked at Ayrmid.

"The weather and crops are not in your control," she replied.

She didn't deny it all. "So I am not his son."

She shook her head. "No. You are not."

He leaned his head back and stared at the ceiling. Tears gathered in his eyes. "Then whose?"

When silence answered, he lowered his gaze. Ayrmid watched him intently.

"I am not certain," she replied. "But I believe you are my son's."

A burst of raw emotion, quickly staunched, filled him. Startled, he glanced at the younger goddess. Her eyes flashed. Before she could say anything, Ayrmid held up a warning hand.

"Birte."

"But."

"Peace."

Anden felt the power behind the command. He placed his hand over Birte's, thinking to soften the older goddess' rebuke. Her surprise quickly became warmth and she squeezed his wrist. He looked at Ayrmid.

"My mother," he said slowly, "laid with a god. With your son." When she nodded, he licked dry lips. "Was she forced? Did she desire it?" His voice shook.

"Child, I know this is difficult."

"Difficult?" he interrupted angrily. "You're telling me I'm not who I thought I was. It is more than difficult."

Ayrmid's eyes darkened. Birte sucked in her breath, fingers digging into his wrist. Anden kept his gaze locked on the older goddess.

Take care. She is the most powerful of us all.

The barely whispered thought broke into his anger. Anden closed his eyes, forcing himself to be calm. After a long moment, he opened them again. Ayrmid still watched him.

"My pardon, Lady." He looked down to where his hand still rested on Birte's. "I was rude."

He heard her sigh. "You deserve explanations I do not have."

He glanced up and found himself caught again by her gaze. Her eyes were still dark but the edges softened.

"I will tell you what I have discerned." She stood and returned to the chair. "Godsblood runs in your veins. For some, it means nothing. For others." She leaned forward. "For others, it changes everything."

Anden moved his hand from Birte's. When she released him, he stood and moved to kneel at Ayrmid's knee. "Everything? Can I go home? Must I stay here?"

Will I see Mother again?

Ayrmid captured his chin in a light grip. "You will, child. None are forced to stay in the Godswood and certainly not in the spirit realm. Most mortals cannot and remain sane."

The question died on his lips when she smiled gently. "You are still mortal, Anden."

He was silent a moment. "You said everything changes."

She nodded. "Are you the same child who worked in the fields and shared a sleeping chamber with his brother? The same who wondered why Rayenn was convinced he was not his son? I think the young man kneeling before a goddess is a changed person."

Anden took a deep breath. "He is changed." He took strength from the sense of Birte standing at his back. "But what now, Lady? What do I do?"

Anden stared toward the bright spot he knew was the edge of the Godswood and took a deep breath. "Go home," Ayrmid had told him. *If only it was that easy*, he thought. He felt more comfortable in the Godswood than he thought possible. *Likely the influence of the goddesses.*

"Not entirely," Birte replied.

Anden turned to her. The goddess had led him back through the spirit realm. Now she stood, one shoulder against the trunk of the tree where they had found him, worry in her eyes. As he approached, she nodded toward the tree. He pressed one hand against the rough bark, unsurprised to feel worry along the connection.

"This is your tree, isn't it?" he asked.

She cocked her head to the side, then smiled. Gentle humor replaced the worry. "It is."

Lightly resting his shoulder near hers, Anden said, "Do I have one?"

Her sigh was warm on his cheek. "No. Only those with a full measure of godsblood have trees."

He glanced away. "Not a bastard like me."

Fingers lightly brushed his chin. "Anden, look at me." Her grey eyes shone as he obeyed. "You are who you are. Do not let anyone's opinion change you."

He nodded and looked down. "It's difficult."

"I know." Her voice grew soft. "Are you ready?"

Anden shook his head. "No. But it's time I go home."

"Welcome, my son."

Jullie smiled and opened her arms to him. Anden took her hands instead, squeezing them gently. Now that he was here, he did not know how to ask her.

He had waited until Rayenn had left for the field, a reluctant Lienn at his heels, after the mid-day meal to approach the cottage. His mother had been waiting at the door.

"I knew you would return today."

"How? Did they tell you?"

She turned and led him through the door. Anden stopped when he saw the table. At his place stood a pitcher flanked by two small wooden boxes. The handle of a scythe showed above the bench.

"I knew you would return," Jullie repeated. "A young man should be with family on his fourteenth birthday."

"But—" Anden stopped. Ayrmid's voice reminded him most mortals could not stay in the spirit realm and still remain sane. He closed his eyes. Only a few watch glasses had passed while in the company of the goddesses but here a half cycle had gone by. What would have happened had he stayed longer? Would everything have changed?

"Your father said I was foolish to expect you to return."

He opened his eyes and turned to face her.

"He said you would never."

"Mother." Anden took her hands in his, forcing her to look at him. "Mother, I know the truth. Rayenn is not my father."

Jullie let out a slow breath. He thought she would argue but she said, "I knew one day you would discover it." She looked away. "How did you?"

He led her to the bench. Once she was seated, hands clasped on her lap, he knelt before her. "When Rayenn came looking for me, Healer Brianne sent me away. I escaped to the Godswood."

She stared at him, eyes wide.

"I met two goddesses there. One said her son was my father."

"Timus," Jullie whispered. "Ayrmid's son."

He nodded. She tensed, her knuckles whitening. As he laid a hand over hers, she slowly began to speak.

"I had gone to the Godswood to pray. I was training to become a healer and thought to ask the Lady for guidance." She stood and began pacing.

"When her son Timus arrived, I didn't know what to do. I didn't wish to anger or insult him so I listened. He told me I could be more than a healer. That he'd been watching me. Waiting for me."

She stopped before the fire, arms wrapped around herself. When she spoke again, her voice was bitter. "He told me I was beautiful, said all the things a maiden dreams to hear."

Anden rose and moved to stand by her. "You are beautiful, Mother."

Jullie didn't respond. Eyes on the fire, she said, "After he . . . seduced me, he vanished but I heard his voice in my mind. He thanked me and laughed as he told me I would have his child."

She turned to face him. "If I wished to remain in the village, I had to wed. Rayenn had asked me from the time I turned eighteen but I'd always said no. I think he wondered what had changed my mind but he didn't question me. Not then."

"Not until he discovered he wasn't my father."

"I don't believe he *knows*. He suspects."

Anden looked past her into the flames. "That is more than enough. Even as a man I cannot stay here."

"No," she agreed quietly. "You can't."

Turning from the fire, she stepped to the table. A padded sack sat on the bench. As she opened it, she said, "The traditional gifts of passage. I never thought you would need them so soon." She wrapped the pitcher in a cloth before placing it in the sack.

Anden picked up the first box and shook it. "Salt?"

Jullie nodded, taking it from him to put it in the sack and picked up the second. "These velen seeds can be sown or traded as spice." She checked the length of old leather securing the lid. "They are yours to use as you require."

When the final item was in the sack, she closed it and handed it to Anden. He slipped its strap over his shoulder and intercepted his mother's hand as she reached for the scythe. "What will you tell Rayenn when he sees these missing?"

She shrugged. "I put them away. He was right. You didn't come." Her voice cracked on the final word.

Anden blinked away tears as he gently embraced her. "I will return again, Mother. I promise."

*   *   *

"You dared come back after all."

Anden placed the sack and scythe beside the rock boundary and stepped onto the field. Lienn worked in the middle of the field, glancing up but not coming closer. Rayenn leaned on the hoe's handle, watching his approach. Only a few rows separated them when Anden stopped and met the older man's eyes.

"I had to."

Rayenn looked past him. "To collect your things, I see."

Shaking his head, Anden replied, "I had to speak with Mother. And with you."

"Me." His voice was cold.

Anden swallowed hard. "Yes, sir." This was harder than he had thought it would be. "I've come to say good-bye."

Rayenn snorted. "Now that the truth is out, you think to find your true father?" He swung the hoe, slicing deep into a weed. "Be gone then." He turned his back and continued attacking the weeds.

Stung, Anden stepped closer, trying to remember the man who had taught him, raised him. Hands clenched at his sides, he said, "In every way that matters, you are my father. Nothing will change that."

The hoe blade glanced off a plant, sending dust into the air. "What do you want of me?" Rayenn demanded.

"For myself, nothing."

The older man turned to look at him.

"Don't hurt her," Anden said quietly. "She isn't to blame." Before Rayenn could speak, he continued, "She told me you'd asked her to marry you many times before she finally agreed to."

Confusion clear on his face, he nodded. "I did."

"See her with those eyes, not ones blinded by anger."

They stared at each other. After a long moment Rayenn tightened his grip on the hoe and turned his attention back to the weeds. Anden watched him, heart sinking. *Have I just made things worse?* he wondered. Shaking his head, he made his way to the row where Lienn worked.

"You're leaving?" Lienn asked without looking up from his weeding.

Anden heard the pain in his voice. "I have no choice," he answered gently.

His brother dropped the hoe and faced him, hands clenched at his sides. "Don't go. Don't let Father make you leave."

Anden rested a hand on the boy's shoulder. "I have to go. I need to find out who I am."

A tear left a trail in the dust on Lienn's cheek. "If I could, I would stay. If you need me," Anden said, "leave word with Healer Brianne. She will know how to contact me."

A second tear joined the first. Anden swallowed hard against the sudden lump in his throat and leaned in to whisper, "Will you do one thing for me, Brother?"

"What?"

"Look after Mother."

Lienn straightened and met his eyes, studying him. After a moment, he scrubbed away his tears and nodded. Anden squeezed his shoulder. "I will miss you," he said as he turned and retreated across the field. He slung the sack over his shoulder.

He had only taken a few steps when the sound of his name broke the silence. Anden looked back to where Rayenn was a silhouette against the setting sun.

"May the gods keep you safe on the road."

Anden ducked his head. "Thank you, Father," he said and walked into the gathering shadows.

Anden stood in the shadow of the Godswood and took a deep breath. "I can think of nowhere else to go," he whispered. "Gods, please allow me refuge for the night." Ensuring the scythe blade was covered, he glanced in the direction of the village before stepping among the trees.

He had only traveled a short distance before he stumbled into a clearing. Light flared, then coalesced into a glowing orb. He took a step back.

"Wait."

He froze. "Birte?"

When his eyes adjusted to the light, he saw her sitting on a stack of wood and stone at the far side of the clearing. She rose and held out her hand. He did not move. After a moment, she let her hand drop to her side.

"Never fear your welcome, Anden. At least," she added with a smile, "as long as I am here."

"I can't remain forever."

The smile slipped from her face. She stepped into the light at the center of the clearing. "I do not expect you to."

Something in her voice told him she was hurt. Leaving the scythe and sack behind, he crossed to her, searching her grey eyes. They gave away nothing but he found his heart beating faster. Uncertain, he asked, "What do you expect?"

"You could stay for a time. The gods have much to teach." She crossed her arms. "We might learn from you as well."

"And then?"

Birte looked at the trees surrounding them. "When that time comes, perhaps you could be an emissary. Speak to mortals about the gods. Teach tradition. Advise those who seek you."

He took a deep breath. "Why would someone seek me?"

"Those who walk with the gods are often sought."

She still stared into the trees, hands tightening on her biceps. Anden suppressed a shiver. Her voice held none of the warmth it had when he arrived. It did hold something he thought he recognized. *Loneliness.*

"Birte? What is your calling?"

Her gaze turned to him. "My calling?"

He nodded. "Ayrmid is the goddess of healing. What are you?"

"Ah." She smiled. "It is my calling to protect travelers. Especially those who are far from home."

He held out his hand. When she took it, he raised hers, brushing it with his lips. "Perhaps the goddess of travelers would walk with an emissary?"

Her sudden blush surprised him but her smile grew. "Perhaps," she replied. "We should discuss the possibility. When you are a little older. For now," she lifted her free hand and the scythe and sack appeared at their feet, "this clearing is safe. Rest. Tomorrow we can begin your lessons."

Birte vanished but the orb remained. Anden lay on the ground, cloak wrapped around him, his head pillowed on the sack. His yawn became a smile as warmth surrounded him and the rustle of wings eased him into sleep.

BASIC MAGIC

Jean Rabe

Jean Rabe is the author of more than a dozen fantasy novels and three-dozen fantasy, science fiction, and military short stories. Her latest novels include *The Finest Choice* and *Return to Quag Keep.* She is an avid, but lousy, gardener; a goldfish fancier who loves to sit by her pond in the summer; and a movie-goer . . . if the movie in question "blows up real good!" Visit her website at www.sff.net/people/jeanr.

"MAYBE IT'S ALGEBRA."

Scotty Wiggapolan shook his head, his carrot-red hair fluttering around his ears. "Algebra? I dunno. But I don't think so, Drew," he whispered. "My big sister took that last year when she was a freshman. Doesn't look like nothin' she ever studied." He grinned and added even more quietly, "not that she ever studies anything all that much."

"So maybe it's geometry, huh?" Drew leaned to his left to better observe the blackboard. By choice, he and Scotty sat in the very back row of Mr. Lawlor's fifth grade class, where their hushed conversations didn't carry very far. And not by choice they sometimes had to crane their necks this way or that to take in everything.

"Geometry, huh? You think so, Drew?" Scotty hadn't known Drew very long, Drew starting at the school only three weeks ago—his family seemed to move around a lot. But Scotty instantly liked him and was drawn to him like the proverbial magnet. Drew was a brain, and Scotty, already considered a geek by his peers, found the newcomer a kindred soul. "Well, I know it's not hieroglyphics. I got a book at home on the Egyptian pyramids. Egyptian hieroglyphics don't look like that. But maybe it's geometry, like you said, or some other kind of fancy math. Geometry has shapes like that, doesn't it?"

Drew shrugged.

There were circles within circles cut by curvy lines that ended in arrows and smaller half-circles, some of them colored in solid. And there were marks that looked like numbers, but not quite—at least not numbers that were written in English—and all of them were sitting inside something that looked like a large rectangle awkwardly tipped up on a point and taking up more than half of the entire blackboard.

"Maybe it's Japanese geometry," Scotty speculated after a fashion.

"Scott-my-man, I don't think Mr. Lawlor knows Japanese, or geometry. He teaches basic math."

"But Mr. Lawlor didn't write it, Drew. So it really might be Japanese." Scotty drummed his fingers against his chin, then brightened and tipped his head up and raised an eyebrow in his best brainy expression. "I got it! Maybe it's German geometry."

"Or German hire-o . . . hire-o. . . ."

"Hieroglyphics." Scotty put on his best serious look. "I got books about hieroglyphics and mummies and stuff. I told you it ain't hieroglyphics."

"Then maybe it's magic, Scott-my-man."

Scotty made a "pfffting" sound through his closed lips. He didn't believe in magic. Magic was the stuff of fairy tales and comic books and movies and wasn't at all real or practical. And Scotty was nothing if not very practical. He'd never believed in the Easter Bunny or Santa Claus, though he played along with the notions until he was seven or eight, as the free food and toys were too good to take a pass on. Still . . . he sucked in his lower lip as a stubby piece of chalk floated silently behind Mr. Lawlor, who was seated at his desk at the front of the room. The teacher was mumbling to himself and busily grading papers, apparently oblivious to the strange marks appearing on the blackboard behind him.

There had to be some logical explanation for what was going on behind Mr. Lawlor's back, Drew decided. *There just had to be.*

The chalk drew an egg-shaped object this time, the narrow part of which almost touched the crooked rectangle.

Drew leaned over farther. "Scott-my-man, yesterday Mary Johnson said weird things were happenin' in her class. Books floatin' around and stuff. The principal checked it out."

"Principal Singleton?"

"Yeah, Simple Single. Mary Johnson said he did a real Law and Order routine on 'em."

Another pfffting noise. "Mary Johnson is a third grader."

Drew mouthed "So?"

"So third graders make stuff up."

Then both boys returned to studying the board.

Next the chalk made a lopsided figure eight in the middle of the egg and more of the marks that looked like foreign numbers. The chalk squeaked softly when it drew something resembling a monkey's tail.

Cindy Baker giggled.

She and the other girls who occupied the first row in Mr. Lawlor's classroom had been watching the blackboard and passing notes back and forth—all oh-so-quietly until this point. Count on freckle-faced Cindy to ruin the moment by opening her mouth.

Mr. Lawlor looked up from the stack of papers and frowned. Giggling wasn't acceptable during what he declared study time. He met Cindy's gaze, she covered her mouth to stifle another silly outburst, and then she pointed at the board in her defense. The piece of chalk glided down to nest in the tray.

Mr. Lawlor wheeled and stood, knocking over his chair when he spotted the strange drawings and earning a few horselike chortles from the Ferguson twins who sat in the dead middle of the classroom. He spun back to face the students.

"Who did this?"

There were a few more giggles. The Ferguson twins rolled their eyes and pretended to be interested in something on their desks. Everyone else had their eyes riveted on the blackboard.

"Speak up. Who did this?" Mr. Lawlor scoldingly waggled his finger and gave Cindy a more intense look, the kind of expression that said "you'd better tell me right now, young lady."

Cindy held her hands out to her sides and made an exaggerated shrug of her shoulders, then her eyes grew wide and she giggled again when the eraser floated up to wipe out one side of the large tilted rectangle.

Mr. Lawlor turned back to the board, but not before the eraser had nested itself. Hands on his hips, he stamped with one foot and then the other. It was a practiced gesture that told his students he was more than a little perturbed with at least some of them.

"Gary Newton?"

"I didn't do nothin' Mr. Lawlor. I've been sittin' way back here the whole time."

"Anything. You didn't do anything, Gary." Mr. Lawlor was always correcting Gary's grammar. "And I find that hard to believe."

Scotty considered rising to Gary's defense, but Gary dumped milk on him a month back, and before that put a wad of gum on his seat. Let Gary hang. The eraser rose again, this time in full view of Mr. Lawlor. It wiped out some of the foreign numbers inside the figure eight. Mr. Lawlor made a swiping motion above the eraser, not trying to catch it, but in an attempt to see if there was something attached to it, like a thread that might also be attached to a prankster student's hand.

No thread. Nothing but air.

He made another swipe at it while the chalk rose to about the height of his nose and scribbled a few more undecipherable symbols before returning to the tray.

Mr. Lawlor sputtered and spun back to face the class, eyes narrowing menacingly and cheeks puffing when he spotted the papers on his desk that he'd been oh-so-carefully grading. They were busily rearranging themselves and one sheet was folding itself into a high-tech looking airplane. His desk drawer opened, a few pencils rolled around, the lid popped off his Tic Tacs and the candy jiggled out. Then the stapler opened, spewing staples everywhere.

"Wh-wh-who is doing this?" he stammered. "Someone's in for a serious amount of after-school time. And plenty of extra homework assignments!"

Cindy and her friends giggled louder. The Ferguson twins horse-chortled. Even Gary was smiling broadly.

"So it's not geometry or hieroglyphics," Scotty whispered to Drew. "But I still don't think it's magic. No such thing as magic. There's a rational explanation for everything. Maybe errant electricity."

"Maybe faeries," Drew pronounced after only a moment's consideration. "I think the rational explanation is faeries. Our classroom must be filled with the fey. Maybe even the whole school."

"Pfffey? What's that?"

"Faeries, Scott-my-man, little magic people. Wizards can summon them to do their bidding."

Mr. Lawlor, red-faced and huffing, slammed his desk drawer closed, the motion sending the papers he was oh-so-carefully grading flying. Pivoting on his heels like a drill sergeant, he marched out of the classroom and straight to the principal's office, mumbling that someone was going to pay for disrupting study time.

The eraser floated across the blackboard, obliterating every mark. The high-tech paper airplane flattened itself. The papers that were scattered on the floor picked themselves up before the disbelieving students' eyes and arranged themselves in a reasonably neat stack on the desk.

"I don't believe in little magic people," Scotty said—after he was certain Mr. Lawlor was long gone and nothing else was floating about.

"You don't believe in anything," Drew returned.

* * *

"Drew summoned us, Elspeth. But to a place with no trees." The voice was thin and soft, sounding a bit like a flute.

"Yes, most definitely he summoned us. But we should have waited." This voice was feminine and insistent. "We should have most definitely waited until the adult was gone. Adults are too serious. They make my head hurt. They don't believe in magic, they drive us away, slay the weakest of us unknowingly."

"Yes, we should have waited," the first voice repeated. "We should have, Elspeth. Should have."

The voices continued to twitter in the hall just outside Mr. Lawlor's fifth grade class. There were no bodies to accompany them, and no microphone or loudspeaker to hint that they were being broadcast from somewhere else in the building. There was just an almost imperceptible swirling of chalk dust in the air, and a scent—that had there been someone present to smell it—they would have thought it perhaps cinnamon.

"Should have waited, I told you. We should have waited."

"Yes, definitely, I agree, Elspeth. We should have waited. But there is just no telling him. He does not listen to a soul. He summons us on a whim and tells us to do frivolous things."

There was a sigh, musical and pleasing. "Ah, but I love doing frivolous things. And there's a purpose to it."

"Getting children in trouble?"

"No, helping the summoner keep magic alive, and thereby us alive. Spreading the arcane to young people with strong minds. The fates know adults can't embrace magic."

"And this place he called us to, what is it, Elspeth?"

"This place," Elspeth returned, "is called a school. According to the sign out front it is called the Green Hill Elementary School."

"But we did not see a hill when we arrived yesterday, a green one or otherwise. The ground looked pretty flat to me. And there were not enough trees."

"A hill or lack thereof is inconsequential. The voice

called Elspeth made a chirping sound. "This is better than the last place he called us to . . . in the last town he visited."

"That place . . ." The second voice produced a nervous hissing noise, like a tin kettle on a high flame. "A moving theater it was."

"Movie theater," Elspeth corrected.

"I had never seen so many buildings blow up."

"It was not real."

"Pity. And, Elspeth dear, we will not be real much longer else we successfully do our summoner's bidding. We must help him spread the belief!"

The voices quieted as Mr. Lawlor returned, still red-faced and huffing, his shoes clicking rhythmically against the tile floor. He was followed by a skinny older man—the same one who showed up in the third grade classroom yesterday.

"Someone is going to get in trouble for what you did, Elspeth, making runes on the black wall. Some nice young boy or girl."

"The summoner is right. Better that someone get in trouble than us and he cease to exist. Trouble is a temporary bother, death is a permanent inconvenience."

That instant the school bell rang, loud and long, clanging so insufferably that the disembodied voices drifted down the hall toward the gym, where it wasn't quite so noisy. Doors were opening out onto the hall and children were pouring out, heading for the exits and their homes. A few drifted toward the cafeteria, mumbling about play practice.

Scotty Wiggapolan stood in front of the tall, narrow mirror that was propped up against the far wall of the cafeteria.

He didn't think he looked much like Robin Hood. Oh, he was dressed in green, all right, practically every inch of him. Green tights, that he was certain were purchased at some girls' dance store, ballet leotards, no doubt. Girls' clothes! A dark green tunic that hung to just below his hips was embroidered around the collar with leaves and vines. It was made of something shiny, satin, he guessed, something that the real Robin Hood would never have worn. Of course, Scotty knew with absolute certainty that there had never been a Robin Hood, or a band of Merry Men for that matter. It was all a story, a figment of a long-ago writer's dyed-green imagination. Richard the Lion Heart? Now, he had likely lived. But no one was portraying him in the play. He was only alluded to in a couple of lines.

Scotty's shoes were green, brighter than the tights. They were a pair of old Nikes that had been dyed personally by the director—right down to the shoestrings. Before they'd been dyed, when they were an off-white shade because of the playground dust embedded in them, they fit him oh-so-comfortably. But in dyeing the shoes, they'd shrunk a size or two. And now they pinched his toes together terribly and the backs were birthing twin blisters on his heels. He vowed to pitch them in the garbage the minute after the final performance was over. He wouldn't be caught dead on the basketball court—or anywhere else for that matter—in these garish, ruined, painfully-too-small shoes.

On his head was a hat, a funny-looking pointed thing made of thick felt, lovingly sewn by his mother, who told him with each stitch how proud she was that he had managed to get the lead in the play. She added a feather, a long pheasant feather she plucked from one of her own hats—one that she had inherited from her grandmother and wouldn't be caught dead wearing. The feather was the only thing not green about Scotty's outfit, and the director had more than once threatened to dye it, too.

Drew hadn't planned on snaring the Robin Hood part. He was more interested in being the Sheriff of Nottingham, who he thought might possibly have been a real person, or at least loosely based on a real person. The sheriff had more interesting lines, and not as many of them to memorize. Besides, the sheriff got to wear black.

It was his friend Drew who should have been Robin Hood. Drew talked him into trying out for this play. And Drew claimed that there was a real Robin Hood, and he'd been blond—said he'd seen a faithful recreation of him in an old Showtime series that a cousin had on video tape. Unfortunately, Drew—who was very blond and who was currently fidgeting several feet away from Scotty—was having a pillow tied to his waist and a wig with a big bald spot in the middle stuck on top of his head. Drew was grudgingly Friar Tuck. A brown robe that was a few inches too long was dropped over his head to complete the look.

Scotty stifled a smile. At least Drew looked nearly as uncomfortable as himself. But Drew didn't have as many lines. "This is all taking entirely too much of my time, Scotty whispered, as he pushed an unruly curl up under his funny-looking hat. Tonight was the dress rehearsal, which meant they would be here until well past what normally would be dinner time. So dinner would be late. Homework would follow, as always. And he probably would miss the Discovery Channel special on pyramids that he'd been wanting so desperately to see. No chance his folks would record it.

Scotty intended to be an archaeologist—after he made his way through the rest of this year and the next at Green Hill Elementary School, then through junior high school, high school, and at least four years of college, eight if he went for a doctorate, which he intended to do. He had his life all pleasantly mapped out for himself. And the only reason it included this play and him portraying Robin Hood was because he had read somewhere that high schools and colleges—the latter with all their attractive full-ride academic scholarships—looked kindly on students who were "well-rounded," participating in lots of extra-curricular activities. So be it. He adjusted the funny-looking hat and grinned sheepishly.

"Gather 'round me, ye Merry Men," he said flatly, rehearsing one of his many lines. "Let us be off to Sherwood Forest!"

One last look in the mirror.

He tightened his dyed-green rope belt and gave himself a final appraising view. "Wonderful," he whispered. Along one edge of the mirror he saw Cindy Baker's reflection. Decked out in her pastel pink Maid Marian dress, she was intently watching him. She smiled sweetly and began walking his way. "Wonderful," he repeated glumly.

"Places!" the director hollered, saving Scotty from a certain-to-be-boring conversation with air-headed Cindy. She was cute, but he wasn't interested in girls yet, and she wasn't interested in him . . . other than to set him up for a prank orchestrated by the Ferguson twins. "Everyone on the stage! Now!"

The Green Hill Elementary School stage opened onto the cafeteria. And when there was no great theatrical production in the works, the curtains were pulled and it stored extra desks and playground equipment.

Scotty wondered where all that stuff was being stored now.

"Apparently you didn't hear me the first time. Places!" the director repeated louder. He clapped his hands and nodded to Scotty, who leapt up on the stage. Cindy Baker extended a hand, expecting him to help her up.

Wonderful, he thought. "C'mon, Cindy." She was almost too quick to take his hand, giggling coquettishly when she took her place near the meager footlights.

The director gathered his face into a point, scowling at Scotty. "Do go backstage for me, Robin Hood, and see if you can find a stiffer sword. The one you're parading around with looks like a wet noodle. This is England— not an Italian restaurant."

Scotty complied, shuffling backstage, which was actually the school's kitchen.

The countertops were lined with props—some of which were moving on their own. Scotty blinked.

"Faeries," he said finally. "Yeah, right." For the briefest moment Scotty considered retreating. The director could come and pick out whatever sword he wanted Robin Hood to have. But curiosity got the better of him, and he edged closer to the moving props.

He stopped in his tracks halfway to the array of spray-painted Styrofoam weapons. He could have sworn he heard something. A buzzing? Like insects? No. Not insects.

Yes, he definitely heard words, he just couldn't make them out. And he smelled something now. He sniffed the air intently, trying desperately to put a label to the scent.

"Cinnamon?" he said. "I think I smell cinnamon."

There was more of the buzzing sound. And now it was coming from the countertop filled with extra scripts and gloves. All of the Merry Men, Robin Hood included, would have to wear green gloves tomorrow night. They weren't wearing them now because the gloves had been dyed this afternoon and were still a little damp.

"Who's there?" Scotty risked. He figured the twins were pulling a prank on him.

The buzzing stopped, but the smell of the cinnamon—or whatever spice it was—seemed a little stronger. He squinted. The air was shimmering. At least he thought it was. It was shimmering right above the recently-dyed gloves.

"Who?" he repeated nervously. He narrowed his eyes until they were needle-thin slits, until he could barely see. There was something there. He was sure of it. A couple of somethings. They were small and indistinct, looking a bit like tiny clouds come to ground and waiting to rain on the gloves. As he stared, they came more into focus.

"Ghosts!" he blurted, instantly covering his mouth.

There were two of them, each a little bigger than his fist. They were white, as he expected ghosts to be. But he had expected ghosts to be bigger—people size. Though after a moment, he decided that ghosts could probably be whatever size they wanted to be.

Maybe they were the spirits of dead cafeteria workers who were angry that the kitchen had been subsumed for the school play. Or maybe they were the ghosts of Indians. There was an Indian burial ground only a mile or two from the school. No, ghosts didn't exist, his practical self lectured. It's a trick. No ghosts. No faeries.

They floated toward him, sparkling motes that looked like movie special effects. He wanted to run—as fast and as far as his dyed-green Nikes would take him. But he couldn't move. It was like someone had super-glued the bottom of his shoes to the floor. So he shook, trembling all over, praying no one was spying on him and seeing him so scared.

The motes circled him, starting first at his head and working their way down to his knocking knees. As they moved, the air stirred around him. It was a chill breeze that brought goose bumps to his skin and made his teeth chatter. One mote touched his hand. It was an odd sensation, that had he not been so frightened he would have better noted it for his memory. Chilly and warm at the same time, and feeling damp.

The Ferguson twins weren't bright enough to put together something this impressive. Definitely not the Ferguson twins. Not anyone in his class that he could think of. The apparitions spun back around his face. They were moving faster now, whipping up the chill breeze and chattering to themselves, sounding like maddened insects.

Maybe ghosts did exist, Scotty thought, letting his mind open just a little to the possibility. After all, he'd watched a special on the History Channel about ghost hunters in Lousiana. And if they were ghosts. . . .

Scotty suddenly feared that they would kill him for intruding on whatever they were doing. Then his spirit would join theirs, trapped in the kitchen of Green Hill Elementary School until the end of eternity. He'd never make it to the eighth grade and then to high school. He'd never attend Southern Illinois University, become an archeologist, visit the pyramids.

His heart was hammering so loudly it was practically drowning out everything. Scotty's fingers had started quivering, and he thrust them into the folds of his tunic. His bottom lip was trembling, and he felt a drop of sweat run down his face.

The apparitions floated closer still, as if they were inspecting every square centimeter of him. One looked slightly bigger than the other. It made a huffing sound, sort of like Mr. Lawlor was prone to make when he was upset.

"We are not ghosts, boy. Elspeth, he thinks we are ghosts."

"No, ghosts do not exist. And we are not dead. Not yet, at least. Not ever if this boy plays his part."

The play, Scotty thought. He heard the director hollering for him.

"Play your part," the one called Elspeth cooed. "Accept our magic. Go on."

Then the motes drifted back to the countertop, hovered above a spray-painted Styrofoam sword, and floated the weapon into Scotty's shaking hands.

He bolted from the kitchen, the rubber soles of his dyed green Nikes squeaking on the tile floor. A heartbeat later he was jumping onto the stage, hand all tingling where it touched the Styrofoam pommel, fingers bone white from gripping it so tight.

Scotty couldn't see the director, and could only barely make out the forms of his Merry Men in the stage foliage which had oddly become thick and lifelike. He heard the paper leaves rustling in a wind that had inexplicably and impossibly picked up, felt a curl stir against his forehead, the sweat drying and cooling him. He smelled flowers, heard a brook, heard something thrashing in the trees and caught sight of a doe sprinting over a fallen log.

"Gather 'round me ye Merry Men," Scotty said.

His fellows came forward, not in the awkward way fifth-graders move, but in a lithe fashion, quiet like thieves. And they didn't look like his class mates, they looked like men—rugged and haggard, with careworn and scarred faces, dirty hands holding bows and brandishing swords.

"We come, Robin." This from a tall man in a tunic so dark green it looked nearly black. "Today we face the Sheriff."

"For Robin! For Sherwood!" Friar Tuck was clutching his belly, smiling slyly and winking with Drew's pale blue eyes, though the form certainly wasn't Drew's. Softer: "For magic and for the fey."

Scotty didn't remember much else about the rehearsal, save for after it was over, on his way across the parking lot, the director caught up to him and said "good job."

Drew met him at the corner, sack swung over his back

filled with Friar Tuck's robes and stomach. "Going to watch that special on the pyramids tonight, Scott-my-man?"

Scotty didn't answer him.

Drew poked him in the arm. "How about the Sci-Fi channel instead? Heard they're showing the first part of a mini-series on Merlin. But then, you don't believe in magic."

Scotty cut across the street, his hand still tingling from gripping the Styrofoam sword. A tiny cloudlike mote sparkled on his shoulder, then melted into the fabric of his shirt.

"Or do you, Scott-my-man? Do you believe in magic?"

"Hey, Scotty, what do you think that is?"

Scotty Wiggapolan tried his best not to smile, his carrot-red hair fluttering around his ears. "I dunno. What do you think it is, Sara?"

"Algebra?" She asked the question more to herself. "No. I'm sure it's not algebra. That has letters and numbers in it, X plus Y equals C-squared and all of that. So I don't think it's algebra."

"So maybe it's calculus or geometry, huh?" Scotty leaned to his right to get closer to Sara's desk and to better observe the blackboard. They were sitting in the third row of Mrs. Pepkin's sixth grade class, where despite the old woman's claim to poor hearing, they had to be quiet.

"Geometry? You really think so, Scotty?"

Sara hadn't known Scotty Wiggapolan very long, him having just transferred here a few weeks ago. Scotty was at Green Hill Elementary last year, but his family moved to the other side of town in the early fall after too many strange things started happening in their old neighborhood. Trees uprooting, sinkholes appearing, things that Sara planned to ask him about after she got to know him a little better. She intended to be a geologist, and maybe he got a close look into those sinkholes and could give her a good accounting.

"Sara, I can tell you what it's not. It's not hieroglyphics. I have a few books at home on the subject."

"Hieroglyphics?"

"Yeah, once upon a time I was interested in archeology. Not anymore, though. But once upon a time."

"So what do you think they are, all those marks?" Sara persisted.

Scotty shrugged.

There were circles within circles cut by wavy lines that ended in arrows and smaller half-circles and ovals, some of them colored in solid, others filled in with a crosshatch. And there were marks that looked like numbers, but not quite—at least not numbers that were written in English—and all of them were sitting inside something that looked like a large hexagon awkwardly tipped up on a point, as if it were rolling along, and in the process taking up more than half of the entire blackboard.

"Maybe it's part of some sort of helix, like for DNA," Sara mused.

Scotty knew she was a brain and probably could draw all sorts of DNA helixes herself. She was far too serious, reminded Scotty of himself a year back.

"Sara, I don't think Mrs. Pepkin would know about that stuff. She only teaches basic math."

Sara tipped her head, still scrutinizing the marks, eyes refusing to drift from the blackboard.

"Maybe it's magic, Sara." Scotty tucked his feet under his chair, the rubber soles of his oh-so-comfortable dyed green Nikes making a squeaking sound on the tile, a tiny cloudlike mote sparkling above the laces.

"I don't believe in magic," she returned.

"You will after play practice," he whispered.

FEVER WAKING

Jane Lindskold

Jane Lindskold is the author of over fifty short stories and fifteen or so novels, including the recently released *Child of a Rainless Year*, the five volume Firekeeper saga (*Through Wolf's Eyes*, *Wolf's Head*, *Wolf's Heart*, *The Dragon of Despair*, and *Wolf Captured*), and the archeological adventure fantasy *The Buried Pyramid*. She resides in New Mexico, where is she is currently writing her next novel.

YNAMYNET KNELT TREMBLING beside the cot on which her eldest brother, Kiriel, tossed with fever. Sometimes the sufferer screamed as if his nerves were on fire. Sometimes he talked animatedly to people who were not there. Once or twice he opened his eyes and then Ynamynet knew Kiriel saw her. His lips tried to curve in a smile, but he lacked the strength even for that.

Finally, Kiriel fell completely silent, and nothing Ynamynet did—not the cool clothes she pressed against his forehead and wrists, not the herbal infusions she forced between his lips, not the prayers she offered to indifferent deities—made the least difference.

Drawing breath in ragged gasps, Kiriel struggled to sit up, then collapsed back. He was dead before his sweat-matted hair hit the pillow.

This was Ynamynet's first such vigil. It was not to be her last.

She was only six years old.

"There is a bane upon those of us who bear the mark of magic upon our spirits," Ynamynet's mother said heavily as mother and daughter knelt beside Kiriel's fresh grave. "You have heard of this bane, but it was time for you to see it at work. That is why I assigned you vigil at your brother's bed, and why I am speaking to you now—as I already have to each of your brothers and sisters."

Ynamynet knew this. It had been explained to her before she went into the Chamber of Transformation, but she knew her mother took comfort in repetition, and so held silent.

"The bane did not always exist," Mother went on. "Not all that long ago, as ages of the world are counted, those who carried the mark ruled all the world. My own grandfather remembered those days. He told stories."

Rocking back on her heels, Mother's eyes glazed with memory, remembering the tales that had been bedtime stories to her, stories which she in turn had related to her children. They were tales of power and glory, of sorcerer kings who rode dragon-back through storm clouds, fearing neither thunder nor lightning for both were theirs to command. Ynamynet's favorite tales began in jeweled halls in which toasts were drunk from cups made from the gilded skulls of defeated enemies while boasts of future daring were made before all assembled. Such settings certainly were far grander than the sprawling, ramshackle farmhouse in which she, great granddaughter of those sorcerers, now resided.

As Ynamynet waited to see if Mother would tell one of those familiar yet always thrilling tales, the girl's vision blurred. At first she thought tears had risen unheralded to her eyes, for Kiriel, who lay so close but eternally distanced by death's void, had loved those tales and shaped his life by them.

But tears were not what blurred Ynamynet's eyes. The air in front of her shimmered, giving way to a vision of

past overlaying present. Before Ynamynet knelt Mother
as a child. She looked very like Ynamynet herself: thick,
straight brown hair, hazel eyes that shifted between blue
and grey, the same coltish body, all angles where just a
few seasons before there had been baby fat. This vision
child was superimposed upon Mother as she was now:
plump again, wide in hip and heavy in breast from bearing many children, her brown hair streaked with white,
the blue in her eyes faded, leaving dull grey behind.

Ynamynet trembled. She knew this vision was no trick
of her imagination. It was a sign, perhaps sent from beyond by Kiriel, so newly dead, a sign confirming what
Ynamynet had long suspected—that her own spirit carried the mark upon which the bane would fasten.

Thus far, the ability to work magic had not manifested
in Ynamynet, not as it had in Kiriel. She knew from
observing others that for years to come the ability would
be an erratic thing, crashing forth, then falling back, like
waves against a shore. For all that it was no less real—
no less inescapable—no less a promise of danger and
possibly death.

Mother did not see Ynamynet's trembling. Her gaze
was fixed on the mound of fresh dirt that covered Kiriel's grave. Did Mother see her son as he had been—a
tall, laughing youth of twenty, favorite of all the girls,
but giving his attention to none because of his obsessive
study of sorcerous lore? Or did Mother see him as she
had imagined him—the inheritor of terrific power, bringing the family into prominence and power that had not
been theirs for over a century?

Perhaps Mother saw Kiriel as he had been on what
proved to be his deathbed, twisted with pain, half-insane,
fighting, fighting ever on not to relinquish his power,
until at long and tortured last that battle had killed him.

Whatever Mother saw, she did not share her vision
with Ynamynet, nor did she relate one of Great-
Grandfather's inspirational tales of past wonder and
glory. Instead, when she cleared her throat and raised
her tired voice, Mother spoke about what Ynamynet
both most and least wanted to hear, about the sorcerer's
bane that had ended their ancestors' reign of glory, a

bane that to this day attacked those who carried the mark of magical talent upon their spirits.

"The bane was worse, once," Mother began. "When the bane first struck, it killed almost everyone it touched. Only those of lesser talent survived, and they were crippled, unable to cast the least spells. Those whose talents were less for sorcery, more innate—such as healers or those with sympathy for beasts—fared somewhat better, but many of these died as well. Those who recovered realized that what had been as a sixth sense to them had vanished forever. At the best, they found the sense diminished to a whisper of what it had been."

Ynamynet had heard this before, but never had she listened with such a feeling of immediacy, knowing the story belonged to her personally, rather than to those distant ancestors. She reached and touched the soft, crumbling earth that covered her brother's grave, but otherwise waited in perfect, listening silence.

"In my generation," Mother said, "things began to change. Still the bane came, bringing with it fevers, chills, and madness, but gradually an awareness spread that more victims were surviving. More importantly, more were surviving with some trace of magical ability intact. Even those who had a gift for sorcery—before this time they had been the hardest struck, and the most certain to die—began to come through. True, most retained only a memory of what they had known, as a blind man may remember color, but one or two found that when they studied the old rituals the intricate workings still made sense. These immersed themselves in the old lore and slowly began to bring alive the wonders that had been.

"Those who lived through the bane spoke of having to fight a terrific battle within themselves. Many admitted to having sacrificed some part of themselves to retain their power. Sterility was common result of these battles, as was loss of a sense or a crippled limb. Even so, those who survived the bane felt this price worth the opportunity to retain their ability to do magic.

"Over time, titles arose to define the different ranks of survivors. Those who lived with power intact were

called Once Dead, for going through the bane was like
dying. Those who lived but gave up their power were
called Twice Dead, for they had died twice: within the
bane, and in the death of their powers."

Mother said nothing more for a long moment, but her
gaze shifted back and forth between the fresh grave and
her daughter.

"Your brother sought to be Once Dead, and here he
lies merely dead. Years ago, when my own time came
to battle the bane, I could not face either my death or
the corruption of my body. I remember little about that
time of fever and madness, but I do recall the moment
when I chose to let the fever burn itself along magic's
mark upon my spirit, burn until the mark was ashes and
fell away. I lived, without talent, but intact. I told myself
I could still serve my ancestors by providing many children to carry on where I could not."

Ynamynet experienced a sudden revelation. She had
imbibed with the milk from her mother's breast the suspicion that Mother felt great guilt about that long ago
choice. For years Mother must have justified her choice
on the grounds that her children would do what she
could not. Now her eldest son, most promising of all her
children, lay dead, victim of the cruel bane Mother herself had shied away from. In addition to her grief,
Mother must be feeling a renewal of guilt—a fear that
she had not made the right choice, but instead had con-
demned her children to a heritage of impotent suffering
followed by a horrible death.

Ynamynet looked at her mother's sorrowing face, at
the tears that tracked unheeded over Mother's rounded
cheeks. In her heart, Ynamynet resolved that her mother's sufferings would not be for nothing, that Kiriel's
courage would be an example to her.

Gripping the damp earth mold in her hand, Ynamynet
swore a vow that when her time came she would be
Once Dead. Young as she was, Ynamynet had the wisdom to keep that vow to herself. Words spoken aloud
have the power to bind beyond reason.

Aloud, Ynamynet said only, "Don't cry, Mama. It's
going to be all right."

* * *

Ynamynet began her studies, first using her brother's notes, and, when she had exhausted those, receiving permission to delve into copies of the few books of sorcery that had been preserved from the days when the bane first struck. Then the vicious commoners had destroyed anything that had held the least hint of magic about it. That many perfectly innocent books and works of art had been destroyed did not matter to these who had—in the modern parlance—"Never Lived." The nonmagical had destroyed for the joy of destruction and the petty power it gave them.

Years passed. Ynamynet's education did not stop with reading. She volunteered for additional vigils in the Chamber of Transformation. She chose to serve as an attendant not just because this was the right thing to do, but because she hoped to learn something from the sufferers that might arm her against failure when her own battle came.

Not all those who came into the Chamber of Transformation were Ynamynet's immediate kin. In the days since the bane had struck, those who retained the mark of magic upon their spirits had formed secret communities. They could not always manage to reside apart from the Never Lived. That would have been both difficult and dangerous, for an isolated community could easily be wiped out. Well over a century might have passed since the sorcerer kings had reigned, but feelings about those with magical talent had not greatly changed. The commoners still hated and resented those with greater gifts, and would gladly destroy any who showed too much interest or knowledge in the vanished arts.

Ynamynet's father had died from such ill-feeling when the girl was only two. Father had not shown any talent—he had none, being Twice Dead—but when in his cups he had spoken in unwise praise of rulers gone by and the order they had brought the land. Happily for his family, Father had been far away from home, and murder did not travel beyond that tavern's own walls.

Instead of living in isolation, those with magic's mark lived cheek by jowl with those who would be willing to destroy them, and the Chamber of Transformation was often nothing more than a spare bedroom consecrated to this purpose. Fevers, even killing fevers, were not uncommon in these days without magic. Ynamynet wondered if in their deepest hearts the Never Lived sometimes longed for the days when a talented healer could ease the sufferer on the road back into life.

Deaf Trolog, one of the Once Dead, often posed as such a healer. Indeed, he was knowledgeable about many forms of non-magical doctoring. His abilities and knowledge made him welcome anywhere illness came, be it high hall or low cottage. Although Deaf Trolog dispensed medicines wherever he went, his real intention was to sniff out those cases when the fever in question might actually be the bane, for the bane did crop up among the Never Lived, although not as commonly as it did among families that knew and revered their heritage.

"The sorcerers took what they wanted in those days," Deaf Trolog would laugh in the flat, braying fashion of those who cannot hear themselves. "They spread their seed around a good deal, so their gifts arise even from dry soil."

But although Deaf Trolog occasionally was able to find and save one of those who bore magic's mark, his most honored role was tending those from families like Ynamynet's own where the spirit mark was common, and the risk of death from the bane was high. Deaf Trolog was the one who brought infusions and other treatments to the Chamber of Transformation, and he was the one who pronounced verdict upon the survivors—often before the pain wracked victims were even sure themselves whether they had retained their gift or not.

"Twice Dead," his voice would croak, or sadly, "Truly Dead." Occasionally with a glow of triumph in his voice, "Once Dead!"

From the time she was six, Ynamynet was present for these proclamations whenever possible, watching, waiting, learning what she could for when her own day came.

Ynamynet's resolve to be proclaimed Once Dead was shaken only once, on the day one of her elder sisters passed through the bane. In the years between Kiriel's ordeal and this, one other sibling had died from the bane—a sister two and a half years younger than Kiriel. Two others siblings had survived, both as Twice Dead, and then Leniti's time had come.

Leniti's gift was slight, manifesting as an erratic ability to divine sources of fresh water, veins of metal, even missing items. Leniti was a cheerful young woman who described the sensation of her talent, on those rare occasions when it flared into life, as if she was hearing the song of the living earth. Even when her talent was dormant, Leniti moved as if a trace of the earth's song still lingered in her ears. Though she was as plain as a sparrow, her movements to that unheard song made her strangely beautiful and loved by all.

The bane came upon Leniti when she was eighteen and Ynamynet was twelve. Leniti went into the Chamber of Transformation almost cheerfully.

"I hardly know my talent is there," Leniti said with a giggle, her eyes wide with fever. "Surely I won't miss it when it is gone."

Ynamynet did not scorn Leniti for intending to let go of her talent. Leniti was in love with her husband, who she had married two years before, and her entire soul was given to him and their infant daughter. There was no room for the intense concentration on sorcery to which Ynamynet had devoted herself. Besides Leniti's talent for divination was slight and erratic, hardly something worth dying for.

But the talent seemed to have other ideas or, perhaps when forced to meet her own spirit face to face in the Halls of Self, Leniti had learned how much that seldom heard song mattered to her. Given no recourse for escape, the fever mounted higher and higher. Leniti tossed and turned, screaming fragments of argument to an unseen auditor. She knew no one, not even her husband or her babe—or the younger sister who knelt at her bedside day and night.

Leniti's pain was so great that Ynamynet found herself praying that death would come as a release. Once she came to herself to discover that her hands had lifted a pillow, and that without conscious decision she was raising it to smother Leniti's tormented screams into silence forever.

Hot with shame, Ynamynet laid the pillow aside, and instead pressed snow packs against her sister's burning flesh, not even pausing to mop away the water that resulted as snow turned instantly into water.

Perhaps it was the snow and winter's cold that saved Leniti's life, their combined force that kept the fever from consuming her. Perhaps it was Deaf Trolog's hovering care, for as the bane grew more fierce he rarely left Leniti's side. Perhaps Leniti's own spirit was equal to the battle against whatever it was that sought to devour her innermost self.

They would never know, for Leniti could not tell them. Although Deaf Trolog pronounced her Once Dead with complete assurance, Leniti came forth from her battle completely insane. She had kept the song of the earth in her ears, but never again did she give the least indication of knowing anyone or anything around her.

Watching Leniti move about to unheard music, Ynamynet doubted her own resolve. She wondered if Kiriel's spirit would forgive her if she broke the solemn vow she had made upon the soft earth mold of his grave.

Ynamynet's time came in a whisper of voices and an ache in her bones. She was fourteen. Despite all the times she had sat vigil in the Chamber of Transformation, Ynamynet did not recognize the signs of the bane's rising when they manifested so intimately.

"She is possessed by the bane," Deaf Trolog said with certainty, and over his shoulder Ynamynet saw her mother's face go dead white.

"It can't be," Mother cried in a voice that said she knew the signs all too well. She added in desperation, as if saying so might make it so, "Ynamynet is too young!"

"Now, Mahlli," Deaf Trolog said, "you know as well as I do that the bane comes when it will with no sense of human time. Ynamynet has shown great interest in all things of sorcery since she was hardly big enough to look over the table's edge. There are some who say that interest summons the bane."

There were indeed some who believed that the bane did come more quickly to those who showed interest in sorcery, but as she was hustled off to her time in the Chamber of Transformation, Ynamynet couldn't help but think that her own circumstances were dreadfully unfair.

Kiriel, she thought, *the very one who got me into this, he lived until he was twenty, untouched and untainted. I bet for all the time he spent with his nose in books and his fingers blue from copying, still he had some fun. I bet he even kissed somebody—probably more than one somebody. I remember how the girls cried at his funeral.*

Pervaded with a deep sense of being a victim, Ynamynet collapsed onto the bed. That sense rose within her as the fever twined into her nerves and sent red hot shafts of pain to penetrate her core. Pain surged up the marrow of her bones and made every beat of her heart undiluted agony.

Ynamynet tried to remember the knowledge she had garnered from her long study of the bane. She struggled to remember her goal. Once Dead. Alive with abilities intact.

Her sister Leniti's voice came to her ears, singing one of the oddly musical pieces that were her only utterances since arising from this very bed. Ynamynet amended her goals, each thought shaped as a hammer blow of pain against the anvil of her fevered body.

Once Dead. Alive. Abilities intact. Sane.

Ynamynet understood now what Leniti had faced, the lure of the song of the mark set in her spirit. That song had been so potent that it had washed away the pain, made everything else unimportant until Leniti had followed it into a place without pain—with power—but with nothing else.

Leniti's song faded, but in its fading notes Ynamynet saw her own spirit mark outlined against a vision of her body. This image stood on outspread feet, head thrown slightly back, arms spread wide. It was a woman translucent: skin a pale glow, holding in taut muscles stretched and red with blood; bones lay beneath, hard, white, and solid. Intertwined within this all, carrying with it a burning fiber of agony, was the mark of magic upon her spirit.

That mark touched every muscle, insinuated itself into every nerve, every bone. It permeated the shafts of her hair and the fluids in her organs. As Ynamynet had vowed to make the magical arts her life, so the spirit mark touched every part of her life. And as the bane fed upon that spirit mark, so it also touched every part of her living self and made that life a throbbing, beating scream of pain.

Ynamynet heard herself scream, heard her mother's voice calling for more ice, felt the sawdust covered chunks set against her naked flesh, but the cold could not soothe her. The pain was inside the skin.

"Inside! Inside! Inside!" she screamed, and tried to rake open her skin with her fingernails, but they were blunt and dull, and would not cut. Deaf Trolog had seen this before. How many times had Ynamynet herself cut some suffer's nails, calm and clinical, never realizing why it was done?

Ynamynet screamed and nearly choked as a fever reducing infusion was poured into her open mouth. She'd done that, too, even feeling a certain gratitude that she need not force open jaws locked tightly shut to get the necessary medication in.

She moaned. Why did they try? Why didn't they just let the fever have her? She didn't want to die, but she didn't really want to live either, not when living meant being Twice Dead and a failure. How good it would be if someone pitied her and took her life. Then she'd just be dead, and not alive and a failure or dead and a failure just dead . . .

Ynamynet remembered holding the pillow in her hands when Leniti had been sick, and wondered if she had been responding to some unrealized prompt from the sufferer who had been in her care.

"Pillow! Pillow! Pillow!" Ynamynet screamed, trying

to make them understand, but her throat was raw and scratched from too much screaming, and all that came out was a shrill, high wail.

Ynamynet looked down at herself and at the spirit mark intertwined with her body, nailed into place with her own hopes and desires. If she let it go, separated it from herself, then the bane would no longer have anything extra to feed upon. Robbed of the extra fuel of her physical self, the bane would burn her talent away, and Ynamynet would be free. Free. Alive. Free.

Twice Dead.

Ynamynet fled into hallucination, but the pain was always with her no matter where she ran or who she sought. Eventually, pain took a face, and that face was that of her brother, Kiriel.

"Hey, Nami," Kiriel said softly with that warm, understanding smile Ynamynet found she still remembered. "Having a hard time of it?"

"You know I am," Ynamynet replied. She tried propping herself up but her tortured muscles wouldn't let her. She fell back against the pillow, cool linen instantly hot against her face. She was vaguely aware of efforts being made to ease her suffering, but she couldn't seem to care. Only the pain mattered.

Kiriel took a seat on one of the chairs pulled up beside the sickroom cot and slouched comfortably. Ynamynet found herself resenting that easy slouch. She found herself resenting Kiriel.

"It's all your fault," she said. "If you'd done it right . . ."

"Done what?"

"You were going to be Once Dead. You were going to be the next sorcerer. You were going to be a king. You failed though. You gave up. You left your destiny to me. I was only six!"

"Did anyone ask you to step in?" Kiriel asked. "Did anyone ask you to be a hero?"

Ynamynet stared at him. "Someone had to do it."

"We all hate you, you know," Kiriel said. "The bane is agony enough—you know that now, don't you? Imagine suffering, imagine dragging yourself to the surface from time to time. Instead of finding loving hands and concerned faces, there's this cold, clinical little girl sitting there. There's not a drop of compassion in you, is there? You're cold. So cold . . ."

"I had to do it," Ynamynet said. "You let us down. I had to learn how to defeat the bane if ever again dragons were to fly and we were to raise jeweled cups on high. You remember the tales. You remember the songs. I had to do it."

"You had to?" Kiriel laughed, the sound short, curt, and bitter. "Well, then maybe you belong in that jeweled hall, drinking wine from human skulls. But we hated you, Ynamynet, hated you to the bone. Ah . . . You were so cold, so cold, so cold . . ."

Ynamynet didn't feel in the least cold. Her body burned and Kiriel was gone, but she didn't even remember his being there. Pain beat at her, thunder drumbeat in every limb, every organ. She summoned the vision of herself, and saw the body was fading, the bane now clearly visible, no longer merely running along her spirit mark, but an entity in itself, burning, burning, burning.

It's going to be over soon, she thought, and felt no surprise. *I can still untack the spirit mark from my physical self—I think. I must. I must try . . . Surely living is better. Didn't I learn that from all those bedside vigils? Living is better, even living without power. Even . . .*

And then Ynamynet remembered what she had learned, and she knew that her only hope for success lay within the very thing for which Kiriel and the others hated her.

Cold.

She was cold. So cold. Cold flesh did not feel. Cold things did not burn. Cold and heat were opposites. Where one was gathered, the other surely could not be.

Ynamynet gathered cold into herself. She iced her flesh, cemented her joints with frost. She forced heat from her bones and her body, channeled it into the burning thread of the bane. Her fingers grew numb, so she pushed with them as if they were sticks strapped to her hands, until her hands were as blocks of wood strapped to her wrists. The wrists grew cold, and then the elbows, but still she pushed, winnowing every ounce of heat from herself, giving heat to the bane, seducing it from herself and her spirit mark, feeding the bane's fire until it burned out.

And left her cold.

Ynamynet came to consciousness to hear Deaf Trolog braying triumphantly, "Once Dead! Once Dead!"

She opened her eyes, and found her mother sitting on the edge of the bed, her gaze alight with hope and joy. Various sisters and brothers, aunts, uncles, and cousins, crowded around the doorway, all aglow with joy and pride.

Mother looked down at Ynamynet. "You did it, my child. You did it!"

Ynamynet managed a faint smile, but although the searing waves of bane agony were gone, she still felt weak, sick, and wrung out . . . All that, and something else.

"How do you feel, darling?" Mother asked.

"Cold," Ynamynet whispered, and knew that never again would she be warm. "So cold."

STARCHILD WONDERSMITH

Louise Marley

Louise Marley is a former concert and opera singer who now has great fun writing fantasy and science fiction, often with musical themes. Her published novels include *The Glass Harmonica*, *The Child Goddess*, and *Singer in the Snow*. She lives in Washington State with her husband and son and a white Scottish Terrier. Louise loves hearing from readers, and can be reached through her website at *www.louisemarley.com*.

"WELL, SON." Puck Smith stopped the car. "Here we are."

Star and his parents gazed out at the glass and steel rectangle of his new school. A crowd of kids were filing in through the double doors. They mostly wore denim, Star saw, and every one of them carried a backpack.

Star had carefully chosen his sunset shirt and his favorite pants, violet with stars on the legs, but he could see now they weren't going to work.

"Mom," he said. "I need different clothes. And a backpack."

"Oh, honey." When she leaned forward, the sleeve of her caftan sent spangles of light drifting over his shoulder. "Maybe you should wait until . . ."

"No, Mom." He took a deep breath, and opened the car door. "I've waited long enough."

Crystal sighed. "Oh, dear. I suppose you're right." She held out one of her special containers. "But don't forget your lunch."

Star took the container. At his touch, wisps of scented steam curled around his fingers, sparkling in the sunshine. Dismayed, he said, "Mom! I can't take this!"

"He's right," Puck said. "It breaks the Rules."

"Oh, the blessed Rules!" Crystal cried.

"We have to protect the Normals," Puck said sternly. "You know that, dear."

Star said, "I'm sorry, Mom."

Crystal's eyes reddened. "But—what will you do about lunch?"

"There's a cafeteria."

Puck said, "It's not too late to change your mind, Starchild."

"Dad. It's Star, okay? Star Smith."

"Right, son. Star. We know." Puck took the lunch container and laid it on the seat. "But you're still one of us."

"I know. Thanks, Dad."

"We love you," Crystal whispered, tears in her voice.

"I love you, too, Mom." Star swung his legs out of the car. The silver stars on his trousers glittered in the sunshine. "'Bye."

Star watched his parents drive away. Then he turned, touched the whistle in his pocket for luck, and started up the sidewalk toward his new life.

It had been a hard decision to change schools.

He had always gone to school with his cousins, and his cousins' cousins, and their cousins' cousins, the School for True Beings. It was a soaring blue and green tower hidden in a little forest of pine trees, with multicolored stone floors, circular rooms, and crazy-glass windows. While the Beings waited for their Talents to emerge, they learned to read and write and do math. When their Talents made themselves known, they practiced using them.

Most Beings found their Talents when they were eight or nine, although sometimes they were ten, or even eleven. Starchild Wondersmith's birthdays came and went, eleven, twelve, thirteen . . . but nothing happened.

He wasn't an Assembler, like his father, who made various materials fasten themselves together into wonderful birdhouses or sinuous garden goddesses or lacy gazebos. He wasn't a Cook, like his mother, who could put yeast and flour and water in a bowl and create bread with a flick of her fingers.

Star wasn't a Finder, or a Seer, or a Rememberer. He waited. His third cousin twice-removed, Joyful Clearwater, found she could dust an entire house with only a few minutes' concentration. His second cousin on his grandmother's side, Seagull Whiteheart, learned he could make any cloud, no matter how small, shed rain just where he wanted it. Star was still waiting when the best Talent of all was bestowed upon Splendor Skychurch, of the honey-colored hair and emerald eyes. Splendor Skychurch could make anything—from a paper clip to a station wagon—disappear. The object, an envelope or a radio or a cherry tree, was still there, safe and sound. It was just invisible.

Splendor's whole family had marvelous Talents. Her mother was a Lightbringer, and her father was a Forger. Her great-great-aunt Charm had been that rarest of Beings, a Gatherer, but Star thought Splendor's Talent was even better than that.

It happened sometimes, though rarely, that a True Being never developed a special gift. Starchild Wondersmith, unhappily, was one of those. Starchild Wondersmith couldn't do anything a Normal couldn't do. And finally, he gave up waiting.

He decided to become a Normal.

Walking the corridors of his new school, Star felt as if he were caught in a spiderweb. Everything was in shades of gray, the walls, the floor tiles, the ceilings. The classrooms were perfectly square, and everyone sat in identical desks. Kids stared at Star's pants, and snickered at his name when he had to speak it. He kept his head down all morning, pretending not to notice.

Except for his teachers, only one person spoke directly

to him. He glanced up at the sound of her voice, and saw
a slight girl with dun-colored hair, dressed all in black.

She held up a fractured pencil. "Do you have an
extra?" she asked.

"Oh," he said. He groped in his pockets, but he
couldn't find anything except his whistle. If only he were
a Fixer. Or a Cutter. He held up his empty hands.
"No. Sorry."

She said, "Thanks anyway," and turned away. He
sighed, feeling he had missed a chance to make a friend.

No one else spoke to him. Most kids acted as if he
wasn't there, as if Splendor Skychurch had rendered him
invisible. By lunch break he felt miserable and utterly
alone.

He followed the crowd to the cafeteria, where everyone sat at long tables. Here and there a solitary student
hunched over a lunch tray. Mostly the kids sat in tight
little groups, their backs turned to everyone else. No one
met Star's eyes, or invited him to join them. He decided
after a moment that he wasn't really hungry.

He turned away, clutching the stack of his new books
under his arm. He found a small patch of lawn outside
the library, and sat crosslegged on the grass. He opened
one of the books and began to turn its pages.

When a shadow fell across the book, he glanced up.

Three boys, looking very large in lettered jackets,
stood over him. "Who're you?" one of them said.

Star closed his book. "I'm Star," he said. "Star
Smith."

"Star?" another said scornfully. "What kind of name
is that?"

"And what's with the pants?" the third said. He wore
enormous high-top sneakers, and he tapped Star's leg
with a rubbery toe.

Star pulled back. He wasn't sure if it was a joke or not.

The foot came again, harder, leaving a dusty print.
The boys giggled. One of them said, "Twinkle, twinkle,
little Star!" and they all laughed loudly at this witticism.

Star jumped to his feet. Some other boys were throwing a football back and forth on the lawn. Several girls

were watching, tossing their long hair and whispering together.

Just as Star bent to pick up his books, someone threw the football in his direction. It struck him in the chest, and he staggered backward, almost falling. "Hey!"

The three closest to him whined, "Hey! Hey!" and laughed again, socking each other in the shoulder, glancing at the girls to see if they noticed.

Star gathered his books, backed away, and retreated into the school.

He wandered aimlessly until he came upon a tiny open courtyard. It held four concrete benches, all the same shape and size, and a few dispirited shrubs. The girl with the dun hair was there, sitting with another girl whose black hair stuck up in stiff spikes. They looked up as he came out into the sunshine.

"Hey, look, Emmy," the spike-haired girl said. "One more for the Losers' Club."

Emmy said, "Shut up, Hannah. He's new."

Hannah squinted at Star. "Didn't take you long to find us, did it?"

He had no idea how to answer her. He sat down on a bench with his books beside him, wondering how much time was left before the buzzer sounded. His fourth cousin, Sweetbriar Goodfellow, always knew exactly what time it was in any part of the world, but Star didn't have that Talent, either. He closed his eyes, letting the sun warm his eyelids, and imagined himself back with the Beings, sitting in a prism of colored light shining through crazy-glass. An idea came to him, and he felt in his pocket for his whistle.

The only thing special about Star, among the Beings, was his music. When Star took out his whistle, the cousins stopped what they were doing to listen. Even at festivals, the Beings would gather to hear Starchild Wondersmith play.

His music was new every time, different every day. He never knew what it would be. He wasn't at all certain even how it worked, but it seemed to him that he breathed in the feelings around him, and then breathed

them out through his whistle. Sometimes, when he
played at a festival, Splendor Skychurch would dance, in
a swirl of scarves and floating honey-colored hair, and
those were the best times of all.

Now, sitting in the little courtyard, Star thought about
Splendor dancing. He breathed in the memory, and then
breathed out a little flight of notes that swirled like bubbles in a glass, up and up and up, until they escaped from
the concrete courtyard to twinkle into the sky above.

"Wow."

Startled, he opened his eyes to the square grayness of
his surroundings. The girl called Emmy stood before
him. He lowered his whistle. "What?"

"I mean, wow. You're really good."

His cheeks warmed, and he dropped his eyes. "Oh.
Well. Thanks."

"What is that thing?"

Star turned the whistle over in his hand. It was just
ordinary, made of tin, with six stops. "A whistle."

"Play it again," she said. "That song."

Star hesitated. "I'm sorry—I can't."

Emmy tilted her head. "Why not?"

"Well . . ." Star hesitated, and then mumbled, "I—I
don't know."

"Try," the girl named Hannah said. Her voice had an
edge to it, like a pair of scissors.

Emmy said, "Hannah, don't be rude."

Hannah grinned at Star. "Don't talk much, do you?"

"No."

"So who are you, then?"

Star stood up, a little wary. "Star Smith."

"Star?" Hannah laughed. "Star! That clinches it!"

"What?"

"You're definitely in the Losers' Club!"

The buzzer announced the end of lunch break. Relieved, Star put his whistle back in his pocket. It had
been an odd way to spend lunch break. But, he supposed, he could tell his parents he had already joined a
club. A club of losers!

The next day Star went to the courtyard again, this
time with a plain peanut butter sandwich in a paper bag.

He had made it himself, since even Crystal's cold sandwiches tended to flicker and glow. He sat on the same
bench, and was opening his lunch when Emmy and Hannah came into the courtyard, trailed by a tall girl and a
thin boy in glasses.

"Hey, Star," Emmy said. "Want company?"

"Sure." She sat next to him. The other kids took
nearby benches, and watched him expectantly. Star
slowly put his sandwich back in the bag.

"Will you play for us?" Emmy asked. She waved her
hand at the others. "I was telling these guys about your
whistle, and they want to hear it."

"Well," Star said. "The thing is—I never know—I
mean, I'm not all that good."

"Liar!" Hannah said. She turned to the others. "He's
fabulous. He's just a big liar."

Emmy said, "Hannah!"

But it was so outrageous Star started to laugh. "First
I'm a loser, and now I'm a liar?"

Hannah grinned, and said in her sharp voice, "You
got it, Starman. Now, will you show off for these guys,
or not?"

Star stuck his lunch bag back in his new backpack,
and pulled out his whistle.

"Cool," the new girl said. The thin boy said, "Yeah."

Star put his fingers on the stops of the whistle, and
said before he began, "It won't be the same, you know."

"What do you mean?" Emmy said.

"I never know what it's going to be. It's different
every time."

"Improvised," Hannah said. "Like in Jazz Band."

"I guess." The word didn't quite fit, but Star didn't
know a better one. He put the mouthpiece between his
lips and closed his eyes.

It was, as he had warned them, different. He breathed
in, and breathed out a long, winding melody that painted
the cement of the courtyard with pink and mauve, washed
the gray walls of the classrooms and the unrelenting corridors in apricot and lavender. His music turned and twisted
until the straight corridors curved, the drab walls shimmered, the plaster ceilings bloomed like flowers.

He finished, and opened his eyes.

"Sweet," the tall girl said. Emmy said, "Yeah." Star blushed.

Hannah said, "I told you he was a liar!"

The next day there were six kids gathered in the courtyard when Star arrived, and the day after that there were ten. The next day there were fourteen, and not everyone could find a seat on the benches.

Hannah said, "Wow, look how many losers there are at this school."

Emmy said, "Hannah! Stop it!"

Star's melody that day was broad and slow, like a sunrise, light flaring over the horizon to banish the darkness. As he finished it, and opened his eyes, everyone was smiling.

Hannah said, "Thanks for the music, Starman," and several others chimed in. Starman, it seemed, had become his Normal name.

He smiled back at them. It wasn't a bad name at all.

That weekend, there was a festival for the True Beings. Star found a moment to be alone with Splendor Skychurch, who was wrapped in lavender scarves and wore a violet in her hair. When she asked him how his new school was, he said, "It's okay."

"What are they like? The Normals?"

He frowned. "It's funny, Splendor. I've been there two weeks, but—I don't have any idea what Normal is." She nodded, solemnly, but Star wondered if she could possibly understand.

"You should come to the school," he blurted. "You and some of the cousins. See for yourselves."

She smiled at him. "That's a nice idea, Starchild. I'll talk to Seagull and Joyful."

By the middle of his third week, the courtyard was so crowded during lunch not everyone could get in. Kids hung about in the doorways and sat on the floor in the corridors. Star's music was quick, rising and falling like flocks of birds wheeling through the sky, descending in clouds to perch, then rising again, all together, the beat of their wings like a thousand heartbeats.

He was grateful that the Losers' Club had set a pattern. No one clapped, which would have been embarrassing. They said short, quiet things like "Yeah, man" and "Love it" and "Cool, Starman." And then they started talking to each other. No one turned their backs on anyone else that Star could see.

Emmy said, "Look at them. You can't tell who the losers are anymore."

Star turned to her. "I thought you didn't like that word."

She shook her head. "I don't. There are still losers, though."

Before he could answer, a voice cut through the chatter. "Excuse me. Excuse me, people. Let me through, please."

Star looked up. The principal, Mr. Lyne, a big bald man, was coming through the crowd like a boat through water. Conversations died away as he passed, leaving silence in his wake. He stopped before Star.

Mr. Lyne said, "You're Star Smith, aren't you?"

Star nodded. "Yes."

"Well," the principal said. He rubbed his hands together, and smiled as if he were trying to be pleasant. "Well, I'm sorry, Star, but we can't have this many people in the courtyard. I know everyone is enjoying your little concerts . . ."

"Oh, they're not concerts," Star began. He felt everyone's eyes on him, and wished Splendor were there to make him disappear.

"That's fine, fine," the principal said. He waved his hand around the courtyard. "But it's too crowded here. The fire regulations are very strict about blocked doors. And these people will never get out in time for class. I'm afraid I'll have to ask you not to do this again."

A second later, the buzzer sounded. No one, Star noticed uneasily, moved an inch.

Mr. Lyne scowled. "Look, young man, I'm sure you mean well, but you can't—"

Hannah's voice cut through the principal's words. "It's not his fault!"

Emmy hissed, "Hannah!"

Mr. Lyne glared at her. "Why are you all still here? Go to your classes!"

Kids began to move, slowly, the ones in the doorways first, the ones in the courtyard having to wait for them to get out of the way. Star could see that the principal was right. It took several minutes to clear the courtyard. If there were a fire, that could be a terrible thing. One of the Beings was a Douser, but he wasn't here. The only Being here had no Talent.

Mr. Lyne stood with his hand on Star's shoulder, so he didn't dare move. Emmy and Hannah left last, glancing over their shoulders at him, Emmy with sympathy, Hannah with eyes glinting angrily.

Mr. Lyne removed his hand, and Star picked up his backpack. The principal said, "What school did you attend before this one?"

Star said hastily, "Pine Tree Academy."

"Ah. Private."

"Yes, sir."

"Well, Star, this is a public school, with a lot of young people. We have to regulate activities, gatherings, you know, where a lot of students are together in one place."

Star said weakly, "It was just the Losers' Club."

"There are no losers here, Star. We help everyone to succeed."

Star looked at his toes, and sighed.

"You're new, and I know it's hard to fit in. But I don't want to have to call your parents."

Star's heart sank. The strictest Rule of all was that the Beings' way of life remained private. No one had said he shouldn't play his whistle, but just the same, this had gotten out of hand. "Okay, Mr. Lyne."

"We could arrange for you to play with the band, maybe."

Star shook his head. "No, thanks, Mr. Lyne. I don't think so."

Unfortunately, it wasn't that easy to quash the Losers' Club meetings. The next day, and the next, Star left his whistle at home, but the courtyard was crammed with kids anyway, the chess club kids, the punk rock kids, the

French club and the Honor Society and even the tennis team kids. They all turned and shouted to him when he came down the corridor. Hannah stood on a bench in the middle, grinning.

Star tried eating his sandwich on the patch of grass outside the library, but the same bulky jocks were there, hooting his name when he appeared. He went to the back of the school, where the smokers hung out, but what seemed like a hundred students gathered around him, asking where his whistle was. He tried the cafeteria, but someone unplugged the jukebox and started chanting "Starman, Starman" until he fled.

And so, although Star had kept his part of the bargain, Mr. Lyne called his parents.

Crystal hung up the phone, looking gloomy. "Starchild. We need to talk to your father."

They found Puck in his workshop, shaking trails of silvery smoke from his fingertips. A birdhouse with slender, slanting turrets stood on the workbench, blue and gold and vermilion paint still glistening wet.

Crystal told him about the phone call. Puck took off his apron, and began tidying things. He said gravely, "What's happening at the school, son?"

"What do you mean, Dad?" Star gave his mother an anxious glance.

"You understand the Rules," Crystal said softly.

"I didn't break the Rules!" Star protested. "I just—it was just—" They were both watching him, trusting him, waiting for him to explain. He sighed. "It was the Losers' Club."

"You're in a club?" Crystal asked, brightening.

Star shook his head. He had known from the beginning she wouldn't understand. "Let's go inside," he said. "It's a long story."

When Star had explained as best he could, Puck said, "Well, Starchi—I mean, Star. Mr. Lyne said he invited you to join the band."

"I can't play that way, Dad," Star said. He took his whistle out of his pocket. "My music—it's like—it's just—breathing music."

"Breathing?" Crystal repeated.

"Yes. I just . . . breathe. In, and out. And the music is there."

There was a pause. His parents looked at him, and looked at each other. Crystal opened her mouth, then closed it when Puck shook his head at her. She excused herself, and got up to draw her fingers over a pitcher of water and sugar and sliced lemons. When she came back with the freshly made lemonade, Star noticed his mother was glowing, not just her fingers, but her face and her hair. She was surrounded by a haze of light. He wondered at that. Making lemonade hardly took any of Crystal's Talent.

Puck distracted him. "I think you should meet Mr. Lyne halfway," he said thoughtfully. "A concert, only not a concert. Just a—" He frowned, looking for a word.

"A festival?" Crystal suggested.

Star said doubtfully, "I don't know, Mom. Festival sounds—I mean, what if it doesn't work? What if nothing comes out?"

"A meeting, then," Puck said.

Star turned his whistle in his fingers, considering. "A meeting. Maybe, Dad." He suddenly smiled. "Yes. A Losers' Club meeting. If Mr. Lyne says it's okay. There are a couple of kids who can help."

"You just need a place."

"Yes. The courtyard is too small, and the cafeteria is busy serving lunch. The jocks will cause trouble if we use the lawn outside the library . . ."

Crystal said, "What about that big meadow? With all the benches around it?"

"The football field? But they have football practice there, or soccer, or whatever."

"At lunch break?" Puck asked. "I'll bet it's free at lunch break. I'll call Mr. Lyne back."

It took some doing, some persuasion of Mr. Lyne by Puck and Crystal, some help from Emmy and Hannah to spread the word, but two days later the Losers' Club was to meet in the bleachers at one end of the football field. Star walked across the parking lot and up the cement ramp with Emmy and Hannah, his whistle in his pocket, his stomach full of butterflies. A few small clouds floated high above, but the day was warm. The usual members of the Losers' Club were already waiting on the benches, and other kids were wandering up to find seats, the tennis team all in a group, the chess club coming in twos and threes, the rockers with their band tee shirts and spiky hair climbing right to the top, waving and calling, "Starman! Cool!"

It looked as if the whole school had come out. There were girls and boys Star had never seen, sitting on the benches, standing on the dirt fringe below the bleachers, hanging over the railings. Mr. Lyne and the vice-principal stood with folded arms beside the empty ticket booth, and the jocks who had driven Star off the library lawn huddled on the field, their heads turning as Star and Emmy and Hannah walked down the aisle. One of the jocks said something to the others that Star couldn't hear, and they all laughed.

Hannah said, "Look, the beef-for-brains guys are here."

Emmy said, "Hannah! Shut up!"

In the shade of the Visitors' Locker Room, Star caught sight of his parents and several of the cousins, come to support him. Seagull Whiteheart was there, and Joyful Clearwater, and Splendor, her hair gleaming in the sunshine. Star rubbed his stomach, where the butterflies swarmed, and sat where Emmy pointed. He drew his whistle from his pocket.

"Hey, Starman," someone said.

Somebody at the top of the bleachers called, "Play for us, Starman!"

The thick-necked guys on the field imitated the call, whining, "Starman! Starman!"

Emmy whispered, "Ignore those guys, Star."

Hannah said loudly, "Losers' Club rule: never listen to anybody whose neck is bigger than their head," and the kids around her laughed.

Star closed his eyes. He felt as if he were at the center of a kaleidoscope, colors and shapes turning around him, shifting and twisting, coalescing, flying apart, coming together again. Everything meshed, his butterflies, the Losers' Club, the jocks, the Beings. He breathed it all in, and breathed it out again through his whistle, almost before he knew he was doing it. The sound was thin and fragile in the open air.

His melody lasted a long time, because there were so many people, so many feelings. There were all the kids, each with their own concerns. There was Mr. Lyne, worried about fire regulations, and about losing control. There were the cousins, marveling at the Normal school. And there were Puck and Crystal, who were full of—full of what?

Star's melody slowed, descended, came to an end. Cautiously, he opened his eyes. Puck and Crystal were full of pride. That had been the crowning touch to his breathing music. His parents were proud. And from both of them, there was a sense of—of joy!

Why?

He looked up, and found Emmy smiling, Hannah grinning. Voices said quietly, "Wow, Starman," and "Best ever." No one was leaving. They were just hanging out together, smiling, beginning murmured conversations. It was just the Losers' Club, having fun.

And then one of the jocks on the field began to tootle on a kazoo.

It was a raw imitation of Star's music, the harsh sound of the kazoo mocking the delicate sound of the tin whistle. Star heard a few embarrassed titters from the bleachers, and his cheeks flamed.

Hannah growled, "Those booger heads!"

Emmy stood up, and shouted, "Stop that! Shame on you!"

They called back, "Shame on you, shame on you," in high falsetto voices. Emmy burst into tears. Hannah put an arm around her. Star sat helplessly, staring at them, wishing the Beings weren't here to see his embarrassment.

And then someone said, "What's that? What's happening?" and he glanced up.

One of the small, high clouds had floated down to hover directly over the boys on the football field. Raindrops began to fall from it, lightly at first, and then hard and fast, great fat drops that splashed on the boys' heads and rolled down their cheeks.

Mr. Lyne said, "What the—".

Hannah said, "Awesome!"

Star was afraid to look at the cousins. Seagull would be glowing. What about the Rules?

The group on the field tried to move away from the cloud. It followed them.

Star knew that once he started, Seagull would not stop until the cloud had emptied itself. The boys began to run, dashing for shelter. The cloud pursued them, the rain falling faster and faster, until their clothes were drenched. The kids in the bleachers and on the fringe started to laugh, and Emmy raised her head, tears forgotten in amazement.

The boys crowded into the Home locker room, and the little cloud evaporated. From the school, the buzzer sounded, and the students all rose. Mr. Lyne and the vice-principal left the ticket booth as the kids, still laughing, began to make their way out of the bleachers. Puck and Crystal and the cousins started across the football field toward Star.

When the bleachers had cleared of everyone except Emmy, Hannah, and himself, Star moved down the aisle to meet his parents.

Somebody called to him, "Later, Starman!" He turned to wave, and then turned back.

He froze.

Emmy and Hannah were just behind him. Mr. Lyne and the vice-principal were approaching at a right angle to the path of Puck and Crystal and the cousins.

But Crystal was glowing like an incandescent bulb. Sparks glimmered from her hair and her hands, and her caftan shone as if it were aflame.

"Mom . . ." Star groaned. The Rules!

He had just reached the bottom fringe of the bleachers, and Emmy and Hannah were about to step down beside him. Mr. Lyne waved to Star as if to tell him to wait. And his mother, all unaware, quickened her step toward her son. Did no one notice, not Puck, not Seagull, not the other cousins? Did Splendor—

And then, all at once, Star knew that Splendor *had* noticed. Crystal Wondersmith disappeared, as neatly as if she had never been there at all. The three little groups converged, the principal and vice-principal, Star and his two Normal friends, the cousins. Introductions were made, hands were shaken, thanks and farewells said. Emmy and Hannah hurried off to class. Mr. Lyne and the vice-principal strolled away to the main office, leaving Star with his father and his cousins.

And his mother. Splendor waved one slender, scarf-draped hand, and Crystal, sparkling all over, reappeared as if nothing had happened. Fragments of light clung to Star when she hugged him.

The cousins exclaimed over the school, the football field, the bleachers.

"But," Splendor said. "They all like you, don't they?"

"Well, I don't think the jocks do."

"I don't know about that," Splendor said. "They came to hear you, after all."

"Oh, Starchild," Crystal cried. Even her happy tears glittered. "You *do* have Talent!"

"What?" Star looked around for his father. "What does she mean?"

Puck's eyes were almost as bright as Crystal's. "Why, son," he said. "Don't you know?"

"Know what?" All the cousins were smiling at Star. Splendor's smile was the widest.

Puck gripped Star's shoulder. "Why, Starchild—son—you're a Gatherer!"

"There hasn't been a Gatherer in a hundred years," Crystal said.

"You can come back to the School for True Beings!" Splendor said mistily. Seagull and Joyful and the other cousins nodded.

Star stared at them, and then at his parents, stunned. "A—a Gatherer?"

"It's your music, son," Puck said. "Your breathing music. It gathers people."

Long minutes passed as Star thought about this. The Beings waited respectfully, understanding the immensity of the moment.

A Gatherer! A Talent after all! Star could hardly take it in. All he did, after all, was breathe in feelings, and

breathe them out . . . but it was true. Here at the Normal
school, where there were so many differences, people
gathered together when he played. Even the jocks, even
though they made fun!

He tucked his whistle into his pocket, and patted it.
"This is wonderful," he said. "But I think I'm in the
right place. I'm needed here."

"That's right," Puck said. "Good for you for knowing
that, son."

Crystal said, "Oh, Starchild. You'll be a wonderful
Gatherer."

"I hope so. But now, I'm late for class," Star said.

Everyone chuckled quietly, and the Beings started off
toward the parking lot. Splendor said, "See you at the
next festival, Starchild."

"See you, Splendor," he said. He waved at her, and
then hurried off to class.

As he went, he shook his arms and hands until the
glow faded, and he looked Normal.

FAR FROM THE TREE

Melissa Lee Shaw

Melissa Lee Shaw's short fiction has appeared in
*Realms of Fantasy; Analog; Silver Birch, Blood
Moon; Sirens and Other Daemon Lovers; Writ-
ers of the Future;* and the French anthology *Il
Etait Une Fée.* She is currently at work on a
fantasy trilogy set in the same world as "Far
From the Tree."

NALIA HURRIED ALONG the road that ran
through Fallon's Bend, picking her way around the
muddy ruts left by ox-carts and carriages headed to or
from the royal city of Kellinvale, or the more distant
ports further up the Laskia River. Long habit guided her
to the trail on the edge of town that led to her favorite
weeping willow, its slender leaves buttercup-yellow with
autumn's cooling.

As usual, her best friend Jemmy sat in a comfortable
niche about twenty feet up, where the willow's massive
trunk split into three. From the slump of his shoulders
and the tightness around his eyes, Nalia knew that his
mama was busy showing her wares to a new customer.

Nalia ducked beneath the long, swaying streamers of
leaves and climbed up beside him. "Been here long?"
she said, bracing her bare feet against one trunk. Jemmy,
as always, wore stiff leather shoes.

Though he didn't answer, he acknowledged her presence with a flick of his leaf-green eyes. He held up a piece of wood the size of two fingers outstretched. "I've been practicing," he said. "Watch." Closing his eyes, he stroked his fingers delicately along the piece of wood. The mildest hum burred from his throat.

Beneath his touch, the wood softened, flattened. Nalia watched, entranced, as the grain of the wood started moving like sluggish river water, curling here, straightening there. So absorbed was she watching the movement that she didn't notice at first the shapes made by the new pattern of the grain. "Oh, Jemmy! Faces!"

He smiled faintly, rubbing his thumb over the smoothed wood a few times. Opening his eyes, he examined his work.

"Let me see," Nalia said, reaching for it.

"In a minute," he said, twisting away. "I have to make sure it's done."

She rolled her eyes, but waited till he dropped his creation into her hands. "Wow," she said, turning it. "It's—Jemmy, it's us, right? You and me?" A boy's face in profile, a few lines suggesting a shock of dark hair falling into his eyes, facing a girl's, her lighter hair tied back with a twist of cloth. "It's lovely."

"It's nothing much," he said, though she could tell he was pleased. He wedged his creation between two close-growing branches, near the trunk. "We'll keep it here," he said.

She nodded. "That way it won't get lost."

And then he was skittering down the tree, quick as a squirrel, shouting, "Come on, Nal! Hurry up!"

"Hey!" she cried, scrambling down, but he was already far ahead. She had to run hard to keep him in sight. Whooping here and there as he leaped a fallen trunk or a small stream, he led her on a convoluted course through the forest. Quick as he was in the trees, though, on the ground, she was faster. Soon she ran beside him.

They turned toward town, and the morning market. Panting, Nalia said, "Who is he?"

Jemmy scowled. "Who?" he said, though he obviously knew.

"The new customer."

"How should I know?" he said, kicking at a small stone. "Some merchant, on his way to Kellinvale. Kept wiping his nose with this disgusting handkerchief."

"Looking for fine garments for his wife. Silks and satins," she said dreamily. "Blues and reds and greens."

"There's Twig," Jemmy said, nodding at a spindly little boy trudging along, a burlap sack slung over one shoulder.

"His name," she said, "is Speare."

"*Look* at him," he said scornfully.

She stopped. "Not everyone is strong. That doesn't make my brother worthless."

"I *know*, Nal, but—"

"He works hard," she said. "It takes him hours to deliver all his loaves, but he won't even eat till he's done. You of all people should know you can't judge someone because of something they can't help."

Jemmy kicked a clod of dirt with the mud-streaked shoes that hid his deformed feet.

"Nor," she said, fixing him with a firm look, "because of what other people say about them."

"Sor-*ry*! I was just kidding and you know it."

"Sometimes people kid about you," she said.

"Sometimes *you*," he said, "are such a *girl*." And he took off running again, weaving between carts and women laden with wicker baskets.

Nalia bit back her indignation and followed. She caught up with Jemmy near the honey-cake stand and its delicious smells. Staring wistfully at the fried, golden-brown treats and the clay pot of honey, the two lingered nearby. On occasion, the vendor gave Nalia a free sample, since her father supplied him with the dough, but never when Jemmy was with her.

The vendor snapped at Jemmy, "Get out of here, you fatherless brat. Go on, get!"

"Don't you talk to him that way!" Nalia cried.

"You need to watch that one," the vendor said. "You're a good girl, you've got a fine father, but that boy—he'll come to no good. Apple never falls far from the tree."

"Then his father was a good man," she said hotly.

"Your own father should be more careful who he lets you keep company with."

"*Oh!*" Nalia grabbed Jemmy's arm and stalked away. "Tomorrow, I *swear*, I'm spitting in his dough." A glance at Jemmy's face showed the dark, brooding look she hated to see, because it meant he was angry and hurting inside. *It's not his fault his father's not around*, she thought. *Why do grown-ups place such importance on the stupidest, most trivial things?*

As the pair wandered through the market, Jemmy relaxed. His whole life, people had treated him with suspicion and disdain. By now, he was used to it.

But Nalia wasn't. She had always sensed that Jemmy was doomed, from the sideways looks people had given him ever since she could remember, the way they muttered under their breath when he passed, raising their hands in signs to ward off ill luck. She couldn't stand the thought that everyone judged him so unfairly, nor that he might someday suffer for it.

For his sake, though, she smiled. The two sauntered through the bustling, lively throngs, past chicken merchants, men with wind-scarred faces and chapped hands selling fish fresh from the Laskia River, farmers selling cabbages and onions and bags of grain, tomatoes and plums and early pears.

A hard shove made Nalia stumble. "Hey!" she said, and spun around, face hot.

It was bad enough to see tall, skinny Cinda standing there, with that vicious grin. It was worse to see Asher, Cinda's chubby twin brother, lounging beside her. Either twin alone was bad news; both together, and only fleet feet would save you from bruises and scrapes. At twelve, they would even take on older kids if they caught them alone. Ten-year-olds like Jemmy and Nalia didn't stand a chance.

"Look, Cin," Asher said. "It's Squirrel and the cripple's brat. How's your mama, Squirrel-boy? Any *customers* lately?" He smirked.

Jemmy's hands clutched into fists. Nalia grabbed Jemmy's arm and pulled him into a nimble, zig-zagging run that took them weaving between market patrons. The cries and cuffs that followed in their wake, though, did little to hide their direction.

"Come on," Jemmy said. "This way!" He led her behind the meeting hall, skirting along two of its sides before darting behind the adjoining wooden shed. Quick as thought, he scaled the wall and flipped up onto the shed's low roof, then reached down and helped her scramble up.

"They'll spot us!" she said, but he grinned and hauled himself up onto the meeting hall's high, slanted roof.

"Are you crazy?" she hissed.

"You want the twins to catch you?"

Nalia took hold of the roof's edge and let Jemmy help her wriggle up beside him.

They flattened themselves against the wooden shingles just in time. A puffing and red-faced Cinda came pounding around the side of the shed, her wheezing brother close behind.

"You said they came this way," Asher said.

"They did!"

"Well, where are they?" He pushed her shoulders.

"I don't know, you stupid goat!" she said, shoving him back.

Before the fight escalated, something caught Asher's eye. His anger dissolved, turning into a satisfied smirk. "Next best thing," he said, trotting around the shed.

Nalia snaked her way to the top of the roof.

"What are you doing?" Jemmy said.

"Some other kid is probably in trouble."

"Long as it's not us." But at her stricken look, he said, "What?"

She whispered, "Speare." Her little brother threaded his way through the market just a few feet below, sack slung over one thin shoulder. She turned to Jemmy, her heart full of need.

"What do you want me to do about it?" Jemmy said, scowling.

With a huff of exasperation, she squirmed down toward the shed. "I can't let them hurt him."

"But they'll smash you to bits!"

"He's only six!"

"Just—hold on, will you? Let me try something."
Jemmy touched one of the wooden shingles beneath
him. It lifted free a moment later. He closed his eyes
and hummed.

"Hurry," Nalia whispered, seeing the twins split up to
trap Speare between them.

"Twiggy!" crowed Cinda. Speare jumped. "You were
supposed to bring us our bread this morning."

"I *did*," he said, backing up. Behind him, Asher
grabbed the burlap sack.

"You didn't," Cinda said. "Mama said so. You're not
calling our mama a liar, are you, you little snot-nosed
weakling?"

If Jemmy didn't do something soon, Nalia was going
to jump down. She glanced at Jemmy and saw the shin-
gle in his hands fall apart into a dozen sharp wooden
darts.

"Be ready," Jemmy murmured. He elbowed his way
to the top of the roof and threw half the darts with a
snap of his wrist. Before they hit, he let fly with the rest.

Asher howled first, then Cinda.

Nalia and Jemmy scuttled down the roof, half-jumping
and half-falling to the shed, then to the ground. They
ran around the side of the meeting hall, in full view of
the twins.

"You *turds*!" Cinda screamed, brushing darts out of
her hair and clothes. "I'll tear your arms off!"

Nalia held back on her speed till she was sure both
twins were pursuing them. Then she sped up and
grabbed Jemmy's arm. "I have an idea!" She led him in
a circuitous route, knocking into market patrons here
and there to be sure muffled cries and curses marked
their path for the twins to follow.

They ran right in front of the honey-cake stand,
Nalia's stomach twisting with hunger at the delightful
smells. Four flattened rounds of fried dough sat steaming
on the wooden rack, already dripping with honey. A few
feet away, the vendor stood watch over his cast-iron fry-
ing pan, stirring a new batch.

Just as she'd hoped, Asher slowed; his sweet tooth

was legendary. He grabbed one of the honey-cakes and
tried to slip away, but the vendor's arm snaked out and
grabbed his wrist. "You're paying for that, boy," he said.

Asher howled in frustration, twisting to free himself.

Cinda said, "You let my brother go!"

"Come on," Nalia said, pulling Jemmy away from the
market, toward the forest. Once they made the trees,
the twins would never catch them.

She'd never been so glad to feel the chill of the forest's shadows.

"That was a good idea," Jemmy said, as the two of
them slowed to a brisk walk.

"Thanks."

"How'd you think of it?"

She shrugged. "I knew they'd be mad as hornets. And
what does Asher do when he's mad as a hornet? He
finds something sweet to eat." A little shyly, she said,
"That was great, making those darts."

He shrugged and kicked at the dirt, hiding a small
grin.

"I never saw you do anything like it before. Did you
learn that from the forest people too?"

"Hamadrians," he corrected absently. She knew he
sneaked off for a few days at a time when his mama was
busy with a customer. Taking Maven's riding horse, he
would cross the Laskia River, heading deep into the forest to spy on the strange people who dwelt in the trees.
She wasn't sure anyone else in town even knew they
were there. He had offered to take her along, but she
knew her papa wouldn't allow it.

"I wish I could do that woodcraft stuff too," she said.

"It's not that hard," he said, but she held up her hand
before he could offer to teach her again. In all the times
she'd tried, she'd never shown the slightest ability.

He said, "You just have to talk to the wood, ask it to
change for you. It's amazing, what the Hamadrians can
do. I even saw one coax a tree to make special sap for
a poultice, for someone who was hurt." His eyes grew
dreamy. "I bet I could do that."

"Jemmy," she said, "what did Asher mean, about
your mama? What's wrong with her having a customer?"

His mood soured. "Nothing," he said, and scaled a nearby oak before she could say anything else. Seconds later, he sat on a branch thirty feet up.

She suppressed a sigh of frustration. He knew she couldn't climb like that.

When she got home that afternoon, Nalia found her papa, Sabaston, sitting at the work table in the bakery's back room. The stump of his left leg rested on a chair kitty-corner to his, a grim reminder of the mill accident that had claimed her mama's life six years before.

While he measured out flour, salt, and potatoes for the next day's deliveries, Nalia gathered up the dirty baking sheets to take them out back to the water-pump and wash them. She wanted to complain to her papa about what the honey-cake vendor had said about Jemmy, but she knew what he'd say: *Jemmy's an odd boy, and people can be suspicious of odd things. Don't fret about it.* How was that supposed to help her, anyway?

A new voice broke the silence. "Look, look!" Speare dashed into the back room, beaming and holding up a grubby coin.

"Where'd you get that, little man?" Sabaston said.

"Maven's new customer," Speare said. "I was kinda out of breath when I got there, so he gave me this and said I was a good boy to work so hard."

"Why were you out of breath?" The question was mild, but Nalia heard the concern behind it. Speare wasn't supposed to overexert himself.

Speare blinked, his grin dying. "Well, um," he said. "I wasn't, till. . . ."

"Till?"

Nalia spoke up. "It was Cinda and Asher. They found him in the market."

Sabaston raised an inquisitive eyebrow and turned back to the unbruised and unbloodied Speare.

"Nal and Jemmy lured them away," Speare said, embarrassed. "Then I ran fast to get out of there, but honest, Papa, I had to—"

Sabaston raised a floured hand. "I think I see." Nodding at the coin, he said, "And what do you plan to do with that?"

Speare's grin returned. "Honey-cakes," he said happily, and dashed back out the door.

Life went on as usual for a few days: Nalia delivered her loaves in the mornings, hurrying in the deepening autumn chill, and spent her afternoons playing in the forest with Jemmy. But a week after their run-in with the twins, she found their weeping willow tree empty. Jemmy wasn't at the market, nor at the bakery.

She found him behind his mama's house, in her small orchard of apple trees, notable for their red-and-yellow-splotched fruits. He lay along a bough of the largest tree, eyes drowsing, fingers stroking along a branch and down one of the apples.

"What are you doing?" she asked, coming closer.

He glanced at the house and then said in a low voice, "Mama's sick. I'm going to make her better."

"How?"

He pointed his chin at the piebald apple beneath his fingers. "I'm asking the tree to put medicine in it."

"How long will it take?"

"Two or three days," he said.

"You can't stay up there for two or three days!"

"I have to. She's sick."

Nalia turned to leave.

"Where are you going?"

"To get you food, and a blanket. You may be crazy, but you can at least be warm."

The next morning, as Nalia gathered more supplies for Jemmy, her father called to her from the bakery's workroom.

"Yes, Papa?" she said from the doorway, hiding the sack behind her.

"Hop-Flea, you need to take Speare's rounds today," her papa said. He looked troubled. "He's ill."

She rushed upstairs to Speare's little cubby of a room. Her brother lay in bed, awake and listless, his breathing raspy. His eyes looked gummy.

"Don't you worry," she said, ruffling his thin brown hair. "I'll see to it you get better soon. Can't have you turning into a lazy lie-about."

He smiled faintly.

She got to Jemmy's apple tree just after noon. "Sorry, I know I'm late," she said. "Speare's sick so I had more deliveries. Here." She handed the sack up to him.

"Thanks," Jemmy said, and yawned.

"Jemmy," she said. "Speare's sick."

"And?"

She lifted an eyebrow at him.

"Nal," he said, "I can't just—"

"He's my brother," she said. "You know he's not strong. He needs all the help we can give him."

"I'm not—" He lowered his voice. "I'm not supposed to."

"Not supposed to what?"

"Do anything out of the ordinary, around anyone."

"You do stuff around me all the time!"

"That's *different*. That's just you. Speare can't keep a secret."

"He'll never know," she said. "Please, Jemmy."

He gave a hard sigh and stretched his free hand to touch another apple.

Throughout Fallon's Bend, many, particularly children, fell ill. Most, including Nalia, felt miserable for a day and then bounced back, but Speare's health ebbed like a slow, low tide. Nalia fussed and fidgeted over him, forcing him to drink broth and tea, putting hot plasters on his chest to ease his breathing, but nothing she did seemed to accomplish more than temporary relief.

The day after Nalia's own brief bout with illness, as she loaded up her sack with deliveries—and another, surreptitiously, with supplies for Jemmy—Sabaston said, "Bring these to the twins' house." He handed her two warm loaves of his braided potato bread. "No charge."

"Why?"

"Asher's sick."

To Nalia's chagrin, part of her was secretly glad. "How sick?"

"Sick. For days now." He shook his head. "Poor Shona, and Frayne."

"I don't understand," she said. "Every time I go there, Asher's mama accuses me of bringing her days-old bread, or says we're using mealy flour or rancid butter. Why do you want to help her now?"

"Well, Hop-Flea, sometimes a little kindness at the right moment can soften a suspicious heart." He shrugged. "Even if it doesn't, it's easy to be kind to your friends. The mark of a truly good heart is helping those you don't get along with when they need it most."

When Nalia knocked on the twins' door, their mama, Shona, pulled it open. Her red-rimmed eyes spoke of recent tears. Without a word, Nalia handed over the two braided loaves.

Shona's mouth thinned. "We didn't order these. I'm not paying extra for them."

"No charge," Nalia said. "Papa says they're a gift. We—we hope Asher's better soon."

"A gift." The look in Shona's eyes said she was trying to figure out how Sabaston was trying to cheat her this time.

"Tell me," Nalia said, "it's what everyone else has been sick with? What Asher has?"

"What's it to you?"

"It's just," Nalia said, and faltered. "Speare's sick too."

Shona said nothing.

"Anyway, I hope Asher gets better soon," Nalia said, and fled.

Speare looked awful, and now Papa was looking awful too, grim and worried. She hadn't seen him like this since Mama died.

After rushing through her deliveries, Nalia raced for Jemmy's orchard.

"Yet?" she called up to him.

"Shh," he said, glancing at the back door to his house. "No, not yet. Took longer to work on two at once. But

I finished my mama's last night. Her fever broke this morning," he added proudly.

"How much longer?"

He let his fingertips drift over the apple, a clouded look on his face. "Another day, maybe day and a half."

Speare would be all right for a day and a half. But—could he wait even a little longer? Nalia hesitated, then said, "What you're doing is wonderful. I just know you'll save Speare's life."

He shrugged.

"You could save another life too, you know."

Twisting his head to look at her, he said, "What?"

"Someone else is very sick."

"Nal—"

"You have such a good heart, Jemmy, I've seen it. Doesn't it make you feel good, that you could help your mama when no one else could?"

He rolled his eyes. "Who is it?"

"Asher."

The look on his face mixed disbelief and betrayal. "You're crazy!"

"He could die!"

"If anyone deserves to be sick, it's Asher."

"Papa says it's easy to be kind to your friends, but the true test of a good heart is helping people you don't like when they really need it. Jemmy—I know the things people say about you. About how you're odd, and fey, about how you don't have a father, about—about how there's something wrong with you."

His glare was so bilious that she knew she'd gone too far.

She knew she should keep her mouth shut, but the words spilled out anyway: "This is your chance to show everyone what I already know: that you're the kindest, most good-hearted person in all of Fallon's Bend."

His fingers tightened around Speare's apple. Nalia made herself walk away before she said anything more.

Just before sunset, after she'd finished cleaning up at the bakery, Nalia skulked near Maven's house, trying to catch a glimpse of Jemmy without being spotted. She crept closer, till she made out his form, lying like a snake along the branch. Her heart lightened when she saw that he cradled not one apple now, but two.

On the second day, when Nalia arrived with supplies for Jemmy, he plucked Speare's apple from the branch and dropped it into her hands.

Nalia was about to thank him, and tell him he was doing the right thing with the other apple, when a sharp voice startled her.

"Hey!" Maven yelled. She stood at the back door in a robe clasped around her stout form, her graying dark hair spilling down her shoulders. "You there!"

"Go," Jemmy muttered.

Nalia dashed off, hearing Maven shout, "Jemiah! Get in here *now*!"

Running home seemed to take five times as long as the walk over had. Speare had little appetite, so Nalia cut the apple into tiny pieces and stirred them with a few drops of honey. She sat by his bedside and nagged and pressed, overcoming his protests and feeding him the apple bit by bit, till he'd eaten it all.

"There now," she said, stroking his hot cheek. "You'll feel better soon, I promise." Relief made her giddy.

The next morning, Speare ate an entire bowl of chicken soup with onions and carrots, and even shakily got out of bed. It was with a light step that Nalia descended the stairs to the kitchen.

Nalia sneaked back to Jemmy's house, but he wasn't in the orchard. She found him high in their weeping willow, yanking off thin branches and hurling them at the ground. Such a big pile had already accumulated at the tree's base that Nalia wondered if he'd been at it all night.

"Jemmy?" she said, climbing up to their niche.

"Go away!"

"I will not. Come down here and talk to me."

A willow whip sailed down toward her, smacking her in the shoulder.

Her flash of anger was quickly replaced by worry. "Jemmy, what happened?"

"Leave me alone!"

"All right," she said, settling in against the split trunks. "But I'm staying right here. You can throw all the branches you like at me. I won't leave."

He kept up his branch-tearing tantrum for another hour; the air around the tree was thick with falling willow whips. Glancing up, Nalia could see sunlight through a denuded spot high above.

When he finally climbed down to their spot, the look on his face was savage. "You want to know what's wrong? Fine!" He whipped off his leather shoes and yanked off the rags that bound his feet.

Nalia braced herself to see toes missing or deformed, a club foot, burn scars—but what she saw perplexed her. Smooth, even feet, with long supple toes. "What—what's wrong with them?"

"The toes," he snapped. "The big toes. Look!"

She looked more closely, reaching in fascination for one of his feet. He flinched, but she lifted his foot into her lap, inspecting it. The toes were unusually long, sure, but—

Jemmy's big toe bent out to the side, like the thumb on a narrow hand.

"I don't understand," Nalia said, touching the thumb-toe.

He stared at her for a long moment, then scurried down the tree and started running pell-mell through the forest.

Swearing under her breath, Nalia shinnied down and started following. Before long, her lungs and legs burned, but she pressed on.

Jemmy finally stopped beside a stream, hunkering down low, wrapping his arms around his knees as he stared down at his muddy, exposed feet. Nalia sat beside him. When he started shaking, she put a hand on his back.

"Mama said," he said, his voice raw, each word like a wound. "Mama said I shouldn't have made the apple for Speare. That I would ruin everything. That she worked so hard to be sure nobody knew the truth, but I was going to throw it all away. So she told me. She told me the truth."

Nalia rubbed his back, gently, like she massaged Speare's when he was coughing.

Jemmy lifted bloodshot eyes to Nalia's. "You know who my father was?"

She shook her head.

"He wasn't a merchant, nor a traveler, nor a thief. He—he wasn't even *human*."

"Oh, Jemmy," Nalia whispered.

"He was a Hamadrian. She fell in love with a Hamadrian, when she was young and the world's biggest idiot, and then I came along. It's why I can do woodcraft magic. And why you can't. It's the Hamadrian blood in me."

"But—why is it bad, that your father's Hamadrian?"

"I'm a crossbreed," he said. "Some of one thing, some of another, but not whole, Nalia, I'm not whole, I can't be, ever! Mama said—she said there's a word for crossbreeds like me. Half-things. And you know what happens to half-things when childhood passes, when they grow up? They go crazy. They lose their minds, because they can't be just human, and they can't be just Hamadrian. And that makes them dangerous, because of the magic. People know that, and it scares them. They'll find out, somehow, in town, and when they do—" His voice closed off.

"What?" she said, full of dread. "When they do, what?"

"They'll kill me," he whispered. "They'll know I'm rotten inside, I'm broken, I'm a danger to everyone, and they'll hunt me down. Like a rabid dog."

"You're not rotten or broken! You're a wonderful person, you've already saved two lives!"

"It's over for me," he said, rocking back and forth. "It's all over."

So this was the doom she'd always felt hovering over him. She took him into her arms. He collapsed against her, sobbing.

Stroking his hair, she said, her voice high and odd,

"Everyone said Papa's life was over, after he lost his leg and Mama died, in the accident. He was a miller then, did you know? They said he was worthless, he'd never be anything but a burden and a cripple. They tried to take Speare and me away—he was just a newborn babe then—and put us in homes with other families. But Papa didn't buckle. He sold the mill and bought the bakery, he cut down the legs of the worktable so he could sit instead of stand. He remade himself.

"Papa says you can let other people's words be the bars of your prison, or you can push free and listen only to the words in your own heart. He says it isn't easy, it's like being a fish and trying to swim up a fast river, but you can do it if you just remember that your heart is smarter than the people around you."

Pulling back, Jemmy looked away as he wiped his nose on his sleeve.

She said, "Maybe those Hamadrians in the forest could help you."

Bitterly, he said, "Hamadrians hate half-things too."

"But your father, maybe he's there—"

"No. Mama moved here from a hundred miles away, just to get away from my father. You know why she became a, a seamstress?"

Nalia shook her head.

"So she'd be spending time with lots of men, so no one would suspect who—what—my real father was. She told me so."

"Well, maybe you can find your real father, maybe he can help—"

"When I was born," he said, his voice tight as a strung bow, "he told my mama to leave me in the forest, let me perish there. He said that was the only merciful thing to do with half-things, that leaving one alive would lead to misery and tragedy. That's why she left."

Nalia could think of nothing to say. She reached over and cradled Jemmy's hand between both of hers.

When Jemmy wasn't at the willow tree the next afternoon, Nalia sneaked around Maven's house till she could see the little orchard.

Jemmy lay along the branch of an apple tree, his face smoldering with resentment. But his fingers were gentle as they stroked a piebald apple.

Without a word, Nalia slipped away again, fetching food and water and blanket. When she handed them up to him, and opened her mouth to thank him, he said, "Shut up."

The next day, in the early evening, a haggard Jemmy came to the bakery door. When Nalia opened it, he put the apple in her hand and trudged away, holding up his hand to forestall her thanks.

Nalia rushed through streets reddened with the setting sun, and was out of breath when she reached the twins' house. Shona opened the door and stared down at her.

"May I please come in?" Nalia said. "I have something for Asher."

"What?"

"It's—" she said, and hesitated. "Something that helped Speare get well."

"And what would that be?"

Nalia held up the apple.

With a bark of laughter, Shona said, "That's it? An apple?"

"It's a very *good* apple."

"It's one of that whore's apples."

Whore, Nalia thought, wondering what it meant.

"Is this some kind of joke?" Shona said, her voice rising. "My little boy is sick, and you're here to play some kind of horrid prank?"

Out of the corner of her eye, Nalia glimpsed Cinda lurking on the stairs.

"It's not a prank," she said. "It helped Speare, I just thought—"

"Take that thing out of my house," Shona said.

Crushed and bewildered, Nalia turned to go.

Stiffly, Shona said, "And—tell your father thank you. For the bread."

Back home again, Nalia got to work. After building up the fire in the oven, she pared and seeded the apple, cut it into small chunks, and boiled them till they were falling apart. With her father's potato masher, she turned the chunks into puree.

The mild snores from her father's bedroom told her he was sleeping, so she dared to pour precious honey and cinnamon, ginger and cloves and nutmeg, into the mashed apple. She fashioned a tart crust, heavy with butter, filled it with the apple mixture, and baked it to golden perfection.

Papa would chasten her about the expensive ingredients tomorrow, but she already had her excuse: Asher loved sweet treats, so this was a kindness like the potato bread, and how could he scold her for doing what he taught her?

At the twins' house, Shona's face looked colder even than last time. "You're becoming quite a nuisance, girl."

Nalia held up the warm, cloth-wrapped package, peeling back the folds to reveal the tart inside. "It's pear," she said, hoping the heavy spice smells masked her little white lie. "His favorite. I felt bad, about earlier."

Shona folded her arms. "How much?"

Nalia shook her head.

"Why all this sudden generosity?"

"I just—we thought, if he's sick, he might like something sweet. Speare had trouble eating, but he got stronger when I found something to tempt him. But if Asher wouldn't like it. . . ."

"He's upstairs," Shona said. She led the way.

Nalia followed, but a harsh hiss from behind stopped her.

At the bottom of the stairs, Cinda stood, face aflame with suspicion, gangly arms crossed. "What are you up to, you nasty little brat? If anything happens to my brother, I swear I'll pull all your fingers off, one by one."

Nalia scurried after Shona, wondering if maybe her father was wrong about the transformative power of kindness.

Asher looked awful, his skin yellow-gray, his eyes sunken. Head propped up with pillows, he lay in his bed, muffled in thick quilts.

"The baker has sent over something new, darling," Shona said, reaching toward Nalia, who surrendered the pastry. "A pear tart. Doesn't that smell good, hmm? Give it a try, love."

She cooed and coaxed till he ate two thirds of it.

"There's a good boy," she murmured, as he rolled onto his side and closed his eyes. "I'll leave the rest here by your bed, little sweeting. For later." Her lip trembled as she ushered Nalia out of the room. "That's the most he's eaten in two days."

"I hope it helps," Nalia said, and slipped downstairs and out.

Nalia spent the rest of the night glowing with a giddy sense of accomplishment. She had helped a boy who'd been nothing but cruel to her, when he needed it most. She was a good person, just like her papa. Better, she'd helped Jemmy be a good person too. Now Asher would recover, and he and Cinda would soften toward Nalia and Jemmy—how could they not?—and everyone would ultimately see Jemmy's goodness, so maybe Jemmy wouldn't have to be doomed after all.

So she was shocked the next morning when a grim-faced Shona, accompanied by the furious Cinda, stormed in through the bakery door. Shona grabbed Nalia's arm from where she stood at the front counter, hustling her into the back room where her papa labored. Speare had already left with his deliveries.

"What did she put in this?" Shona demanded, throwing a cloth-wrapped package on the table beside Sabaston's hands.

He said, "What are you talking about?"

"Your daughter brought my son a pastry last night, claiming kindness. She said it was a pear pastry, but it wasn't, was it? It was apple, the same apple, I daresay, that came from that whore's orchard, the one your brat tried to give my Asher earlier." Her voice turned cold as icicles. "A poisoned apple."

Nalia was shocked. "But—" She fell silent. If she told the truth, Jemmy's secret heritage would be exposed.

Sabaston pulled back the layers of cloth to reveal the remnants of the apple tart. He sniffed it, then lifted a morsel to his mouth and touched it to his tongue. He turned to Nalia. "You made this?"

She nodded.

"Why did you tell them it was pear?"

"Because," she said, feeling like she was spinning down the white-foamed rapids of the Laskia River, "because they wouldn't take the apple, and I knew it would help, might help him get better—"

Shona turned on her, mad triumph in her eyes. "Why would *that* apple help him? What lies did that fey bastard boy tell you?"

Sabaston's face tightened.

Miserably, Nalia said, "Apples are good for you." Then, "Isn't he getting better?"

Cinda cried, "You *know* he's not, you evil thing!" and shoved Nalia.

"Enough!" Sabaston said. "Shona, you will restrain your daughter in my house or you will leave it."

"Watch yourself, Sabaston," Shona said. "When everyone hears of what that brat of yours has done—"

"All she did," Sabaston said, "was try to help your ailing son."

"With a poisoned apple, given her by a wild boy whose father could have been any one of a thousand drunkards, thieves, or murderers." Her eyes narrowed. "Or worse."

"He didn't do *anything*! He only wanted to help!" Nalia ordered her mouth to stop speaking, but it had a mind of its own. "Anyway, it wasn't even his apple."

"Of course it was, you lying brat!" Shona said.

"It wasn't! I swear it wasn't! It was—" Her voice trailed off.

"Go on," Shona said.

"When Speare first got sick," she said desperately, "I had to do something to help him, so I—Jemmy showed me—there are these people, living deep in the forest, across the river."

"People?" Shona said.

"They live in the trees, they're called Hamadrians." Her tongue and teeth formed words so fast she could

barely comprehend them. "Jemmy said they knew
things, they can do magic, they could make medicine, so
I—I baked some of papa's special potato bread, I
brought it to them and begged them for medicine for
Speare, and they, they gave me an apple—I mean two
apples—they said if one didn't do the trick, give him the
other, but the first cured him, so I still had the second,
and when Asher wasn't getting better, I thought perhaps
it would help him too—" The words finally trailed off
at the rising looks of horror on her papa's face and triumph on Shona's. "What?" she whispered.

Shona grabbed Cinda's arm and stalked out so fast
the air eddied behind them.

"Oh, Nalia," Sabaston said, shaking his head. "You
don't know what you've done."

But Nalia did know. She wasn't supposed to mention
the Hamadrians at all; the townsfolk hadn't known about
them. Now they'd figure out that Jemmy was half-
Hamadrian, a half-thing.

Now he really was doomed, and it was all her fault.

She raced to the willow tree, finding Jemmy in its
branches, morosely tracing circles on the rough, grooved
bark. "Jemmy!" she cried. "Jemmy, they know!"

At the look on her face, he skittered down to the
ground. "What do they know?"

"I panicked, I was trying to protect you, I told them
I got the apple for Asher from the Hamadrians in the
forest—"

His face grew white. Without another word, he took
off toward his house. For once, she had trouble keeping
up with him.

When he got to his doorway, he turned to her, out of
breath. "Go back," he said. "Get in their way. Slow
them down."

"What's going to happen?"

"Just go. You shouldn't be here when my Mama
finds out."

"But Jemmy. . . ." Her voice trailed off; she knew
he was right. "I'm so sorry," she whispered. "I never
meant—"

"Go!" he snapped, and darted inside, slamming the door.

Nalia intended to go to Shona's house, try to explain everything, fix what she had broken, but streams of townsfolk were headed toward the meeting hall, which couldn't be a good sign. She ran toward the bakery, but a sharp voice cut through the air:

"There she is! Bring her too." It was Shona, and before Nalia knew it, both her arms had been grabbed and she was being hustled along.

"Let my daughter go!" rang out Sabaston's voice. He came stumping along with his crutches. Nalia, near to tears, had never been so glad to see him.

"She's a witness," Shona said. "And possibly a conspirator."

"We don't know for sure that anyone has done anything wrong," Sabaston said.

"Perhaps you don't," Shona said. "It's not your boy barely clinging to life after being poisoned!"

"Papa, it's all right," Nalia said. "I'll go with them. We'll straighten all this out." *Get in their way. Slow them down.*

What followed was a blur to her. She found herself inside the town hall, being pelted with questions like small, stinging rocks. She stammered and struggled, clinging to her story about the Hamadrians, which no one believed.

"What would Hamadrians do with bread, anyway?"

"Where did you say they lived, exactly? How long a journey? Where did you cross the Laskia River?"

"Why was the apple splotched with yellow, then? Everyone knows only Maven grows apples like those."

"So Jemiah gave you an apple for Speare too?"

"No!" she said. "The Hamadrians did!"

"What has Jemiah told you about his father?"

"Has Jemmy ever told you he was a half-thing?"

Nalia wanted to scream. She kept saying, "Don't you understand, it was me, it was my idea, he had nothing to do with it!"

The truth didn't matter to these people. She could see

from the fervor in their eyes that they were building to a fever-pitch that meant, guilty or not, someone would have to die.

But still she kept answering as best she could, evading, trying to draw out her explanations, trying to give Jemmy the time he needed to—what? What woodcraft magic would save him from this?

And then she stood in the meeting hall, alone except for her father. She looked up at him, stricken. After all that talking, she had no more words.

"Come along home," he said heavily. "What will happen will happen."

She felt exhausted down to her toenails. But she ran out the door, ignoring her father's shouts.

An angry throng milled around outside Maven's house. Sick with worry, Nalia sidled closer to a loud group.

". . . believe it? That slattern, gone so fast . . ."

". . . left most everything . . ."

". . . stable empty, horses and cart gone . . ."

". . . crossbreed . . ."

". . . half-thing . . ."

Nalia slipped away, toward Maven's stables. The door stood open; the cart and both horses were gone.

Like lines of ants, streams of people jostled their way into the house empty-handed, coming out carrying silk scarves, glittering baubles, anything of value they could find. The killing anger in the crowd seethed around Nalia, only partly sated by the looting. It wasn't long before someone threw a torch onto the roof, then in through a window, and the house began to burn. Nalia worried that the angry townsfolk might chase after Maven and Jemmy, but they stood transfixed and muttering, staring at the curling flames.

It dawned on her: *He got away. They got away.*

And then: *My best friend is gone. I won't see him again.*

A firm hand settled on her shoulder. She blinked up at Sabaston.

"Come on home now," he said.

* * *

She barely remembered walking the streets, but then she was in her own room, Sabaston tucking her into her bed like she was a little girl.

"I don't understand," she said, half to herself. "Why didn't it work?"

"What?" Sabaston said, sitting on the edge of the bed.

"The apple, it worked for Speare, it worked for Jemmy's mama—" She stopped, realizing what she'd said, but he looked unsurprised.

"There was something in those apples," he said. "Some medicine."

She nodded miserably.

"Sometimes cooking can make medicine not work as well, or even change it into something else."

"I didn't know," she said. "Papa, I swear, I only wanted—"

"I know," he said gently.

She must have slept, because a rap at the bakery door startled her awake the next morning. She heard the door open, and a moment's silence.

Shona's voice drifted up the stairs. Nalia crept from her bed to listen.

". . . were kind to us," Shona was saying stiffly. "So here's a kindness for you. Asher's fever broke. His appetite is back."

"That's good news," came Sabaston's voice.

Asher was all right. Jemmy and his mama had been chased out of town, their belongings stolen, their house destroyed—all for nothing.

The sharpness of Nalia's grief surprised her. She fled down the stairs and out the back door, finding the fastest way into the forest. Her feet took her to the willow tree; her hands took her up it, to her accustomed perch.

Jemmy was gone. She'd seen him for the last time already. He probably hated her now.

She didn't deserve to live. She had goaded him, pushed him, been the end of him. She should have left him alone, left Asher to his fate. Wretched and sour with guilt, she wrapped her arms around the willow's rough, gnarled trunk.

Beside her leg, wedged between two close-growing branches, she spotted the little carving Jemmy had made with his woodcraft. She remembered the two faces, boy and girl. Gently, she worked the bit of wood free.

It was snapped in half. Only the boy's face remained.

Her heart broke open, the tears spilling afresh, as she realized Jemmy had left her a part of himself, that he bore her no grudge.

And he had taken her with him the best way he could: her, his best friend, his conscience, his compass. She could only hope that in the life that lay ahead of him, it would be enough.

THE WEIGHT OF WISHES

Nina Kiriki Hoffman

Nina Kiriki Hoffman has sold more than two hundred stories and a number of novels. Her works have been finalists for the Nebula, World Fantasy, Mythopoeic, Sturgeon, and Endeavour awards. Her first novel won a Horror Writers Association Bram Stoker Award. Her young adult novel *A Stir Of Bones* is out in paperback, and her next YA, *Spirits That Walk in Shadow*, will be published this fall. In addition to writing, Nina works at a bookstore, does production work for a national magazine, and teaches short story writing through a local community college. She lives in Oregon and has cats.

BETH AND I PLAYED rock-paper-scissors to see which of us would have to take the Christmas stocking into our daughter Lisa's room this year. As usual, Beth was paper and I was rock. Dang! We knew each other well after twelve years of marriage, yet I always expected Beth to choose something new, so I stuck to the same strategy.

Beth put a big candy cane into the red stocking and handed me the bulky thing. "Good luck, Will." She kissed me. She grabbed the green stocking, the one we'd put together for nine-year-old Tim.

Tim was our easy child.

I glanced around the master bedroom, which, on normal days, was a clash of Beth's and my versions of clutter amidst white-and-green bamboo print wallpaper. Tonight's clutter was clutter on top of clutter. Wrapping paper, ribbon, tape, and wrapped gifts all over the bed. The closet door gaped: there were still a few hidden gifts on the upper shelves to wrap, but we needed a break.

I suspected Lisa had been in our room in the weeks leading up to Christmas, snooping through the closet, and nothing we had gotten her would surprise her. Had she wrecked Christmas for Tim, though? Had she told him what she had found? I considered. Lisa was in one of her hate-Tim phases. Was she Machiavellian enough to know that she could spoil Christmas by telling Tim about the bike, or was she petty enough to enjoy knowing without telling? I prayed for petty.

"Don't forget the costume," Beth said.

I wasn't fat enough to make a good Santa, and neither was Beth. We had an elf outfit that would fit either of us, though the red velvet pants only came down to my knees.

We'd had a theological argument about whether elves ever went on the sleigh to help Santa out. Canon said No. Convenience and sense of being less ridiculous dressed as an elf than dressed as Santa said maybe. Beth had insisted we buy the costume after Halloween when there were tons of costumes for sale at half price, because last year, when I chose rock and had to take the stocking into Lisa's room, I had gone as myself, and Lisa had been awake. I hid the stocking behind my back before she saw it, and escaped by convincing her I was sleepwalking to the bathroom. Then I waited outside her door for two more hours, and finally went in while she slept. I spent Christmas in a state of unpleasant exhaustion, even though the kids were happy.

But Lisa was ten now, a whole year more sophisticated than she had been last year, not to mention a year more powerful. The costume, Beth's brainstorm, was supposed to protect me from discovery; if Lisa saw me and thought "Santa's Helper," so what? I could place the stocking and get out, leaving us enough time to finish wrapping the presents and decorating the tree.

That was the plan, anyway.

I changed into the red velvet pants, pulled up red-and-white striped stockings, put on curl-toed velvet slippers with bells at the upturned tips, and donned the red velvet doublet with its puffy sleeves and frill of lace down the line of silver buttons. I finished up with the fur-trimmed red velvet cap with a white furry ball at the dangling end, which draped over my shoulder and dropped halfway to my waist. I felt almost as stupid as I had in my sixth grade play, when I had to dress up as broccoli and deliver doggerel about the benefits of vegetables in a healthy diet.

"Come on, honey. Sit here. There's more to do." Beth made me sit at her vanity. She got out spirit gum and a black beard and mustache. She smiled fiendishly while she stuck fake hair to my face. "You're devilishly cute," she said. "I'd kiss you, but I don't want to end up with the mustache."

I glanced in the mirror and saw a me I didn't recognize. "Ho, ho," I said. My voice lacked Santa authority; I was too unnerved by my transformation. I hadn't realized I could change so much without Lisa having anything to do with it.

"It ought to confuse her, anyway," said Beth. She kissed my cheek, while I tried not to wiggle my lips; the spirit gum made my upper lip itch.

I stood. "Okay, let's get this over with so we can get at least four hours' sleep."

Beth saluted and grabbed Tim's stocking. We left the master bedroom and headed our separate ways.

Lisa's room was toward the front of the house, a mistake whose magnitude we had only lately come to recognize. She looked out her window a lot, and if she saw things she didn't like, or saw things she liked too well, well. . . . It would have been safer if she had Tim's room, which looked out over the back yard, a region that belonged to us—but she was stubborn. She liked her room and didn't want to change it.

The bells on my toes were ringing. It irritated me. I had hoped Lisa would be asleep when I got there, a vain hope, I knew, but still a tiny hope. She was a light sleeper—often woke me and Beth because she heard a dog digging in the yard, or kids necking in a parked car in the street. The bells would wake her up for sure.

I eased her door open anyway, as if I were really a sneaky Christmas elf. I crept across the carpet toward her bed, jingling softly. I hoped she hadn't redecorated the room since the afternoon; I didn't want to trip over anything.

When she'd gone through her swamp phase, Tim had actually been bitten by a poisonous snake in here.

It was close to Christmas; Lisa had been acting Good for more than a week, a relief to everyone. If she'd changed her room around, it should still be friendly.

The bedside light snapped on. Lisa was sitting up, blankets bunched in both fists under her chin. She stared at me.

My daughter had the loveliest soft dark hair; it clouded around her head like glory. Her face was round, her cheeks rosy, her dark eyes wide and brilliant. She sucked on her lower lip.

As my eyes adjusted to the onslaught of light, the first thing I felt was a rush of love for my daughter. The fear took a couple seconds to kick in.

"Wow," she said. "Wow! You—"

Her shifter power flooded through me. For the first time I realized what a dumb idea the costume had been.

"You're an elf!" cried my daughter.

Why did they call them elves when they were obviously dwarves? I wondered, as I dwindled down to the height of a five-year-old child. My ears pulled up into points, and my muscles bunched and tightened as my arms and legs and torso contracted. The outfit shrank with me. The beard and mustache rooted into the skin of my face, and my hair, usually short, sprouted into dark curls that tumbled down around my now-compacted shoulders.

The good thing about the change was that it was almost painless. Earlier shifts Lisa had put on me had hurt. One or two of them were even life-threatening, but that turned out to be a good thing, though I didn't think so at the time. My being rushed to the hospital in an ambulance had convinced Lisa not to throw her power around carelessly.

"Yes," I said. My voice sounded different, deep and gruff. Dwarf, I thought. An elf should sound like someone singing. Oh, well; my daughter and I were fishing different myth streams. I would find out first hand what she thought of elves now.

My new shape didn't hurt, but there were strange warm spots in my chest and forehead I didn't understand. Was I going to sprout horns? My costume was now spangled with small gold balls. Were they real gold? Why did my tongue taste of peppermint?

Something flowed into me, something warm and strong and scary. It flowed into the spots on my chest and forehead, then spread through me, rushing out to the tips of my fingers and toes, crackling like static in my new wealth of hair. Some of it flowed out of my hands and into the stocking I held. The bumps in the stocking shifted, some shrinking, some expanding. I remembered what Beth and I had put inside it, but I was pretty sure that wasn't what was in it now. This was the shiftiest shift Lisa had ever cast on me. "Yes. I'm an elf. What are you doing awake, little girl? You're supposed to be asleep."

"I wanted to see magic," she said in a half-swallowed voice.

"Christmas magic happens while you're sleeping," I said. My voice reminded me of frog croaks.

A tear trickled down one of Lisa's flushed cheeks. "I know," she said. "The magic other people believe in happens while they're sleeping. I'm the only one magic happens to while I'm awake. I just thought . . ."

"All right, all right," I said. "Now you've seen me." I walked to her bed and set the stocking down on the foot. Something moved inside the red velvet, squirmed toward the opening; the stocking looked longer, more ornate, with a gold-embroidered star on it; the white fur around the opening looked like rabbit fur. "You take a peek in here." I patted the squirming part of the stocking, wondering what kind of food we'd need to get for it. It had better be able to eat human food for at least a day. The pet stores would be closed on Christmas. "Take care of what needs care, but then close your eyes and settle down. It's going to take me a little while to prepare the rest of your Christmas, now that you've delayed me."

"I'm sorry, Mr. Elf." She sniffled.

"It's all right, honey." I patted her hand. "Oh, one more thing. You be nice to Tim today."

She nodded.

Jingling, I left the room. The door closed silently behind me before I had a chance to pull it shut, and my hands prickled.

The upstairs hall was lit by a nightlight so the kids could see their way to the bathroom, or sleep with their doors ajar for comfort. In that dim light, I stared at my new hands. Squat and sturdy and strange, different from the long fingers I used to play guitar or massage Beth in foreplay. Something prickled under my skin. I rubbed them together, trying to ease the itch. When I pulled them apart, sparkling flecks of light flew out, red and green, blue and lavender, danced in the air, then flattened in glowing snowflake patterns on the wall.

"Will?" Beth murmured. She stood just outside of Tim's room. "What?"

I strode toward her. My head was waist height to her now. I grabbed her hand—so big!—and pulled her into our bedroom.

She dropped to her knees on the carpet at the base of our bed, so our heads were level. "Oh, Will, I didn't know—"

"It's all right." I shrugged. "She wanted to see an elf, and the costume clinched it."

"What were those snowflakes?"

"Good question." I looked at the chaos of our room, mid-wrap, and the heat in my chest burned hotter. "I'm a Christmas elf," I said. I pressed my squat hand against my chest. The warmth was still flowing into me, moving up my arms and buzzing in my fingers. "So I might as well use what she gave me—" I gestured, and the other presents wrapped themselves in paper we hadn't had before. Bows in red and gold foil frothed up from the tops of gifts. More things flew out of the closet and wrapped themselves before I could even see what they were. Small already wrapped gifts appeared out of the air. The presents stacked themselves on the bed, a lovely pile of loot. I could swear we hadn't bought so many presents. Brightly colored cards fluttered from nowhere to land like paper butterflies on the gifts.

Beth knelt beside me, her eyes wide. "Oh," she said. "Oh, no. Oh, wow."

"Now the tree."

She followed me downstairs. While I poured warmth toward the tree and watched it manifest as spun glass ornaments, filigrees of tinsel, small wooden birds with feathered tails, gilded nuts, giant iridescent bubbles, Beth wandered into the kitchen. She came back with two mugs of cocoa with marshmallows; I could tell by the smell.

"Wow," she said.

I gestured, and the presents we had wrapped upstairs flocked down through the air and stacked themselves around the base of the tree.

I flicked a finger at the tree lights, and on they went, a blinking multitude of colors that sparkled through the clear ornaments and glittered reflections off the opaque ones.

I could get used to this, being able to remote-control everything by lifting a finger. I had had really good dreams like this.

Then I looked at my wife. She stood there with steaming mugs, her expression a mixture of pole-axed and irritated.

"What?" I said.

"I thought we were going to put the family ornaments on the tree. Together." She turned and sat on the couch facing the tree.

I went to the couch and climbed up next to Beth. She handed me a mug of cocoa. We sipped in silence.

"There's still room for our other ornaments," I said. I felt an edge of an ache in my chest that had nothing

to do with Christmas elf magic. Beth was right. Our
Christmas Eve preparations were something we had
shared with each other since before the kids were born.

"Oh, come on. It's perfect. You don't want to add old
junk to something that's perfect."

"Beth." I put my hand on her thigh. Warmth pooled
under my palm. She was a big, solid presence beside me;
she smelled like lilies and gingerbread, and she looked
like the woman I had loved all my life, even before I
met her.

Beth set down her mug and put her hand over mine
on her leg. She leaned over. Her mouth tasted like
cocoa.

Something passed between us, flavored with desperation and excitement. We went upstairs to bed.

Tim woke us up later by pounding on the locked door.
"Hey!" he called through the wood. "It's Christmas!
Come on!"

Beth's blonde head was resting on my chest, her arm
across me. Her brow furrowed, and she snorted. I raised
my hand to stroke her hair and saw I'd gotten my guitar-
playing fingers back.

Lisa's shifts could last an hour, a day, a week, or forever. I was glad this one had been so short. And so fun.

"Will?" Beth mumbled.

I sat up, gripping her shoulders so she wouldn't fall.
"We'll be right there," I yelled to Tim, "after we shower
and dress."

"Do it later!" he yelled back. "Santa came! We have
to see what's here!"

"We sure do," Beth muttered to me. "Do you even
know?"

"Lisa has a new pet. I don't know what kind."

"A new pet?" Beth frowned as I handed her a robe.
"We decided against that six times, didn't we?"

"You and I did, but the elf—"

"Oh, come on, Will. That was you."

"Not entirely." As I spoke, I knew I was being ridiculous. Who else could the elf have been?

The contents of Lisa's stocking had changed in my

stubby hands before I knew what I was capable of doing. Something had made decisions about what I was giving Lisa, and it hadn't felt like I was the one in charge.

Once, Lisa and changed me into Say Yes Dad. Whatever she asked me, I said yes. Yes, I would take her to the ice cream parlor and watch, smiling, as she ate the biggest sundae on the menu. Yes, I would buy her that expensive doll with huge wardrobe and dream house she'd been lusting after for two months. Yes, I would sit on the floor with her and play dolls. Thank goodness Beth came home before I said Yes to anything worse. Beth had talked Lisa into turning me back into myself.

One of Lisa's rules was that she could only experiment on one parent at a time, and she had to obey the other parent. When she'd started shifting us, about the time she was four, and we couldn't stop it from happening, we'd drummed that rule into her. She was going to break it, probably someday soon. The teen years were coming. All we knew how to do in advance was lay a groundwork of love, discipline, and hope.

While I was Say Yes Dad, I hadn't realized I was someone other than myself. Every Yes I said felt like the right choice. Maybe the elf had had elements of some Not-Will person in him. He had known how to do magical things, something with which I had no experience.

What could we do now but go forward? "I'm sorry, Beth. Lisa has a new pet." I shook my head and tied the belt of my robe.

Beth brushed her hair and sighed. "All right. Somehow we'll make it all right. We always have so far."

"An elf came last night," Lisa told us when we opened the bedroom door. Tim was already racing for the stairs.

"Really?" Beth asked.

"Really and truly. He brought my stocking. Look, Mom. He gave me a kitten."

"A kitten," Beth said. She glared at me, slitty-eyed.

"It's just what I always wanted," Lisa said.

The kitten was adorable, in a big-pawed, lavender-eyed, lilac-furred way, with darker points at nose, ears, and tail, like a designer version of a Siamese. It rode

Lisa's shoulder, and its eyes looked too intelligent. "His name's Singer," Lisa said. The kitten let out a musical meow.

"Lisa, you *know* you're not supposed to shift animals," Beth said.

"I didn't shift him, Mom, honest I didn't. This is what he looked like when he came out of my Christmas stocking. I know I'm not allowed to shift living things without permission."

I hooked my arm around Beth's neck, drew her close so I could whisper in her ear, "We did put a stuffed kitty in the stocking, and it was those colors." Like a fool, I had thought maybe a plush cat would satisfy Lisa's eternal hunger for a kitten. In a way it had.

"Damned clf," muttered Beth.

I let her go and squatted in front of Lisa. "Well, merry Christmas, honey. Hello, Singer. Welcome to our house." I held out my hand, and the kitten deigned to sniff it. He meowed a musical question and pressed his paw on my hand.

"Sorry," I said. "I don't speak song." I looked at Lisa, who shook her head.

"Mrrp," said Singer.

"Mom! Dad! Lisa!" Tim yelled from downstairs. "If you don't get down here right now, I'm going to open something without waiting for you!"

I straightened. Lisa took my hand as we went down the stairs, tugged me to a stop while Beth continued past us. I stooped so my head was even with Lisa's.

"Singer's the best present in the world," she whispered. "I don't care what else I get. I'm already happy, Daddy."

I lifted her in my arms, even though she was too big for that. I prayed I wouldn't throw my back out. She put her arms around my neck; Singer clung to both of us without breaking the skin, and I managed to walk downstairs carrying all three of us without tripping. I wanted to stretch any sweet moments Lisa offered as long as I could. She was heading at breakneck speed toward teen, and I wasn't sure how much longer I'd be eligible for father benefits.

"Come *on*, Dad," Tim said. He jumped up and down by the tree. "Look at it! Look at it!"

I set Lisa down and sat on the couch beside Beth to stare at the tree. Had the ornaments lasted after I lost my power? They had. Beth and I had never gotten around to putting up the family ornaments. The tree was beautiful, almost unearthly—and unhinged from tradition. I took Beth's hand, and she squeezed mine.

"Oh, Daddy," Lisa whispered.

I swallowed. "Who wants to play Santa?"

"I'll do it!" Tim cried. That surprised me. Whoever played Santa had to hand out a gift to everybody before he got to open his first one. We did the opening in cycles. One gift for everybody, a wild ripping of wrapping paper, and everybody got to admire each other's gifts before we moved on to the next round. Tim had always been too impatient to play Santa.

He handed Beth a medium-sized present, me a small present I didn't recognize, and Lisa a medium present before rushing to the bike, which he had obviously scouted before he came upstairs to wake us. "Ready?" he cried. He was tearing paper before anyone else got a chance to answer. In seconds the blue ten-speed stood revealed in its scattered shell. "Oh, boy!" Tim cried. "Oh, boy! Oh, boy! I want to try it now!"

"Tim, calm down. You're not the only one who got a present," said Beth.

Tim hugged his bike, then turned to see what we had gotten. Beth held up a glazed clay handprint Tim had made her at school. I showed off my new red and purple tie from Lisa. Lisa held up a book by one of her favorite authors; I couldn't remember if Beth or I had gotten it for her. We all thanked each other and Santa. Singer watched from Lisa's shoulder.

"Next round," Beth said. Tim gave his bike another hug, then distributed more presents.

We had bought the kids more presents than we got for each other, so the distribution network broke down before the end of the present opening. Tim gave Beth and me small unfamiliar gifts last, before he and Lisa plunged into an orgy of what-else-is-there.

Lisa's big present was art supplies—an expansive set of tubes of acrylic paints, a selection of brushes, a palette, a fancy paint box with compartments for everything, and some pre-stretched canvases.

Beth and I had debated over that one; Lisa had done some paintings at school with poster paint, and we both thought they were promising, but there was no guarantee she wanted to do more. Was she happy with the gift? I didn't know. We had given her a bike last year. There was no way for us to give the kids equal gifts, their interests were so different. Was she going to be mad that Tim got something more spectacular than she had this year? If she got mad, how would that manifest?

I saw Singer on her shoulder, remembered she had said that Singer was a good enough gift.

My final present had a note on it, one of the butterfly cards, and it was wrapped in red cellophane that crinkled as I untied the golden bow.

"Read the card, Will," Beth murmured.

I did. It said: "Don't try one until you're alone." It was signed ELF. Inside was a round brown tin the size of my palm with a red spot on the lid. I touched the spot. It felt hot. The lid popped up. An array of small ruby hard candies lay inside, glowing with light of their own. I lifted the box to sniff and smelled cinnamon and peppermint. A blue snowflake drifted out of the box and melted on my chest, and for a second I felt the return of pizzazz.

I closed the tin and tucked it in my pocket.

"Oh, boy!" Tim cried. He waved the card from a small gift wrapped in blue cellophane. "It's a spell, Dad! My first spell." He ripped off the cellophane, opened the jewelry box that had been inside it, took a silver ring out, slipped it onto his left middle finger. He held up his left hand, middle finger extended. The ring gleamed. "It's called Turnback. Just try anything on me now, Lisa. Just you try."

"What? I'm not allowed to shift you, Tim."

"Like that ever stops you. Come on. Turn me into a dog."

Lisa glanced at me. "Daddy?"

I looked at Beth.

"Turnback? A spell?" Beth asked.

I shrugged. "News to me."

"Special permission, Lisa," Beth said. "One small, short-term shift that doesn't hurt."

Lisa's smile was blinding. She set Singer on the couch, rubbed her hands, and sent shifter energy at Tim.

His new ring flared with blue light. He laughed as Lisa dwindled down into a chihuahua. Singer darted to the back of the couch, lavender eyes glowing as he watched the small dog. Lisa barked and raced around, trapping herself in wrapping paper. Her barks rose in pitch and frequency. She was scaring herself.

I lunged forward and caught her. "Hey, honey." I sat on the couch, cradling her in my arms. Her trembling rocked me. After a minute or two it slowed. She looked up at me with large black eyes and licked my nose.

"It works. It so works!" Tim cried. He hugged himself, then ran around the room flapping his elbows like chicken wings and crowing. "I am so gonna celebrate!"

Lisa suddenly shifted from dog to herself on my lap. I still had my arms around her. She sat with her back to my front, watching Tim. "Daddy," she whispered. She turned her head so I could see her profile.

"It will change things," I said, "but maybe that's better." We worked hard to keep her from mistreating Tim, but we couldn't watch them all the time. Something in her seemed to restrain her from doing things that would really hurt him; she had been fascinated by him when they were both babies, before her powers manifested, and perhaps that affection had transformed into a guardian mindset. Beth and I hoped so, anyway. We knew Tim's life was haunted by strange changes coming over him at odd times, and we weren't sure how to take care of him. We picked up the pieces after every shift we knew about and tried to sort them out. There weren't any manuals for this that we could find. Tim had friends, and spent a lot of time with them instead of Lisa. He was boisterous and happy most of the time. He seemed well adjusted, but who could tell?

The ring would definitely change the way he and Lisa related.

Lisa sighed. She had two friends of her own, but the need for secrecy about her skills meant she held a large part of heself back from her friendships. Tim was the one person close to her age who knew everything. She depended on him more than she knew.

Tim, crowing, raced up to us and waved his beringed finger in Lisa's face, then ran away again. I wished he'd put the ring on a different finger, but for all I knew, there were instructions included in the note that specified the middle finger; we'd probably have to apologize for him to the public at large until we got him tamed down. "Mom, can I have some cookies?" Tim yelled.

"Not until you've had a normal breakfast," Beth said. "You're hyper enough as it is." She held a small yellow jewelry box in her hand, the orange cellophanc it had been wrapped in folded neatly on her lap. She tucked the box in her bathrobe's pocket. Curiosity bit me. What had the elf given Beth for Christmas? For that matter, what had he given me? I guessed I'd have to wait to find out. Christmas morning was kids' time; parents would have the afternoon, while the kids broke or got tired of their presents.

Then again, we had the traditional Christmas afternoon visit to my sister Vicki's house to look forward to. She only invited us over every year because she felt the holiday called for her to be tolerant and generous, but in reality she and her husband were terrified of Lisa, like most of my family, and the visit would be agony for everybody, including Vicki's two kids, who had been warned to be very, very quiet while Lisa was in the house.

"It's Christmas," Tim said. "Today, everything's different. I vote we have cookies for breakfast!"

"I vote we don't," Beth said. In our household, a grown-up's vote counted twice as much as a child's vote, one of the things Lisa kept trying to adjust before we convinced her to stop that. "Will? Lisa?"

"Cookies," Lisa said.

"Pancakes," I said. Everybody liked those, though not as much as cookies. The sugar-free syrup tasted pretty good, too.

"I change my vote to pancakes," said Beth.

"Awww," Tim said. He grabbed the handlebars of his bike, ready to push it outside for a try.

I set Lisa on the couch beside me and stood up. "I'll make the batter. Beth, you watch Tim try the bike, okay?"

"Can Singer go outside?" Lisa asked.

"Will he stay with you and not run away?"

Lisa reached up to the back of the couch, where Singer crouched. She stroked the kitten's head. "Will you stay with me? Not be a wild thing?"

Singer meowed a short snatch of melody. Lisa looked at me, and I shrugged. "I bet he'll be a wild thing no matter what. Just ask him to stay. I wish I knew what he wants to eat. We need supplies for him, but we won't be able to buy anything until tomorrow."

"Daddy, can I do a special-permission shift again?"

"What kind?" I asked. Beth, who was holding the front door open for Tim and his bike, paused before following him outside.

"I want to understand Singer."

I checked with Beth, who nodded. "Okay," I said. "Let's give it a shot. Don't make it permanent until you know you like it, though; maybe he's saying things you don't want to know. Oh, and what if he's not really communicating at all? Put a parameter in about not forcing you to understand if there's nothing there to decode." Mental shifts were even trickier than physical ones; unexpected side effects abounded.

"Okay." Lisa sat with Singer in her lap, closed her eyes, frowned. She cocked her head. The furrow between her brows deepened, and then prickles of shifter energy needled my face and scalp.

"Hey!" I said.

Lisa opened her eyes. She rubbed her forehead and frowned.

"Did it work?" asked Singer.

Lisa and I stared at each other. We both nodded.

Beth said, "What did you do? Lisa, did you shift your father?"

"Yes," Lisa said in a small voice.

"What have we told you?"

"No shifting other people without asking. He said 'let's give it a shot.' "

"Lisa. You know he didn't mean it that way."

"I know," Lisa whispered.

"One hour of alone time," Beth said, "but you don't have to pay until tomorrow." She went outside, letting the door slam behind her.

"What's that about?" Singer asked.

"That's my punishment for shifting Daddy without permission," Lisa said. "I hate being alone worse than anything."

"Let's go to the kitchen," I said.

"Is it okay if I carry you?" Lisa asked Singer.

"Better than okay, gifa," Singer said. "Let me up on your shoulder. I love your head. It's got woosa around it."

"What's woosa?" Lisa asked.

"Delicious," said Singer as we crossed the dining room. I held the kitchen door for Lisa, then followed her in.

"Singer, what are you?" I asked. I got out a bowl, ran water in it, and set it on the floor.

"What am I? You should know." The kitten blinked both lavender eyes.

Uh-oh. Don't go there. Maybe Lisa knew I had been the elf, and maybe she didn't. She usually knew when she shifted something or someone, though she had occasionally done a shift in her sleep before she got her powers under control. Fortunately, that was before she had the oomph she had now, and the shifts had usually been short-term and minor.

Shifting me into the elf was a big one, but I could just barely believe she had done it in a sleepy state, without noticing. She had really wanted to see an elf. She might have mistaken shifting for longing.

Whatever the elf had done to bring the kitten to life, I didn't want to find out, not until Lisa was out of the room.

"But I *don't* know." Whatever Singer was, I hoped he could take a hint. "Are you really a kitten?" I asked.

"I have the body for it." Singer broke into a melodic purr. "Woo!" he said above his own purring, "you should try this. It's like being massaged on the inside."

I got the feeling Singer wasn't really a kitten.

"What do you eat?" Lisa asked. I got out the Bisquick and a mixing bowl, milk, eggs, the eggbeater.

"I'm not sure," Singer said. "I think I'd like . . . meat. Any kind of meat."

Lisa went to the fridge, opened the door. "Daddy, can I give him some turkey?" We'd had a big feast over at my mother's house last night, and Mom sent us home with loads of leftovers. She made a giant turkey and gave us leftovers for almost every holiday, convinced that Beth was a terrible cook and nobody in our family got enough to eat. Beth didn't mind. Much. It was true Mom made excellent turkey, and Beth loved turkey as much as I did.

"Sure. Put some on a plate on the floor. Singer, whatever you are, you're going to have to act like an animal while you're in that body. You're odd enough already to give the neighbors things to talk about."

"We'll see," said Singer.

Lisa forked some turkey onto a plate and set it on the floor next to the water bowl. Singer jumped off her shoulder and stuck his nose into the turkey. "Heaven," he said, and ate. He lapped up some water, too.

I whipped up some pancake batter and pondered the kitten. I had liked him better before I understood him. Now I didn't know who he was, or whether he was a safe companion for my daughter.

She knelt on the floor next to him and stroked his back, and he purred and ate—for the moment, a perfect picture, if you could get used to a purple kitten.

"If I take you outside, you won't run away, will you?" Lisa asked Singer.

"Are you kidding? Leave you, gifa? Never." He rubbed his head against her hip, then returned to the turkey.

Beth and Tim came in through the kitchen door, Tim hauling his bike right into the kitchen. I knew I had forgotten something: a bike lock. Well, the bike could live in the robbery-safe garage at home, but for now, Tim wasn't letting it out of his sight. Should make for an interesting bedtime.

"How'd it go?" I asked. I set the skillet on the stove and turned on a burner.

"This is the greatest bike in the world," Tim said. "I rode around the block and saw Ricky Davis on his new bike. Mine's much better. These racing stripes. And the Turnback ring. This is the best Christmas ever!"

"Glad you're enjoying it." I dolloped pancake batter into hot oil in my skillet. "Lisa? How you doing?"

She sat back on her heels and picked up the kitten, hugged him to her chest. "Thanks, Daddy. Thanks, Mama. It's my best Christmas, too."

Beth knelt and kissed Lisa's cheek. Lisa set Singer down and reached up to hug her mother.

I dished up pancakes, and we all ate. Afterward it was time to clean up all the wrapping paper. As the four of us wadded paper, threw the wads toward wastebaskets, and high fived if we scored, I found some purple cellophane near where Lisa had been sitting when she opened her gifts. The kids had already stacked their gifts and carried some up to their rooms. Under the tree, there were only a few presents for the grandparents and of course Vicki and her family. "Lisa? Honey, what came in this wrapping paper?" I asked.

"It's a present I don't understand," she said. "I thought maybe it was a joke."

We all stopped cleanup and gathered to look at Lisa's mystery present, which she pulled out of the middle of her stack of books, art supplies, clothes, stuffed animals, and board games. MAGIC KIT, it said on the brightly colored tin box. AMAZE YOUR FRIENDS! CONFOUND YOUR ENEMIES! A magician in a turban waved a wand on the box top; a rabbit was emerging from a puff of smoke in front of him.

"Wow, is that ever a dumb present for you," Tim said. "Like you need stupid tricks! Who gave it to you?"

"What did the note say, honey?" Beth asked.

Lisa unstuck the note from the gift and handed it to

her. "Use this to build your reputation as a magician," Beth read aloud. "Signed, Elf."

"I get it," I said. "I think I get it. You practice doing tricks from this box, Lisa. They'll look like other magicians' tricks. Everybody knows those are just tricks. You tell people you're studying magic, and show them some tricks, and then if they see you do other things they can't explain—"

"Oh, yeah," said Beth. "I love that elf!" She beamed.

"I tell people I'm a magician?" Lisa said slowly. "I tell people I'm a magician. But I'm not supposed to tell anybody anything."

"This would be okay to tell," I said. We'd had to change Lisa's school several times to cover up mistakes she'd made. These days I drove her six miles across town to Hillside Elementary, where she hadn't messed up yet. She'd only been going there since mid-October. If she decided to be a magician now, maybe she could stay all the way through sixth grade. "You have to teach yourself the tricks the hard way, though. No real magic, just imitation magic."

"That's weird, Daddy," she said.

"Can I try?" Tim asked.

"No!" Lisa said. She hugged the box.

"Why not? You don't want it."

"Yes, I do." She stared at the floor, her arms tight around the magic kit, then looked up at Tim and relaxed. "Okay. You can try. We'll both learn it."

"Yahoo!"

She opened the clasp and raised the lid. Inside was a manual with a magician on the cover. She lifted it out. Beneath it was a compartmentalized box with all kinds of tricks—a deck of cards, shell game shells, red and yellow juggling balls, steel rings, a traditional magic wand—black, with a steel cap at either end, a bouquet of feather flowers, a collapsing top hat.

"*I* get to try them first. It's *my* kit," Lisa said.

"Well, try something, then, so I can try it next," said Tim.

Beth and I rose, finished cleanup without any more scoring, and retreated to the kitchen.

"What was your elf present?" she asked.

"I don't know," I said. I showed her the candy tin and note. "What was yours?"

She got out the yellow jewelry box, handed me the note. "This ring's name is Bendshift. Love, Elf." She opened the box to display a slender silvery band nesting in yellow velvet. She took out the ring and slid it onto her ring finger, where it dropped into place above her wedding ring without being noticeable. "Bendshift," she said.

"Sounds promising." If she could bend Lisa's shift power, the way Tim could now turn it back—

We'd spent all of Lisa's life trying to get her to respect other people enough to leave them alone. If she wasn't such a good kid to start with, one of us would probably be dead by now. With the new ring powers, maybe everybody could relax.

"I love that elf," Beth said again. She gave me a kiss.

"I'm not—it wasn't—I didn't—I don't remember putting these gifts together," I said.

"Well, I love you more, Will, but I love the elf anyway. This is going to change things for all of us."

"I wonder if you can bend a shift that's already taken place," I said.

"Which one? Lisa's been so good today."

I took Beth's hand and led her to the kitchen table, where we sat facing each other. "I don't know about the kitten, Beth. He's not originally a kitten."

"She loves him. We can't take away something she loves." Her eyes looked hollow. We'd had some very difficult fights with Lisa in the past about things she loved that were bad for her. Lisa was better about such things now; she listened instead of throwing tantrums, and we didn't end up in the hospital after the fights. There were other kinds of scars, though.

"Not take him away," I said. "Understand him. She gave me the power to understand him; I wonder if you could extend that to you."

She consulted the note from her present, frowned. "It didn't come with instructions. I thought it would work like Tim's, protect me when she was shifting me. Let me see. Where did you feel the shift?"

"Face and the top of my head."

Beth laid her hands on my face; they felt warm. I smelled Christmas perfume I'd bought her on her wrists, something by Givenchy I'd noticed her trying more than once when we went to the department store. It carried a different kind of warmth, full-bodied and enticing. I wondered how soon we'd be able to get some real time alone. Probably not until after the kids went to bed.

"Oh," she said. "There's kind of a—" She moved her hands over my face, across my scalp. My skin prickled in the wake of her touch. "—a tingling. Ring, bend this shift so it touches me, too."

My face and scalp went pins and needles. Beth gasped. She sat back, her hands dropping from my head. Her face turned red; the color faded.

"Are you all right?" I grabbed her hands.

She took a deep breath, let it out, nodded. "That was just—so strange. Will. I did magic. I did magic. Oh, my, god."

"Let's see if it worked." We stood together and went back to the living room.

"Alakazam," Lisa said, and tapped the wand on one of the three yellow shells she had set on a table. "Your penny!" She lifted the shell and showed Tim a penny.

"Hey, how did you do that? It wasn't there a minute ago."

Lisa laughed and handed him the manual. He studied it, then turned the shell over, discovered the fake inside shell. "What a gyp!"

Singer was curled up on the couch beside Lisa, purring.

"Singer?" I said.

The kitten stretched, rolled over, looked up with half-lidded eyes. "Will?" he said.

"This is Beth."

"I know."

I checked with Beth, who nodded, her smile small. "He's kind of snotty," I told her.

"Oh," said Singer. "That was a formal introduction? Excuse me." He stood up and walked over to us, his fluffy tail hooked at the end. Beth stooped and held out a hand, and Singer smelled it. "I don't know why I feel compelled to do that. You smell very nice."

"Thanks," said Beth. She stroked his head, and he purred.

"Mom?" Lisa jumped up, scattering plate-sized steel rings and rubber balls. "Can you understand him? I didn't shift you, honest I didn't."

"I know, honey. I got a spell for Christmas, too. I can bend the shifts now. I bent Daddy's Singer-talk spell to me."

"Wow. Everybody got magic for Christmas? Wow! Daddy, what did you get?"

"I don't know yet."

"Everybody can understand the kitten but me?" Tim said. "That's not fair. Lisa, shift me too."

She looked at us. "May I?"

"You remember what you did last time?" I asked.

"Of course, Daddy."

I exchanged glances with Beth, something we did a lot of. "Well, Tim gave you permission, and we do too," Beth said.

Lisa closed her eyes and concentrated, then sent a shift at Tim. His ring flared blue and the shift bounced back, enveloping Lisa, who blinked in confusion.

"Oh, I forgot," Tim said. He pulled off his ring and set it on the table. "Do it again, Lisa. Please."

She rubbed her eyes, wrinkled her forehead, and focused again. She sent the shift.

"Ouch," said Tim. "Oh. Kitty, do you really talk?"

"Sure," said Singer. "Do you understand me now?"

"Oh. Yeah. Wild. Thanks, Lisa. Hey, can I try a card trick next?"

They started squabbling about things in the magic kit again. Beth nudged me toward the door. "Go try one of your elf presents," she whispered. "Find out what they do. I'll keep track of the kids."

I slipped out of the living room and went up to the master bedroom, shut the door, locked it—not that a lock would keep Lisa out. It added to my feeling of being alone, though, per my instructions.

I sat on the bed and opened my tin of Christmas candies. They were small—I counted, and there were thirty of them. Maybe I should save them for emergencies. But heck, if I didn't even know what they did, how would I know which emergencies to use them for?

I took one out and put it in my mouth.

Flavor exploded across my tongue, peppermint, cinnamon, sugar, ozone. Heat gathered around me, wrapped me up. I felt again the flowing inrush of energy and the contraction of my muscles and bones. My ears pinched and pulled, and my beard and mustache grew. Hair pushed out of my head to tumble in dark curls around my shoulders.

I wasn't wearing the costume this time. My bathrobe didn't shrink; I was lost in its folds by the time the transformation finished with me. I fought my way free and did what I had been too busy to do the night before. I looked carefully at this alternate self in a mirror.

Stocky. Muscular. Small. My head was big in proportion to the rest of my body; my face looked nothing like the clean-shaven, taller Will. If I didn't know it was me inside, what would I think of this person?

I turned my head, pushed hair aside, revealed my ears. Foxy points. I leaned forward, stared into my eyes. When I was tall Will, my eyes were dark brown; as Elf, I had tawny eyes under heavy brow ridges.

"Why did I give myself this gift?" I asked out loud, my voice gruff.

I felt tides of power shift under my skin. "Remember," said my new voice.

We had always wondered where Lisa's powers came from, once we got over the shock of their appearance. At first Beth and I had not been able to believe what was happening. We moved from denial to unconscious acceptance. So stuffed animals and cookies flew across the nursery to the crib. Deal with it. Lock up anything Lisa shouldn't have, and if she shifted one of us through the air toward her, try to land without cracking a shinbone or breaking a finger. The awareness snuck up on us in increments, even as we learned all kinds of defenses (only show her off to the relatives when she was asleep, for instance. Daycare was impossible, so Beth and I adjusted our jobs so one of us would always be home with the baby). We didn't get around to asking why us until Lisa was two years old, and we never got any answers.

"Remember," I said again.

I'd seen a face like the elf's before. Old Uncle Darius, a short-statured man, who had lived in the attic of the house where I grew up. He had his own staircase to the outside world, and kept to himself most of the time, but once in a while I climbed up on the roof and he came out too, and we watched the stars together, he smoking some fragrant tobacco in a small pipe. He wasn't a very conversational person. "There's hope for you, young Will," he told me once, "though the rest of the family has gone water weak." I never did figure out what he meant.

Uncle Darius died when I was fifteen; he had grown more taciturn as time went on. Now I couldn't ask him my questions.

My sister Vicki had seventeen volumes of our grandmother's journals from the nineteen-twenties and thirties. She liked them because Grandmother had a taste for expensive gilded Florentine leather book bindings. I wondered if there were any family secrets inside. Maybe Grandmother wrote about the family before it went water weak. I didn't think Vicki had ever read them.

"Remember."

I closed my eyes and tapped into the power flowing through me. *Help me remember*, I thought, and then the answers came.

Not so long ago, powers ran through my family—not as strong as Lisa's, but a little in everyone. Something about the twentieth century had driven them all underground, as though someone had set a mimic curse on us to help us blend with everyone around us. I remembered, though I didn't know how, that Beth's great-grandmother was from a different lineage of power, healers or harmers depending on their natures; shifters.

Though neither Beth nor I had manifested any powers, they lay latent deep inside us. Lisa's elf-shift had finally forged a link from her invading power to my own source, opening gates that had been closed all my life.

"Do I have to shrink to use this knowledge?" I asked, and I laughed, then realized that being short *did* put me closer to the source. Once I grew again, my powers would retreat to somewhere I couldn't touch them.

The elf had given me magic candy. How long did one hit last? I had fallen asleep last night before the shift ended, so it might be hours. On the other hand, with the powers I had in this form, I could shift myself back to tall Will right now. I would lose my powers, though.

A knock sounded on the door. "Will?" Beth called.

I was going to ask if she was alone, but my voice had changed. I didn't want the kids seeing me like this. I grabbed the robe and shrank it to fit me with a thought. I put my stubby, short-fingered hand against the door and felt outward through the house. The kids were in their rooms, getting dressed to go to Vicki's.

Vicki's. Oh, yeah. Wouldn't she get a kick out of seeing me like this?

I opened the door to Beth.

"Oh," she said. She smiled, knelt, hugged me, drew me into a long, exquisite kiss. Man, she smelled good, and tasted better.

Beth kicked the door shut behind her. "So this is what happens when you eat those candies?" she asked. "What would happen if I ate one?"

"Whoa," I said.

"Can I try it tonight after the kids go to bed?"

I considered this with all the skills at my disposal, figured it couldn't hurt, or if it did, I could fix it, provided I ate a candy first. "Sure."

"Can you give magic presents now?"

"Do you need something?"

"No, I was just wondering."

"I get the feeling I could whip up a lot of mischief, yes."

Beth grinned. Then frowned. "Can you explain the cat to me?"

"Where did that cat come from?" I asked myself.

"He's a helpful spirit," the elf voice answered.

"What?" asked Beth.

"Lisa needs some extra help," said the elf. "That was everybody's Christmas wish. I brought my friend here—Singer—he's probably laughing about that name—to watch out for her. If Bendshift and Turnback don't work, Singer can help."

"But who is he?" asked Beth.

I waited for an answer. We both did. Finally I said, "I guess we'll find out by talking to him. Just now, though, I guess we need to get ready to see Vicki and Clive." I looked down at my elf self and frowned.

"You could go like that and say Lisa did it."

"Lisa thinks I'm a Christmas elf. Besides, I don't think Vicki and Clive need anything else to be scared of."

"Maybe you better hide until this wears off. I'll tell Vicki you're sick."

"It's all right. I can shift myself back from here." I slipped the tin out of my pocket, though, opened it, conjured a candy to replace the one I had eaten. I wanted the power to become this self. "I've got something to tell you."

"Does it have to be now? We better get ready for the visit. Let's take a quick shower," Beth said. She took my hand and led me to the bathroom. I didn't shift back to my taller self until after we dried off.

Things were different at Vicki and Clive's.

They always received us in their living room on Christmas. Maybe it was because the tree was there, but I thought it was because they didn't want to let Lisa any farther into the house than that. The kitchen, the bedrooms, the rec room, all the rooms where they did their actual living, were too precious to allow an invasion by such an unpredictable force. I could understand that.

It still made me mad.

The living room was, as usual, magnificent in its decorations and decorum. Vicki and Clive sat on the couch, with their children, Art and Nellie, to either side of them. All of them looked posed and polished in really

nice clothes, unlike us; Tim's socks didn't match, his hair
was still wet, his shirt buttoned wrong, and Lisa had
chosen a red dress and a chartreuse jacket.

We all said Merry Christmas and sat in our usual
chairs, chairs that saw our asses only this time each year.

"Children," Beth said as Tim grabbed a plate, "ten
cookies each. I mean that. Choose carefully."

"Oh, Bethie," said Vicki, "don't be so strict. I love to
give your children cookies. They seem so appreciative."

Beth heard implied criticism in anything my family
said to her, and usually I feared she was right.

Beth shifted her rings and straightened. "Vicki, you
make great cookies, so the children always eat too many.
Today we're starting some new rules. Ten each, kids."

Lisa opened her mouth, closed it. She looked at me,
and I smiled at her. Tim picked all the biggest cookies
with chocolate in them, stacking them high on the tiny
plate.

Lisa picked ten cookies and sat back. She lifted one
and took some tiny nibbles.

"Punch?" said Vicki brightly.

We got the cookies, punch, and coffee portion of the
visit out of the way in ten minutes. Art and Nellie had
two cookies each. I had never noticed, but I suspected
they always had two cookies each. Then we had the gift
exchange, which was painful. None of us knew what to
get for Vicki's family, so we settled for knickknacks,
which didn't go with anything they had. Their gifts to us
were just as pitiful. I got my third tie of the day, in
colors so neutral I couldn't tell if they were gray or blue.
Beth got a cookie cookbook. Lisa and Tim got educa-
tional toys that would teach them to read below their
grade level.

We were out of there in half an hour.

"Oh, boy!" Tim said as we drove away. "Oh, boy!
You mean, we didn't have to stay there hours and hours
every year, trying to play with those awful, boring toys?"

"Let that be a lesson to you," Beth said. "It's good
to take less food. You pay less in time."

"Art asked me if I was sick," Lisa said.

"He did? When?" I asked.

"While you and Mom were telling Aunt Vicki about Christmas Eve at Grandma's."

"He say why he asked?"

" 'Cause I wasn't having a tantrum and scaring them. That's not fair, is it, Daddy? I didn't have a tantrum the last two years."

"True, but you did fly the plates and cookies around, and you spilled tea on the carpet from a cup floating through the air. We know you were trying to help, but they don't understand it."

"Oh."

"So what did you tell him?" Beth asked.

"I said we were all getting better."

Christmas night, Beth and I took turns saying good-night to the kids. While she was in with Tim, I sat on the edge of Lisa's bed, patting Singer, who, when he wasn't talking, did a passable imitation of a kitten.

Lisa's art supplies covered a desk she had made larger to accommodate them. Some of the brushes stood up-right in a jar of water, and some colors sat in three-dee oodles on the palette: red, blue, white, purple. She'd started painting on one of the canvases, outlined and half colored in a shape that might be a cat.

"You never told me what your elf gift was," Lisa said. "Did he give you magic, Daddy?"

"Yeah. Mine's different from Tim's and your mom's—it doesn't work all the time—but it's pretty good."

She sighed and snuggled deeper under her covers, her smile wide. "Now everybody has magic I can see in the daytime. This is the best Christmas."

I kissed her cheek.

We locked the door and I got out my tin. I ate a candy. I needed to be an elf for what I had to tell Beth.

"I learned something else while I was working on this today. We both come from magical families, Beth. Your great-grandmother was a healer."

"Sure, Granny Nightshade. She died when I was ten. How could you know about her?"

"I asked the right questions." I placed my hands on

her shoulders, closed my eyes, and looked inside her for the hidden spring of her lineage. Barely a trickle, but there. I primed it with some of the magic I could draw in this form, strengthened it. "Do you feel that?"

"What? Oh. Yes." She stroked a hand down her front. "What is it, Will?"

"It's your power. I have some, too, but I can't get to it unless I'm in this form. Lisa got her magic from us."

She placed a palm on my chest. I felt a flow of warmth there that didn't come from me. "Will?" she said, fear and wonder in ther voice. "Will?"

This didn't feel like Lisa's shifter power, a rain of pins and needles directed toward whatever part of me Lisa wanted to shift. It was more like a warm bath, being enveloped in pleasure. I closed my eyes. When I opened them, I had returned to my large self, the person Beth had married. She stared down at her open palm, then up at me. "Oh, Will," she said, and hugged me.

THE TRADE

Fiona Patton

Fiona Patton lives in rural Ontario, Canada with her partner, a fierce farm Chihuahua, and inumerable cats. She has five novels out with DAW Books: *The Stone Prince*, *The Painter Knight*, *The Granite Shield*, *The Golden Sword*, and *The Silver Lake*. She has twenty odd short stories published in various DAW/Tekno anthologies including *Sirius the Dog Star*, *Assassin Fantastic*, and *Apprentice Fantastic*.

THE CITY OF Cerchicava had been struck by the plague. The oppressive summer heat, hanging over the streets like a pall, kept the purifying air from the Ardechi River from reaching the sick and spread the disease like wild-fire. All those who could, had fled, leaving the poor and the infirm to die by the hundreds. While the gravediggers and the ragged priests who served the city's most desperate citizens struggled to bring the sickness under control, the nobility and their servants spent a peaceful, isolated summer amidst the sweeping trees and cool river banks of the surrounding countryside.

In the ornate glass conservatory of his family's summer palazzo, three-year old Montifero de Sepori sat on his nurse's lap, turning the pages of a large picture book while she read the story aloud to him.

"And the man asked, what is the greatest power in the world?"

She glanced down, an indulgent smile on her face.

"And what do you think the answer is, young master?"

Running one finger along the next word, Montifero sounded out each letter carefully.

"Faith?" he asked.

His nurse beamed down at him. "Yes, that's very good. Your lady mother will be so proud of you. Yes, faith will sustain you when all else fails. Faith in the Church and in its priests," she said fingering the Church made charm around her neck reverently. "Their magics can work miracles."

Later, that afternoon, however, as they passed the open doorway of the crofter's cottage they'd often brought gifts of food and clothing to, his nurse drew him away fearfully. In the parlor he could see the body of a tiny baby laying in its cradle, still and silent, while its mother sat beside it, weeping inconsonantly.

"The child is dead, young master," his nurse said in a hushed, frightened voice. "It's not safe. Come away and leave the family to their grief."

He looked up at her, his dark, intense eyes confused. "But can't the priests use their magics to bring it back to life?" he asked.

Horrified, his nurse bundled him back to the palazzo at once. His mother sent for the family priest who stared reprovingly down at the boy from beneath his thick, graying brows.

"Death is final, Montifero," he said sternly. "And it's heresy, sacrilege, to tamper with a dead body, magically or otherwise. Anyone who visits spellcraft upon the dead is dammed for all time. Remember that."

Later, his father's footman had explained it better.

"Only the Death Mages work spellcraft on the dead, young master," he said as he polished Montifero's new riding boots. "They work terrible necromantic magics that attack the living. They call it the Trade." He leaned forward conspiratorially. "And they're everywhere. They come and go like ghosts in the night. They can snatch a corpse before the priests have a chance to even begin the purification rituals or break into a poorly protected crypt to do their evil work, and then vanish again like smoke."

A week later, the footman brought word of plague in the local village.

"Your lady mother is very ill, young master. You cannot see her today. Come and play with your hobby-horse like a good boy."

Montifero had tried to tell them that he had to see her, that he needed to tell her that faith would sustain her and protect her, but his words, like his screams of rage, went unheeded. Later, when the house had grown quiet and his nurse slumbered in the hot stifling air of his nursery, he'd crept away, down the wide, richly carpeted stairway to his mother's apartments. Pushing the white and gold-painted door of her bedchamber open, he'd slipped inside.

The room was shadowy and dark with the curtains drawn, and it smelled of incense, magic, and sickness. A figure, his mother, lay stretched out on the silken sheets of her bed, dressed in her finest linens, her palms laid across her bosom. Her face, although peaceful in expression, was covered in red, pus-filled sores, already gone sunken and black.

Montifero stood guard over her body until the priests came to take her to the family crypt, and even then, it took the strength of three footmen to drag him away, screaming in fear, that the Death Mages would steal her body.

"The Death Mages are everywhere."

His father returned from the fighting against neighboring Pisario as soon as he received the news of his wife's death. He took young Montifero to visit her tomb but, as the summer passed into autumn, he saw less and less of him. Consumed by grief, Lord Ramiro de Sepori's health began to fail.

* * *

"Oh my sweet boy, what is to become of us now? What is to become of you?"

This time his nurse and the other servants had been too distraught to stop him. Across the wide hallway from his mother's apartments, the dark, paneled door stood slightly ajar, inviting him inside.

The figure, his father, lay on his own bed, his arms flung out, the blood and sweat-stained sheets in disarray beneath him. The smell of disease was strong, much stronger than the masking scent of incense and failed magics, a biting, acrid odor that scratched at the back of his throat. Montifero stared at the body suspiciously.

His nurse had told him that his father was a soldier, a general, a man the duc of their city relied on to keep them safe from all their enemies; an undefeatable giant and a pious lay member of the Church. But the man in the bed was no undefeatable giant; the man in the bed had been defeated by plague; defeated by death. Faith had no more sustained him than it had Montifero's mother.

Turning away, the boy returned to his nursery.

"What is the greatest power in the world, Piero?"

Seated in the large glass conservatory of the Palazzo de Sulla in Cerchicava, seven-year-old Montifero, ward of his uncle, the great General Matteo de Sulla, glanced over at the retainer charged with his education.

"What do you think it is, young master?" Piero replied.

The boy stared out the window at the great spire of the San Dante Cathedral just visible above the line of cyprus trees that marked the borders of his uncle's home.

"Death," he said simply.

Giving him a shrewd glance, Piero nodded. "And so the man who can harness the power of death is . . . ?"

"The most powerful man in the world."

"Yes."

After a long moment, Montifero turned his darkly, intense gaze on Piero's face. "I want to be the most powerful man in the world," he stated.

The retainer nodded. "And you shall be, young master."

And so at the age of seven, Montifero de Sepori accepted the binding spells of Piero Bruni, one of Cerchicava's most talented Death Mages, and entered into the study of the Trade.

"The most powerful components are those collected from corpses no more than a few moments dead, and they include in descending order: organs, muscle, skin, bones, fluids, and hair. They may be stored for up to one year but every moment they spend in preserving solution leaches their potency away. The best storage is always the mark's living body."

Another hot and stifling summer had descended on the city. Seated on a high stool before a corpse laid out on a spotlessly clean worktable in a warehouse in Vericcio—one of Cerchicava's most destitute housing districts—ten-year-old Montifero removed an example of each component, sealing them into individual ceramic urns before glancing up at Piero, his intense eyes ringed with the red glow of a death spell.

"What about the earth from a freshly dug grave?" he asked. "It's on the Church's list of proscribed items."

Piero snorted in disgust. "Earth, young master, is not flesh. It's used by amateurs and charlatans and is not to be bothered with by serious practitioners of the Trade."

"Then why does the Church believe it otherwise?"

"Because amateurs and charlatans are generally the only ones the Church is able to catch. The most powerful Death Mages act behind the protective screen of the nobility and their subordinates carry binding spells so strong, they can restrict the breathing passages at the first hint of betrayal. The less powerful hide themselves in Vericcio and Bergo where the Church rarely bothers to go.

"But we're not invulnerable, young master," he continued. "The priests are powerful mages in their own right and they have powerful identify and locate spells. The best deflecting wards include hair and skin boiled in urine, then thrown on a fire. Urine collected from a corpse related to the enemy priest is best, but liquid mediums do not have to be necromantic components; any urine will do. Except your own, young master. Never use anything of your own in any spell-casting. It will lead the priests and their Order of the Holy Scourge right to you. And then you'll hang, be you nobleman or pauper."

"The touch of a dead man's hand will not cure goiter as some believe, however, the fingernails from a dead man's hand will locate the last piece of precious metal he ever touched; a much more useful bit of spellcraft, when even a second-rate physician can cure goiter."

In the enshrouding darkness of Debassino's Heretic's Cemetery, eleven-year-old Montifero listened with half an ear to the lesson as he watched two of Piero's markers carry a shrouded corpse from a crumbling mausoleum.

"And if the dead man was a Bergo thief cut down off a gibbet and tossed into an unprotected crypt?" he asked, pulling his scalpel and moving swiftly forward, "how useful a spell can that be?"

"If that thief was hanged because he robbed a richly furnished palazzo in the Carmina District, a very useful spell indeed, young master," Piero answered. "Gold buys more than fine clothing and beautiful homes, it buys loyalty and it buys silence. In the most extreme cases it can even buy access or egress from prison."

Slicing open the shroud to reveal one, blacked hand, Montifero nodded his understanding before removing each fingernail, one by one.

"And so a potion of lemon, honey and cinnamon will not only soothe the throat but, when used in concert with a mirror and a silver key, can predict the most advantage time to engage in . . . well to produce an heir. The silver in the mirror and key promotes the banishment of all save the magical intent. Do you see, young master?"

Thirteen-year-old Montifero indicated his understanding of his herbal master's words with a wave of one hand. Everything a young nobleman of Cerchicava needed to take his place among the rich and powerful members of his class had been made available to him in the glittering halls and richly paneled studies of the Palazzo de Sulla; dancing, swordscraft, riding, magery, theology, trade, and politics.

Everything he needed to take his place among the rich and powerful members of the Trade had also been made available to him in the stinking alleyways and silent, shadow-draped cemeteries of Vericcio and Bergo: marking, collecting, creating and unleashing offensive spellcraft, and the tactics and politics of avoiding detection.

The individual lessons often had just enough similarity to be amusing.

His dancing master on the art of the waltz: "You hold your partner lightly but firmly with your hand in the small of her back, young master, then as the music directs you, you turn fluidly, guiding her steps to flow in tandem with your own."

Piero on the art of collection: "You hold the scalpel lightly but firmly, young master, cutting with just enough force to part the skin but not so deeply as it pierces the desired component beneath. Then reaching in with the left hand, position the organ like so and slice it cleanly through."

Other lessons had just enough difference to color that amusement with practicality.

His uncle's swords master on combat tactics: "Slash to kill the enemy."

Piero's marker on setting a mark for a collection: "Thrust to kill the mark." And sometimes there was no similarity at all.

"Or you could just bash his brains in. Whichever works best," the huge marker added, holding up a heavy jack.

"Make no mistake, the Holy Scourge—may they be blessed in their most sacred mission—will ferret out the defiling heresy of necromancy, no matter where it might be found. Cerchicava will soon be free of the Death Mages so that all its people may walk safely and freely without fear of damnation."

Seated in his family's pew in the San Dante Cathedral, fourteen-year-old Montifero listened intently to the Bishop Enrico Sebesti's sermon. The Scourge had a zealous new Captain, Lord Romuald Croce, a fiery-tempered cousin to the Achivescovo himself. Under his leadership a dozen necromancers and their subordinates had been arrested in the past week. The shocking news that one such Death Mage had been Lord Guido Peruzzi, a high ranking member of the duc's court, had rocked the nobility. Standing with a group of youths before morning services, Montifero had maintained a distant air while paying very close attention to the buzz of rumors and accusations that swirled around him.

"It's said they found a secret workshop beneath his palazzo filled with the most vile accoutrements."

"The house servants have all fled into Bergo and Vericcio of course. Half of them must be necromancers themselves."

"The Scourge should burn them all out."

"I heard that the duc has expanded the powers of the Scourge and that Captain de Croce is looking for a dozen new novices to train in his holy crusade."

"It's true; my own son has been named lieutenant."

"And they say there's going to be a new tax to maintain the wards on the city's paupers' cemeteries to put a strangle hold on the supply of bodies to the Death Mages."

"What? It's all one can do to afford the wards on one's own family crypt."

"The Death Mages are everywhere."

Watching the Bishop gesticulate with every forcefully delivered denouncement of the Trade, Montifero considered the situation from each angle. He needed to know where the Scourge was holding Peruzzi and how much they had forced him to reveal and the only one who could tell him this was the Bishop Enrico Sebesti.

At the reception held afterwards in the cathedral's expansive gardens he mingled casually with the rest of the richly garbed congregation, all the while keeping a sharp eye out for the Bishop's distinctively brocaded church robe. He finally spotted him by the long, linen-draped buffet table, and after exchanging greetings with a young woman whose eyes glowed with the bright, anticipatory green popular among the city's youth that season, he positioned himself beside the older man and helped himself to a thin slice of melon.

Behind him, he heard the expected guffaw.

"That miserable bit of nothing won't hold you for an instant, lad."

Montifero turned, a perfectly crafted expression of polite respect on his face.

"My Lord Bishop," he said formally.

Holding a plate overflowing with confectionaries, the man waved a glass of wine in his direction. "How can you break your fast on such a lovely day eating such poor fare," he almost bellowed. "Take a pastry or two before your health fails you." He peered at him in what Montifero assumed was supposed to be mock suspicion. "You're what fourteen, fifteen now?"

"Fourteen, sir."

"Ah, yes, a young man with a keen intellect and an accomplished rider and swordsman to boot, or so I'm told."

As Montifero widened his eyes in feigned surprise, the Bishop chuckled heartily. "Didn't think I kept my eye on you, did you, lad? But of course I did, for your dear departed mother's sake. A fine woman," he added thickly. "And a powerful court mage. She's missed terribly, terribly. But then I advised her not to bring so many servants from the city during that frightful summer. The lower classes have no understanding of cleanliness," he declared, slopping wine down the front of his robe. "They brought the plague to the countryside with them no doubt. It's a wonder you survived. A miracle." He took a large swallow before continuing. "As I said, I've kept my eye on you as you've grown, and here you are nearly a man. So what's it to be then, magecraft like your sainted mother?"

"I'm afraid I haven't the skills necessary for magery,"

Montifero began, his eyes glowing a faint, washed out green.

"Limited power eh?" the Bishop interrupted tactlessly. "Well, so what? I haven't much myself, but I do well enough. So what then, the Church perhaps?" He winked broadly. "I think I could find a position on my staff for a talented and pious young man with the proper breeding and background."

"I should be only to grateful, My Lord Bishop. I'd have to write for my uncle's permission, of course."

"Yes, yes, of course. He's not home much, I understand. The duc keeps him busy directing the offensive against Pisario."

"Very busy, My Lord, but we keep in touch by letter. His last missive suggested that he was considering finding me a position as a military aide, or possibly even a novitiate in the Scourge."

"Hm." The Bishop made a show of considering his words. "The Scourge is a blessed calling," he agreed. "But it's a terrible business if you haven't a true vocation. Weeding out heresy among the degenerate creatures of Bergo or Vericcio is one thing, finding it in Carmina is something else again. Could you arrest a member of your own class boy, a peer, a friend?" He gave him a shrewd look. "A relative of beautiful young Charlotte d'Angasi over there? The Death Mages are everywhere and the dungeons beneath the San Dante are a dark and terrible place."

Montifero made himself cast a horrified glance towards the cathedral. "San Dante?" he asked in a hushed whisper. "But I thought . . . I never would have believed . . . Beneath?" He shuddered.

"Beneath," the Bishop repeated, enjoying Montifero's supposed squeamishness. "Right underneath the very nave where you hear services. Why at this very moment Captain de Croce is interrogating old Peruzzi and I think you can very well imagine what's transpiring. He grew careless you see, they always do. So." He gave him a bright smile belied by the triumphant expression in his eyes. "Shall I make an introduction to the Captain for you, lad?"

His face a similar shade of green as his own eyes, Montifero gave a shaky bow. "I think perhaps it is as you say, My Lord Bishop, the Scourge demands a true vocation. With your permission, I shall write my uncle regarding your very generous offer of a position on your staff."

"A wise choice," the Bishop agreed magnanimously. "Although not nearly so exciting as the Scourge, the prelacy can always find a place for a serious scholar and you could do worse than ally yourself with the San Dante. After all, the Achivescovo was a scholar before he took on the leadership of the Church. A young man could go far in such company."

"My thanks, My Lord Bishop." Bowing, Montifero retired from the conversation and returned to the coquettish company of Charlotte d'Angasi waiting patiently to one side.

An hour later, feeling a low grade love spell tingling against his fingers, he accepted a silver token in exchange for the promise to attend her and her family at supper later in the week and took his leave of the reception.

He found Piero bent over a length of intestine in the Vericcio warehouse an hour later. Holding up the tiny, silver key, he laid it carefully on a shelf neatly stacked with necromantic components.

"Charms," Piero said disdainfully, wiping his hands on his long, leather apron. "Worthless trinkets sold in the marketplace to gullible marks from the country or to the foolish members of the nobility who don't know any better."

"It's the third one this week," Montifero noted, slipping his own apron on before he approached the table. "A gift from Charlotte d'Angasi."

"You'd make an advantageous match, young master. The ladies of Cerchicava are well aware of this."

"So is the Bishop. He offered me a position this morning."

"He would ally himself with the house of Sepori."

"He would ally himself with the money of Sepori. I

come into my inheritance in less than six months. The carrion are already gathering." He glanced down at the intestine. "A divination spell?" he asked.

"Yes, young master. Guido Peruzzi's been arrested by the Scourge."

"Your first teacher. I heard. The Bishop announced it from the pulpit this morning. He's being held in the San Dante dungeons. They're questioning him as we speak." He handed the older mage a fresh scalpel. "Exactly how much danger are we in, Piero?"

"It's hard to tell just yet. No one of his stature has ever been taken before and my usual contacts are too frightened to be of much use." Slicing down the length of intestine, Piero inserted a number of small finger bones inside. His eyes glowed red for a brief moment, then he picked up a needle threaded with a length of plaited hair. "His protections are considerable," he continued, sewing up the cut both deftly and swiftly. "However, if the Scourge can break him, he'll name every subordinate who ever served under him. Masters do not wear binding spells."

"Then we have to make sure they don't break him."

The intestine began to burn with a dull, ruby glow, then suddenly turned to ash. Piero stared down at the blackened finger bones for a long moment before gathering them up again. "His protections are still in place," he noted. "But they're weakening."

"Then we have time to formulate a plan."

"We can't kill him in any conventional manner, young master," Piero warned, noting the finality in Montifero's voice. "No amount of money would be enough to gain access to him in the San Dante. And the priestly containment spells around him will be both subtle and powerful. The result of any offensive spell would be traced right back to the originator."

"A conventionally offensive spell, yes," Montifero agreed, glancing towards the shelf with a thoughtful expression. "But I have something a little more unconventional in mind. Charlotte d'Angasi is related to Guido Peruzzi, is she not?"

"Distantly, young master."

"How quickly could the components for a banishment spell be collected?"

"From Charlotte d'Angasi?"

Montifero chuckled at the worried tone in the man's voice.

"No, Piero, from someone both more closely related and less likely to arouse suspicion and outrage."

"His cousin Fernando is a worthless drunkard who frequents the wrong sorts of taverns," Piero offered at once. "I could have a marker and a cutter on him before the sun finished setting."

"Do it."

The components arrived before nightfall. Accepting the three ceramic urns from Piero, Montifero emptied the contents directly onto the table. "Charms are worthless trinkets sold in the marketplace to gullible marks from the country or to the foolish members of the nobility who don't know any better," he said, repeating the older man's words from earlier. "And in the case of protection or love charms, I agree." He picked up a cleaver and began to mince the components into a fine paste, using the side of the blade to mix them together. "But the foundation of an Intent Charm such as this," he held up the silver key, "is a watered-down banishment spell strangely enough. Banishment for rats, toothache, disease, impotence, or in this case, thought or attention to anyone save the token's originator, they're all basically the same. Now supposing you lay a necromantic banishment spell onto the charm and direct it along the duel blood link from the token's originator and the mark who supplied the components?"

Piero smiled. "The duel blood link would be powerful enough to overcome any protection spells Peruzzi had in place."

"Exactly. The Scourge can only identify a necromantic spell signature and trace it back to the Death Mage once the spell has taken effect, but with the original spell still in place within the charm . . ."

"The Scourge will be lead to Charlotte d'Angasi."

"Who may spend a rather uncomfortable night in their care but as she carries no taint of necromancy, they probably won't hang her. And if they do," Montifero shrugged as he dropped the key into the mixture. "I still have two others tokens should I wish to take a wife.

"No one will make the connect through the token because the Church has no idea how necromantic spells actually work, and no one will assume that Montifero de Sepori could enact such a spell at all, since it's well known that *my power is limited*," he added with a snarl.

"It's sound thinking," Piero agreed, "but what are you planning to banish, young master?"

His eyes glowing a red so dark they were almost black, Montifero scooped the mixture into a heavy, iron box. "I'm going to banish the breath from Peruzzi's body," he answered. "You might want to stand back."

In the dungeons of the San Dante Cathedral, the violence of Montifero's spell slammed Lord Guido Peruzzi against the bars of his cell hard enough to snap his spine, his cry of pain and surprise cut short as his windpipe collapsed. The conflagration that discharged from his dead body as his wards cut off flung Romuald de Croce against the far wall. By the time the Captain of the Holy Scourge was able to rise, there was little left of the city's premier necromancer but a smoking shell.

In the Vericcio warehouse the iron box held for less than a single heartbeat before it too vaporized in an explosion of crimson shards. After the dust had cleared, Piero Bruni, his ears still ringing from the force of the blast, knelt and removed his binding spell from Cerchicava's newest Death Mage.

A week later, seated amidst the profusion of roses in his uncle's conservatory, Montifero read through Matteo de Sulla's recent letter with a satisfied expression.

"The duc's cousin, Franco de Messandi, has offered me a position on his staff as a research scholar," he said. "Should I be willing, my uncle has agreed."

"The Bishop will be disappointed, My Lord." Piero noted.

"No doubt, but it suits me well enough. Messandi's

no fool, but he's easily distracted by books and scrolls. It affords me a ducal shield and the time I require for other pursuits."

Standing, Montifero walked to the window, staring out at the darkening gardens beyond.

"The Trade is powerful, but it's not invulnerable, Piero. The Death Mages are indeed everywhere but they have no order, no hierarchy and that makes them weak. Peruzzi was stupid, he was careless, and he nearly destroyed us all. Masters do not wear binding spells? Well, soon there will only be one master in Cerchicava."

Staring out at the line of cyprus trees, his intense gaze glittered like fire.

"You're to take charge of Peruzzi's subordinates and whatever minor necromancers operated under his control or protection," he ordered. "Those you believe to be the most trustworthy can carry your own personal binding spells. Any you believe to be a liability are to be executed at once and components from their bodies stored for future use. Once that's finished, I want the names of every Death Mage in the city, their contacts, cutters and markers, and every member of their families, no matter how distant."

Beyond the line of cyprus trees, the setting sun reflected off the copper roofs of the San Dante Cathedral and he frowned. "Faith," he sneered.

"The Church is also weak, Piero," he continued. "It too believes it's invulnerable, and so it too has grown stupid and careless."

He fell silent for a long, introspective moment until Piero finally coughed faintly, then he gave a cold, decisive nod almost to himself.

"In five months time I come into my inheritance. On that day I want a dozen setters sent into the Carmina District to collect and catalogue the names and movements of every relative of every leading Churchman in Cerchicava from the Achivescovo and the Bishop of San Dante to Captain de Croce and his Holy Scourge. Storable components that may be gathered without raising suspicion are to be collected. I want solid, reliable people, Piero, with the strongest possible binding spells you can apply. Nothing must threaten the security of the Trade ever again."

"Yes, My Lord."

Turning from the window, Montifero glanced across the length of the conservatory, his crimson gaze introspective once again.

"What is the greatest power in the world, Piero?" He asked almost gently.

The man went down on one knee, feeling his master's new binding spell constrict about his throat ever so slightly.

"You are, my Lord," he answered.

Montifero smiled, his eyes glowing hotly. "Not yet, Piero, but very, very soon I will be."

SHAHIRA

Michelle West

Michelle West is the author of several novels, including *The Sacred Hunter* duology and *The Broken Crown*, both published by DAW Books. She reviews books for the online column *First Contacts*, and less frequently for *The Magazine of Fantasy & Science Fiction*. Other short fiction by her has appeared in dozens of anthologies, including *Black Cats and Broken Mirrors*, *Alien Abductions*, *Little Red Riding Hood in the Big Bad City*, and *Faerie Tales*.

THE EGG IS ROUND. Perfectly round, tinted a salmon and gold that blend to make the eye water. It is larger, and in the darkness of a room that might be finely appointed or utterly empty, it is the only source of light; they find their way in the dark, drawn to it. The floor is warm beneath their feet, and sandy.

Here, at last, the priests draw braziers close to their chest as they approach the egg; their robes, red and gold, have dwindled in the shadows to a type of grey. They wear tall hats, carry tall sticks upon which the empty braziers hang; they walk in silence and frown several times when the silence is broken by the voices of those they lead.

Shahira knows, for hers is one of the voices raised at times in the darkness; her toes are stubbed and bleeding because she does not know the way. Nor do the other children, boys and girls, her age and younger. They have been gathered in this long summer, this year of endless heat and dry, dry grass, from their village homes.

Where water was not plentiful in the wells or the shallow lakes, in the empty trickle of river beds, it was shed in abundance by parents and grandparents, by siblings older and younger, all made gaunt by hunger in the sparse time.

Shahira does not like the priests. Nor is she fond of the priestesses, for although many of them are round and ample, there is no warmth in their cold smiles, their shining eyes; they have either pity or disdain for the children, and not one of them offers comfort. They offer, instead, scant foot and harsh words, and many open handed blows. They offer no more harm than this; they would not dare.

This is the year of the harvest, after all. And until the choice is made, they do not know which of the children they have taken will be the key, the awakener.

Shahira's grandmother makes baskets, and in her youth, when her hands were stronger, wove other things besides; many old blankets and cold clothing—which Shahira has seen but has never used—were made by her hands for the villagers, in trade for food and wood. Her grandmother, seeing in Shahira's hands some memory of her youth, began to teach her these things only last year. She has learned them well enough, and on the road here, takes dried leaves and twigs with which to occupy her hands.

But her thoughts are not occupied, and they turn—as they often do—to the children, the younger ones, born as she was born, to the moon and stars in their ill-fated positions. Marked at birth, branded and scarred although none remember the pain of that heat, they have waited, most in ignorance, as she was ignorant, until their coming.

But she remembers asking about the brand, the white network of scars on her inner wrist. Like serpent coils, it rides her skin, moving as her skin moves, stretching as she grows. Her mother was silent, and her father left their home; but her grandmother, withered and old in the face of her father's heated words, caught her wrist, and told her.

"It is the mark of the Summer," she said softly, her hands shaking as she traced it.

"You don't have it."

"No, Shahira, I don't. Nor do your fine brothers—or Otto, that lout—and sisters. Only you." And she had hugged Shahira for a moment before she spoke again. "You were born to the face of moon and moon, the meeting of moon and sun," she said quietly, after some time had passed. "And the eye watches you. We all watch," she added.

"For what?"

"For Summer." The old woman looked away. "For the searing that does not end."

"But—but why?" She remembers, now, that it was stories of Winter that were a comfort. The long winter, when people worked together against the cold and the white, against the hunger of wolves and bears and the thin season of rabbits and starving deer.

"Because if the Summer comes that does not end, it is time."

"Time for what?"

"For the birth," she said quietly, "of the fire."

In winter stories, Fire was their friend and savior, but even so, it burned and killed the unwary. "We don't want the fire to be born."

"No. But if the Summer that does not end comes to us, we will in the end pray for the Fire's birth, for if it is not born, if it is not captured and made living, it will devour us; the field will bear no food, and the lakes will dry, and the animals will starve."

"But in Winter—"

"Hush," the old woman replied. "For there are other serpents, and other stories. Your story, child, is the Summer story. Yours, and the children who were born to the same signs. They will be your brothers and sisters for a short time."

"What will happen to them?" These unknown brothers and sisters.

Her eyes were shadowed and hollow. But she did not flinch and did not stoop to lie; the winter was in her still, strengthening her against the coming of Summer. "The fire will devour them," she replied, "all but one." She caught her granddaughter's face in her withered hands and said, "You must be that one, do you understand, Shahira? You *must* be that one."

"Why?"

"Because if you are not, you will never come home to us."

"And how, grandmother, can I *be* that one?"

"I have taught you about the Winter," her grandmother said sternly, "and you must hold it in your heart. Let nothing melt it, and you will be safe."

And the others? She thought, but she did not ask, for the Winter was in her grandmother's voice and hands.

Two years passed, the first normal, and the second—warm. The passage of the winter season had been fast, and spring was heady, as it always was. There was song, in their long house, and celebration, and the spring songs were the songs that were best loved, although the old ones said it was not a *true* winter.

But the Summer that followed was long, and it did not end. Months passed, and in those months, the rain dwindled, and the heat grew; the ground hardened against their feet. And Shahira knew what it meant. Her parents knew as well, and grew somber; her brothers and sisters were somber as well, but it was hard to be happy when her parents were so grim.

They made offerings at the temple; all of the people did, although her grandmother resented it loudly and bitterly; of what use was this waste of food? The priests would eat it, and get fatter, and that was all that would come of it. The gods, after all, had no interest in food, no interest in these pathetic offerings.

And perhaps grandmother was right.

For at the end of a year, the priests came to the temple. They came, they said, from the city, speaking as if the villagers were so ignorant a city was beyond their comprehension. They had received the sign and the blessing, and they spoke of it in stern tones, their red robes so perfectly clean it looked as if they had never laboured a day in their lives. But their skin was smooth and pale, and in their fashion, unbent and unbowed by labour in the fields or in the small rooms of the long houses, they were beautiful.

But they came with armed men, men who wore steel instead of shaping it, and those men came to the long-house of Shahira's father, a priest by their side.

"We have come," they said quietly, "for Shahira a'Lebann. She is to accompany us when we leave."

Shahira was not in the longhouse, and it took them some time to find her, but when they did, she left off her weaving and came to where they stood, sweating in the dry sun's heat. "Let me see your hands," the priest commanded, and Shahira held them out for his inspection. But although his hands were perfect and clean, he caught hers, dirty and pale, and turned them over; he pushed back her right sleeve, and stared at the mark made their. "This is the child," he said.

Her father was there, and her mother, and the swords of the men in armor—for it was armor they wore—were no longer housed in their sheaths. As if they expected a fight. They were grim, these men, and yet she did not dislike them as much as she disliked the priests; she could not later say why. The priest nodded, and one of these men came forward.

"We will protect your daughter," he said, which was not what she expected, "while she lives, we will lay down our lives for her. But you must give her into the keeping of the priests.

"If you fight us, we will fight. I am a father," the man added, with just a twist of lips, "and were there any other way, we would not now be called upon by the King to perform this duty." He paused, measuring her father's grim silence, her mother's stiffness. "You have many children," he said at last, "and they need you. There are those whom we have visited who have only one, and we have taken that child from them."

It was a threat; she could hear it. But could hear more

in it than threat. It confused her, but she understood some part of it clearly, and stepped forward.

"I will go with them," she said, her voice quiet and clear.

Her father touched her shoulder. "Shahira—"

"I will go and I will return," she continued. She searched for her grandmother, but she did not see her. It caused her some pain, because there was no good-bye she could offer. But she understood that her grandmother did nothing without reason: if there was no good-bye, then it did not exist.

She hugged her brothers, even Otto, and her sisters, younger and older, and then she added, "we need the rains, and an end to this Summer."

And her father met her clear, calm gaze. He did not smile; he didn't have it in him. But he said, "I see my mother in your eyes," and nodded grimly. "Winter in your heart, Shahira mine."

"Winter," she whispered softly as she hugged him.

And the water that the sky would not shed, was shed then.

She was not the first child to be gathered, nor was she the last, but of the first—five in all—she was the oldest. The younger children were not so young as the baby; they could speak and think and walk, and they did not need to be fed or carried. But they were afraid, and she understood why: they had no home and no family here.

Remembering some part of her grandmother's words, she knelt by them, learning their names: Ademi, and Kyle, Lorna and Kerri, and also the silent Eleni. She gathered them to her side and she said, "We were born on the same day of different years; we share a birthday, and also this journey.

"We are not family," she added softly, "but we are like brothers and sisters here, because we bear this mark."

"But what does it mean?" Ademi asked her, for he was quick with words and questions.

"It is the symbol of fire," she told him gravely. "Because if we had no fire, we would be animals, or corpses. But fire in the dry time is the most dangerous thing of all."

"Then we're dangerous?"

"Us? No. No, we're not. We're the ones who—" she looked at them all. The priests had told them nothing, of course. "We're the ones who can bring the rain," she said. "If we're good, and if we're strong enough, we can bring the rain."

"I'm not very strong," Eleni said quietly.

"But you will learn to be stronger," Shahira said, with a confidence she did not feel. "I will be your older sister while you learn this."

"For how long?"

"I don't know. I don't know how quickly you learn." She smiled at the girl's frown. "But we will be together, I think, for as long as we live."

"Promise?"

She nodded. She knew that she should have spoken of death, and of sacrifice, but she couldn't; they were just children, younger than she, and they did not have her grandmother to give Winter to their hearts. If they didn't, she would have to do.

They did not reach the city quickly, and the walk was long and dry. Everywhere they went they could see the evidence of the long Summer, and nowhere was it more evident than the burned and blasted stretch of land that had once been forest. Fire there, she thought, uncontained. If there was life in the black lands, as she would ever after call them, it was theirs: they walked through the ash in a cold silence.

But surrounding the charred vale were other villages, and their number grew in ones and twos as they journeyed toward the capital. The priests were not patient with either thirst or hunger, and they hated tears; they were like the harshest of parents without the love of other actions to sustain them.

But the men with the swords did not let the priests' anger grow too hot, and if the priests did not love the children, they little loved the men they seemed to command, and they were—as the man had promised her father, safe in a fashion.

That man's name was Adelos, and in the evening light ten days after Shahira had said good-bye to her family, when the children gathered to be fed, and the men joined them—eating no more and no less than the smallest of their prisoners—he offered them his name.

As they were all very young, they were honored, and knew it. And they were fascinated by his armor and his sword, and asked him if he knew how to use it. He told them stories of war against raiders and bandits, and they watched him, willing captives. Shahira, understanding that some of his stories were outrageous—for she had her grandmother's way about her, and thought much was nonsense—also understood why he told them, and she thanked him for it after she had seen the children to the tents and put them to bed. That was her job, the job she had undertaken. The new children understood it because the children she had first met expected it, and they, too, were told Shahira's story about Summer and birth.

He looked down at her, for he was tall, and said, "it's the least I can do."

"Because you lead us all to death?"

His brows rose as he met her clear eyes, but he did not step back or falter, and he did not offer her false laughter or mockery. His silence lasted for a moment, and then he said, "Because I lead you all to death. And know it."

"And will not turn from it."

"How can I?" He said bitterly. "For I, too, have children, and the Summer will devour them all if it does not end." But he looked at her for another long moment. "You are trying to protect them," he said at last, "when you know that only one of you can survive."

She shrugged. "None of us will live forever," she said at last, her grandmother's words. She borrowed a few more, and added, "And only a fool tries."

"Aye, there's truth in that, in the old tales. Only a fool," he said, nodding. "But it's bitter."

"Death is," she replied.

"Theirs and yours," he answered. "For you've hardly lived at all. But the truth of it is, girl, that you remind me of my daughter, and the reminder both softens and hardens my resolve. She's not lived either, not truly, and without this—" he held out his hand, lifting it from the pommel of his sheathed sword, "she'll have no chance." He left her then, but as he turned away, she said, "Come back to us. At the evening meal. The children are happy when you are here."

"You place a burden on me," he replied, with a slight smile. "But I will shoulder it."

He could. She saw that clearly, who saw much clearly: he could bear the burden of loving these children who he was escorting to death. He was a strong man, and a kind one, not unlike her father. Memories could cut two ways.

At another time, she might have hated him.

"There is a great magic," he told the children, "in the heart of the Empire, and it rests upon the shoulders of the King and his priests." There was no fire here, but none needed; fire was a danger where the winds were high, and across the flats, they could be high indeed. Yet the lack of firelight did not dim his face; his eyes seemed to sparkle with reflected light, and if the light came from within, and not without, it was still bright.

"The King," Ademi said, shoving Systeri aside in his impatience, "have you seen him? What is he like?"

"Aye, I've seen him, and *do not shove* Systeri."

"She was sitting on my hand!"

"She is half your weight; a strong boy like you should be able to have her sit on your head without noticing it."

Ademi's expression was a mixture of sullen and eager, an odd one. Systeri took the opportunity to hit him. Very like younglings, Shahira thought, her lips pressed together in her grandmother's stern frown. She separated them, putting them to either side of her.

Systeri instantly leaned into her side and looked up, and Shahira's frown stayed only on her lips.

"What is he like?" Adelos said, pausing for a moment. "He is a man," he said at last. "Older than I."

"Very old?"

Adelos laughed. "He is not considered very old, no."

"But if he's older than you—"

"Ademi," Shahira said, "if you interrupt Adelos you will never hear the rest of his story."

"He is a stern man," Adelos said, "But very handsome. He wears a great sword as if it were a dagger, and he fights like a demon. He can be kind, and he is always fair."

A small voice said, "But he took us away from our parents."

"And we will go back," Shahira told Trystera quietly. She made a place on her lap for the youngest of the children, and put her arms around her when she crawled into it. "But I told you why we go, Trystera. I told you why we are important."

"I don't want to be important," Trystera replied.

No, Shahira thought bitterly. None of us do. Not this way. But she smoothed dirty, dry hair around a winding part, and kissed the top of the girl's head. "Sometimes we don't," she conceded. "But the King must think of every single man and woman in the Empire as if they were all his children."

"And we're the ones he doesn't love?"

"No," she said. "We're the ones he will love more than any, because only we can save the Empire from the scorching Summer."

"But *how*, Shahira?"

"I don't know yet," Shahira replied. Because it was true, because she was careful to speak only truth, Trystera quieted. "But Adelos was speaking of magic."

"Aye, I was. When the first King lead his people to these lands, they were barren, or so it is said. All of them—like great, vast wastes, without even the burned trunks of trees to mark them. Nothing grew here, and nothing lived."

"Then why did we come here?"

"It is not written," he replied. "And I'm not a sage; I don't know why. But I know that the first King brought with him the power to make these lands grow, and they offered life to those who followed him. Fields," he added, "and forests. The animals came, and with them, much else.

"It was long ago."

"And the magic is forgotten?"

"No, Ademi, it is not forgotten. All Kings hold the magic within them, with the help of the gods. But it is a hard magic, and sometimes—"

"Sometimes," Shahira continued, when Adelos faltered, "the land seeks to take back its shape, and rid itself of life."

"Why?"

"Because living is hard."

"I'd rather be alive than dead."

"The old ones say death is peace."

"That's because they're *old*."

She had no ready answer to that, and imagined what her grandmother would have said, discarding it. "Sometimes," she said quietly, "the land takes Winter into its heart, and there is a long, long cold. The rains freeze as they fall, and everywhere you look, there is white, white as far as the eye can see.

"Then the men who farm must learn to hunt, in the cold, and many perish. And the people of the villages must cut down old trees, and make fires in the longhouses, and live very close together. They sing, then," she added.

"Have you seen Winter?"

"I? I have seen a small winter, just like you. The long Winter, I have never seen."

"But you're older—"

"Not old enough."

But Adelos was gazing at her, his eyes almost wide. "Shahira speaks the truth," he told them softly, "for I lived in such a Winter when I was a boy."

"And—"

"And during the Winter, if it lasts long enough, the King summons his priests, and they speak with god, and he creates a great magic, a magic of warmth and sun, and he calls it Spring." She looked at her wrist. "And there are children born, like us, who are also called to the King, and they, too, must leave their families and go."

"And what happens to them?"

"They are born," she said quietly, "in time of need and peril, as we were, and they must help the King to bring Spring to the rest of their people." She ran her hands through Trystera's hair. "Is this not so, Adelos?"

"It is, Shahira. Your wisewoman must be very wise indeed to have told you this."

"She was my grandmother," Shahira replied.

"But how can we help?"

"We are part of a great magic," was Shahira's careful reply. "Come. Let me teach you a song. It was a Winter song."

In this fashion, Shahira kept Winter in her heart.

They were twelve when they reached the capital city, and twelve very dirty, very hungry children at that. Even Shahira found it hard to be cheerful; her feet were raw and her throat was parched, and the approaching city lay across the landscape like looming spires that spoke only of the shadow of death.

As well, winds brought unpleasant smells across the great furrow that had once been a river, and several of the children were sick with it. Three of the children who joined them were Shahira's age, and she was happy to have their company, for the younger children grew more frightened and therefore more difficult as the days grew. Because Shahira was there, she greeted the newcomers, even the sullen Estavos, and asked them for help, giving them some of her work: the children.

Estavos was not particularly kind; he was used to field labor, and not the more subtle labor involved with the care of children. The priests disliked him, but not with the intensity of his own disdain for them. He spoke to her, as they reached the city, of escape, for the streets were many and the people unimaginable in number.

Shahira watched him for a long moment after he had finished speaking. "You could run," she told him at last. "And even escape. But the younglings would be lost there."

"Better there than in the hands of men and women such as these."

She shook her head. "Do you not believe that without us, the Summer will last forever?"

"I don't care."

"Your people will die—"

His eyes burned; he was lost to Summer, then. "They killed my father," he said, his voice low. "And my mother is certain to follow. They had no one but me. They didn't care for us—why should I care what happens to them?" And he threw his arms wide, to encompass not only the city, but the whole of the world.

"You should care," she told him gently, "because you are better than they are." For it was true, what he said; the priests did not care. "You spend all your time in your tent."

"With guards."

"With guards," she said. "But you could join us. Not all of the Priests are like the ones who came—"

"Don't make excuses for them."

She nodded again. "I don't care for them," she said at last, meaning it. "I don't care if they die, and the Summer scorches their flesh from their bones. I don't care if they freeze in the long Winter. And home is far away," she added, looking back over her shoulder, "and it is hard to care for it, although easy to miss it. I miss the longhouse greatly."

"You aren't angry?"

"I am," she said, "and with less cause."

"You talk like an old woman."

"I talk like my grandmother." She paused, and then added, "but I care about these children. Because if I don't, who will? You?"

"They're just sheep," he said bitterly.

She nodded.

He shoved his sleeve up with a savagery she had seldom seen. "And we're branded, like sheep. Don't you understand? We are walking to our deaths!"

She almost hit him, then. But the children were not present, and they had not heard his words.

"They will kill you, if you escape," she told him quietly. "And they may kill my children, as well. Yes, I know why we were branded. I know that we face death."

"Then will you not—"

"But my grandmother said we are walking to death from the moment we open our eyes and draw breath. Sometimes it's a long walk, and sometimes it's a short one, but it's always, always toward death."

He looked at her and shook his head.

"We are the only warriors they have," she countered, trying a different tactic. "And if we have no swords and shed no blood, it doesn't change the truth. We should have been escorted in honor," she added, "and your parents honored as well. But should have doesn't matter. The children don't know," she added. "You could tell them; I can't stop you. But if it's true that we face death, is it better to face it screaming and crying? Is it better for their last days to be spent in terror and dread?"

"It's better to know what we face."

"But we don't know," she replied, matching his intensity, but wrapped now in layers of cold chill. "We don't know what we face. If it was just our deaths they wanted, we would all be dead already. They could have just sent men with swords to kill us."

He stopped for a moment, then, and studied her face as if it were new to him. At last he said, "You don't believe we will die."

"I don't believe we will all die," she replied calmly. "This is a magic meant to save life."

"Aye, and in the old stories, the greater the magic, the greater the cost."

She nodded, but added, "not all of the price paid is death."

"Sometimes it's worse."

She nodded again, thinking of her grandmother, and their bitter Winter. "We have each other, and only each other," she told him quietly. "We who are marked and bound for the city. These children are my brothers and sisters, and you, Estavos, like my brother Otto, are one of us, whether we will it or no."

"You had a brother?"

"I have four," she told him. "Otto is always in trouble. He is a great trial to our family."

"You sound like an old woman again."

"I hope so."

"All right."

She looked at him.

"I won't tell the young ones."

"And what do you want from me in return?"

He shook his head, like a wild thing, his shoulders bending toward the ground. "I don't know," he whispered. "I want justice, I want vengeance, I want death."

"But not your own."

"I want to live to see it," he replied. "No one else will give me what I want."

"Then if it is in my power, I will help you. I told you, I don't care about these men and women—well, maybe one of them—but I care about us."

All true, and truth could be bitter in unforeseen ways.

They entered the city, bedraggled, bruised, tired, and they were led through it like an odd procession of beggar children. There were other children here, in the streets, sitting in the scant shade of tall buildings, pressed together in a huddle that made the longhouse seem empty in comparison.

"Why are they here?" Shahira asked Adelos. "Where are their families?"

"Most of them are probably safer here than with their families," he replied. "But it's not so bad today."

"But they're so young—look at that boy—"

Adelos caught her hand and pushed it back to her side. "They'll not come near you while we're here," he told her, "but they're like starving dogs; they're dangerous in packs. It doesn't matter how young they look to you, Shahira. You've the children in your care, and these—these are beyond you. Accept it."

She held her arms stiff by her side as they walked. It was true; the boys and girls shied away from the armed men who walked through the streets, and the priests and the priestesses did not seem to notice them; they were less than ghosts, although they were alive.

She wondered if any of these men and women had ever held a child.

"I see you've taken Estavos into your fold," he added, lowering his voice. "It was a messy business, that."

She said nothing.

"Shahira."

"Don't, Adelos. Don't excuse them."

"Girl, I don't. But the father drew sword against the men, and he would not be—"

"Adelos. My father would have drawn sword against you, and you know it; you knew it that day. But he didn't because you understood him. If you had been sent for Estavos, his father might still be alive."

"I don't know that, girl. Had your father chosen to fight, we would have fought, and all of us are better trained than one desperate man with a weapon." His voice was low and bitter. "We've made our vows, and been given our swords; they are blessed, and they will not fail us. Or so we're told. But it was a bad business, all round."

She said nothing as the streets widened. It was hard to talk, the stench was so overpowering. But Adelos did not seem to notice it.

Ademi pushed himself between them, catching Adelos by the hand. "Will we get to see the King?" he asked.

"Aye," the man said wearily, "You'll see the King, that's a certainty."

And from his tone, Shahira had something new to worry about, for she knew that he was afraid. For them.

But they did not see the King that day; they saw instead the rise of the most beautiful building that Shahira had ever seen. It was made not of wood, but of stone and glass, and it rose up, and up again, as if it would go on forever. It cast a long, long shadow as they approached it, but even in shadow, it was like a story, like something too grand for a story, as it stood in the center of large, empty circle.

The children were awestruck, save only Estavos, and they spoke—when they could—in a hush.

"Is this where the King lives?" Ademi finally asked, but he asked Shahira.

Shahira looked at Adelos, and Adelos shook his head.

"Not here," she said quietly, finding words with difficulty. Song, she might offer, but even that would come out quavering. "I think this is the place where people try to speak with gods," she added. "For the gods themselves would be impressed by such a place as this."

"Gods live here?"

"No, don't be silly. Gods live here," she told him, placing one hand firmly over her heart.

"But sometimes they're hard of hearing," Estavos added.

"Because they're old?" Ademi asked in reply. Estavos batted him gently on the top of the head, and offered a warning nod at the back of a nearby priest. If Ademi was not afraid of Estavos, he understood that the priests were different, and fell silent.

They loved any silence but their own.

It was to silence that the children were led at last, in this grand building, with its cold floors and cold walls. Even the color of tapestries that lined those walls for what seemed miles did not diminish the chill here. It was not a Winter chill; it would not kill, and it was not the cold against which men gathered. Rather, it was a cold they esteemed, even revered. Shahira, from the wood and smoke of the longhouse, hated it, even as she loved its beauty. She held the hands of the children prone to wandering or touching things, for she knew that the Priests would not tolerate it; this gawking wonder was evidence of their inferiority.

But to Shahira, it was different; she wondered at men and women who could walk in such a place and feel no true wonder, could offer only the mockery of reverence without the substance. Her children—they understood that there was a magic in this place of stone, in its height and its echoing stillness. Had she not been escorted by priests, she would have encouraged them.

As it was, she attempted to play by the rules they set; to say nothing, to notice little, to be above it somehow.

It was difficult, but difficult, as her grandmother said, was beside the point. It was necessary.

They were led to a large, large room, one bigger than the longhouse in its entirety. It had only a small window, and none of the coloured glass that made light so beautiful; it had a large, solid door with a big ring that opened from the outside. Like a cage door, she thought, but without the obvious bars.

There were, however, beds, stacked in twos, against the walls, and these beds had blankets—which were pointless in the swelter of the heat—and pillows. By the foot of each of these beds was a chest into which the children were to place their belongings, the last word said with a barely concealed sneer.

As their belongings consisted almost entirely of the clothing they wore, the chests themselves were cavernous and empty.

"You are in the temple now," the Priest who was oldest said sternly, "and while here, you will wear the robes of the most junior of our servants, and you will comport yourselves with dignity. Do you understand? You will eat in the hall after the novitiates, and you will speak to no one."

They nodded.

Adelos was still with them. "Do not attempt to leave the grounds," the Priest added, "or we will be forced to lock the doors."

So, Shahira thought, with the slightest of glances at Adelos' face, it starts. But after the priest had closed the door, she said, simply, "They are afraid we will get lost in the big city, and if we are lost, we will not be able to find one another."

Estavos snorted, but said nothing.

Winter, she thought, braving the cold that *could* kill.

She gathered the children around her in a large circle, and she began to sing; they joined her, unaware of the way their voices blended. It wasn't harmony, but the cacophony was soothing and sweet nonetheless. While the world raged without, they could find some comfort and safety within their walls, and if the walls were of stone, it signified nothing.

Thus, Shahira kept Winter in her heart.

*   *   *

The robes came in the morning. They were not perfect, and they were overlarge, but they were soft and fine, and the children were—once the boys had been convinced that these were not *dresses*—happy enough to be free of the dirt and dust of the long voyage. The beds were neither soft nor hard, and the food *was* food, and better than they had had in village or on the road for many days.

But they were not allowed the company of any but their guards, and even these had been winnowed. The gods were kind, in this; Adelos was allowed to remain. Or, Shahira amended, as the days passed, the gods were kind to the children; for Adelos, they showed little mercy.

At seven days, they were taught to sing a song whose words were not, as far as Shahira or any of the children were concerned, words at all. They were nonsense, and the priests were unkind; the nonsense *must* be sung in the correct tones, the correct harmonies. They were quick to anger, the men and women who came, and Shahira took great care to memorize their faces; she refused them the honor of remembering their names.

But it was Adelos who at last pulled her aside. "It is not easier for them," he said quietly, "to do what must be done."

"They show no kindness and no understanding—"

"They cannot afford kindness, Shahira. Understand that," he was weary. "And if you must hate, hate them, hate the gods, hate as will. When men are forced to acts of barbarism, they deal with it as they, too, must."

"I would not."

"No, you would not. And I can only hope that my own daughter would suffer as you have suffered, Shahira. Your parents must have been proud of you."

She offered him a slight smile, then. "Not always."

"Not always, but no parent is always proud, and no child always worthy of pride. We are all tested," he added, "and if failure marks a man—or a woman, or even a child—forever, than we are all marked. Life is unkind, but some men are fortunate enough to be tested again, and to pass what they failed in ignorance before. We learn humility that way."

She saw no humility in the Priests, but took care, when Adelos was present, to school her face, to relax her expression. And when they left, she worked with the children, schooling her expression more easily. "We do not all have fine voices," she told them, "and we do not always remember what we are told."

"I do," Ademi said. She batted the top of his head and frowned. But the expression had no ferocity in it, and too much affection; he smiled at her before her hand had reached her side.

Three days of lessons, the same song over and over. At night, she would sing different songs, pulling the children into a huddle; she had used a circle on the road, but the circle that the priests had drawn was so rigid she thought to break it or soften its lines. There was always a scuffle for her lap, or the lap of the other girl her age, and there were often tears, for the priests little valued their sleep, but in the end, sleep overtook tears, and Shahira was last to succumb to it, protecting them, watching over them as she could.

On the fourth day, they were brought different robes, much finer than the ones they had yet worn. They were cautioned to silence, and formed up into two neat lines, and for once the priests looked almost human; they were worried, and it showed. They did not lift hand, although their words were sharp; they gave orders, and the children, entranced by their finery into an awareness of the importance of occasion, followed those orders without exception. Even Estavos, although he was the only one who managed to be sullen.

Excitement and fear were twined as they walked the long, tall halls, their steps echoing in the harmony of sound their voices were only barely capable of producing. It was hot, but the men and women suffered the heat more prominently than the children, who had become accustomed to the sting of sun and the lack of water in their homes. Were it not for the absence of their parents, their whole families, they might have felt only excitement.

They were led from the long halls through a garden that the sun and the wind did not touch, and they were allowed a moment to marvel at the fountain which sat in its center, spouting water as if water were not of more value than gold or grain.

And then the moment passed, and they were led once again past this garden and into another hall. But this hall had an end, and it was a dais, and the floor was marble strewn with gold and smoke and fire. There was a long, crimson carpet, edged in the same gold, that seemed narrow until Shahira stood upon it; it was wide, but the room was wider still, and no ceiling she had yet seen was taller. This one was also round, like the inside of a cupped palm placed with care over something fragile and vulnerable.

Thus it was that the children were led into the presence of the King, and they knew him as King by his raiment, his crown, and the distant beauty of his expression. By these things and the throne upon which he sat, finer by far than the room, and more intimidating than the height of its ceilings, the utter silence it contained.

The guards knelt the moment they halted, and the children were for once of the same mind; they knelt as well, their robes spilled about them as if they were the petals of an odd, rectangular flower that was only beginning to blossom.

The King was silent as he rose and walked across the long platform which held his fine chair; silent as he came down the steps which led to it, approaching the Priests— who remained standing—and the people who knelt.

The oldest of the priests bowed low to the King.

"These are the children?" The King asked, although he did not look at the Priest.

The priest, however, did not look away from the King. "Your Royal Highness," he said, executing the same perfect bow, "these are the children. We surrender them to your keeping."

He nodded, this man with his golden hair and his sky blue eyes. "I accept them into my keeping; your duty in this regard is done." He paused. "Twenty-four," he said quietly.

"Your majesty."

"And the other two?"

"They did not survive their early years."

"Very well. What the gods decree, they decree." He now looked at the children, as they knelt, and said, "You may rise."

But it took them some time to rise, and in rising, they became children again, lost and unruly. Shahira spoke to the closest in her low, sweet voice, and they quieted. Taking her example, the other girls sought to do the same, but to her surprise, Estavos did likewise, calming them by being, somehow, calm.

"You do me honor," he told them, when at last they stood again in two orderly rows, "and likewise, the people of my kingdom, even if they know it not. Have you learned the song of awakening?"

The looked at each other nervously. Shahira stepped forward boldly and lifted her chin. "We have," she said quietly, and stopped short of saying more.

"Good. It is three days hence that you will be called upon to sing, and when you do, you must sing perfectly. It is the only thing I will ask of you, but I must ask it. While you dwell under my care and protection, you will practice, and I will be your only audience. Come the third night, I must be satisfied."

There was no threat in the words he offered, although his voice was grave.

But Shahira nodded again. He frowned at her boldness. "Your name, girl?"

"I am called Shahira by my kin," she replied with care. And then, discarding care, added, "but it is seldom that we are called upon to give our names to one who remains nameless."

"Indeed. It is an act of subservience," the King replied, "or obedience."

And it came to her that Kings must be hard and cold,

like their thrones, and just as splendid, as distant. She
would have knelt, but he did not demand it, and her
legs were stiff.

"Very well," he said. "You will now follow me, for
we have begun our work, and your presence is re-
quired." He paused and added, "You may speak among
yourselves, but you are not to speak of this to any other
living person; it is a great secret, and it is not one that
can be safely shared."

Again, he offered no threat, but Shahira was old
enough to hear the threat beneath the surface of words,
and she marveled that words could be like a dagger,
sheathed but waiting, edge only hidden, but never forgotten. She did not ask him what would happen to those
the children she might speak to; she had no need. It
was evident.

"You were born," he said, "for this; you are a part of
the magic, and a gift in need to the people from whom
you came." He gestured, and guards appeared, as if by
the self-same magic; they were not Adelos, and they
were as finely attired as the King himself, or so they
seemed; grim and cold and somehow perfect.

To the Priests, he now bowed, and if the bow was not
low, it was still clear. "You will attend," he said, "three
days hence. Take your leave and be at peace; you have
had a long, long journey."

She was forced to bite her tongue and clamp her jaw
to hold her peace; the words seared the inside of her
mouth as she contained them. He had offered no like
words for the children who had been taken from their
families. Even his honor was cold. Her grandmother had
been cold and stern, but never like this, and she would
not soon forget.

But if they had dreamed of palaces, the truth was like
waking; they were now led from a room that had seemed
a place for penitents, to someplace that was like a dun-
geon. They were led, first, to a door that was old, and
surrounded by rough, pocked stone into which were en-
graved shapes and symbols. Shahira could not read; she
thought, however, that had she the skill, it would have

made no difference. There was something about these
marks that was old, older than the barrows in the hills
in which all her ancestors of note had lain for hundreds
of years.

Here, torches were lit, and they were needed, for sunlight did not penetrate the darkness into which they
stepped; there were stairs that went down in a winding
spiral, and the guards ordered them to stay close to the
walls; they themselves walked upon the outside of the
children, enforcing that order by their presence.

But the children—except perhaps Ademi—did not
need to be told twice; there were no rails here, and steps
such as these had never been seen by any of them in
their lives. Down they went, and were it not for the
presence of the King and his guards, they might have
wept or stopped. But if they dared the anger of Priests,
not even the youngest dared the wrath of Kings, and
this was wise.

This man, Shahira thought, had seen the long Winter,
but he had not been part of it; he had crested above it,
oblivious to the cold and the danger of death that lay
waiting outside his walls.

As if he could hear the thought, he paused to look at
her, and she realized that he had chosen to walk, to
place his feet, beside her. His gaze was keen and clear
as he assessed her, barren as the fields. And it came to
her then that he was weary, as weary as Adelos. She felt
no pity for him; pity was not a thing to offer Kings. Nor
did she feel any warmth, or even compassion. He was
not hers.

Only the children were, in this place, and she could
count the length of days that that responsibility would
last, for he had named them himself: three.

Three days.

The Winter in her heart grew cold as she met his gaze,
and colder when he at last looked away. In the darkness,
she dared this much, and in the darkness, he allowed it.
"You are their keeper," he said quietly. His voice did
not carry, and given how loud their steps were, she was
surprised, but she should not have been; she thought the
heavens themselves might bend at his command.

And that he might be cautious before the giving of it.

"I am their eldest," she replied with dignity, "and they are the brothers and sisters of my spirit. We were born to the same fate, and for the same reason; we are bound together."

"You are a strange girl," he replied. "For I feel you understand some of your fate."

"Only some," she told him softly.

"And you walk without fear?"

"I am never without fear. But it is better spent for them, than upon myself. Or so I've been taught."

"Then you have been well taught, child."

She said nothing. She had been taught more, besides; that fear itself was foolish, but that it might be honed and used if one were cautious and had ones wits about one. Her grandmother's voice was strong in this place.

"You have heard stories about the magic in this place?"

"We have all heard stories," she answered cautiously, lowering her voice.

"Then you will see the truth of them—or the lie—for yourself. I can offer you no comfort, but you do not ask it."

"Not for myself."

"Not at all."

She nodded again and continued to walk, as he did.

They came at last to the end of these stairs, the torches flickering brightly. He led them to another door, older still than the one above; she could see a glimpse of similar carvings in it.

"We delved here, when we came," he told her. "To plant our roots and take our place. This is the heart of my kingdom, and it is laid bare to you for these three days; make of it what you will."

And so Shahira looked first into the heart of a kingdom and blinked, for it was dark here, and the walls had given way at last to stone that had no discernable shape and no end; it went up into a blackness that torchlight was too meagre to penetrate. Sunlight would have been too meager; here there was only the shadow that no light casts.

She was afraid, then.

And because she was Shahira, she clung to old stories and the harsh affection of her grandmother's longhouse voice. And the King said, "here we first woke the sleepers at need. And here, in return, once we had paid their price, we were offered a Kingdom.

"But here," he added softly, "when the time has come, we must renew old vows if we are to keep what we have built."

"What vows?" she whispered; she could not raise her voice.

But the King did not answer, and she did not ask again. Instead, listening to the voices—and the silences—of the younglings, she moved away from the man whose word was both life and death, and returned to the duties she had chosen.

"Here," the King told her, "you will reside. Here, you will practice, and eat, and sleep. For it is here that you will be heard, and here, in the end, that your fate will be decided. In three days, you will understand what you cannot understand now, and in four, you will be allowed to leave in honor."

"How many of us?" Estavos asked.

Shahira would have hit him, had she been close enough.

The King did not even glance at the boy, but after a moment he said, "All that remain."

She hated the King, then. She understood the allure of the hatred that drove Estavos, and it burned her, and she stood shaking with it, her hands in fists, her lips a tight line that threatened to swallow all of her words and songs forever.

But Ademi caught one fist, and Kaylarra, so quiet, the other, and she was torn a moment between a helpless rage and a helpless fear.

Which will you choose, daughter?

The strong voice her grandmother's voice.

And Shahira, who had accepted her fate, struggled to shoulder it once again.

Between love and hate, which will you choose?
Can I not have both?

At your peril, both. But not at the same time. Choose one and hold it fast. Choose quickly.

She swallowed, and as Kaylarra's little voice rose in a quick series of panicked breath, the choice, she felt, was made for her; she gathered the girl in her arms, lifting her from the rough rocky ground and burying her face in the soft, fine hair.

She had sustained them all the way here, leading them at last into darkness, but she realized as she held the girl and felt the steadying comfort of that embrace, that these children had also sustained her; truly, they were bound.

Her eyes were wet when she lifted her head; she allowed herself this weakness because it was so hard to see in the gloom. "This is a poor place for children," she told the King, "but it is cool here; the sun does not reach this far."

The King did not smile or falter. "The Summer's heart," he told her, "is in this place. And the coming of autumn and the rains. But I am not yet finished, child. Come, all of you, and gather round me." He lifted both of his hands, and light grew in his palms, a light that was pale and more radiant than the meager torches. The hands of the King, ringed with gold, caught them all as if they were moths and he, fire.

He led them, by this light, this fey fire, into the heart of a cavern, the darkness pushed back by his presence, and at last, where the ground was warm beneath their feet, to a smooth flat place where sand had been scattered.

And in the centre of the sand, smooth and large, something white and round and larger than any of them.

"You must touch it," he told them, although he himself did not move towards the object that lay before them. "Touch it, and offer it your names."

"What is it?"

"Salvation," he replied gravely. "It has been waiting for you here, while you lived with your families in distant villages, and it will not wake without you."

They were afraid now, for the King did not move. And so Shahira, holding Kaylarra in her arms and trailing Ademi, who could not be dislodged by anything short of force, walked across the sand toward the thing that lay there. If this was magic, it was an odd magic to demand so much and offer so little.

She laid her hand upon the white surface and drew back in surprise, for it had looked hard to her, and it was not; it was nubbled and strong, but it felt like . . . skin. Like living skin.

She spoke her name slowly, lingering over each syllable, and almost wished it were longer. But she spoke, and after a long moment, when she had not been devoured or destroyed, Ademi followed, placing first one hand and then the other, and then his cheek, against the surface. He whispered his name to a wall, and the wall, she was certain, absorbed it—but it did not answer.

Kaylarra looked up at Shahira, and Shahira nodded. So Kaylarra offered what Shahira had offered, and after a moment the children flocked toward her in a huddle to one side of this white monument, this living egg. They offered their names, staring in wonder. Estavos came last, and he placed his hand upon the egg, but he did not speak.

"Estavos," Shahira began.

"I want it to speak its name first," he replied with a strained dignity. "It is not my father, nor my King; it is not my god."

She glared at him over Kaylarra's head. Thinking if one and only one survived, it might well be Estavos. Winter was not strong in her heart, and she did not desire death—but more than life she desired the comfort of these children and the easing of their fear.

"You must choose," she told him gravely, her voice a whisper.

"What must I choose, Shahira?"

She started to answer, and then shook her head. "The children are waiting, Estavos, and the King is waiting." And her tone implied that there would be no peace while both were true, and she did, indeed, intend as much.

He met her eyes and held them with his, and she felt again the flare of anger and hatred that had held her immobile; felt it as if it were her own. It was part of her, and she accepted it. Swallowed it. Held it as she held Kaylarra.

And waited.

Estavos was as cold and hard as the Priests for a moment longer, and then he exhaled and said, in a low, low voice, "I do this for you." As if it were an accusation. She did not much care why he did it, and her glare told him as much. He touched the egg, and he whispered his name, and his name was long indeed, and heated, before he withdrew.

The silence that followed was broken by the King. "I will come myself," he said quietly, "when food is brought, and I will join you in the song of awakening."

"You know it?"

"By heart," he told her, and a hint of bitterness was in the words. "It is in my dreams, these days, and it is the only thing I hear. Better to hear it sung in your voices than in the voices I hear." He offered them no comfort, and she realized, finally, that he never would.

But he left them, then, with torches and instructions on how to keep them lit. "Do not let them die," he told Shahira, "for when they go out, they will not be lit again before the time."

"What's in the egg?" Ademi asked, when the King and his men had left them in the darkness of torchlight. They were huddled about her, and around each other, beneath the small wells of light the torches cast, and they stared at the egg as if it would crack open and something terrible would emerge to devour them.

And as Shahira herself felt the same, it was difficult to cleave to her purpose. But she smiled at him. "Salvation," she said.

"What is salvation?"

"For us? An end to Summer," she told him firmly.

"But what kind of end?"

"Ademi, enough." She remembered her grandmother's words, and she found the Winter in her heart, and held fast to it, for here, at last, she could feel it howling around them all, beyond the walls of ragged stone. "We must sing the song we were taught, and we must sing it well—but there are other songs we must sing tonight."

"Harald?" He asked, his eyes bright and shining. Ademi was a boy who loved the long, old songs about bright heroes and shining swords.

"Harald," she said, although it was not her favorite. "And then the others. And any voice is good enough for Winter songs. Remember why we sang, in the Winter: to raise our voices against the howling death that waited outside. We worked together, and because we could, the cold did not kill us; it made us stronger."

"It's not Winter," one of the other children began.

"It is Winter in our hearts," she replied. "And if we remember that, we will sing the right song, and we will see Spring."

"I want the song about the rabbit and the moon."

"But that's a *girl* song!"

"I'm a *girl*—"

Estavos hit Ademi on the hand with his knuckles. "Men know how to wait," he said sternly. Ademi subsided, but he made a rude gesture behind Estavos' back. Estavos, an only child, hit him again. He had come far, in his long journey. It made Shahira smile, and so little else could she felt comforted by the bickering that erupted around her. Because the longhouse had been full of it; people sounds, happy and sad, joyful and angry by turns.

That night, they dreamed about flight and heat and fire, and they woke in wonder and fear, babbling each to the other as Shahira walked among them, tending the torches. She did not demand that they sleep apart; in the Winter, all warmth was good warmth. She did, however, demand that Ademi take his elbow out of Estavos' face before Estavos' hit him again.

With no priests and no guards, they were happy in their fear, and the only absence she regretted was Adelos, but he did not come. She wondered if she would see him again.

And she sang, to the children, not a song of wakening but a song of slumber and safety. It was a lie, but some lies are so strong they become an oasis of truth.

It was hard to tell morning from night, and it might have been impossible, were it not for the arrival of the King. Food and water were brought, and the meal was fine indeed, for even in this wilderness beneath the city, a King expected to eat well.

When he was present, they sang the song the priests had taught them, and by his frown or his nod, they corrected their errors. He did not raise hand against them, and the guards did not threaten them; without such threats, they relaxed, and their voices became less quavering and less uncertain. Singing the Winter songs had robbed them of some of their fear and if this song had no words, it was still familiar.

Shahira made up a story to go with the words when the King was absent, and this helped. But the lack of sunlight, the lack of moonlight, wore on her, for she had no way of counting the days, and the doom, and time became a thing to both treasure and dread.

But she could hide this because she had to. Well fed, the children were less fractious, and became bold enough to play other games; there was less weeping, less fear. She was grateful.

But when they slept, and they did, she left them and once again touched the egg with both of her hands. *Serpent*, she whispered, her lips pressed against it. *Swallow Summer if you must, take it and devour it. Fly where you will. But these voices, do not still.*

For she knew what lay within the egg, although she did not speak of it, and she knew that death, if it came, would be brutal and terrible. Her grandmother had desired that she remember Winter and cold, and she understood in this silence what that desire meant: acceptance of death.

But the Winter in Shahira's heart was not the long Winter that had made her grandmother's life what it was; she did not want to live to see these children die.

If you must, she said, her lips tasting of salt, *take me first. Spare me what must follow. Grant me at least this.*

And then, because the gods did not listen, she added, *take only me. Wake now, and I will be silent; devour me whole, let them see nothing, and I will not fight or run or cower.*

But the egg was silent, and at last, defeated, Shahira sang her Winter songs to its silent shell, thinking that it, too, was a child, and at that, one not yet born. In darkness it lived, and this shell was its isolation; it was not hers, and not of her. What it needed, it would take, as all children did who were born whole, and Shahira knew well that sometimes the life demanded was that of the person who had birthed the infant.

But to hate the infant for the mother's death was beyond her people, and Shahira was of her people. After the salt had left her lips, she decided. Her hand on the egg was gentle, as gentle as it might have been had she rested it upon Kaylarra's head.

"Tonight," she told the children, "We will gather round the egg."

"How do you know it's night?"

"It's *always* night here."

She waited for the bickering to subside; she hadn't the heart to end it.

"What will we do?"

"Sing," she told them quietly. "It is a baby. A very large baby, but still a babe. We will sing it our songs, because it is one of us."

Ademi looked dubious.

"It is," Shahira said quietly. "And it waits the same moment that we do. If song is needed, let us sing the songs *we* like; let it learn the words and the deeds of our ancestors."

"But they're—"

"Hush, Ademi," Estavos said severely. "If you want to hear Harald again *ever*, you'll listen to Shahira."

So they gathered, and they sung, and they argued about where Shahira would sit, and in the end, she roved among them, keeping her voice steady as she did.

                              *   *   *

Estavos woke her in darkness, and the darkness was
final. She had not let the torches gutter but they were
guttered; night had fallen and it was starless. She startled, and he caught her. Held her for a moment, offering
her what she offered the children. Comfort.

"Footsteps," he whispered. He did not point out that
the torches were gone.

"The children—"

"Sleeping."

"But you—"

"Shahira," he told her quietly, "I chose. I hated it,
and I chose. They will come now, and we'll let them."
His breath was soft against her cheek for all its harsh-
ness. He was afraid, she thought.

But the Priests came in the darkness, and they woke
the children and said "It is time." The King was with
them, so silent and dark that she did not at first recognize him.

She nodded at the sound of their voices, although they
couldn't see her, and she whispered the names of the
children, one by one, touching them as she stumbled in
the darkness. They woke to it, but also to her, and chose
her without being aware that they chose at all.

She had earned this trust, and felt the enormity of the
lie at its foundation, but to beg for forgiveness would
have destroyed what she had built. She offered them the
lie instead, and found strength in the act of offering. She
gathered them as she could; it was harder here.

But the King said, "You must stand around the egg.
You must touch it."

And they were led, stumbling, until this moment.

And now, the egg. Shahira can see it, and it has
changed in color, but not shape; it is glowing with the
light that once—and only once—limned the King's
hands. The shell seems almost translucent; they can see
the shape of what lies within, waiting.

The children should be afraid. But they are not afraid.
Two days they have spent around this egg when the King
has been absent; two days, they have listened to the
stories of the longhouse while the egg lay in the sand

that clings to robe and foot and hair, and sometimes mouth.

She has led them this far, and she will lead them at last to the end of this road. Estavos is by her side. Ademi and Kaylarra and all the rest of the children allow this, because they know that Estavos will cause trouble if they don't. He is like a boy, she thinks, with both gratitude and fondness.

She starts the song, for she is so very, very weary, and with the song, there will be an ending.

Only one of you will survive, her grandmother says. *And it must be you. You must come home to us.*

But, Shahira thinks, are we *not* one, now? One family, one tribe? Were we not all chosen to share this fate? Will we sunder what we've made? For she can no longer imagine a life without these lives about her. The longhouse is gone, or rather, transformed: it is this cave, in the end, this Winter place in the middle of a killing Summer.

She starts the song, and she expects to sing alone for some time, for the priests make the children nervous. But it is Estavos who joins her first, his low voice singing the harmony to the melody she must carry. That she has carried from the beginning. The children join her before she has finished the first phrase, halting and hesitant—but their voices are sweet and their notes are true. They touch the egg with one hand, and they touch the child nearest them with the other, making small anchors of themselves for reassurance. It has been three days since any of them have spoken of home. The words fill her mouth, and with those words, she lets go of her fear. The egg is beautiful and glistening and round, and it has been part of her Winter here, and if Winter ended long before she was born, it is part of her still.

She does not notice, at first, that the priests have withdrawn; does not notice the absence of the King. She is aware of the song and the egg, and she is aware—perhaps they are all aware at the same moment—of a foreign voice that has joined theirs, singing another harmony, a low thrum that is wordless and pleasant and terrifying.

For it grows, and it grows loud, threatening to drown out their voices, their own small parts. They *are* small. She realizes it, and she denies it by lifting her voice, by forcing it to be heard. Estavos' is defiance personified, and he finds the same strength of voice, joining it to hers, and urging the children to do the same; his hand does not leave the egg.

It cannot. Nor can hers; she has tried to lift it. It will not come. As if it is no longer hers, it remains there, anchored. But the song is almost done, and she does not give in to the panic she might otherwise feel; does not allow weariness to quell her voice. The song itself is beautiful, and if it is hard to hear over the growing thrum of this last, new voice, she listens anyway for the other voices that she knows she can hear, and she names her children, her brothers and her sisters, as he picks their voices out of the whole.

And when the world shatters, when the final note attenuates, held at last by only the one voice, she shifts her song, her low song, and she sings a song that is Winter and comfort and hunger and death, for in the Winter there were only these things.

Glowing pink shards pulse and break, and were it not for the familiarity of the Winter song, the children would cry out or break or run—she knows this because it is her own desire, and one she masters with difficulty. The torchlight is no longer necessary; she can see every child in the room clearly if she swivels her head; can see them as the small helpless creatures they are, Summer things and hungry and terrified and yet—and yet—

She can feel her limbs pinioned to her sides and she struggles to free them. And she speaks their names in one breath, all of them falling together like the syllables of one *long* name, each a part of the whole, and each, important to her.

She feels hunger, a terrible hunger, and she has known hunger for years. But hunger did not kill her and hunger did not drive her to kill; it drove her to tears at times, and waste of water, but she was younger then, and it was expected. She swallows the hunger as it grows, and Shahira understands, for as she stretches her limbs, they are *not* her limbs; they are thin, wet wings that go on forever, up and up, bound by gravity.

Bound by hunger.

She sees as the dragon sees, and she hungers as the dragon hungers, and for a moment, they are the same creature.

But she is Shahira, and Winter is in her heart. The Winter that withstands the howling and the hunger of the world.

She is Shahira who is standing upon the rough ground of the cavern looks up at the swirling eyes of the dragon who is, for a moment, also Shahira, and she sees herself as frail and faltering and weak, and more, she hears the promise, at last, of strength.

And she wants it. To have an end and have peace, and more besides; to have flight and freedom and a full belly.

This is no infant, no delicate babe, and yet it is no adult, and she does not hate it for its driving need, as she thought to. She asked it for mercy, and she understands that mercy is a concept that it cannot see or know, not yet; what babe does?

But she is Shahira, and she hears the dragon's voice, and she says, *you will feed on Summer*. And it sings to her, deafening, its great thirst, and she knows what will quench it. But she says again, *you will feed on Summer. You are cold, and warmth is waiting*.

Jewelled eyes now, hardening into shape. Her eyes and not her eyes. She sees her children as it sees her children, weak and helpless and waiting. And she opens her mouth, her small mouth with its flat teeth, and she sings in her weak thin voice, and the song she sings is not the song of wakening, but a Winter song.

Yes, we are weak, she sings; yes we are frail. But together, no Winter or Summer can kill us.

I can kill you, the dragon says.

She does not argue; who argues with a child? But she sings again, fighting hunger with years of long practice. And in a sly voice, it tells her that it cannot consume Summer if it is weak.

It does not lie.

Nor does she. *I do not care if you consume Summer;*

I care only that you do not kill your brothers and your sisters. I will go with you, and if you must, you can consume me.

Brothers. Sisters.

Yes. You are of the longhouse, and we sang to you while you slept. You were born, as we were born, to save our people. And it rises shedding the last of its shell. *I was born*, it tells her, *to fly and eat and grow warm; it is cold in this place, and the cold kills.*

It is cold, she whispers. *Outside of this place, and the cold kills. Sing our songs, and I will sing with you.*

And it sings, as if song is a surprise.

And she hears the shouts of men in the distance with her own ears and with dragon ears, and she hears the rough cadence of voices she detests and understands the words that have always been nonsense to her.

"We offer you this.

We offer you this in keeping with our vows, child of the ancient world. Go forth and keep yours."

Brothers. Sisters. The dragon hisses and rises, thinking of hunger and cold. Winter creature, yes, and Winter is in Shahira's heart, and it is her own Winter, for she has made it so. And she turns to Estavos, her throat raw, her song coming to an end: "The children," she whispers. The dragon is shining a blinding white gold, a light that the eye cannot hope to contain. They close their eyes, all of them, but they are not yet terrified.

Estavos stares at her.

"The children," she says again, her voice louder. It might be the last words that she speaks, for the dragon's throat is thrumming and it thrums in keeping with her own.

She says it again, and this time it is the dragon's jaw that forms the words, and they are a command and a plea. And he finally understands her, and he grabs Ademi, all of the children whose hands now hold fragments of dead shell, useless harbor, and he drags them away from the light, the jaws, the waiting death—and the dragon allows this, but barely.

She wanted to spare them.

But the dragon must feed, for promises made in blood

are bound by it. And beyond them all, the Priests are chanting, and she knows they will be a harder meal, for she is not yet strong enough to fly on the wings of a dragon; not yet strong enough to break free.

But she is strong enough to lurch away from the circle of children because the dragon knows their voices, and their song, and he understands that the Winter holds food if one knows how to hunt. The strong hunted. The weak remained behind, waiting, singing, hoping.

They are singing now, the songs that she loved. She is both with them and beyond them. She is Shahira, and she accepts that those who leave the longhouse to face the storm—to stand in it—might never return alive.

Thus with the Priests and the guards and even the King, and as she rises at last, as the dragon rises, she does not fight him at all. Instead, she croons her love of her family, his family; she speaks to him of the warmth that waits, and she goes as far as she can from her children before she at last lets him give way to hunger and the desire for blood.

She hears the screaming and the terror, and it feels both wrong and right; she hopes that Estavos can somehow protect her children from the knowledge of what she is doing. Taking what must be taken. But not from her family, not from her kin.

When it is done, she is injured, but she is whole and strong, and she knows no pity and no mercy; she knows only the drive to survive and protect what she has built.

He is giddy, this child she has sheltered, and they are without Priests or guards and the King is bleeding but not yet dead, and his eyes are bright, his sword brighter.

And she says "For your people," and means it, although she speaks with dragon's voice. But she does not kill him; his wounds might. The cold is strong, and the dragon is strong, and he is tingling with a frenzy of desire as he rises up and up into a darkness that cannot be dark in his presence, like the moon itself stretching toward the sky.

Save us, she sings, *and we will never leave you.*

And in the cold of this night, the dragon begins to bind the scorching heat of Summer into its scales while below the children sing in voices so pure and clear she can sing with them.

And if they sing a song of blood and death and glory and battle, well, that's Ademi, and besides, the dragon likes the song better than the rabbit song; he *is* a boy. She is Shahira. She can feel the land beneath her as it stretches out farther than her eyes could ever see, and she can see the roots of Summer in the hard earth, and it is this summer she takes, with a frenzy of joy.

She is free here.

But hours later, when she is warm, she is lonely, and the dragon is lonely, and it stretches its new wings out as it flies.

Yes, she says, weary and content. *Home, now, hunter, and we will sing for the joy of your return.*

And he whispers, crooning, *brothers. Sisters.* And it is to them that he goes, replete, and they are waiting for him, and they are waiting for Shahira, and they are not afraid as he lands.

Come, he tells them, and her own voice fades, and her vision diminishes, and she returns to darkness and frailty with a pang of terrible loss, *I will take you home.*

There is a small pause and then he says, *I will stay with you all.* It is a question, a child's question, and Shahira, with her own arms, reaches out to embrace its closed jaw and chide it gently about its wings and its claws and the danger they might pose.

TAD WILLIAMS

TAILCHASER'S SONG

"Williams' fantasy, in the tradion of WATERSHIP DOWN, captures the nuances and delights of feline behavior in a story that should appeal to both fantasy and cat lovers. Readers will lose their hearts to Tailchaser and his companions."
—*Library Journal*

"TAILCHASER'S SONG is more than just an absorbing adventure, more than just a fanciful tale of cat lore. It is a story of self-discovery…Fritti faces challenges—responsibility, loyalty, and loss—that are universal. His is the story of growing up, of accepting change, of coming of age."
—*Seventeen*

"A wonderfully exciting quest fantasy. Fantasy fans are sure to be enthralled by this remarkable book." —*Booklist*

0-88677-953-7

To Order Call: 1-800-788-6262

DAW 43

TAD WILLIAMS

Memory, Sorrow & Thorn

"THE FANTASY EQUIVALENT OF *WAR AND PEACE*...
readers who delight in losing themselves in long complex
tales of epic fantasy will be in their element here."
—*Locus*

THE DRAGONBONE CHAIR
0-88677-384-9

STONE OF FAREWELL
0-88677-480-2

TO GREEN ANGEL TOWER (Part One)
0-88677-598-1

TO GREEN ANGEL TOWER (Part Two)
0-88677-606-6

To Order Call: 1-800-788-6262

Tad Williams

THE WAR OF THE FLOWERS

"A masterpiece of fairytale worldbuilding."
—*Locus*

"Williams's imagination is boundless."
—*Publishers Weekly*
(Starred Review)

"A great introduction to an accomplished
and ambitious fantasist."
—*San Francisco Chronicle*

"An addictive world ... masterfully plays
with the tropes and traditions of
generations of fantasy writers."
—*Salon*

"A very elaborate and fully realized setting
for adventure, intrigue, and more
than an occasional chill."
—*Science Fiction Chronicle*

0-7564-0181-X

To Order Call: 1-800-788-6262